THE VIRILITY FACTOR

A NOVEL

Works of Robert Merle

Novels
Malevil
Weekend at Dunkirk
La mort est mon métier
The Island
The Day of the Dolphin
Behind the Glass

Contemporary History
Moncada, premier combat de Fidel Castro
Ahmed Ben Bella

Plays
Volume I: Sisyphe et la mort, Flamineo, Les
Sonderling
Volume II: Nouveau Sisyphe, Justice à Miramar,
L'Assemblée des Femmes

Biography
Vittoria, Princesse Orsini

Essays
Oscar Wilde, appréciation d'une oeuvre et d'une
destinée
Oscar Wilde, ou la "destinée" de l'homosexuel

Translations
John Webster: Le Démon Blanc
Erskine Caldwell: Les Voies du Seigneur
Jonathan Swift: Voyages de Gulliver

Translations with Magali Merle
Ernesto "Che" Guevara: Souvenirs de la Guerre
Révolutionnaire
Ralph Ellison: Homme invisible

THE VIRILITY FACTOR

A NOVEL BY
ROBERT MERLE

Translated from the French by
MARTIN SOKOLINSKY

MCGRAW-HILL BOOK COMPANY
New York / St. Louis / San Francisco / Düsseldorf / Mexico / Toronto

Originally published in France under the title *Les Hommes Protégés,* copyright © 1974 by Editions Gallimard.

1 2 3 4 5 6 7 8 9 B P B P 7 9 8 7

Library of Congress Cataloging in Publication Data

Merle, Robert, date
The virility factor.
Translation of Les hommes protégés.
I. Title.
PZ3.M547Vi3   [PQ2625.E5278]   843'.9'14   76-58513
ISBN 0-07-041496-3

To Catherine or to Sébastien

1

A windowless, air-conditioned room. Oak wainscoting halfway up. Above this, the walls were white with a single print depicting a scene from the anti-smallpox vaccination in Cuba in 1900. Thick carpeting that I sank into up to the ankles. A big, comfortable armchair in which, at a wave, I buried myself.

Then, a long silence. I had come there to speak, but they didn't look like they were about to let me. Letting people speak isn't something the important people of this world like to do. They prefer hearing themselves rather than listening to others. On top of that, as I knew all too well, I wasn't *persona grata*. Not me; not what I had to say. They let me stew. That way, I would understand my own insignificance right from the start.

There they were, all three of them, silent, on the other side of an oval table whose uncommon width symbolized, I suppose, all the distance between the Administration and the ordinary citizen. I had the impression (which made me feel younger without pleasing me) that I was taking an examination. Besides, although I'm a neurologist with years of practice, it *was* a bit like an exam and I wondered if I were going to flunk. The irony of it was that my career wasn't at stake. I had come there to defend the general interest to the very people who were responsible for it.

Three men faced me. In the middle, as massive and square as HEW's "Fascist Federal" architecture, Secretary of State Matthews. To the right of Matthews, Skelton, the Director of Health—health that he didn't have, judging from his emaciated physique. To the left of the Secretary of State, and considering him with a look of discreet contempt, Cresby, one of the President's brilliant advisers.

Of the three, I knew only Cresby. He was alert, small, slight, with jet-black eyes.

"He pretends to be a genius," my second wife, Anita, told me, not without a trace of bitterness. She had the feeling that, if it weren't for the misogynic culture of our times, she would also be one of the President's advisers instead of his secretary.

And, certainly, she's right. The word "competent" becomes almost pejorative when applied to Anita. Her knowledge is vast, and behind her lovely forehead, her superb dark auburn hair and her green eyes there is a miniature computer operating at a high level of efficiency.

I speak in all objectivity. I didn't see enough of my wife Anita to be truly in love with her. Careers came first with us, so we didn't live together. She came up to see me at night at my apartment in Wesley Heights two or three times a week and not at all when the White House was plunged in some crisis or other. I must say that I was always surprised at the repercussion of matters of state on the frequency of my orgasms.

It was through Anita that I had alerted the President to the dangers of Encephalitis 16 and the President had reacted—without going through HEW—by ordering Cresby to put me in charge of a commission of inquiry on the disease.

My confidential report was there, on the enormous table, between Matthews' big hairy paws. He was thumbing through it, both to show me that he hadn't read it and to make me feel his hostility by openly trifling with me. Although his silence was becoming more and more oppressive, I didn't put all the blame on Matthews. The President had started, God knows why, by going around him, and when the time had come to take action, he had put him back into the circuit. It was worse than offhand—it was humiliating.

Before that day, I had once seen Matthews on television: He

had the optimistic look of a politician and one of those square jaws that are supposed to reassure you about the future of the United States. His jaw hadn't changed, but his eyes, under his bushy black brows, were totally disagreeable—especially when he stared at me. I knew quite well how he saw me: a little wop the President had appointed out of the blue—without HEW's knowledge—to head a medical commission, just to please his secretary.

As to Cresby, the balding young genius, Matthews liked him still less. Cresby, active in all the undertakings that the President carried on behind the backs of the Cabinet, was the kingpin of what Matthews and his peers termed bitterly "the parallel administration." Matthews' only hope—quoth Anita—was that Cresby, arrogant with everyone (at times even with the President), might fall into disgrace. Anita shared that hope.

As to the Director of Health, the emaciated and yellowish Skelton, he looked as though he had been eaten away by his own vinegar. It was obvious that he hated everyone: Matthews, Cresby and me.

There was a fifth person in the room, one who took up little space—a woman. On entering, I had heard someone call her Mrs. White. A fairly ironic name, for Mrs. White was gray from head to toe. Dress, complexion, hair, it was all the same mousy shade. She was ageless and sexless and busied herself, wearing earphones, around a tape recorder. Like all very self-effacing people, she gave me the impression that she had erased herself out of life.

"Dr. Martinelli, I give you the floor," Matthews finally said, not with the look of giving it to me but of lending it to me—and for as short a time as possible.

I wasn't going to be intimidated. After all, it wasn't my fault if the President acted like an autocrat and governed without the knowledge of his Cabinet members. And it wasn't my fault either if they preferred to pocket affronts rather than resign. You have to pay a stiff price for Cabinet greatness.

I looked Matthews in the eyes and began in a firm voice: "The commission was set up by myself at the President's request on July twenty-seventh. Its purpose was to make a study of the facts now known about Encephalitis 16."

"Why that name?" asked Matthews abruptly.

I felt like telling him that he would know why if he'd read my report. Instead, I told him without impatience but without excessive amiability, "The first case that I observed was in room sixteen of the Georgetown University Hospital."

"Go on," Matthews said.

"In view of the fact that we had so little time, our study, up to now, covers only the major cities of the United States and foreign countries."

"Skip the foreign countries," Matthews said.

"But that part of the report could be of political interest."

"And just what might that interest be?" asked Matthews haughtily, as if I were too ignorant to venture into that domain.

"To the best of my knowledge, all big epidemics have spread, up to now, from east to west. This one is an exception—it's spreading from west to east. That's why Western Europe has a smaller number of cases than we do; as far as we know, the U.S.S.R. hasn't been hit as hard as Western Europe; and Asia is hardly touched. Furthermore, the study we've carried out shows that Japan and China are presently taking steps to prevent their populations from coming in contact with Westerners."

I had hit the nail on the head. Matthews raised his thick black brows interestedly and was about to pursue his questions when Cresby said, in a polite, quick and incredibly sharp voice, "Mr. Secretary, we won't dwell on that point. I've gone to the trouble of reading Dr. Martinelli's report"—a brief, treacherous smile—"and I've already briefed the President on its political implications regarding Asia."

As harsh to me as he was, I felt sorry for Matthews just then. No one could have let him know with less elegance that he was judged worthless and that everything important was done without his knowledge.

I could see Matthews grit his teeth. After pocketing affronts, now he had to swallow them.

"Go ahead, Dr. Martinelli," Matthews said, glancing at me furiously.

Naturally, he could treat me any way he wanted. I wasn't anybody important.

I went on: "Our inquiry showed that, in the large cities of the United States, seventy-three percent of the neurologists contacted were already aware of the problem. Two of them—Dr. Pierce of Los Angeles and Dr. Smith of Boston—had begun virological studies just like me. Unsuccessfully up to now."

"Why *unsuccessfully*?" asked Matthews with a note of shock that I found rather naïve.

Matthews must have thought that U.S. science could never meet defeat.

"Well, as far as I'm concerned, I've taken samples from encephalons affected by the disease and have tried to cultivate them."

And as Matthews (who felt he was out beyond his depth) was looking at me without speaking, under his thick black brows, I added, "The aim of this culture is to isolate and define the virus. But the seedings have failed up to now, probably because the sown media weren't adequate."

I stopped speaking. I looked at Matthews. He understood the seriousness of my words and felt like asking other questions. But since he also was afraid of betraying his ignorance, he made the wisest move. He squared his shoulders and jaws in that responsible-looking way that must have been so useful to him in his political career. Then he turned to Skelton in one monolithic block, as though his neck were screwed right into his trunk, and said, "Mr. Skelton, would you like to ask Dr. Martinelli some questions?"

I don't know what Skelton nourished himself on, but it certainly wasn't the milk of human kindness. He considered me. What little yellowish skin he had on his face wrinkled and his teeth appeared. A death's-head that smiled. An icy smile. Now it was my turn to look at him. He had such a narrow torso that you wondered how nature had managed to put a heart and lungs in there. Nothing but spite kept all that standing. The man's eyes! As yellow as a cat's! And they matched his skin! And, deep down, aside from his natural venom, he was angry with me, too. He had also been given a back seat. In terms of the chain of command, he was the one who should have given me that assignment, not Cresby. And I'm sure that this affront, just at that second, counted more than anything I might say about the nation's health.

"Dr. Martinelli," he said in a weak, cracking, wheezing voice, "I'd like to ask you a few questions. They might have the merit of shortening your oral report."

How courteous. I had hardly begun and I was already talking too much.

Skelton went on: "According to what you've just said, it's been impossible to develop a vaccine against Encephalitis 16 in the United States."

"In the United States and, to the best of our knowledge, abroad."

"Have tried and tested drugs had any effect on Encephalitis 16?"

"No, not to the extent we've been able to use them."

"Why the restriction?"

"The incubation period of the disease is about a week. During that time, it shows itself only by disturbances in sight, speech and motility. But these disturbances are minor. They aren't accompanied by fever and don't prevent the victim from engaging in his usual activities. Most of the time the people don't even see a doctor. And when the disease manifests itself, it's too late."

"How does it manifest itself?"

"In an extremely brutal manner. The victim loses consciousness and falls into a coma. That's the reason we concluded we were up against a new disease. No known encephalitis develops in such a startling way."

"In cases where the disease was treated right from the onset of the minor disturbances that you've described, did antibiotics or cortisone succeed in checking its development?"

"To the best of our knowledge, no."

"When the victim lapses into a coma, is there anything you can do?"

"No."

"Could some people have recovered spontaneously?"

"If they have, it happened before the coma and wasn't reported in our study."

"Then, am I correct in saying that, in all of the cases you have observed or have been reported to you, the outcome of the disease has always been fatal?"

"Yes."

Skelton moistened his lips and went on: "How does Encephalitis 16 spread?"

"The disease is contagious from the first day of incubation." I added, "Because the victim doesn't quite realize that he's got it and since the incubation period lasts a week, he can go on contaminating a great number of people during that time."

I had a special reason for saying that. The press still hadn't gotten wind of Encephalitis 16. They didn't even know what name we'd given it. This silence seemed disastrous to me. I would have liked the Administration to make my report public and to take the necessary preventive measures at once. It was obvious that the free movement of people had to be restricted as much as possible—no matter what the economic harm resulting from such a decision—if they wanted to keep the epidemic from spreading like wildfire.

I went on: "I'd like to point out an important fact. At first sight, the number of cases doesn't seem high. One thousand two hundred and seventy-five cases in two months isn't enormous for a city like New York. But I want to warn you against optimism. It's not the number of cases that's alarming but the rate of increase in all the towns surveyed. If this trend continues in the same proportions, we may be up against an epidemic."

I hadn't minced words. On the contrary, I'd thrown them on the table with all desirable force and in so doing I had obviously pierced the hide (thick as it was) of Secretary Matthews. Although his eyes were hidden under his beetle brows, I read in them a certain degree of emotion. After a moment he spread both arms away from his body and, his hands open, said with a mixture of fright and incredulity, "Is a big epidemic possible?"

I was going to drive the nail home, since it had to be done.

"Mr. Secretary, if you'll allow me to be frank, there's an optimistic supposition in your question. You think actually that, in view of the progress made by the medical profession, it shouldn't take long to stop such an epidemic."

"Well, am I wrong?"

"You may be. Let's suppose that we're dealing with a virus that can't be isolated or identified."

"For example?" asked Skelton with his weak and squeaky voice.

"The Spanish flu of nineteen-eighteen."

"Dr. Martinelli," said Skelton, looking as though he'd caught me in error, "I'd like to point out that immense progress has been made in virological research since nineteen-eighteen."

"That's true," I said sharply. "But it doesn't mean that we're going to find a vaccine against E-16 overnight. The Asiatic flu took only a few months to cause twenty-two million deaths."

"How many do you say?"

"Twenty-two million."

"That's a lot more than the number of deaths for all the countries combined in World War One," Cresby said.

What Cresby said was correct, but, judging by his triumphant tone of voice, all those dead meant little to him, except to score a point against Matthews.

"Please continue, Dr. Martinelli," said Matthews with a gesture of his hand, as if he were brushing off a fly.

"There's another point I'd like to emphasize—the age of the victims. According to the statistics we've come up with . . ."

"Just a second, please, Doctor," Mrs. White said. "I'm having a little trouble with the tape recorder. It isn't recording anymore."

The eyes of the three men facing me turned at the same time to Mrs. White. Being neither young nor pretty, she had not, as yet, attracted their attention. For them, she was a woman between two ages who performed a lowly function and had scarcely more importance than a table. Except that a table didn't get itself all fouled up and Mrs. White did. Because, naturally, she didn't know how to use a machine. For once, all three of them agreed on something. I could read it in their eyes, along with the superior indulgence with which they accepted the fact that feminine ineptness might halt the progress of important business. If it hadn't been for their dignity, they would have gone over and gotten that damned tape recorder going again in three shakes of a lamb's tail.

I was sure that Mrs. White could sense everything that those gentlemen were thinking just then. She knew that it was wrong, but she let herself be influenced by their judgment to the point of really getting fouled up. I saw it from my seat. Blushing, tears in her eyes, she had to exert an enormous effort to rectify her error, doing a great deal of fumbling and spending twice as much time as necessary.

"I'm ready," she finally said, straightening herself, crimson-faced, her eyes wet.

A little silence. Those sitting across the table again turned their eyes to me. Since everything was working once more, Mrs. White was tossed back to nonexistence.

I resumed: "I was speaking about the age of the victims. There is one thing I'd like to point out in this regard. In the twenty-nine cities we surveyed, the cases fell within a bracket ranging from twelve to seventy-five years of age."

Which meant nothing to my audience—except, of course, to Cresby, since he had read the report.

"I'd like to point out that this observation is surprising. What our study shows is that no boy under the age of puberty appears in the cases that have been counted in the United States or in foreign countries. On the other hand, we have very few cases over seventy years of age, and these were vigorous old men who still led an active sex life."

In Skelton's long, gaunt face I saw a gleam of derision. In a weak voice but one loaded with venom he said, "Dr. Martinelli, you seem to find a connection between Encephalitis 16 and sexuality. Aren't you just going along with the times?"

His tone of voice was so aggressive that I had an urge to answer with some insolent remark. For instance: If sexuality is a fashion, you couldn't have gone along with it very much. Instead of that, I placed my hands flat on the table and replied evenly, "The connection between spermatogenesis and ailments at first sight foreign to the genital system is undeniable. You know as well as I do that, according to an inquiry of research workers from the Syracuse Medical Center, men who underwent vasectomy were particularly vulnerable to arthritis, articular rheumatism and to multiple sclerosis."

"I'm familiar with the Syracuse study," Skelton said. "The

team of researchers doesn't present its conclusions as certain, in view of the small number of cases examined."

"Neither do I," I answered curtly.

"After all," Matthews said then with a common sense for which I was grateful, "the nature of the connection between the two phenomena is unimportant—facts are facts. Dr. Martinelli, you said that, according to your statistics, no boy under the age of puberty appears among the victims of Encephalitis 16. Would you say as much for girls?"

Just then Cresby turned to Matthews and, with an arrogance that disconcerted me, gave a little sneering laugh. He, of course, wouldn't have raised that question; he had read my report. I looked at him. He was exultant. The fellow was an imperialist. He didn't just want to know. He wanted to win and jeer.

His reaction had little bearing on the seriousness of the problem. After all, we weren't there to thwart Matthews but to convince him to take the action required by the situation.

I looked at Matthews and said in a courteous tone of voice, which he had hardly granted me, "I'm glad you've raised this point. It's a very important point. Whether in the United States or abroad, not one victim of Encephalitis 16 has been a woman."

Skelton and Matthews were petrified, and the more petrified of the two, without a doubt, was Secretary Matthews. Square and monolithic, he pressed his big hairy paws one against the other and, elbows on the table, he thrust forward his carnivorous jaws, looked at me from under his thick brows and said harshly, "Encephalitis 16 doesn't strike women? Is that possible?"

Although he hadn't framed his question very scientifically, I answered patiently, "This isn't the only instance where women are immune to a disease found in men. For example—hemophilia."

"What? What?" asked Matthews in utter bewilderment. "What's the connection between hemophilia and Encephalitis 16?"

"There isn't any," said Cresby squashingly. "Dr. Martinelli is making a comparison between two immunities. Women enjoy total immunity with regard to hemophilia and Encephalitis 16."

"And how do you explain this immunity?" asked Matthews with that note of shocked naïveté I'd already observed in him.

"I'm not explaining it," I said. "It's proven data."

There was a long, oppressive silence. And they needed it. It took time to absorb a fact like that. What astonished me wasn't the silence but Mrs. White—or, rather, the way she was contemplating us. She was stupefied to see all those masculine eyes converging suddenly on her. Oh, she had no illusions. In her fifties, gray from head to foot, with not even the vestiges of a former beauty, she wasn't used to being looked at—neither with such insistence nor by so many gentlemen at the same time. She turned crimson. She felt a vague guilt about her immunity and attempted a timid smile of apology in the Secretary's direction. For once Matthews didn't react with the toothy and dazzling smile of a politician. He stared bitterly at Mrs. White for a long time.

Actually, I'm sure this all took no more than two or three seconds, but later on, when I recalled that session, it was always this moment that I saw again.

Nothing came of my meeting with Matthews. Three weeks after our encounter he hadn't warned the public, and none of the prophylactic action that I'd called for had been taken. What really surprised me was the fact that the press still hadn't been aroused. As was frequently the case, foreign affairs kept them from seeing domestic affairs. At the time, the mass media had eyes and ears only for Thailand and the consequential initiatives that the President had just taken there. As to Encephalitis 16, there wasn't just silence; there was utter apathy. Oh, I did read a few little articles on the disease here and there but nothing really reflecting the gravity of the situation.

But it hadn't escaped the attention of neurologists. My mail and the phone calls I got bore that out. But these doctors, just as I had been three weeks before, were very respectful of the Administration, trusted it and relied on the commission that I headed to take the necessary action. As to the public, I made a sickening observation: The number of fatal cases wasn't high enough for them to become aware of the problem. What's more, people had the impression that an epidemic was the "kind of thing" that could still break out only in Africa, Asia, at the worst in Latin America. Certainly not in the United States. When I mentioned my uneasiness to an editor from the Washington *Post*, I ran into polite skepticism. In him, as in many others, I discerned two convictions that combined to have cumulative effects: blind faith in the U.S. medical profession and another faith, no less blind, in the ability of the Administration to mobilize against any national danger.

I'll admit I was amazed and frightened by the responsibilities burdening me and for which nothing in my life had prepared me. I was uneasy to the point of losing sleep, and I spent my nights wondering what I should do. I noted uneasily that Anita was no help to me. Since the presidential elections were approaching, I saw her less and less, and when I did see her she only spoke to me about the elections or Thailand. When I finally managed to get the conversation around to Encephalitis 16 and the urgent need for prophylaxis, she became very evasive: "HEW," she said, "won't be long in taking the action that you recommended. A little patience, Ralph. 'Your' epidemic isn't the only thing on their minds."

I wound up thinking that my commission and myself served as an alibi for an Administration that, for reasons that escaped me, couldn't or wouldn't do anything. On September 28, without saying anything to Anita—who would have fought it tooth and nail—I made a decision. I communicated it to my collaborators and asked Cresby for an appointment so that I could let him know about it.

The prematurely balding man wasn't as nasty as usual. Oh yes, his little eyes, intensely black, were still as keen. But his features were rather drawn, his nose anxious, his lips bitter. I told him straight off that I no longer wanted to be an accomplice to HEW's silence and inaction. I gave him my resignation from the commission over which I presided.

A surprise: Cresby didn't try to dissuade me. On the contrary, he shared my point of view. With perfect coolness he made revelations that, coming from him, astonished me. HEW's inertia wasn't Matthews' doing, as I had thought, but the President's. The latter had been caught in the trap of his own cleverness. At first he had capitalized on the lack of interest that the press had shown for E-16. He'd hushed up my statistics and put my report on ice. Why? Because if he had revealed its existence, he'd have been forced to take action that would have made him unpopular. And he was already unpopular enough because of Thailand, where he was waging one of those clandestine wars that everybody knew about. Besides, if he revealed my report now, it would touch off a storm. Everybody would rake him over the coals for this tardy revelation; they would blame him for all sorts of deaths, and he would lose the presidential elections to Senator Sherman.

I listened. I stood there gaping. It astonished me that being reelected was more important for the President than the human lives that he could have saved by taking the necessary action sooner.

Cresby started to laugh. "Doctor! You're doing the President an injustice. Do you think he's only considering his reelection? Not at all. Don't you know the great mission that the President believes God has given him—to preserve American influence in Southeast Asia? It's quite simple. If Thailand goes, it's like a house of cards—the whole thing will collapse. And only the President can save Thailand. At least, that's what he thinks. In this light, you understand, what's a little epidemic that, here in the United States itself, has still killed only forty thousand people—less than highway accidents in a year?"

Strange political philosophy. What counted was never what we were upset about here but what was going on at the other end of the earth. Then, too, I didn't really care for the cynical way in which that sharp young man was talking about his boss. Cresby had a high-handed way of talking about everything, including Encephalitis 16. He was wrong. Maybe he'd been born with a silver spoon in his mouth, but disease isn't like poverty—it's something you catch.

I told him so. I also emphasized that the important thing wasn't the number of cases but the speed at which they multiplied.

Cresby then made a suggestion by innuendo, one that left me aghast. Since I planned to hand in my resignation, who was stopping me from making my confidential report public? After all, the report was mine, since I'd written it.

I gave this surprising proposition a chilly reply. The report wasn't an individual effort but the collective work of a commission that had been sworn to secrecy. Betraying that secrecy would not be ethical.

Then, without going into greater detail, I left Cresby, his ear cocked and his fur bristling. I began to suspect that the wonder boy had fallen out with his President and was manipulating me. His aim was clear: He was trying to use my scruples to play a dirty trick on his former boss. And he would manage to come out innocent as a lamb, while I was incriminated.

I called Anita on the phone and asked her to come up to my place. She began by saying no—too much work. I mentioned my meeting with Cresby, and at once she told me in a hurried way, "Okay, Ralph. I'll be at your place at ten."

At night, of course. I had time on my hands. I discreetly supervise the bedtime of my son, Dave, age ten. He isn't Anita's child. Her career plans exclude children. Dave is the son of my first wife, Eileen, who died of septicemia at thirty-two, when Dave was four.

I showered and got into my pajamas, which always amused Anita because I had them tailored. In vain I'd explained to her that people on the short side, like me, can't afford to have drooping pajama bottoms.

At nine-thirty I moved into Dave's room to persuade him to turn off his light. A peaceful scene. The Airedale, "Buzz," (a temporary boarder at our house; he belonged to a neighbor lady) was stretched out at the foot of the bed, his snout on his paws. Already dozing off, he gave a minimal welcome—one eye opened and his tail slapped the rug. Dave didn't move. Sitting up against a bolster folded in half, he was reading. His black lashes made a bushy shadow on his cheek. I sat at the foot of his bed and looked at him. He was rather small for his age but nicely built, with an oval face, mat skin and wavy chestnut hair. His size, the outline of his face, his complexion and the lashes came from me. His eyes were Eileen's. Every night, for six years, I had come back to that face.

Arranging my life hadn't been easy. I had an excellent neighbor lady who took Dave to school in the morning and brought him home in the afternoon and another neighbor lady who, being childless, was happy to keep an eye on him until I got back from the hospital.

Since I'm talking about my neighbors, I note (now I can laugh about it) that when I had just moved into our house in Wesley Heights, they used to wonder "if they should invite the Martinellis," when they gave a party.

This hesitation didn't last. They accepted me soon enough. Thanks to Eileen. Thanks, too—and I quote them—to my "Latin charm." Which means that they wound up assigning a *plus* sign to what they had assigned a *minus* sign before knowing me. It's racism but in reverse. From the moment it's friendly, I'm not one to be fussy. When my neighbors are around I'll even put on an act and be more Italian than the Italians. They eat that up. Especially the women.

"I'm turning off the light, Ralph," said Dave, rewarding me for the tact with which I'd waited—without saying a word—until he was ready.

I got to my feet. I ran my right hand over Dave's hair, resisting the desire to kiss him (he disapproved). Back in the living room, I waited for that other half I so rarely saw.

To my friends—and, in particular, those who had known Eileen—my remarriage under such conditions didn't seem justified. They were right. My excuse was that I had no choice. I married Anita because, having learned of my affair with her, my ex-mother-in-law, who wanted custody of Dave, accused me of immorality. Now, between that accusation and me stood the thickness of a marriage license.

It was rather thin. Our married life wasn't very everyday. Me, "the mother hen," as Anita put it, me who had acquired the love of family from my Italian ancestors, I stamped and fumed over that disappearing wife. But Anita was entirely satisfied with the situation. And why shouldn't she have been, since she was the one who'd forced it on me?

Ten o'clock: There she was—a delicious thirty-two, auburn hair, green eyes, her nose "delicately chiseled." At least, that's the way she described herself in her moments of vanity.

She came rushing in and, very excited, threw herself at me. She was so greedy to hear me that she hardly let me speak.

She was horrified twice, but to different degrees. My

resignation—she could accept that. But give my report to the newspapers! I couldn't do that! That would be awful! A few weeks before the presidential elections! Besides, I didn't have the moral right to do it. The report didn't belong to me!

I let the flood go by—a bit surprised that Anita invoked the idea of moral right for an Administration that wouldn't move a pinky to defend public health. When she had exhausted her invective, I pointed out to her that, in this case, there were not one but two duties: the format duty that she had so clearly described, which I myself had cited in objecting to Cresby's suggestion; and the real duty toward the people of this country—namely, that of alerting them at any cost to the danger that threatened them.

This done, I allayed her fears. I had made a Xerox of the one copy of my report that the commission held, but it would stay locked up in my safe-deposit box at the bank. I wasn't going to publish it under any circumstances. I'd have been too afraid of touching off a nationwide panic. What I planned to do, on the contrary, if HEW went on marking time, was to contact the press—but as a doctor and a private individual, not as the ex-chairman of the commission.

Anita looked at me. That's what reassured her and set her at ease. She sat down on the couch at my side. Her green eyes changed—and in a way that I knew quite well. I must say this for Anita: The most serious problems, political or private, never robbed her desire for sex or food for long. At the first respite, each of the two hungers whetting the other, she would devastate my bed and plunder my refrigerator.

So I wasn't surprised to find her, a few minutes later, in my kitchenette, devouring ham and eggs that she had just cooked. I took advantage of the fact that she had her mouth full and so was forced to listen. Again I pleaded with gravity, with passion, the urgency of the action I had called for. Her meal over, I followed her, still pleading, to the bedroom.

"Ralph, dear," Anita said, stretched out across my bed in the first contentment of digestion, "you know the latest news from Thailand as well as I do. We're ripe for a second war in Southeast Asia. Result: A few weeks before the presidential elections, Father's popularity—" she refers to the President that way for fear of being bugged, even in my apartment—"has gone way down. Of course, I'll give Father a report. He must know the part that Cresby is playing in all this. In my opinion, Father shouldn't have fired Cresby before the elections. That little snake knows too many things. Ralph, please, don't make that face! You've got to understand! In politics, you have to make choices. There'll always be priorities. First, save Thailand and, to save Thailand, win the election. But we can't raise the issue of your encephalitis right now. We've waited too long. It would be the worst possible mistake. Everyone would say: *Now* you decide to tell the public? Everybody would let us have it, and Sherman would be elected."

I went on pleading, but it was hopeless. Politely or to change the subject, Anita asked me for news about Dave. It wasn't very good. Dave was a bit anemic. Now that I had resigned and was unemployed, I would probably take a week off—to get a change of scene. Anita smiled, and as that smile irritated me (I knew what she thought of my relationship with Dave) I asked her, rather aggressively, if she thought it was entirely normal for a woman not to have children.

"Normal?" she asked disdainfully. "I don't know what normal is. And I don't see why my ovaries should run my life. For me it's the brain that runs the show."

Having spoken, she fell asleep instantly, like a faucet that you turn off. Besides her great talents, Anita had a hardy nature. But perhaps not overly sensitive. When, in describing the spread of Encephalitis 16 to her, I spoke about the death of Dr. Morley, who headed the reanimation center at the hospital where I worked, she hadn't shown much emotion. Nevertheless, she knew him. She had gone with me to his place for lunch on several occasions.

Clearly, in this affair, we weren't, we couldn't be on the same wavelength. Morley's death had in itself overwhelmed me, so why not say as much? Because his fate could have been mine if I had stayed at the hospital instead of chairing a commission.

I looked at Anita. Her dark, brownish hair scattered in a halo, she slept, right where she had dropped, across by bed. As I didn't want to wake her, I was going to make do with the living-room couch. She slept in perfect peace, her face firm, even in her slumber. Naturally. She wouldn't die of Encephalitis 16. That thought didn't disturb her waking or sleeping. Anita had no anxiety on that score. Neither for herself nor, I fear, for me.

The following day I sent my letter of resignation and, at noon, received a phone call from Anita. The phone call was elliptical (still her fear of being bugged). "Ralph, I've spoken to Father. It's out of the question to publish the report, but Matthews could make a television appearance to alert the people and give them some recommendations."

I hung up. It was a half promise announcing halfway action. All right. I would go away, as planned, for a week. If on my return nothing had been done, I would have to do something myself.

In Jamaica, in a remote spot in the Blue Mountains, at medium altitude, I rented a little peasant shanty without plumbing, without radio, without television—in fact, without electricity but boasting a splendid view over the southeastern part of the island.

After this cure of primitive living, from which Dave and I returned in high spirits, I landed in Washington and there, baggage collected and customs cleared, I bought the New York *Times*. On the second page I read with stupefaction long excerpts from my report.

Feverishly, I bought all that day's papers. I leafed through them. What an amazing change! A week before, the papers had spoken only of Thailand and the elections. And now one single subject, only one: Encephalitis 16. Long quotes everywhere from my confidential report, and the White House was under indictment—implicitly or explicitly—for its concealment, its failure to act and its incompetence.

Sure enough, there had been a leak and, for the newspapers, since they had been unable to reach me, there could be no doubt: I was the source and I was on the run. Of course, no one expressed it in those terms. It was enough to say that I had resigned and had disappeared.

Back in my apartment—it was 9:00 P.M.—I phoned Luigi Fabrello, my lawyer. There were strident howls in the receiver: *"Where the hell were you?"* What's more, I didn't have the time to open my mouth. Luigi roared again: "Shut up. I'm coming over."

An hour later he was there at my door, his eyes dark, his hair tragic, his face Roman and, on his cheeks, whiskers so dark and so thick that he looked as though he had never shaved. "You can expect to be arrested at any time," said Luigi.

After finishing his dramatics, Luigi got a grip on himself. He listened to me. Then we drafted, weighing each word, a written statement for the New York *Times* in which I set the record straight. After that he went away majestically, carrying off the statement and advising me not to contact Anita before the next day, when my statement had appeared.

But the next day—a Saturday—I didn't have the time to inform Anita of my return. At 8:00 A.M. two policemen showed up—fortunately, Dave was still sleeping—and the older one (who looked a lot more like a college professor than a cop) said politely, "Dr. Martinelli, I have only one question to ask you. Is it true that after resigning you made a photocopy of your report?"

"That's right."

"Can I ask you to show me that photocopy?"

"That's impossible today. It's in my safe-deposit box at the bank. And the bank is closed."

"When did you put that photocopy in your safe-deposit box?"

"The day of my resignation: September twenty-eighth."

"Have you been back to your bank since?"

"No. I left for Jamaica on the twenty-ninth and I didn't get back until last night."

He nodded with a friendly look. An odd cop. Fifty or so, thoughtful eyes behind thick glasses, high forehead, benign face and manners that couldn't have been more courteous.

"Well," he said, "we'll come back for you on Monday morning to open your safe-deposit box at the bank. And until then, Dr. Martinelli, would you be good enough to stay in Washington and keep your door closed to reporters?"

They left. I was beside myself. Apparently the fact that, after my resignation, I'd Xeroxed my report had incriminated me. I'd talked to no one but Anita. Obviously, she'd betrayed me. I picked up the phone and called her.

"Anita?"

"Is that you, Ralph?"

The amused tone of that voice broke my heart.

"Anita, I have one thing and only one thing to tell you. After the little informing job that you've just done, it's out of the question for me to go on seeing you, listening to you or talking to you."

I hung up. My legs were trembling and sweat ran down my cheeks.

I spent a rotten weekend. I didn't like the looks of that suave cop. I expected to be arrested on Monday, and, if not for the advice that Luigi had given me, I might have tried to escape immediately and hide out someplace with Dave. I saw a horrible injustice in the fact that I was the only one in this business to have tried to do my duty and yet the only one being threatened by the long arm of the law.

Besides, on Saturday afternoon, while taking a taxi downtown, I saw a man suddenly collapse on the sidewalk. Of course, this could have been something other than E-16. But I didn't tell the cab driver to stop. The instinct of self-preservation had been stronger than my professional duty. Afterward, I couldn't stop thinking about this betrayal and wouldn't forgive myself.

Finally Monday rolled around and, at 9:00 A.M., the older cop showed up alone. He reminded me of his name, V. C. Moore, in a friendly way, but he remained silent at my side throughout the drive to my bank. When my safe-deposit box had been opened, I handed him the Xerox of the report.

He flipped through it, but not just any old way. On a scrap of paper he had page numbers, and those were the pages of my report that he studied carefully. His examination lasted five minutes, no longer. After which he shut the file and handed it to me with a bitter smile.

"Dr. Martinelli, that puts you entirely in the clear. I never really believed you were guilty. Your psychological profile—such as we know it—would make that highly improbable. So long, Dr. Martinelli."

With that, abruptly, he went away. Perhaps it's an understatement to say that he went away—he disappeared as though he'd gone through a trapdoor, and I remained alone before my open safe-deposit box, stupefied at being free again. Moore hadn't told me, and his disappearance had been so prompt that I hadn't had time to ask him just why my photocopy exonerated me.

This wasn't to be the last of my surprises. Back at my apartment I was called by a White House secretary. Mrs. Martinelli was expecting me at 1:00 P.M. in the Chinese restaurant. I didn't have time to say yes or no—she hung up.

Despite this offhand way of making the appointment with me, I was going to go there, for I'd begun to regret the phone call that I had made on Saturday.

In the old days, Anita and I used to go regularly to the Yenching Palace, but since the Peking Chinese began eating nearly all their meals there Anita, who had an abnormal fear of being spied on, had dragged me to Mr. Twang's, who, aside from his fine cooking, offered the additional advantage of reserving us a cozy little room upstairs. And there, enthroned on a red velvet seat, her forehead lighted up by a little painted lantern with gilded fringe, I found Anita, exquisitely dressed. I apologized for being late, I sat beside her, I praised her clothes. A waste of breath. I don't know any more who had said that men, never women, could be disarmed by a compliment. Anita looked at me with her green eyes, without saying a word.

Truce. Mrs. Twang had come to take our order. She wore a black silk dress with a little slit that revealed her right leg up to the calf and, on her lips, an archaic smile. It never left her face as long as her little paper wasn't filled. After which she folded it, bowed her head and withdrew. My eyes followed the little slit of the dress.

"Still fascinated by those big calves?"

The attack was sharp and her green eyes pitiless.

I remained silent. I wasn't going to cross swords over Mrs. Twang's calf.

"What a surprise!" Anita said. "I certainly didn't expect to see you. I was getting ready to die of loneliness."

"Listen, Anita . . ."

"What's that—you're talking to me? And I thought you never wanted to see me again or talk to me or listen to me! Have I repeated your brilliant formula in the right order?"

"Anita, please."

"You say *please* to me? What a promotion! It looks like I can be seen again, heard again. I'm endowed with speech again!"

"*And how* you are!"

"Naturally, I can keep quiet if the fact that I open my mouth displeases you."

"No, I think, on the contrary, that an explanation is quite in order."

"An explanation! With an informer!"

"As far as I'm concerned, at least, I have something to tell you."

"Another little informing job that you've uncovered?"

"Stop, please, Anita. It's important."

"Important—who for?"

"Anita, there's something new."

"I know what's new. It's the way you're treating me."

"This new something doesn't involve you."

"Oh, God, another woman!"

"Anita, stop!"

"No phallocracy, Doctor! Outcast that I am, I still have the right to express myself."

"Anita, tell me, yes or no—did you tell Moore that I'd Xeroxed the report?"

"Yes, Your Honor. And that's how I got you cleared."

"Then you know?"

"Of course. Moore phoned me after leaving your bank."

"And how and why was my photocopy enough to clear me?"

"Slowly, mister. First apologize."

"Apology before an explanation?"

"Naturally. What good would it do you to apologize afterward?"

"I apologize."

Her green eyes gripped me. They weren't in the least pacified. Anita said with vehemence, "Ralph, you were awful on the phone, absolutely awful!"

"I've already said that I'm sorry."

"Oh, it's so easy. You just say, I'm sorry, and then we're even. It's all washed away."

"Oh, no!" I said in exasperation. "Apologies or no apologies, it looks as though we're going to discuss that phone call forever!"

Mrs. Twang made her appearance, beaming, carrying a tray loaded with bowls and small plates which she placed on the table. Her movements were of the same kind as her smile— precise, quick, light, with a sort of a polite straightforwardness that honored her quests.

She left. What my apology couldn't do, the egg rolls could. Anita ate and her mood softened.

"Of course," she said with her mouth full, "I never for a minute believed that you were responsible for the leak."

"Why?"

She chewed, she swallowed and she said in an imperceptibly disdainful tone, "Dave."

"What about Dave?"

"Did you want to go to jail and let your mother-in-law get her hands on Dave?"

"I hadn't thought about that."

"You didn't think about it *consciously*."

She pounced on a second slice of egg roll with her chopsticks and gobbled it up. I still hadn't begun to eat. I was looking at her. She fascinated me, both by her appetite and by the knowledge she had of my reactions.

"Second point: In the photocopy that the New York *Times* has, the typographical errors have been corrected by hand."

"So?"

"You're lazy."

"I'm lazy?"

"Yes, when you have a report or an article typed in three copies, you never correct the typos on your personal copy. So I was sure that the Xerox sent to the New York *Times* hadn't been made from your copy and I asked Moore to check on that."

I felt a bit crushed. She never missed a trick. She remembered everything and, when the time came, she made her move. And while she was saving my neck, I was dragging her through the mud.

"Anita," I said, "now that I know, what do I have to do? Do you want me to get down on my knees?"

She placed her left hand over my right hand and said with an affection bordering on condescension, "You're charming, Ralph—that's your only excuse."

With that, she downed a quarter of an egg roll. I kept still, not very happy. I was inclined to think that her generosity humiliated me. I resumed: "Who sent that Xerox to the New York *Times*? Cresby?"

"Who else?"

"Moore has proof?"

"No. Besides, what does it matter? Father is sunk at any rate."

And "at any rate," curiously enough, she didn't look like it bothered her much. On the contrary, there was a zest, a cheerfulness about her. I looked at her. I still hadn't made up my mind about starting my meal. Yet it was supposed to be urgent. Having devoured her share of the egg rolls, she was attacking mine. Which didn't prevent her from talking at the same time.

"You've been away for ten days, Ralph. You don't know the latest figures on Encephalitis 16 any more than the papers do. It's frightening (she looked only moderately frightened). And that's not the worst of it, Ralph, not by a long shot. We know that the big insurance companies are planning to cancel life-insurance policies."

"Do they have the right to do that?"

"They'll take the right. Father's goose is cooked, Ralph. According to the last Gallup poll, only thirty-two percent of the people are behind him."

"But Senator Sherman is in trouble, too. I read in Saturday's papers that his running mate had just had a stroke. Sherman's got to come up with another Vice President as soon as possible. That isn't so easy."

"He's already found one," said Anita.

"How do you know?"

"She phoned me."

I looked at her.

"*She?* It's a woman? The Vice President a woman?"

"I think," Anita said, considering me with solemnity, her two chopsticks in midair, "that *under the present circumstances*"—she was the one who gave it the emphasis—

"Sherman has shown himself to be very realistic and very wise in selecting a woman as Vice President."

She trapped a section of egg roll between her chopsticks and swallowed it.

"Who is she?"

"Sarah Bedford."

I frowned. There were several shades of women's libbers, and Sarah Bedford belonged to the hard-liners.

"So what did she say to you over the phone?"

"That she understood very well if, for the time being, I stayed at Father's side to see him through his defeat but that, after the elections, she was counting on me."

"As her secretary?"

"As her adviser."

A little silence.

"That's a promotion," I said more coldly than I'd meant to.

But Anita didn't sense my reticence. She wasn't listening to me. She hardly saw me. Her green eyes shone brightly; she tossed back her dark, brownish hair with a triumphant look and said fervently, "It's a magnificent promotion, Ralph. Not only for Sarah and for me. For women! Ralph, think of it! If Sherman died, Sarah would be the first woman President of the United States."

I thought of it, since I'd been asked to do so. I felt no special sympathy for Sherman. I'd seen him two or three times on TV. He was a man of forty-five, athletically built and didn't look his age. No one would have ever thought for a second that death might threaten him in the near future. And Anita wasn't the only one—I would have sworn to it—to have imagined, foreseen and even wished for that death. Misfortune was good for something, then, since it had produced—what were the exact words again?—that "magnificent promotion."

"Come on, leave me an egg roll or two," I said after a moment.

Anita stopped chewing, glanced at the dish, looked at me and broke out laughing. I laughed, too, after a time lag—mirthlessly.

A wish come true. A prophecy fulfilled. One month after his

election, President Sherman fell victim to the epidemic, and Sarah Bedford took the destiny of the United States in her small hands.

As for me, I wasn't in Washington on that day, so I didn't attend the inauguration of Sarah Bedford or Anita's installation which accompanied it. I had been hired by the Helsingforth Company and was heading a laboratory for virological research into Encephalitis 16, located in Blueville, Vermont. Dave was with me.

2

Blueville, Vermont

I've survived—that's something. But it doesn't give me any guarantee for the future. Until further orders I belong to the handful of Americans that the newspapers call *P.M.* (Protected Men). This designates economically or scientifically important men placed in a *P.Z.* (Protected Zone) specifically set up to isolate them from the contagion.

As I emphasized in my report, Encephalitis 16 is not transmitted by a vector agent—like the mosquito or the tick—but by contact and only from a subject in incubation to a healthy person. Accordingly, persons enjoying biological immunity to the disease—women, boys under the age of puberty and old men—can approach P.M.s without contaminating them. On the other hand, an adult male can only be considered healthy enough to be allowed into a protected zone after undergoing a quarantine covering the incubation period. And that's just what happened with me on my arrival in Blueville.

The state of Vermont, which owes its name to the Frenchman Champlain, shares, with its neighboring Maine, a number of localities or place names that end in "ville." I like to think that in the case of Blueville (which isn't a town but a ranch) the English colonist who took over from the French anglicized *bleu* to "blue" and stopped there, too bored to translate *ville* to "city" or "town." The climate is rather cool in Blueville—especially for somebody who has been living in Washington for ten years. But, at least, when they aren't covered with snow, the tiers of plains are greenish. And the hills, also green (but a darker green), bear admirable coniferous trees.

Blueville is a rather incongruous cluster of buildings. There is nothing about the house itself to suggest what is ordinarily meant by a ranch. It's a mansion in that pseudo-Gothic style affected by a great number of colleges in this country. It has the defect characterizing that type of building: lack of authenticity.

I doubt that it will ever be found beautiful—even 300 years from now. Because of its enormity and overelaborate style, we call it, a bit sneeringly, "the castle." At least it has the merit of being spacious and of housing all our common activities: cafeteria, a library very well stocked with scientific works, meeting rooms, lounges and, in the basement, a heated pool.

Very few people live in the castle: Mr. Barrow, the administrator, and his wife; Dr. Rilke, the physician; the personal secretary of Mrs. Helsingforth, Emma Stevenson. As to the cook, Mike; his two helpers; and the three maids—they live in the basement. All of them are white. Even on the ranch, no blacks are to be seen. They say that Mrs. Helsingforth, the sovereign of these parts, can't bear the sight of them. What's especially strange, with regard to her, is that we never see her at all.

The laboratories and quarters for the research workers are wooden barracks, set up around the castle in what must have once been the grounds of a lavish estate. To make room for the frame houses many trees were cut down, and the buildings in general are enclosed by a high barbed-wire fence that does nothing for the scenery.

The militiawomen's post guards the only entrance to this compound. Their barracks building differs from ours in two respects: It is longer and flanked at one end by a wooden observation post that looms over all the buildings. At the top of the tower, covered by a roof of boards but open on all four sides, is a lookout post defended by a heavy machine gun that can swivel in a complete circle. In winter I've often felt sorry for the militiawoman on duty who, buried in a fur-lined overcoat, with a fur hat pulled down to her eyes and field glasses hanging around her neck, must stay up on her perch two or three hours at a stretch in the Siberian cold. At night a powerful searchlight, connected by some system or other to the machine gun, follows its rotation.

The ranch itself, Stienemeier told me, is sealed off by miles of barbed-wire fencing. I saw nothing of all that. I got there at night by car, asleep, Dave's head resting against my shoulder. I've never even seen the fence around the ranch, although I go on long horseback rides with Jespersen and Stienemeier over acres of fields and mountains.

Jespersen is at the head of a project different from mine. Stienemeier, too. I don't know what they're doing. We are supposed to say nothing among ourselves about our respective work. I don't know why Mrs. Helsingforth has sworn us to secrecy, but, up to now, while finding it absurd, we have respected her dictum. Jespersen, a chemist, is just over thirty. He is tall, with Scandinavian blond hair, a transparent complexion, eyes that are icy blue. Belying his appearance, he has a cheerful and carefree manner.

We call Stienemeier "Stien" because he hates his first name, Otto, and his wife "Mutsch" because he calls her that. Jespersen says that Stien is "full of years, white hair and dandruff," but actually he can't be more than sixty. He has a face furrowed with deep wrinkles and two or three successive bags under his eyes. The latter, which are gray-blue, imprisoned below by these bags and above by multiple folds drooping from his eyelids, seem to have a great deal of trouble fighting their way to you. But his gaze is keen, youthful and pugnacious. Stien is immensely cultured outside his specialization. Physically, he doesn't seem to have a particularly stunning shape. He's short, even shorter than I am, stooped, with narrow shoulders and a hollow chest. Nevertheless, he goes horseback riding with Jespersen and me on Sunday afternoons, and once he manages to perch himself on the little mare that has been set aside for him, he stays in the saddle. He has a marked preference for the gallop, perhaps because he doesn't like walking. His gait as a pedestrian is most individual. He takes very short steps that start from the knee, without seeming to bring his hips into action. He throws his feet—which are very small—from right and from left, the tips of his shoes pointed slightly inward.

Although Stien—like Mutsch—has a soft heart, he has a rough exterior. Always in a bad mood, his brows quarrelsome, his mouth sneering, he raves, scolds, swears, grumbles—all this in several languages. During these paroxysms he shouts in Yiddish. His face is a mass of tics, and he has lots of little obsessions, the most annoying of which is to remind you constantly that he's Jewish or, what amounts to the same thing, *that you aren't.* Which he does with a look that is at once piercing, provocative and suspicious, as though he were trying to spot in you an infinitesimal trace of anti-Semitism that had, so far, escaped him.

Stien is an eminent biologist, one who has published a great deal, but I admit that I haven't read any of his work, whereas he had the curiosity to stick his nose in the books and publications that I'd had the "castle" library acquire. He is therefore quite well informed about the project that I'm heading, although he makes a point of not referring to it in order to respect the secrecy that has been required of us.

I speak of Jespersen and of Stien because they've become my friends, but there are quite a few other research workers spread among the three projects. Their wives and their children live with them, each nuclear family in separate barracks. But we take our meals together at the "castle." And at night, in the lounges, we have little family parties that we try to enliven. At times we sing, dance, laugh and even put on plays. But all this entertainment—like that, I suppose, of prisoners—has a forced, rather unreal look.

Of course, I'm not a prisoner. I'm a *protected man*, a P.M. But I'm not oblivious to the fact that, at Blueville, everyone, except the parties concerned and their wives, utters these initials, P.M., with a kind of contempt. It's not a lack of courtesy. If it had been a failing of that kind, it would have been easy to spot. No, it's a lot more subtle. They give us the feeling that we are tolerated because of our work but that we rate no esteem or, still less, friendship.

Moreover, the protection we enjoy is revocable. In the

leonine contract that we had to sign with Mrs. Helsingforth—without seeing her; none of us has ever set eyes on her—she reserved the right to terminate it at any time and throw us at will into the shadows outside.

As far as I am concerned, I feel that sentence has only been deferred, even more so for me than for my companions. Nevertheless, the importance of my research should reassure me regarding the possibility of being sent away. It doesn't. I don't feel at all safe from such a fate. I say "feel," for my intuition is based on intangible indices. Yet the feeling keeps growing stronger. I have survived but live in fear of tomorrow.

Despite Dave, I feel rather lonely or, better stated, abandoned. Anita, who sits now at summit conferences on President Bedford's right, comes to see me once a month. Each time I have the same impression as any convict: The intervals between visits are long and the visit is short. That's why I greet Anita with a feeling of sadness and almost with reluctance. No sooner does she arrive than it seems that she has already gone away.

There is something military about Blueville, not only because of the armed militiawomen who guard us. The schedules are rigid, and there are many restrictions.

A siren wakes us up at 7:00 A.M. At eight, each of us is supposed to be in his laboratory. Lunch at one o'clock sharp. Supper at seven. Lights out at ten.

That means that at ten o'clock you must be in bed. Furthermore, it's a good idea to be in bed, for, five minutes to ten, two whistle blasts warn you that the electricity in the individual barracks is about to be turned off. Only the campus lights stay lit and the powerful searchlight on the lookout tower that illuminates, in turning, the lanes between barracks. If the beam catches you out of your residence after hours, you are requested by loudspeaker not to move until two mounted militiawomen take your name and lead you back to your quarters. The militiawomen are polite but contemptuous. It's pointless to try to talk to them. When they escort you, they take up positions on either side of you, and you walk with your head at the height of their boots, and you suddenly get the feeling that you're a black arrested by the mounted police in a Southern state.

The next day you find a note from Mr. Barrow, the administrator, on your desk. He is sorry to have to withhold ten dollars from your salary as a fine for violating Blueville's rules.

If you repeat the offense, you receive a second note from Mr. Barrow and a second fine, amounting to twenty dollars, but this time the measure is increased by a brief letter worded as follows:

Dr. Martinelli:
There is something that disturbs me about your case: your inability to conform to the discipline of Blueville. From now on kindly make a serious effort to remedy this laxness.
Hilda Helsingforth

Imagine the effect such a note can have on you, especially when it comes from a person you've never seen but who can decide at any time about your life or death.

I believe that the militiawomen—it's the official line at Blueville—are here to protect us from the gangs that, in the anarchy of the times, might try to break into the ranch to raid our provisions. The latter are, in fact, stored in a barracks adjoining the lookout tower. I also understand that we must economize electricity. Blueville produces it from a stream that flows down through its lands. So the curfew is legitimate, as is also, to an extent, the restriction placed on us about moving around the barracks at night. After 10:00 P.M. the administration wants to be sure that no research worker is in danger of being taken for a marauder by the militiawomen.

What is harder to understand is the strict way in which the regulations are applied and the small regard they have for us.

After all, we aren't parasites. We are working on jobs that call for great scientific specialization. What sustains the big company that employs us? To whom does it owe its power and assets, if not on research workers like us? If I managed to develop a vaccine against E-16, this discovery, when placed on the market, would bring Mrs. Helsingforth an immense fortune. And yet, for the slightest "offense," I am taken to task like a schoolboy who has misbehaved and am threatened in no uncertain terms with being kicked out if I don't mend my ways.

We are also subjected to petty, inexplicable hazing. We are forbidden to own a transistor and, at the castle, we have neither radio nor television set—at least not in the rooms assigned to us. Nevertheless, when we go past the militiawomen's barracks we can see the blue-and-white images on their screen through an open window. Mrs. Pierce's son, Johnny, an eight-year-old, once stopped at the window, fascinated, and Mrs. Pierce didn't think she was doing anything wrong to let him watch. At once a militiawoman got to her feet and, without so much as a glance at Johnny, slammed the window shut and lowered the blinds.

We do get newspapers, but three or four days late and only a few copies. What's more, certain editions are missing, without explanation, so that we have come to believe they are censored. We wonder why, for while the newspapers may have lost pages, their main loss has been in quality. We are disconcerted by their total insipidness. The news is skeletal, and opposition to the Administration, once vigorous, has given way to a sort of official purring.

In the publications we receive, I have noticed that Encephalitis 16 is mentioned less and less and that figures are never given. On this score, President Bedford has proven more efficient than her predecessors at suppressing news. We are no less struck by the apathy of the mass media toward the epidemic. I fear—and Stien shares my opinion—that people have grown inured to the problem. People get used to anything—to dumping tons of filth in the world's rivers and oceans and seeing people die like flies all around you. Yet these men who perish have fiancées, mothers, wives. How, then, is it possible for the public to be apathetic to such wholesale slaughter?

For it is a slaughter; there can be no doubt about it. True, we have been deprived of any real means of information. But as long as we go through the Blueville switchboard operator and submit to monitoring (we can even hear the little click of the tape recorder) the phone is available. I used it at first, but, one by one, my friends' voices ceased to answer me. I no longer dared to call the ones who were left. I prefer to remain in the dark.

According to Anita, right here in the United States millions have died. But Anita herself, who must know the figures, doesn't disclose any. Which leads me to believe that they are still rising. So I'm held in Blueville by two solid chains: the urgency of a task which, if I accomplish it, can check the epidemic; the thought that if I were thrown out of Blueville, I would resume medical practice and, like Morley, as so many other colleagues, meet death in so doing. To tell the truth, I'm so deeply disturbed by the conditions imposed on us in Blueville that I'd be prepared to run that awful risk. But there's Dave. I'm almost certain that, if I died, Anita, despite the promise that I extracted from her, wouldn't take care of him. Even if she wanted to, she couldn't. And then Dave would fall into the hands of my ex-mother-in-law, Mildred Miller.

Before living at Blueville I didn't know how deeply attached I was to my dignity as a man. Certainly, I wasn't always fond of the way men reacted to my physique. But there was compensation: I wasn't oblivious to the fact that women found me attractive. And most of all, at the hospital, within my profession, I was highly regarded. At Blueville, my material conditions are good, but in a million ways I sense that, as a human being, I have only inferior status.

If I feel diminished as a social being, what am I to think, on the other hand, of Anita's triumph? When she comes to see me, I find her radiant, sure of herself, proud of her high office, proud also of the efforts that her sex has made to take over the work of men.

She explains to me that, from the economic standpoint, the situation is serious but not as catastrophic as one might have feared. In the big corporations the death of a large part of the white-collar people has not had many tangible effects. Actually, it led to a simplification of the bureaucracy. In the beginning the labor drain disorganized production. Various means were used to cope with this: with women, of course, but also with massive imports of male labor, "which is replenished as it dies off" (sic).

Despite everything, production has gone down, but, owing to the death of a great number of men who leave their widows destitute, consumption too has fallen off sharply, and an equilibrium in the poverty has somehow or other been established.

I asked Anita about the effect that the massive entry of women into the country's economic life had produced. She revealed some bitterness. First, she pointed out that there had been far more workingwomen, in all fields, before the epidemic than she had supposed. And, most of all, many of them performed jobs far below their actual ability. Their rapid promotion did not, therefore, catch them unprepared. And, by and large, they were remarkably adaptable.

Anita did, however, point out with honesty some failings. In manual jobs, women work faster than men but take fewer initiatives, and, at higher levels, women are less likely to be perfectionists. They also have a tendency to be less punctual and be absent more often.

But, according to Anita, these weaknesses are due—and I quote—to "the historical sabotage of women's lives by family slavery." When they have been relieved of this burden, it is probable that this type of defect will die out.

On the other hand, she said, when women are appointed to managerial positions or inherit large businesses, they reveal themselves to be less emotional and less likely to give in to discouragement than men. The serious losses of money that, at the start of the epidemic, produced so many male suicides are far from having such disastrous effects on women. Less proud than their husbands, women are also less sensitive to financial failure and are less likely to grow tired of living because of it.

The male hecatomb has been felt hardest in terms of scientific knowledge. In this area, very old men have been pressed back into service. Their new responsibilities, taking them away from the melancholy of retirement, had apparently restored their zest and vigor. And, most of all, a new caste had appeared that was taking on growing importance in the economy.

And, with that, Anita, retracing her steps, gave me a brief and exciting account.

Just about the time I'd been in quarantine in Blueville, cut off from all news, an itinerant lay preacher was scoring a huge success in one city of the United States after another. His name was Jonathan Bladderstir. The almost exclusive theme of his sermons, enhanced by an impressive physique and acting ability, had the merit of simplicity: Since a connection, however obscure, had been revealed between spermatogenesis and Encephalitis 16, any Christian could see the truth as plain as day. The Lord, in striking men, had sought to punish them for the way in which they had abused their sexual power. At best, that power should have been used for procreative purposes only. Alas, that had not been the case. Impelled by the selfish pursuit of pleasure, men had imposed frequent intercourse on their wives—at times, he was sorry to say, daily.

Bladderstir was a fine-looking man around forty, and when he described these excesses—and he described them in all their detail—his magnificent dark eyes and his warm voice magnetized his audience. In short, Bladderstir concluded, Encephalitis 16, in punishing most particularly the sin of the flesh, showed men the path that they had to follow to win their pardon. For himself, he had inferred the blinding lesson from the facts and asked his brothers in Jesus to infer it with him. By mutual agreement with a wife fondly cherished (at this point Mrs. Bladderstir, a dimpled, sexy blonde, came forward on the stage and, with a ravishing smile, took her husband by the hand) he had decided to abstain henceforth from all carnal relations and to live with her as brother and sister in the bonds of pure affection (frantic applause followed by hymns).

Bladderstir proclaimed loudly that abstinence, aside from its spiritual value, represented, when all was said and done, the best preventive measure against E-16. Although this view of things is in no way scientific, for spermatogenesis does not cease as a result of disuse (and it has not even been proved that it slows down over the years in chaste clergymen, even if the accompanying desire eventually grows dull), there was a Paulinian aspect in the proposed asceticism that could not fail to impress an audience trained in Christianity. In fact, Bladderstir was very quickly accepted as an article of faith by a great number of men who, in defiance of the heightened risk of contagion, mingled with vast crowds to hear the preacher.

Two events occurred that were to undermine, and even throw down, Bladderstirism. Mrs. Bladderstir initiated divorce proceedings against her husband. She accused him of bringing onto stages, under a name and title that belonged only to her, a pseudo Mrs. Bladderstir that Mr. Bladderstir had recruited in the course of his preaching. She further accused her husband of having had sinful relations with that person. To confirm at very least the usurpation of identity, Mrs. Bladderstir published a photo of herself in the newspapers. I didn't see it. I was, as I've said, in quarantine at Blueville, but Anita assured me that Bladderstir would have greatly diminished the herosim of his abstinence by exhibiting his real wife at his side on stage.

Mr. Bladderstir protested vehemently against these "calumnies," but he didn't have the time to do much protesting. An event occurred that no one had expected—not even Bladderstir himself, who was so close to God: Bladderstir succumbed to Encephalitis 16.

No matter how the facts are considered, this should have been the death knell of Bladderstirism. Either Bladderstir had been having extramarital relations with the blonde that he was passing off as his wife and, in that case, he was, of course, nothing but a charlatan; or he'd really practiced the chastity that he had recommended to others, and, in that case, abstinence didn't have the prophylactic value he had attributed to it.

But logic and truth have nothing to do with popularity. In the United States, it was often said, and not without sadness, that the more a politician was lying, crooked and crafty, the less he had kept the promises made during a previous election campaign, the better his chances were of being triumphantly reelected against the most honest rival. This held true for the new prophet. Bladderstir, dead, breathed new life into Bladderstirism.

But the succession of the Master was not without a commotion. His disciples fought over both his spiritual heritage and the enormous receipts that he made out of his preaching. When all was said and done, Bladderstirism broke up into two different camps—the "Continents" and the "Ablationists."

The former, faithful to Bladderstir's supposed practice, advocated chastity both as a prophylactic precaution on this earth and as an asceticism rewarded in the Hereafter by the Lord. The Ablationists, much more radical and very much in the minority at first, had the ablation of the testicles performed on themselves and recommended the same surgical excision to their followers.

From the religious point of view, the thesis of the Ablationists could scarcely be recommended by tradition. In general, the churches oppose castration. They prefer keeping the tool and limiting its use, even willing, like the Catholic Church, to forbid it totally to its priests. It was only to sing the praises of creation—which had, for the parties concerned, a poignant irony—that the young male singers of the pontifical chapel were deprived of their virility.

But, from the scientific point of view, Ablationism, though traumatic, humiliating and irreversible and, for this reason, not recommended by doctors—did at least offer the advantage of eliminating spermatogenesis forever and actually gave the castrati the same immunity to Encephalitis 16 that boys under the age of puberty enjoyed on a temporary basis and the elderly on a permanent basis.

In a materialistic society, nothing succeeds like success. In the struggles inside Bladderstirism, the Ablationists, in a minority at first, gained simply by the fact that they weren't dying. Vainly the Continents tried to exploit the hecatomb thinning out their ranks by arguing that the Lord recognized his own since he was calling them to him in order to reward their chastity. The Ablationists pointed out that he had also called back to him the wanton and the dissolute.

Like Abraham of old and in a sense going him one better, the Ablationists had sacrificed more than the flesh of their flesh—the very possibility of fatherhood.

All over the United States, the list of new members grew longer with each passing day, members they couldn't satisfy for want of surgeons. For death hadn't spared the medical profession, and, owing to the reduced number of specialists, the rates for operations got higher and higher. It reached the point where they were asking exorbitant sums for ablation and scarcely smaller amounts for a routine bistournage. *The Able*, the weekly publication of the Ablationists, protested against this exploitation and asked vehemently, in one issue, if castration were becoming a luxury for the rich. Action was taken in some states to freeze rates. These measures served only to promote a black market in ablations and, on the other hand, led to low-priced offices where the operation, performed by unqualified charlatans, often resulted in fatal accidents.

It should be noted that, in the beginning at least, the Ablationists were opposed to chemical castration. Since they were imbued with religious spirit, it didn't strike them as sacrificial enough. But the scarcity of doctors finally made it necessary to have recourse to sterilizing drugs. At first, the applicants used an anti-androgen, cyprotero-acetate, but the demand was so heavy that the product, dispensed in the form of 50-mg pills, to be taken morning and night for a month, disappeared from the market. After that a drug was discovered or, rather, rediscovered, which, also administered orally, produced all the effects of the cyprotero-acetate, but much more quickly.

On that score Anita had nothing to teach me. I knew about that drug, although it wasn't sold in the United States at that time. I had discussed it at length in the book that I had written on the Nazi doctors in World War II concentration camps. Those doctors (if the term can be used for such monsters) had, at one point, thought of importing the drug and using it on a large scale to sterilize the Jewish men that Hitler had rounded up all over Europe and kept in his prison camps. In the end, the Nazis had given up on this project, for they would have had to transport the raw material in considerable quantities from Latin America, and at the time (1941) their freighters couldn't have ventured across the Atlantic without enormous risks.

This raw material, *Caladium sequinum*, is a herbaceous plant of tuberous origin from the family of the araceae. It grows wild in Brazil, in wet or swampy places or in heavily shaded forests. But of course, for the massive use of the substance that the Nazis were contemplating, intensive cultivation would have been required, for neither the roots nor the fruit interested them but an extract prepared from the sap.

The properties of this extract, no doubt first obtained by primitive means, had actually been known since time immemorial by the aborigines of the hemisphere. According to a tradition handed down by word of mouth among the Indians of equatorial America, their ancestors had used the substance to reduce captured enemies to impotence and turn them into docile slaves. Violence must have been used to get those poor wretches to take the *Caladium sequinum*, for the extract itself (at least as sold in the United States by the Ablationists) appears as a viscous, greenish liquid, the odor and taste of which are in no was enticing. But the effect is swift and sure, without the outer appearance of the organs being altered in any way. The *Caladium sequinum* acts within those organs. The testicles, the epididymis and the prostate are affected by necrosis, a phenomenon that, in its first phase, brings on a complete halt of spermatogenesis and, in a second phase, the irreversible destruction of the spermatogenic tissue.

The United Caladium Sequinum Company (or UCASEC) founded in Boston for the purchase of suitable farmland in Brazil, as well as the planting, growing, harvesting and local processing of the plant, was created by the Ablationist F. M. Hammersmith, who was to survive his corporation's colossal success by only three months. He died at fifty in his office of a heart attack, the victim of overwork and, most of all, his obsession for doing several things at once. It was revealed that, at the moment of his death, Hammersmith had been drinking a glass of whiskey, smoking a cigar and, while caressing the breasts of his young secretary of Cuban origin, had been dictating letters to her. It was the secretary herself who confirmed the active and passive part that she'd played in the brief tragedy. Besieged with questions by the reporters as to why she allowed her employer such intimacies, she pointed out that they were harmless, since Hammersmith was an Ablationist and, moreover, that, despite their difference in age, she'd had almost maternal feelings for him. "Why not let the *pobrecito* play?" she said, tears streaming down her cheeks and falling one by one on her opulent bosom.

The deceased was scarcely in the grave when his widow, Dora Magnus Hammersmith, had to cope with a situation that threatened to ruin his empire: Taking advantage of the momentary weakness of the army and the police, a left-wing government seized power in Brazil and demanded that UCASEC turn over 51 percent of the corporation's shares, while a still more leftist faction insisted on immediate nationalization. The situation was even more embarrassing for Dora, as the CIA, reduced by the epidemic to a fifth of its strength, was in no position to exert an influence, with its usual discretion, on Latin American affairs.

Dora reacted with the utmost vigor. She went to see President Sarah Bedord, explained forcefully the dangers that the confiscation of UCASEC's assets in Brazil would mean for the health and foreign trade of the United States and got her to intervene energetically. Tremendous pressure was exerted on Brasilia, pressure that even went as far as the threat of atomic reprisals, Anita assured me.

Brasilia gave in. It was learned shortly afterward that the extremist faction of the Brazilian government whose threats of nationalization had prompted the President to take action had, in fact, been bought and manipulated by Brazilian agents of the UCASEC. The President, far from being angry with Dora Hammersmith for her tactical ability, came to respect her and, when the Secretary of State died, called on her to take over that high position. Dora immediately resigned from UCASEC and was replaced as its leader by the Ablationist P. J. Barry, to whom she gave her orders over the phone on a daily basis.

This story, from Anita's lips, resembled the success stories that have sickened us in so many novels and films. Anita told it to me, I believe, to convince me that women, at the head of big businesses, were as efficient as men. She didn't need to go to all that trouble. I was already convinced.

While UCASEC had managed to gain a foothold and increase its exports in the industrialized countries of Europe, it was having great difficulty marketing its goods in Latin America and, generally speaking, in all the underprivileged countries of the world, in Africa and in Asia. The closer you went toward the sun, underdevelopment and poverty, the more men clung to their virility and preferred to risk death rather than lose it. Having learned about them through Anita, I had only scorn for the grotesque efforts that Dora Magnus Hammersmith, in her official and unofficial role, was making to force on those poor souls, by any means—including pressure inadmissible at the governmental level—that drug they considered to be shameful.

Shameful may be a bit strong, but, for my part, if I were thrown out of Blueville, I wouldn't agree to taking the drug. It isn't that phallocratic pride of which my sex is so often accused. I don't deny that phallus worship exists, but it exists in neurotic individuals whose manhood is necessarily suspect since it is narcissistic. But on the other hand, nothing can excuse the voluntary mutilation of a function which, quite aside from biological necessity, is indispensible to a man's enjoyment of life's pleasures and to his creative urge.

I'm only repeating obvious facts here, but facts that are ignored by men who have stampeded by the thousands—soon it will be hundreds of thousands—to join the ranks of the Ablationists and who, after a ceremony reminiscent of a baptism, were allowed to drink *Caladium sequinum* in the company of their peers. Furthermore, they might have dispensed with these rites, as *Caladium sequinum* is freely sold in all drugstores. But very few consumed it alone. The new members found a kind of justification in the strong religious coloring of the Ablationist initiation and also in the comfortable feeling of belonging to a powerful group that was playing an increasingly important part in the country's economy.

The study made by a team of psychologists from Columbia University, headed by professor Harriet Steinfeld, further showed that, in the motivation of the new converts to Ablationism, economic survival and moving up the social ladder meant more than fear of death. Very soon, in fact, demand on the labor market for men that were designated as "A's" (and which some practical jokers among the intact nicknamed "A-minuses") would increase. The A's offered every advantage for the employer—job stability and docility in the performance of their work. Furthermore, their technical know-how, which the women, by and large, still lacked, made them quite valuable for filling the gaps left by the epidemic. Thus, in one fell swoop, the A's got positions and salaries that they had never before dreamt possible.

Among the many interviews that Professor Harriet Steinfeld published in her study, that of Mr. C. B. Mills, an engineer, from Cleveland, Ohio, is perhaps the most revealing. Mills received Harriet Steinfeld in a recently redecorated living room.

Seated in a brand-new armchair, Mills, prosperous and stout, seemed relaxed and sure of himself.

"Believe me," he said with a little laugh, "I'm not one bit sorry. First of all, because the A's are quite different from, say, the Rotary Club, A's never let one another down. They really stick together. Better than the Jews! But, most of all, when I think about my former life, I can only be thankful that I did what I've done."

"So your living conditions were really that bad, eh, Mr. Mills?"

"No. They were actually quite good. But in order to get them, my life had become hell. I was swamped, all I did was pay off loans and bills. There was the house to be paid off, the three cars—mine, my wife's and my oldest daughter's. There were the outrageous premiums on my life insurance, the two color TVs, that's all I did—pay, pay and pay. And, naturally, to pay for all that, I worked! I worked like crazy! So, at forty-five, I had a stroke. And I spent a fortune on doctors, which put me deeper in debt."

"So then, you're happier now?"

"There's no comparison. I made a fantastic leap forward. I'm earning infinitely more. As you can see, I've just had the house done over, I'm planning to buy a fourth car and a third color TV set."

"So, then, there's nothing to spoil your happiness?"

"No, nothing."

"Mr. Mills, I'd like to raise a rather delicate question. You're forty-eight, you aren't old and you're married to a very attractive woman . . ."

"Oh, that," said Mr. Mills with the same little laugh, "that doesn't bother me at all."

"If you don't mind, I'd appreciate if you would explain why."

"Listen, I'm going to let you in on something. Before my initiation into the A's, I was so overworked and I had so many worries about money and was always in pretty bad shape on account of my stroke that an awful long time had gone by since I'd even touched my wife—two years maybe. So, you see, there isn't much of a change."

In her study, Professor Harriet Steinfeld followed this interview with a commentary that I found unkind at first. She pointed out that, even before his initiation, Mills—like quite a few of his fellow citizens—had traded his manhood for cars, TV sets and freezers, since the burden that such expenses involved led him to so exhaust himself working he could no longer make love. In short, she concluded, Mills hadn't hesitated about castration because he was castrated already. I found some harshness in these remarks, but when I saw, in the appendix, that the interview and the commentary had—prior to publication—been read and approved by Mills himself and the other interviewees and that they had, furthermore, supplied photos of themselves to the lady interviewers without seeking to hide their identity, I understand that their condition wasn't a source of shame for them but that, on the contrary, they saw it as the turning point in their success.

I also noticed that, at Blueville, where there were many more A's than P.M.s, without exception they all wore a big green rosette on their lapels; in the center a Gothic "A" stood out in gold. The first time I saw that insignia, I thought, *mutatis mutandis*, of the unfaithful wife in *The Scarlet Letter* sentenced to embroider on her dress an "A" for her adultery and who purposely added arabesques and fioriture to the embroidery, turning a mark of infamy into a badge of honor. The difference, of course, is that the insignia of the Ablationists is highly regarded everywhere, opening all doors for the ambitious, having become the emblem of a certain moral distinction.

3

We're off on Sundays at Blueville. In the morning, at the castle, there is a religious service given by a woman missionary, never the same one but belonging to some Protestant church or other, as it appears that the Catholic Church, still a victim of its secular misogyny, hasn't been able to bring itself to ordain a woman.

Attendance at the service isn't mandatory, and we never see Hilda Helsingforth there. Nevertheless, almost everybody attends regularly—including me, despite my skepticism—for at the end of the service there is generally a rambling discussion with the missionary, and, as she comes from the outside, we hope to learn interesting things from her. Deprived of radio and television, the newspapers being what they are, we are hungry for news about the world, the real one, the one that lies beyond our barbed-wire fence.

In particular, I remember the missionary who officiated on Sunday, May 5. She was a woman so gaunt that any shape she might have had once was gone forever, leaving a morphology that I can only qualify as neuter. Furthermore, Reverend Ruth Jettison had short hair and wore an anthracite-gray suit with an ecclesiastical collar that made her sex still harder to define. Yet, with her hooked nose, her long chin and her big eyes—dark, staring and fanatic—her face did not lack force.

The service and sermon took place in the castle's meeting room, a hall that could seat one hundred people and we could not quite fill. I say "we," but it should be pointed out that there was an order and precedence in the seating arrangement that I found already in use on my arrival in Blueville and that didn't change while I was there.

In the first row sit the VIPs who live in the castle. Mr. Barrow, the administrator, and his wife; Dr. Rilke; Emma Stevenson, the boss's secretary; and three or four persons whose positions and names I don't know. In the middle of them, in a position of honor, is an armchair, respectfully left vacant and which is, if I dare say, filled with Mrs. Helsingforth's perpetual absence. I'm not saying that the people of the castle salute this armchair as they go by, like the Swiss saluted Geisler's hat, but I notice that they go around it with pious faces, as though it were occupied.

In the second and third rows sit Blueville's "single women," very different in age and physical appearance but homogenized by one common attitude: They never so much as glance at a P.M.

In the third, fourth and fifth rows sit the A's, all wearing in their buttonholes the green rosette with the gilded letter of their sect. A close-knit group, very smug and self-satisfied and one which, in public, also pretends to ignore us, whereas most of them, in the labs, are our subordinates. I want to emphasize here that a goodly number of the A's are married men, but, unlike the P.M.s, their families have remained in the outside world, where the A's, sure of their immunity, may go from time to time without danger for themselves, although, I suppose, without much excitement for their wives.

Finally, in the last rows of the hall, on the bottom rung of Blueville's social ladder too, inferior in number and even more so in rank to all those who precede, sit the P.M.s with their wives and their children.

Reverend Ruth Jettison's sermon treated a theme that resembled Bladderstirism in its premises but differed in its conclusions. Clearly, Encephalitis 16 was nothing but punishment from God. The Lord had brought his right hand down on the sinners to punish them for their errors (how often I've heard that refrain since then!). Nevertheless, by "error," we were not to understand what Bladderstir meant. Man's great sin, since earliest times, had been to reduce woman to slavery.

Here Ruth Jettison drew a picture that, despite some exaggerations and a lack of nuances and historical perspective, included a good deal of truth. But after this denunciation, justified though it may be, of male misogyny over the centuries, the sermon became absolutely frenzied. Ruth Jettison, her eyes ablaze, her speech jerky and her movements vengeful, tried to show the point to which men "hated" women.

With the aid of little facts laboriously sewn together, authenticated or supposedly authenticated statements but without precise references to persons, places or dates, mainly by means of a series of anecdotes in which the neurotic and sadistic attitudes of wayward adolescents regarding girls were presented as the male norm, Ruth Jettison claimed to prove that men harbored a profound disgust for women's bodies. This disgust culminated in "vagina hatred (although she used a much earthier term)."

I must say that the coarseness of the term, the paradox of her thesis and, above all, the haphazard way in which the missionary proposed to prove it provoked smiles, laughter and various movements among the P.M.s. For it was obvious to the research workers present that, in working out her thesis, Ruth Jettison had not done the slightest scientific research, that she had not conducted numerous and exhaustive interviews but had proceeded by the most barefaced and the most illegitimate of extrapolations. Like an inverted pyramid, her thesis was based on a few isolated facts, and, replacing the modest method of surveys by dogmatic affirmation, she had built an enormous mountain out of a few molehills.

Religious (or parareligious) thinking is most convenient. It makes up for everything. So, with blazing eyes, a voice quivering with sacred rage and devastating terms, Ruth Jettison finally reached her conclusion: Men, she declared, consider women as lowly receptacles into which to discharge their sperm or, to be more exact, a kind of spittoon that they turn away from in disgust after use.

The audience's reactions were remarkable and subtly differentiated. The administration in the first row and the "single women" in the second row applauded warmly and, it seemed to me, with ostentation. The A's, for their part, remained silent, with a look of contrition, as though overwhelmed by the memory of sins that had been theirs and of which they had, fortunately, been absolved. But there were murmurs among the P.M.s, their wives included.

Ruth Jettison knitted her bushy brows and, staring at our little group with her intense, dark eyes, cried out almost menacingly, "Does anyone want to ask a question?"

There was a rather long silence, of a kind that struck me as un-American, as if we had already begun to give up our freedom of speech.

I was so disgusted by the missionary's fanaticism and by the challenge she had hurled at us that I decided to speak up. But I hadn't had the time to get to my feet when my neighbor, Mrs. Pierce, tugged the sleeve of my jacket and whispered intensely in my ear, "For God's sake, Ralph, don't get involved. It's asking for trouble."

Later on I'll speak about Mrs. Pierce, my closest co-worker's wife. She doesn't have much to boast of physically, but I have the highest regard for her clearsightedness. Seething with pent-up rage, I remained silent.

There was a stir in the row behind us. I turned around. The same situation was being reenacted, only the other way around. Stien, clutching his wife's hand, was doing his best to get her to keep still.

He might as well have tried to stop a bulldozer. Mutsch broke away, got to her feet and said in a clear voice, "I don't have any questions to ask, but I'd like to make some remarks."

"Go ahead," said Ruth Jettison disdainfully.

It's true that Mutsch, although she had a degree in psychology, wasn't much to look at. She was short and dumpy, and, under her white hair, her face wore an amiable, almost self-effacing expression. But as far as we were concerned, we knew how we felt about Mutsch. On a volunteer basis and with indomitable energy, she had taken charge of educating the children of Blueville's P.M.s—a heroic job, for there were twelve of them, ranging in age from five to fourteen.

"I agree," said Mutsch in perfect English but with a rather strong German accent (which, unfortunately, had begun to rub off on her pupils, Dave included), "about the limitations that men have imposed on women in the economic and social area. But this doesn't stem from the hatred they feel for our bodies. Quite the contrary, men overrate the female body to the detriment of our other qualities. Anyone can see this overrating. It's everywhere—in fashions, advertising, the arts, literature. I think that the examples you've given are biased. The gangs of boys you refer to, who rape girls, curse them and beat them, probably have a strong homosexual element in their makeup, something that they repress but which is expressed by this type of behavior. Anyone who calls women "spittoons" is a neurotic and a sadist. This just isn't a typically male attitude. Far from it. And I don't see how there can be any mistake about it. Women who speak of 'vagina hatred' as though it were universal among men lead me to suspect that perhaps they themselves have penis hatred." (Laughter among the P.M.s.) "In any case, they aren't doing a very good job by trying to convince women that men hate them. This can only lead women to hating men and so forth. And let me tell you that it's a shameful thing, right now when men are dying like flies. I find it particularly amazing to hear a Christian woman stirring up hatred among the sexes like this. Furthermore, I may be a little old-fashioned, but I admit that it also shocks me to hear a clergywoman use the word 'cunt' in her sermon." (Mutsch uttered the word with Germanic energy.) "Furthermore, Reverend, I don't think you really know what a couple is. I can assure you that I'm not my husband's spittoon. I'm sure he loves me totally, 'cunt' included." (Laughter among the P.M.s. "My little treasure!" murmured Stien in hushed tones, lifting his arms heavenward.)

"Well, that's what I had to say," added Mutsch, blushing and sitting down abruptly. (Murmurs in the front rows, loud applause in the P.M. group.)

During Mutsch's speech, Ruth Jettison's bearing had been nothing less than evangelic. Squaring her shoulders, clenching her fists, she glared at the P.M.s in a way that, in former times, would have spelled burning at the stake.

When Mutsch was seated again, the missionary was unable

to react for a few seconds, but when she regained the power of speech she could barely make her way through her clenched teeth.

"This speaker," she hissed, "is remarkable for her ignorance, her arrogance and total uselessness. The person who has just spoken belongs to what I would call the satisfied slaves. She mustn't count on me for a reply. I speak only to free women. Our meeting is over." (Protests and cries of "Reply! Reply!" among the P.M.s.)

The sanctions—that's the point we've reached!—fell on us the very next day. Mutsch was reprimanded for her "discourtesy" with a nasty letter from Hilda Helsingforth. As a husband responsible for his wife's action, Stien had two hundred dollars withheld from his salary, and as for the P.M.s, who had been Mutsch's accomplices by their impolite behavior, they were forbidden for a week to gather at the castle after lunch as was their custom. Mr. Barrow even made it known that, if the offense were repeated, these little gatherings we liked so much would be eliminated permanently.

We were all disgusted. If it had been possible to get out of Blueville without risking the death sentence, we would have done it there and then, giving up jobs which, for each of us, were a reason for living. To see freedom of thought and speech flouted so openly at Blueville, we wondered if we were still in the United States or if we had been transported, without our knowing, to one of those Latin American dictatorships American democracy has always backed.

When our little familial gatherings at the castle resumed a week later, I decided to stay away from them. Not that they bored me, but Dave was giving me cause for concern. The two of us lived in a little barracks with two rooms separated by a kitchenette and a bathroom. At night I left the doors open to hear Dave. Almost every night he had been waking me and calling me with anguished cries. I would run to him, and, huddled against me, in a voice broken with sobs, he would tell me his nightmare, almost always the same.

Dave is walking alone in the midst of a crowd. Without knowing why, he feels sad. The people who are walking along the sidewalk with him are very pale. All of a sudden one of them stumbles and falls down unconscious. Then a second, then a third. Soon they are falling by dozens, by bunches. No one dares to bring them help or even go up to them. The crowd contents itself with making a detour around the bodies. Although he knows that he himself runs no danger, Dave feels very anxious, he's afraid, he starts crying, no one pays attention to him. He goes up to a red-haired woman. He takes her by the hand, but the woman shakes herself free and pushes him away. Dave cries. Suddenly, among the people who are walking ahead of him, he recognizes me from the back. I'm about twenty yards ahead. He feels immense relief, calls me with a happy voice. I turn around and smile at him. He sprints toward me, and, for my part, I walk briskly ahead of him. But when I'm two yards away, I collapse. He rushes to me and falls to his knees. I'm pale. My eyes are closed. He shouts, he calls, but the people go around us without stopping, without even seeing us.

At Dave's first scream I go running in. The little lamp on the night table is alight, and I find Dave sitting up in bed, covered with sweat and tears. I take him in my arms. He sobs convulsively and it takes quite a while to calm him.

Dave, who lived in Wesley Heights, never saw the scene that he describes, but, although he magnifies it a great deal, it is true. Shortly before coming to Blueville, I saw men fall in the street. Bystanders didn't just go around them. They ran away. I never breathed a word of this to Dave, and I don't understand where he got the material for his nightmare. Another fact amazes me. Dave doesn't know that I can be thrown out of Blueville's protective enclosure at any time and that I live, therefore, obsessed by fear—not so much the fear of dying as of leaving him alone. And yet his dream expresses harrowingly the anguish of being abandoned.

Tonight I'm writing to Anita, my ear cocked. For I've noticed that the great cry for help at the end is preceded by little, almost inaudible sobs, and if I get to him just then, I eliminate the most frightful part of Dave's dream—my dying and his being alone. At least that's what he told me that night when he woke up. After a moment, I leave him and go back to my little desk. Although the wooden partitions of the barrack are doubled and very well insulated, it's cold and the heating is inadequate. They are saving fuel at night in Blueville. I put on a sweater and, over that, a thick bathrobe, which I pull around me. I scarcely have time to pick up my pen when Dave comes in, all bundled up, too.

"Am I disturbing you, Ralph?"

"Not at all."

He sits on my bed. I turn around and look at him. He has grown taller, lost weight. He's rather pale. In his thin, triangular face, his dark eyes fringed with long, curved lashes take up an enormous space.

"Are you working, Ralph?"

"No, I'm writing a letter." And as he remains silent with his usual discretion, I add, "To Anita."

A little silence and Dave says, in a cracking voice that has already begun to change, "Don't you miss the little meetings at night, Ralph, at the castle?"

That's the Dave who's already an adult, sensitive, full of concern for others.

I tell him casually, "Oh, they weren't much fun."

He goes on without transition, but it seems obvious to me: "What about Anita? Is she coming soon?"

But this time I understand faster. I know the context: Dave is worried for me, not for himself. Proof of this is that part of his nightmare where a reddish-haired woman pushes him away. Dave was disappointed by Anita. When she comes she pays as little attention as possible to him; she keeps him at a distance. It's as if she were afraid of growing attached to him. Nevertheless, she brings him or, rather, she used to bring him (you can't find anything any more with these shortages) sumptuous gifts but always, alas, unsuitable—either too childish or too adult— and which, in both cases, humiliated him. Furthermore, Dave is shrewd. He knows quite well that all those presents rain on him for lack of warmer feeling.

"I don't know," I say casually. "She hasn't phoned. She must be very busy."

A silence. I don't know if Dave has been taken in by my casual manner, for he's studying me attentively. Then he blinks, he yawns, he stretches.

"I'm going to bed," he says.

I nod my head in agreement, and all of a sudden Dave says in an entirely different voice—soft, plaintive, childish—"Will you carry me, Ralph?"

I'm annoyed by this return to babyishness when he has just been so adult. I feel like saying no. But I don't dare. I know the effect a refusal would have on Dave. I may not be very good at raising children, but I have one rule: I don't repair a watch with a hammer.

I give in. Perhaps the hesitation I've betrayed, despite myself, is enough to show that I'm not in agreement. I grab Dave under the arms, lift him, heave him against my chest. At once he throws his arms around my neck and leans his face against mine. As ever, I'm touched. This fleeting moment gives me strength in an existence that isn't easy.

I don't want to paint the picture all black. Although anguish in Blueville is my real trade, since it fills me more continuously than any concern, strong as it may be, for my research, one gets used to anything—including fear. Even a condemned man in his cell must have moments when the future relaxes its vise grip on his thoughts. Without these breaks he could not go on living. And at least I can say this about our existence at Blueville: Our execution is not certain.

Meanwhile, what is most unbearable about our situation is its basic unintelligibility.

Jespersen, Stien and I often talk about it, taking a few precautions, as we're sure that the place is bugged. None of us three and no one among the P.M.s has ever seen Hilda Helsingforth. We know that she's here—and close by—because Mr. Barrow, before us, communicated with her by an inside telephone. But she remains invisible, like the Lord. And, like him, omniscient, all-powerful but not infinitely good.

We've had only snubs and reprimands from Helsingforth in little notes stripped of any salutations and whose very brevity is an insult. On my arrival in Blueville I wrote her a letter in which I asked if it wouldn't be possible to get a pony for Dave, making the purchase by withholding money from my salary. In my naïveté, I went so far as speaking about the emotional gap that the death of his Connemara had left in Dave.

After a week I received the following note:

Dr. Martinelli,

Please take note of the fact that P.M.s are not to write to me, telephone me or ask to see me.

As to the subject of your letter, please note that your family problems do not concern me.

Hilda Helsingforth

I read this note to Stien. He contented himself with saying in a hushed voice, "How typical!"

As to the attitude of the "single women" with regard to us (we give them this name because they have no companions at Blueville and without prejudging, of course, their former lives), it is identical to the attitude of the A's. At work, inside the lab, we have relations with them and with the A's that I'll go into later on. But outside the lab the women and the A's ignore us. If we made advances, these are rejected at once, mouths close, eyes are averted, backs are turned. Not only the P.M.s but also their wives—except Mrs. Pierce!—are subjected to nonexistence. We don't exactly live in a ghetto, as there is only a single cafeteria for all at the castle, but if, after filling your tray, you inadvertently sit down at a table where A's or single women are already sitting, the conversation stops and the silence becomes glacial.

In my moments of insomnia, toward the morning twilight, I ask myself the same questions over and over: Why are they treating us this way? What have we done? What crime have we committed? What threat do we represent? I say all this to Stien, but, on this particular morning, he's in a rotten mood and tells me to get out. "You're a real goy, you're soft, you complain about everything. What do you have to complain about? You're well fed. Nobody's beating you. Nobody's spitting in your face. You've got interesting work, so just do what I do. Don't worry about the rest." He added gravely, "I've been through worse."

I'm sure he had been through worse before leaving Germany in 1936. But I doubt that he isn't worrying, for he is in a lousy mood. He explodes more and more often in Yiddish, and Mutsch has trouble calming him down. Apparently he hasn't got the patience he's recommending to me.

The "single women"—I note bitterly, for they aren't all ugly, far from it—agree to social relations with the A's during and after meals. From my table in the cafeteria or my armchair in the lounge, I grow furious watching them smile and even flirt with those castrati. But I notice they still remain distant and quite formal. It looks as though, in their eyes, the A's, though cleansed of their original sin, are still somewhat suspect.

The A's are all people in their fifties. Any children they have had are already grown and scattered over the globe. In any case, they are no more gentle to our kind than the "single women." For the discrimination that faces us also extends to our children and, curiously enough, without any distinction being made between boys and girls. Apparently, the fact of having been engendered as they have condemns them to a discredit of sorts. Yet, neither the "single women" nor the A's came into the world differently. Are they thinking about changing a method which, for two million years, has been tried and true? I wonder, because I read yesterday in the New York *Times*—which is only a shadow of its former self—an article signed by Deborah Grimm, in which I read this amazing line: "The sex act should cease to be the means employed by society to renew the population."

You feel like shrugging your shoulders. I'm not doing anything about it. I've learned through Anita that Deborah Grimm is part of President Bedford's immediate entourage and that her influence on the President is tending to supplant Anita's own. Anita feels—and I'm with her on this—that it isn't up to the state, nor to its laws, nor its repressive machinery, to decide if a woman is to have a child or not. Woman's right to dispose of her own body is inalienable. True respect for life means respect for woman as a free agent and not as an object through which pass, whether she likes it or not, the future citizens needed by the state. Woman is not a machine for producing soldiers, workers or loyal supporters. The decision belongs to her—to her alone.

What strikes me as serious in Deborah Grimm's position is that, in seeming to go further than Anita, she is actually falling back into the old rut. It should be noted that her sentence is imperative and that no option is granted: "The sex act should cease to be the means employed by society for renewing the population."

What terrifying power Deborah Grimm entrusts to society! In this way, wouldn't society—which was made, if I'm not mistaken, to serve man and not to subjugate him—have the right to turn nature upside down and make it impossible for people to copulate in order to reproduce? I must be dreaming. What becomes of the freedom of woman in this perspective? Condemned by the reactionary state to being a mother against her will, is she now to be condemned not to be a mother although she wants to be one?

If Deborah Grimm's program were to be implemented, what a sad world this would be! Intercourse between men and women abolished, the concept of motherhood outmoded, babies manufactured artificially and placed from birth in nurseries where they would live an anonymous life twenty-four hours a day . . . What a forlorn desert! What inhumanity! What would be the point of life then? What good is it, as Deborah says, "to renew the population"? Why perpetuate the human race? What is that animal need to have descendants when man is a manufactured product? What sense could it possibly make to have these products renewed? If I understand correctly, men would be produced in order to produce objects—and to consume them! What monstrous absurdity! Ersatz children would be manufactured in order to drink pseudo-milk.

In the evening at the castle I talk to Stien about Deborah Grimm's article, and I draw his attention to the sentence that I underlined with a pencil and that I read to him aloud. He raises his brows and says irritably, "I don't know if it's desirable in human terms, but it's possible scientifically."

I'm on the point of questioning him further, but Mutsch glances at both of us in fear and I keep quiet. Apparently, Mutsch thinks that we've been imprudent: Stien has said too much, and, for my part, I shouldn't have spoken so openly about the article.

I don't know if I should attribute this to our double indiscretion, but since that day the copies of the New York *Times* have been getting scarcer.

I've already spoken of the meagerness, of the silences and the insipidness of the newspapers. When you read the New York *Times* or the Washington *Post* nowadays, you'd think they had been emasculated too. God knows how, in former times the press used to make life unpleasant for the occupant of the White House. Those days are over. In the few editions that do reach us at increasingly odd intervals, I find only insipid, nauseating praise accompanied from time to time by hagiographic portraits that make Sarah Bedford out to be a model of virtue for Sunday school.

I'm flabbergasted. Just five or six years ago she made a name for herself in the mass media by parading down 14th Street in Washington, leading twenty or so of her girl friends, all brandishing placards on which could be read:

WE'RE HOMOSEXUALS

—WHAT OF IT?

Not that this kind of placard shocks me. And it's not that I see any valid reason for persecuting homosexuals, as was done for so long in this country and with such a clean conscience. What I don't like is that devout, sanctimonious way people have of speaking about Sarah, as though she had suddenly become the Virgin Mary—minus the child.

It wasn't through the press itself—they must have censored the editions at Blueville—but through Anita that I now know how things reached this point.

When the epidemic began to lay waste to our Congressmen, Sarah Bedford had a law passed, the so-called Substitutes' Law, which provided that each Representative or each Senator should be seconded by an elected substitute of the female sex who, in the event of death, would *ipso facto* take his place in the House or the Senate. Unfortunately, the parties concerned changed the law by an amendment that took all democratic character out of the female elections: They gave themselves the right to choose their substitute themselves and to present her for the approbation of the electors. The idea was to maintain the numerical ratio between the two great parties. In this way, the Democrats brought in Democratic women and the Republicans Republican women.

That wasn't the worst of it. As if the mandate that they had from their electors was a kind of fief that mustn't go out of the family, most of the members of Congress chose their own wives as substitutes. Perhaps they thought that, in so doing, they had found the means, even in dying, of perpetuating themselves. At any rate, this was a miscalculation. The widows, who in growing numbers invaded Congress, had very little training politically, seldom attended sessions and saw in their positions mainly a kind of pension granted by federal authority. In the beginning, at any rate, they provided the President with a majority of an exemplary docility.

Thus it was that the widows, who, at the time, composed more than half of the legislative body, blindly passed a law on the mass media, triggering desperate clamors from the male survivors. The efforts of these veteran male politicians proved vain. Still, they denounced the "Security Law" (Sarah Bedford gave it that name) as a criminal attack on the Constitution of the United States and, in particular, freedom of the press. But the widows saw in their vehement opposition a chauvinistic reaction against the President's sex and overruled the men.

The law stipulated that any organ of information publishing a new article or commentary likely to sow panic, disturb order or demoralize the public—a definition so vague and so general that practically any article might come under the law—would face temporary or permanent suspension and would be liable to a fine ranging from $10,000 to $50,000.

This law, which was immediately applied with the utmost vigor, soon succeeded in stifling freedom of speech. Deprived of advertising, because of the economic stagnation, the mass media were on their last legs. The dailies, in particular, saw their readership, primarily male, dwindling from day to day and couldn't risk the double threat of a suspension and an enormous fine. They submitted.

From that point on, Sarah Bedford enjoyed power that none of her predecessors in the White House had ever had: The powers the Constitution confers on the President had, until then, been throttled by the mass media, public opinion and the Congress. Now, Congress was nothing more than a collection of yes-women. The Supreme Court had been decimated. The public, traumatized by so many deaths, did not react, and the press was muzzled. Two laws, the Substitutes' Law and the Security Law, had been enough to strangle democracy.

It seems more than likely that what's happening at Blueville is only the harshest reflection of the tyranny that now characterizes the outside world.

Dave devotes his Sunday afternoons to long training sessions in the castle pool, and during that time Jespersen, Stien and I are authorized to go horseback riding beyond the first enclosure and within the boundaries of the ranch. The horses we ride belong to the ranch, and we must pay to ride them—and pay plenty. It is still a privilege and it surprises me. I suppose that, in Hilda Helsingforth's mind, it's worthwhile to maintain us in good physical condition to keep our output up.

The only trouble with these rides is that we're followed everywhere by two mounted, armed militiawomen, always the same ones. With the coming of spring, their uniform has changed. Except for their boots, which are black, the militiawomen are dressed in petroleum blue from head to foot, carbines slung across their backs and revolvers in their holsters. Their faces, on the other hand, do not change. Their eyes remain frozen and their lips sealed. We have finally learned their first names, or, rather, their surnames, which they use between themselves. They are both blond, and the taller one (but they're both tall) is named Jackie and the smaller, who reminds you of a cat the way her eyes recede toward the temples, Pussy. To Jespersen, who is young and single, and to myself, who sees Anita less and less, they look very beautiful. Even their uniforms aren't dissuasive. And, most of all, we can't get it through our heads that these young, well-built women could really be our enemies, even if our gaze bounces off their implacable eyes and falls back down at our feet.

When we ride out of Blueville's first barbed-wire fence, Jackie and Pussy go ahead of us and give our names and identity badges to the militiawoman on guard at the foot of the lookout tower. This sentry, almost never the same, looks us over as though she wanted to memorize our hated features. Then she lets us through, calling us both by our surnames and our

registration numbers: Dr. Jespersen, 235. Professor Stienemeier, 226. Dr. Martinelli, 472.

As you see, she doesn't forget our titles, nor the subtle
differences that they bear. When we return, each in turn says
his name and his registration number, and, as we go by, the
badges are handed back to us. Each time I notice that the
militiawoman on duty manages not to touch our hands.

Once past the lookout tower, Jackie and Pussy no longer ride
ahead of us. They follow us discreetly, about twenty or thirty
yards away, and we are the ones who plan the itinerary of our
ride. We talk over this choice solemnly the day before, as it is
about the only freedom we have left. But our decision hardly
varies. We'll do a short trot and gallop over the fields, then we'll
take the mountain trails to the north.

The latter are lumbermen's roads winding among beautiful
firs. They are wide enough for trucks to pass through. So we
have room to ride three abreast, boot to boot and without fear of
the horses becoming restless, even if the mare that I'm on trots
in the middle.

Her name is Chouchka. No horse at Blueville would ever fail
to show her respect, and I don't know to what I can attribute
this mastery except her determined nature, for Chouchka is
small, standing no more than five feet high and, without a
doubt, much lighter than the big horses that she terrorizes.

As soon as the trail starts uphill, we settle down to a walk.
That's when Jespersen, Stien and I chat. Or, rather, Stien
listens to us, as Jespersen, who is young, impetuous and a bit
harebrained (although an excellent chemist), talks endlessly
about Jackie and Pussy and I give him tit for tat. Stien, on his
mare Myrta (he had plenty of trouble heaving himself aboard
her), knits up his brows, grumbles, shrugs his shoulders, pouts
and keeps on adjusting his Tyrolean hat peevishly.

After a moment, I half-turn to him and try to get him to
participate.

"What about you, Stien, what do you think about it?"

"Personally," said Stien with a scowl," I don't have that kind
of trouble. I'm married."

Jespersen breaks out laughing. It's a pleasure, in the situation
that is ours, to see such carefree mirth. There's an expression

that I love: "Split your sides laughing," although it's absurd, since sides don't split. But its absurdity conveys the extravagant mirth in a strong, zestful young person like Jespersen, with his blue eyes, his clear complexion and his hair so blond that it is almost white. He doubles up laughing on the saddlehorn and then straightens up again, broad-shouldered, slim-waisted, with that flat, muscular belly of young men—totally given up to his childish glee. I know what he finds so funny. He has just remembered Mutsch's diatribe against Ruth Jettison last Sunday and, in particular, the last sentence. When we're alone he repeats it and finds it extremely funny. In his naïveté, he can't imagine that a couple of Stien and Mutsch's age can still make love.

"Me too," I say, turning to Stien. "I'm married, but if this conjugal absenteeism keeps up, it's going to be a problem for me."

Jespersen says, laughing, "In that case, I warn you—I've got Jackie!"

This, it strikes me, is the essence of the magical thinking of children: *having* someone or something without being able to have it. But I'm a good companion. I'm going to enter into the spirit of the game, and—why not admit it, even though it's childish—I have fun at it, too.

"I prefer Pussy," I say. "Pussy has a ravishing face. She's feline and treacherous. For me, make it Pussy, if you please. With or without uniform."

"You're both retarded," said Stien scowlingly. "Jess is twelve and you are twelve and a half."

"Oh, come on, Stien," I say. "Even at sixty you can take an interest in girls."

"Not those two."

"You don't think they're pretty?"

"I don't give a damn if they're pretty."

To see Stien, who I'm screening from his view, Jespersen bends forward over his saddlehorn and leans both hands on the neck of his mount.

"Do you have anything against them, Stien?"

A silence, and Stien says, tight-lipped, "They're too goyische."

Jespersen looks at him, his blue eyes opening wide. "What do you mean by that?"

"Well, they're tall, blond, arrogant-looking . . ."

Jespersen laughs. "Come now, Stien, what racism! I'm also tall, blond, et cetera."

"It's not the same," says Stien solemnly, staring straight ahead. "Those girls bring back memories. I've seen enough of that kind of face and that kind of eyes."

All right. I understand, I sympathize. But it wasn't a reason for spoiling Jess's fun. Besides, Stien contradicts himself. Yesterday he criticized me for dramatizing, and today he goes a good deal farther into tragedy than I. Another contradiction, but I emphasize that one because of the comic effect.

"Stien, you call anybody a goy. The other day I was a goy because I was 'soft.' And now a goy has a tough hide. We've got to get it straight: Is a goy hard or soft?"

"He's both," Stien says unflinchingly.

Jespersen laughs. Then silence settles over us, and in the silence I hear the measured sound of the hooves on the stony road. I remember just then—a Sunday in May; the sun through the firs whose branches divide its rays; the grass, a beautiful green, shining on the shoulders of the road and yet, despite the season, a dry cold. Stien was bundled up in his Mackinaw and his little Tyrolean hat pulled down over his eyes. I myself, full of gratitude for my turtleneck sweater and admiring Jess, who contented himself with a thick woolen checked shirt, wide open at his muscular neck. Let's not forget the two militiawomen thirty yards behind us, the barrels of their carbines projecting beyond their backs—as Jess said, "our Cossack guards."

I remember that moment, because what followed happened so fast and in such a totally unforeseen way.

A hundred yards ahead of us the road forked. The road on the right went straight north, and the one on the left described a curve that inclined to the west and, farther on, to the southwest. That was the one we always took. It led us back to Blueville.

"Ralph, do you remember the Frost poem 'The Road Not Taken?'" Jesperson asked.

"Yes. I used to know it by heart."

"Me too."

"Why don't we ever take the road that goes to the right?" Jess continued, turning to Stien.

"Because it's forbidden," Stien grumbled, and the word *forbidden*—in his mouth—had the ring of finality that the word *verboten* has in German.

"*Who* has forbidden it?" asked Jespersen. "I don't see any sign."

"The Cossack guards," said Stien.

"They never told me about it."

"They told me. That was six months ago. And I was supposed to tell you that or, rather, repeat it to you."

"How sad it is," Jespersen said, "a road that will never be taken." And he did look sad. He added, "And what if there were a girl at the end of that road. A real girl, one who smiled?"

Stien shrugged his shoulders. I didn't say anything. I was thinking that it was a pity to be thirty like Jess and be penned up behind barbed wire with women who hate you, God knows why. We started up the road to the left, and all of a sudden Jespersen made his horse circle, retrace its steps and walk up the road to the right.

"You're out of your mind!" Stien said, reining his horse in. "It's forbidden!"

"I'm taking the road that's never been taken!" shouted Jespersen, and he began galloping, his red-and-blue checkered shirt shining in the sun.

I shouted, "Jess! Come back! Don't be an idiot!"

A strident whistle blast shattered the air. It was Pussy. She came up at a gallop, her face livid with rage, several lengths ahead of Jackie. A second whistle blast. Jess was still moving. And all of a sudden I couldn't believe my eyes. Pussy reined in her gelding, dropped the reins on the animal's neck, ducked her head through the sling, gripped her carbine and threw it to her shoulder.

I screamed, "Don't shoot him!"

I didn't have time to make up my mind. My legs, quicker than my thinking, hurled Chouchka against Pussy's gelding. Terrified, the horse reared up, the gun went off. I heard the bullet whistle, and I saw Pussy thrown and fall as if in slow motion, letting go of her weapon.

The gelding fled, kicking its hooves once or twice out of Chouchka's reach to cover up its cowardice and stopped twenty yards farther on, grazing on the grassy shoulders of the road. I had trouble reining Chouchka in, and as I struggled with her I yelled something or other. Stien also cried out, and finally, coming back to us at a gallop, Jess hurled himself at Jackie, screaming, "You shot at me!"

Jackie panicked, pulled out her revolver with a trembling hand and leveled it at Jess. I shouted, "It wasn't her! It was Pussy!"

I think what saved Jess just then was the fact that our horses were getting out of hand, backing into one another in a limited space, Chouchka taking advantage of this to bite and to kick anything that moved within her reach. Then there was a moment of extreme confusion during which we milled around amid cries and curses. It was a miracle that Pussy hadn't been struck by a hoof. She was still on the ground, in a sitting position, a wry expression on her pale face, holding her right elbow with her left hand.

It was that grimace and her withdrawn attitude that restored my composure. An old reflex: I became a doctor again. I dismounted and tied Chouchka to a supple branch, which put an end to her bites, thereby steadying the horses. I went up to Pussy. She also reacted with fear. Fortunately for me, her revolver was out of reach of her left hand. She nevertheless made a try for it with her right. She let out a scream and bent double, her face ashen, biting her lips. But she didn't lose consciousness and cried at me in a toneless voice, "Don't touch me!"

"Don't be a fool," I said, kneeling beside her. "I'm a doctor. Let me see that elbow."

Behind my back I heard Stien bawling out Jackie (who had holstered her pistol) and, in almost the same terms, Jess. I released the hand that Pussy had clamped over her elbow, and very tenderly, through the sleeve of her uniform, I felt the articulation. A simple dislocation, I thought, but an X ray was going to be necessary. As she made no attempt to stand, I supposed that she also must have sprained an ankle. Just then I lifted my eyes to my patient. Pussy was looking at me. A curious look: fear, revulsion, horror—it was all there. It was disappointing. Even a dog would have been grateful.

I stood up and headed toward Jackie. The storm of abuse with Stien had calmed her down. Or was it Stien's age and his white hair? Or Jess's silence? Or the fact that I had neither strangled nor raped Pussy, as she might have expected?

Just as I drew near Jackie, she spoke to Jess with pent-up anger. "And don't tell me you didn't know the road was forbidden. Professor Stienemeier told you! I heard him!"

I traded a glance with Stien. She had "heard" us thirty paces away? With her ears, or with one of those damned gadgets for long-range eavesdropping? Among other things, this is what the "Cossack guards" were good for! I plunged anxiously into my memories of previous rides. No, I couldn't come up with anything damaging, except for some off-color jokes about Pussy. And which she must have taken for gospel, the way she hated us.

Jackie intercepted the glance, understood the slip[1] and blushed, which didn't make her less beautiful. She is a tall, handsome girl with a straightforward face and well built, along the lines of Ingrid Bergman, and she was far from being as inhuman as one might think at first sight of her cold eyes and her icy silence. She had been caught in the open by the enemy and she was talking to him; she was looking at him. Stien trapped her in a discussion of this type: Are we research workers or prisoners of war? Are you here to protect us or to shoot at us? She tried to vindicate herself and lost her countenance and, at the same time, control of the situation.

When I went up to her to talk about Pussy, I noticed that she was looking at me without any hardness. My head was at the level of her knee, and although such a thought at a moment like this was incongruous, the idea crossed my mind that I would have liked to give that girl an unselfish caress—if there is any unselfishness in that domain, something that I doubt. The particular hatred that Ruth Jettison spoke of in her sermon must not be my forte.

"We've got to get back," I said. "Pussy has dislocated her

[1] Or what I took for a slip. Actually, I realized afterwards that it had been a veiled warning (Dr. Martinelli).

elbow. It's got to be put in place right away. Jess and I will help her onto her horse. I hope she'll be able to stay in the saddle. I suggest that Stien and you ride alongside her to prevent her from falling. Jess and I will ride ahead of you."

"O.K.," Jackie said.

Catching up with Pussy's gelding was no easy matter; getting Pussy aboard wasn't either. When it was done Stien called me and said, "Ralph, be a good fellow and pick up my hat. You know the trouble I have getting back up on this nag when I dismount."

I looked for the Tyrolean hat, and as I did I found Pussy's carbine in the grass. In her confusion the "Cossack guard" had forgotten it. I snatched it up and handed it to her, by the barrel, with a little smile at Jackie, who grabbed it with embarrassment. I would have liked to point out to Pussy that I had saved her from a court-martial, but I didn't have the heart to do it. Her right foot wasn't in the stirrup, and her right arm was folded over her stomach. Her hand clutched her uniform. She was very pale, and three or four miles in the saddle wasn't going to do her any good.

"My hat," Stien said.

There it was. I handed it to him absently, and all of a sudden Stien bellowed. Everyone turned to him, except Pussy, who was in no shape to do anything on her saddle. Stien brandished his Tyrolean at arm's length. Two holes had been drilled through it—Pussy's stray bullet.

Stien moved his horse before Pussy and, without a word, with mute rage, showed her her handiwork. Pussy said nothing, far too busy with not fainting. As quickly as he had risen to the boiling point, Stien calmed down. Then wheeling Myrta around, he ranged up alongside Jackie and told her in a rough voice, "Aside from Pussy's fall, which has left marks, and the accidental shot" (he stressed the "accidental"), "I'm of the opinion that we should keep this incident to ourselves. As far as I'm concerned, I won't make a report. What you decide to do about it is up to you."

I looked at her. Between the drooping flesh of her eyelids a little gleam shone in her eyes. "The Cossack guard" had gone beyond her orders, that was clear. And, on our side, Jess was manifestly in the wrong. Old Stien was concluding a compromise with the enemy. Silence in exchange for silence. He was trying to save the future of our horseback rides and to trap the militiawomen in a tacit complicity.

The girls kept quiet—one, because she was suffering; the other, because she was bewildered, at least I thought she was. But a few weeks later I would change my mind about Jackie.

4

In the castle's infirmary there was a great commotion. Dr. Rilke—who the P.M.s nicknamed Dr. Hyde, owing to his apelike ugliness—was absent, the nurse too. They were A's, and they were away visiting their families somewhere in the United States. The arrival of Pussy, borne by Jespersen and myself, plunged the administrator, Mr. Barrow, into perplexity—I should even say into anguish.

He was a man of great stature, with broad shoulders, but whose weight and breadth promised no strength. He was flabby, potbellied. His complexion was oily, his eyes bulging, his hands limp. His knees, for some unknown reason, buckled at each step, making him seem like he was bouncing on the ground. His skull, absolutely denuded of any trace of hair, gleamed with sweat. What was worse, this appearance could not be attributed to the Ablationist initiation that he had undergone, since I'd seen, on the wall of his office, a photo of young Mr. Barrow, hugging a university diploma to his chest. He was already what he is.

Make no mistake about it: Mr. Barrow was full of thankless qualities. He was a good administrator, a zealous bureaucrat. His servility to Hilda Helsingforth astonished me. When he spoke to her over the phone, I always had the impression that he was going to spread himself out at her feet like a carpet.

Nevertheless, hidden under this viscous appearance there was an inhuman or, rather, *ahuman*, hardness. A soft robot. But the core was made of metal.

For me, having crossed the threshold of the infirmary, the situation seemed simple. Since Dr. Rilke wasn't there, since the nearest city was a hundred miles away and because treatment could not wait, I was going to do it myself, with the aid of Mrs. Barrow, who would take a few X rays of the elbow beforehand. Actually, I knew quite well that she was Dr. Rilke's X-ray assistant.

What was I thinking? It was even out of the question to place Pussy on the operating table. She had to make do with a chair! Without any treatment! And during that time, Mr. and Mrs. Barrow argued, bitterly and under their breath, an argument that Mr. Barrow interrupted to tell Jespersen without the least tact that his presence was no longer necessary. Jespersen turned livid with rage and went out at once without a word, slamming the door.

It was my turn to get angry.

"I can go, too," I said coldly, "and leave the patient with her elbow dislocated, a situation for which you will bear the entire responsibility."

"Dr. Martinelli," said Mr. Barrow, turning his soft belly to me and staring at me with his bulging eyes, "you must understand that your intervention raises a delicate administrative problem for us, given your special status in Blueville."

Mr. Barrow had a voice that was special, unctuous but with a little threat in it: steel ballbearings rolling in a vat of oil.

"Do you mean to say that, being a P.M., I'm not supposed to treat people?"

"Exactly!" answered Mr. Barrow. "That's exactly what I mean!"

"I confess that I don't understand."

"It's really quite simple," Mr. Barrow said. "Your contract with us defines you as a research worker and not a doctor."

"But this is an emergency! And my duty, as a doctor, is to give help to a patient. Contract or not, I find it inadmissible that this girl be left sitting on a chair with no one to take care of her."

"Dr. Martinelli," said Barrow, "it's not just your contract.

There's also, as I've just told you, your special status. Would you please wait a few minutes and give me time to settle a problem that concerns only me?"

This was said with crushing politeness. Mr. Barrow repeated the formula "your special status" with a contemptuous face, as if it were a defect for a man to keep his reproductive organs in working condition. With that, he turned his back on me and resumed his argument with Mrs. Barrow.

No mistake about it: I'd been given the cold shoulder. And by whom! I looked at Pussy. She was very pale, her features taut, and just as my eyes came to rest on her she closed hers. Thank you. And thank you, too, Mrs. Barrow, who, since I'd entered the infirmary with Pussy, hadn't looked at me once, even during the battle with her husband. I took my distance from this trio of lunatics. I isolated myself, going to stand in front of the window. I was shaken by a fit of mute rage, the impotence of which I knew all too well.

At the same time I kept my eyes open. The Barrow couple's *sotto voce* argument went on. If I understood correctly, Mr. Barrow was for transporting Pussy to the city and Mrs. Barrow for immediate treatment, even by impure hands. I thought she would have her way. Which proved that, even on an A, a wife's influence was considerable. Mr. Barrow picked up the receiver and, just by his groveling voice, I knew that he was speaking to Hilda Helsingforth. I could easily imagine him lying flat on his soft belly, running his tongue between his boss's toes.

"You may treat her, Dr. Martinelli," said Mr. Barrow with an imposing air as he hung up the receiver.

That slug still astonished me. I wondered how he managed to go so fast from drooling to arrogance.

I turned around and said coldly, "Provided that I'm assisted by Mrs. Barrow."

"Of course, Doctor," said Mrs. Barrow, anticipating her husband's decision but still not granting me a look.

I told her to undress Pussy. During that time I pulled off Pussy's boots. When I got to the left foot she let out a cry. I examined it: a minor sprain. I left her there and washed my hands. Mrs. Barrow ripped open the right sleeve of the uniform. That took some time. I noted, as I dried myself and returned to the table, that Mrs. Barrow was very competent. On the whole, I liked her a lot. She was a woman who was gracefully approaching the fullness of her forties. She was rather short and plump, solid, her feet solidly on the ground and her round head well screwed onto her robust shoulders. Dark with short hair, a strong jaw to chew with, and bright, sparkling eyes. Entirely reassuring good health, balance and realism emanated from her. I was convinced, just glancing at her, that she had a heart to last a hundred years, that she had good digestion, that she had regular bowel movements, that she took no sleeping pills and that her ovaries didn't bother her. I was ready to swear that complexes, neuroses and anxiety were foreign to her and that she walked through life, pushing her furrow straight ahead of her, happy, active and altruistic, at the side of that slimy, bureaucratic monster she might love—who knows?

Under her uniform, Pussy had a crew-necked woolen shirt, the sleeves of which couldn't possibly be rolled up. I helped Mrs. Barrow take it off her. Breasts that had no need of support appeared, and while Mrs. Barrow rolled the X-ray machine toward us, I feasted cautiously lowered eyes on them, impassively.

I became conscious of a presence behind me. I turned around. It was Mr. Barrow, and I had an absurd reaction: I was jealous.

"Mr. Barrow," I said in a rather unfriendly voice, "allow me to tell you that you have no right to be present at a medical examination."

"I'm here by virtue of the instructions that were given to me," replied Mr. Barrow, who had only seen my words in their proper light and was refuting them in the same fashion.

I shrugged and said with severity, "It's true that your presence isn't very important."

This was actually meant to be venomous, but Mr. Barrow missed the venom and replied prosaically, "No, on the contrary, it is very important." A half smile, it seemed to me, ran fleetingly across Mrs. Barrow's lips.

The X rays were most reassuring. There was no fracture or osseous wrenching. A simple rear dislocation. The humerus hadn't even come all the way out of the articular cavity. I put it back in place. Three events occurred in rapid succession. Pussy let out a scream and went into a half faint. Mr. Barrow left the infirmary, called away by the outside telephone. And Mrs. Barrow, who was facing me, raised her head, looked me right in the eye and smiled at me.

I wouldn't want there to be any misunderstanding about that look and that smile. They were not provocative, even if they contained that non-negligible degree of erotic charge that travels in an almost innocent way between a woman and a man in the course of social contact, but without ulterior motive—or, rather, without the thoughts that are in back wanting to come up front and be converted into a definite plan. In this way, Mrs. Barrow looked at me and smiled at me—let's say, with sympathy, with impulsiveness, with complicity. And at once, overflowing with gratitude for this most unexpected of gifts, I returned the look and smile in an outpouring of tenderness for which she thanked me by fluttering her eyelashes and turning her head away.

All that had lasted barely half a second. When Pussy reopened her eyes, it was all over. Mrs. Barrow had changed back into stone and Pussy into concrete, for I got no reply, no thanks, no look when, having massaged and taped her ankle, I went away wishing her a speedy recovery. It is true that Pussy may have realized that I had caused her fall.

When I went down the castle steps, remembering Mrs. Barrow's smile, I had the urge, like Christian in *Pilgrim's Progress*, to "hop three times to express my joy."

Naturally, within P.M. circles at Blueville, I'd had normal relations up to then with the wives of my colleagues. But that hadn't prevented me from feeling how my status, professionally high, was socially low. Now I felt that I had gotten out of my ghetto. Oh, of course, that wouldn't change things; it had been only a flash of lightning. I didn't have the slightest intention nor the slightest chance of laying a bridge between Mrs. Barrows and me. But her clandestine message was for me a priceless treasure. I would remember it and cherish it. I rediscovered, in a fleeting glance, the old complicity between the two sexes that had been for me one of life's daily pleasures.

And, most of all, I had a better understanding of the situation at Blueville. With regard to the P.M., there was a *line*. It was imposed tyrannically from outside; it wasn't interiorized. It was untrue that all women hated us.

My rejoicing was short-lived. A few minutes later, Dave raised a serious problem for me.

When I got back to my barracks late in the day, I found it plunged in darkness, including Dave's room. I switched on the light, and, on his little desk, I didn't find the note that he usually left to tell me where he was. I grew uneasy. On this campus surrounded by barbed-wire fences, the only entrance was guarded by a lookout tower. Running away was impossible. I phoned the castle pool. I was told that Dave had left there an hour before. There were no telephone lines between my place and the other P.M. barracks, and I decided to go from one door to another, looking for Dave.

I finally found him—in Mutsch's kitchenette and in the absence of Mutsch, whom I had just seen at the Pierces. He was reading, seated on a red plastic chair, and when I entered the room he never even lifted his head.

"What are you doing here? I've been looking all over for you."

He didn't look at me, either. His delicate, triangular face was bent over his book, and his eyes, with immense, curving black lashes, were lowered, shading his cheeks.

"I feel good here," he answered in a cold, toneless voice.

"But this is Mutsch's place and she's out."

"What does that matter?" he answered. "Mutsch doesn't give a damn. And neither do I."

I didn't like that tone of voice. That wasn't Dave who had spoken; it was someone else they'd put in his place. I sat down across from him.

"Of course, you must have been terribly bored," I said. "But one of the militiawomen fell off her horse. She dislocated her elbow, and, with Dr. Rilke away, I had to operate."

He didn't bat an eyelash. He had no eyes. Now he had no ears.

"Do you hear me, Dave?"

"I hear you," he answered with cold insolence while studiously turning a page in his book. I was sure just then that he hadn't read a single line of it.

"I'm trying to explain that I couldn't help being late."

"I understood," he replied in the same tone of voice.

I thought I'd better explain my explanation. "It couldn't wait. A dislocation of the elbow requires immediate reduction. When we got back from riding, Jespersen and I both went straight to the infirmary."

"I know," he said. "Stien stopped by the pool and told me."

"Well, in that case, if you know, stop giving me the silent treatment."

"I'm not giving you the silent treatment," he said with an air of icy dignity.

"Yes, you are. You aren't even looking at me. It's not very exciting—talking to a brick wall."

"I *am* a brick wall," he replied without raising his eyes.

He emphasized "am" and, with a brutal finger, turned another page. Silence. I didn't quite know what to do. Dave had already been through some little fits of hostility toward me but never so strong or so long. It looked as though the onset of puberty was intensifying all his reactions. What's more, I had a great deal of trouble retaining my composure. I had a lump in my throat, and my mind went whirling a hundred times around the insoluble and worn-out problem of raising children: Wasn't I an overly permissive parent? Shouldn't I have given Dave a more authoritarian "father image" and, therefore, one that gave him more security? I just didn't know. I didn't trust those peremptory psychologies.

I got to my feet and, forcing myself to keep a brave face, said, "Come on, Dave. Let's go back to our place."

"I'm very comfortable here," Dave answered without moving, his eyes still lowered on his book.

What was I supposed to do? Raise my voice? Give him a slap? Throw him over my shoulder like a sack? I gave in.

"What are you reading?"

He dog-eared the page and, still without looking at me, handed me his book, closing it as he did.

"Oh, yes," I said. "*Huckleberry Finn.* That's an old friend."

I admired Dave for his taste in reading. And it also worried me, being the story of an unloved boy who ran away from home. True, no one ever ran away from Blueville.

I gave him back the book and said to him, "What part are you up to?"

But Dave refused to be trapped into a literary discussion. He replied without moving his lips, "The beginning."

And, at once, he went back to his pseudo-reading, pale, cold and determined.

"Come on, Dave, don't keep me waiting."

A silence.

"Well, Dave?" I raised my voice.

Dave lifted his brows and said in a distant voice, "I've already told you—I like it here."

Silence. I said in a neutral tone, "I'll wait for you in the cafeteria."

No answer. I closed the door behind me, but, before leaving the place, I made my way noiselessly into the bathroom. I opened the medicine chest and, after examining its contents—sorry, Mutsch—I randomly stole a box of sleeping pills.

Since I knew that I would find Mutsch there, I went straight to the Pierces. Pierce worked with me at the lab. He was a good research worker, nothing more, but Mrs. Pierce, now, she was unusual. Although unschooled, she had a mind sharp as a knife. Physically—tall, skinny, long nose, long chin, both having a tendency to meet, giving her the profile of a hawk. A deceptive appearance. She was good, and her prey wasn't humans but events. Always on the lookout, poking her beak everywhere, she saw, heard and understood ten times as much in one day as an ordinary person. At first we had the tendency to dispute Joan Pierce's deductions or intuitions, but they proved, day after day, so accurate that our skepticism ceased.

Wherever she went, Mrs. Pierce carried a big black leather bag containing, oddly enough, little dolls that she made herself and, in with all those dolls, a big pair of binoculars. Often, in the midst of a friendly conversation, she would steal away to the window and there, binoculars glued to her retina, she would painstakingly observe the surroundings.

But Mrs. Pierce didn't need lenses to see into the future or through walls. She combined the gift of prophecy with the gift of clairvoyance. She had warned me at the start of my stay in Blueville that Anita would come to see me less and less often. This prediction, unfortunately, proved correct. So I was inclined to believe her when she described Hilda Helsingforth, who nobody here had ever seen, as being, and I quote, very tall and very beautiful. Her features are classical; she resembles a stone statue. "And yet, all that is spoiled, I don't know exactly by what."

Jespersen had nicknamed Mrs. Pierce the Sorceress. More modestly, Mrs. Pierce spoke of her intuition. But "sorcery" or "intuition" are only words. I rather think that in Mrs. Pierce's case there was reasoning so quick and so astute that Mrs. Pierce herself wasn't aware of the results yielded. The enormous work of accumulating, analyzing and synthesizing facts escaped her in part, probably because it was the only sensual delight of her life.

When she opened the door, her face sharp as a bird's beak searched my eyes and she said, laughing, "Poor Ralph, I see that you're still worried about Dave. But it isn't serious. Have you come to see Mutsch?" And gripping my arm in her talons—her fingers were also very long—she led me into the room where her son, Johnny, slept and which served as a living room during the day, the bed folding up in a closet.

Mutsch was seated at a table, a schoolbook in front of her. Under her thick white bangs, her round, wrinkled face gave a pleasant impression of serenity. Mutsch, in fact, was as peaceful in her bearing and speech as Stien was excited. I sat facing her, and I told her about my meeting with Dave. Apparently, this account didn't interest Joan Pierce, for, after a moment, she got to her feet, took up position at one of her windows that looked out over the militiawomen's barracks and, binoculars at her eyes, watched at length what went on over there.

Mutsch had a rare quality: She listened well. She moved ahead step by step in what you were telling her. And when she didn't understand, she asked questions. My account ended, she smiled at me and told me with that Germanic accent which, for some strange reason, I find comforting, "First of all, Ralph, stop blaming yourself. It isn't your fault that your wife died." (I note once more—neither Mutsch nor Joan considered Anita as really being my wife.) "You're doing everything you can with Dave."

"Ralph is too softhearted, that's all," said Mrs. Pierce half ironically, half affectionately. She said that without interrupting her spying on the militiawomen's barracks. Proof that her ears could do one thing while her eyes did another.

"No, no, Joan," said Mutsch, "don't say that! No one is ever too soft. A child has an absolutely unlimited capacity to absorb love. They drink in love. They never get enough of it."

I brought her back to my problem: "How do you explain Dave rejecting me the way he did tonight?"

"But, Ralph, it's normal."

"Normal?"

"Yes, Ralph. If you could only put yourself in the position of a child. Dave has lost his mother. He's terribly afraid of losing you, too. That's why he's clinging to you. When you go off horseback riding, do you think he's having fun at the pool? Not at all. He waits for you. And when you're late, he becomes frantic. That's why, as soon as I heard that you'd come back to the castle for Pussy's operation, I sent Stien to let him know." (She said "Stien" just like the rest of us.)

"Thanks, Mutsch. Dave told me."

"Unfortunately, it didn't do any good. He'd already overheated."

"What do you mean by that?"

"That Dave was no longer able to come out of the state of anxiety your absence had put him in."

"In that case, he should have been relieved to see me."

She shook her head. "That's your adult logic. The child can't check the momentum of his anxiety. The reflexive brake is too weak. And what happens then is this: Dave breaks away. He breaks away all the more violently as he's more attached to you. He breaks the bond."

I looked at her. "Do you mean that he's broken with me so he won't have to lose me?"

"Exactly. It's the behavior of despair."

"It's bewildering," I said under my breath.

"No, it isn't," Mrs. Pierce said without turning around, her eyes still glued to her binoculars. "You worry about Dave much too much, Ralph. It isn't that serious. There's a certain amount of play in all this. Dave knows quite well that this break-up isn't serious. Mainly, he's trying to punish you."

"And put your love to the test," said Mutsch.

I thought, and the more I thought, the more it seemed that they were right. I looked at them. Or, rather, I looked at Mutsch's face and Mrs. Pierce's back. I was full of gratitude and, at the same time, somewhat overwhelmed by the almost excessive dose of female wisdom that I was taking in.

"Now what?" I asked, a bit on edge.

"Now I'm going to take Dave to my place," Mutsch said. "I'll take him to the cafeteria, and when our trays are full we'll go over and sit at your table."

I got to my feet. "Thanks, Mutsch. Thanks for everything. And excuse me for taking this out of your medicine chest."

As I didn't say what it was, Mrs. Pierce, carried away by her curiosity to see, detached the binoculars from her hawk eyes, left her observation post and came hopping up to us. When she saw the tube of sleeping pills she burst out laughing.

"Dave isn't the only one who's nervous!"

"You think my fears are unfounded?"

"Of course they are," she said.

Mutsch took over. "You've got Blueville sickness, Ralph. You're worried and so is Dave. What is a child like Dave to think when he sees that neither the A's nor the 'single women' consent to look at him? But kill himself—no. Naturally, Dave thinks about death—yours, his—but he won't kill himself. Absolutely not. Relax. Get rid of ideas like that!"

"Think about pleasant things instead," Mrs. Pierce said. "Like the militiawomen, for example. Some of them are pretty."

She laughed with a mischievous laugh. So did Mutsch. And they looked at each other and looked at me in a mocking, affectionate way. And their laughter and their looks gave me the feeling of being a character like Charlie Chaplin in *The Gold Rush*—comical and touching.

Ingrate that I am, I left rather abruptly. Perhaps it's my small size that's made me hypersensitive, but I hate people to make fun of me, even in a friendly way. I thought a lot of those two, but they got on my nerves a little. Always so sure of themselves. One of them with her brilliant intuition that she didn't explain and the other who explained too much. And most of all, I knew what they were going to talk about now or, rather, about whom, and in what terms, and lamenting about the lurch I'd been left in. I knew what I thought about Anita's prolonged absences and the scarcity of her letters, but I didn't like anyone to criticize her or feel sorry for me.

Jackie and Pussy must have accepted the implicit bargain proposed by Stien and have kept the incident quiet or, at least, minimized it, for none of us, not even Jespersen, received a note from Mrs. Barrow announcing a fine to be withheld from our monthly salary check. And the ride, the next Sunday afternoon, took place as usual, except that Pussy was replaced by a tall dark woman, clumsy and out of proportion and just as icy. Curiously enough, I missed Pussy, from whom I'd never had the slightest glance or the least trace of a smile. Whatever she did, at least she gave me something—the pleasure of looking at her.

When we started up the mountain, I turned around, brought Chouchka to a halt, awaited the Cossack guard, and when Jackie drew up to me, quite normally, I asked her how Pussy was. She was so stupefied by my audacity, so embarrassed by the tacit agreement made with us and so disturbed by the surprising fact that I had given medical treatment to her comrade that she answered, "Pussy will be back on duty next week."

When I rejoined Jess and Stien, Jess began to sing. It was a process that we'd found for jamming the Cossack guard's listening device. When I reported my conversation with Jackie to Stien, he shrugged, shook his white hair and grumbled, "What the hell do you have to do with that girl?" To which I retorted: "After all, she's my patient." Which got me a rather sardonic sidelong glance. But Stien was nonetheless satisfied. Now, he said, they were going to be forced to talk to us. And, sure enough, the following Sunday, as soon as we entered the forest, we let ourselves be overtaken by the Cossack guards. Stien placed himself before Pussy, looked her in the eye and said in an accusing voice, "When you aimed at Dr. Jespersen, did you intend to kill him?"

Pussy blushed deeply and said in a trembling voice, "I didn't aim at him. I was going to fire in the air! Everything that happened was Dr. Martinelli's fault for driving Chouchka against my horse."

I said dryly, "How was I supposed to know that you weren't going to kill Jespersen? You've always been so mean to us."

Her gaze was blurred with tears but didn't avoid mine.

"We're not mean," she said defensively. "We're following our instructions."

"That's enough talk!" Jackie said harshly.

I looked at her with anger and said, "Why—because your instructions also forbid you to talk to us? What are we in your eyes? Monsters? Outcasts? Criminals?"

She was thrown by my brusque attack, and I capitalized on this to say to Pussy, "You have the gall to say that you aren't mean when you haven't even thanked me for the treatment I gave you."

"I wasn't going to thank you for throwing me off my own horse!"

"You know perfectly well I didn't mean to do it. And you're forgetting that if I hadn't insisted on treating you Mr. Barrow would have sent you into town. A hundred miles by car! Three hours! Driving! You would have felt every minute of it!"

"All right—thanks," Pussy said furiously but without averting her eyes, and since she was looking at me I met her gaze for a full second.

"That's enough now," Jackie shouted. "Please stop this conversation."

We turned our horses and resumed our advance. I had the exciting impression of having scored a victory, but that impression didn't last, nipped in the bud by Stien. He signaled Jess to sing, and I was submitted to a torrent of abuse uttered in a hushed, hissing voice, in an increasingly Germanic English.

"Ralph, I'm not going to mince words with you. You're just as crazy, just as rash, just as irresponsible as Jess, and that's saying something. What's going on between you and that girl? Under the pretext of bawling her out, you're making advances to her! And that idiot gives you tit for tat! Talk to them—yes. Any time. But not this stuff! Where's it going to get you? Into more trouble and we'll be in it, too. If you won't think of us, think of Dave! I for one have made up my mind. If you do it again, if I spot you looking at that girl again, it's all over, count me out of the horseback riding, you can go by yourselves!"

I replied in a furious voice, "Stien, you're taking advantage of your age. It doesn't give you any authority over me. I don't need a daddy to tell me what to do."

Stien fell silent. Jess stopped singing. And I was astonished by the suddenness and the violence of my own rage. Worried too. To my mind, there was something abnormal in that reaction. A sign of neurosis or of the start of neurosis. Oh, I knew well enough the strained situation with Dave, the social devaluation that I'd undergone, my forced chastity, Anita's silences. All right. I didn't believe—at least, not in my case—in the value of psychoanalysis. I believed, on the contrary, in the therapeutic value of behavior. I thought that, by correcting my conduct, I could, to some extent, mitigate the frustration that I was suffering from.

I made a hand signal to Jess, which meant that he was to cover our conversation again. This time he didn't sing—he recited—"The Road Not Taken" by Robert Frost, which might to the eyes or, rather, the ears of the "Cossack guards" pass for treacherous irony.

I turned to Stien and said to him in a perfectly calm voice, "It never dawned on me that I was making advances to that girl. You're right. It's crazy. I'll stop."

Stien raised his brows and, between the flesh of his eyelids, gave me a penetrating glance. He didn't say anything, not a word, but I knew exactly what he was thinking: nice boy, abandoned by his wife, etc. I controlled my irritation, leaned forward, patted Chouchka's shoulder, then I drew in my reins and said, "Let's go, Chouchka, gallop!" I brushed her flanks with my boots. She tore herself away from the ground, I tore myself away with her, and we ran in unison toward a horizon that couldn't be more limited. But as long as she moved beneath me and the wind whistled in my ears, I felt free.

The next day, I received a short note from Anita. She would

come next Saturday without fail, and this time she meant it. I didn't believe a word of it. I crumpled the note in rage and stuffed it into my pocket. Then, remembering my therapy, I withdrew it at once with slow movements, smoothed out the wrinkles, folded it up again and tucked it away deliberately in my wallet. But that didn't do at all. I had an oppressive tightness in the chest, my palms were sweating, my legs shook. Anita wouldn't show up, I knew it. And I had an endless week of waiting ahead of me until she called it off.

For six months now my research work has been slipping. I'd like to turn back the clock and explain why. Ah, certainly, there is an abundance of raw materials. They bring us as many encephala as we want, we aren't short of laboratory animals, the equipment is magnificent. The weakness stems from the staff. Not that they're incompetent, nor that we're shorthanded. But the staff is separated from me, and they themselves are divided by problems of caste. There are three P.M.s in my lab—Pierce, Smith and myself—twelve A's and five women. Technologically speaking, these women are at the bottom of the ladder. But socially, in Blueville, they are at the top—ahead of the A's, ahead of me.

It's an injustice in both cases. At least two of the women workers deserved something better than the limited knowledge to which the misogyny of our culture confined them. But on the other hand, I can't accept the anti-male racism to which I've been subjected. The resulting situation is intolerable. I feel as if I'm a black lieutenant commanding a platoon of white soldiers. I'm obeyed and scorned.

A lab, first and foremost, is a team, and, for the team to click, the current must flow; there must be a bit of human warmth among its members. This just isn't the case. Under these conditions I simply am not a good leader, nor can I be one. It's easy to understand the reason for this.

Among my co-workers the most brilliant, the most fruitful in ideas, the most creative, is Grabel. He's a vigorous man on the good side of fifty. He's tall, thin, his body stiff yet agile, a bald head topped by a mathematician's oblong skull, little black piercing eyes constantly on the lookout, a long nose, thin and straight, narrow lips and a sharp chin, his face as long as a knife blade.

Under normal conditions, Dr. Grabel, by virtue of his experience, his intelligence, his gifts, should be my closest collaborator and be well ahead of Pierce and Smith, good research workers to be sure but of whom all I can say is that they don't abound with ideas. In fact, I intended, after my arrival in Blueville, to give Grabel that promotion, but I couldn't make up my mind right away, and I did the best thing.

Grabel is an A. I point out in passing that the legend according to which a castrated man must necessarily become adipose is just as wrong for men as for horses. Another myth that I want to debunk: the passivity of the castrated individual. Although his spermatogenesis has ceased forever, Grabel still has an aggressive personality. What's more, as an A, he is very much imbued with his privileges of caste. He sports—even on his white lab coat—his green rosette with its gilded letter, and in a thousand little ways, he's made me feel the inferiority of my status. I've also become certain that he's spying on me. I've therefore isolated him in a narrow, subordinate specialty by trying to set up an airtight partition between him and the actual status of my research. I've required the same secrecy from Pierce and Smith. I never leave my office without double-locking the door and pocketing the key. The last few nights I've even been carrying home the little notebook in which I enter, from day to day, in cryptic writing, progress (when there is any) in our work.

Obviously this distrust, tension and deceit inside our lab is bad. It's regrettable that I can't use a mind as brilliant as Grabel's for a more creative task. It's even more heartbreaking that I can't discuss openly with all my co-workers problems confronting us. The division of the staff into three castes and the scandalous inferiority of my status have therefore made me a bad leader: hard, unfair, authoritarian, secretive—just the opposite, actually, of what I am and what I've been up to now in the departments that I've headed.

At first sight, everything seems to be in order inside the lab. We speak to one another politely, the instructions that I give are executed, work is done or looks as if it's being done. But there is veiled ill-will, on both sides, that rots—like a worm—the task before us.

Grabel hates me, this Grabel who, by dint of his talent and strong personality, has a great deal of influence over the A's and even over the women, to the point that they forget their privileges and talk to him as an equal. For this reason we are both stuck in the dismal machinery of hostility. First phase: He scorns me and spies on me. Second phase: I distrust him and keep him in a subordinate position. Third phase: I become certain that he's writing up reports on me. Fourth phase: I can scarcely stand to be in the same room with him, and when I have something to tell him I go through Pierce. Fifth phase: Grabel starts to undermine me with the A's, the lab women and the administrator, a campaign aimed at my dismissal.

Pierce and Smith have already complained that their viral strains are being sabotaged. I really think that they're mistaken. But their suspicions are symptomatic of the state of mind prevailing in the lab. For my part, I'm on the lookout for all errors and all misbehavior that the A's and the women from my lab may be guilty of, and I painstakingly keep track of them.

It's not in my nature to be this way. I've been forced into it, so to speak.

Three months after my arrival in Blueville, on January 26, to be exact, the crisis took shape. I received the following note from the castle:

> Dr. Martinelli:
> Your attitude to female co-workers and A's in your laboratory does not meet with my approval. Kindly change it.
> Hilda Helsingforth

This message, which terrified me, left me no way of justifying myself. As I've known since the first memo that Hilda Helsingforth sent me, we are forbidden to write to her or ask her for an audience. So I went to see Mr. Barrow. He received me with contemptuous politeness. A written complaint had been given to him about me. He read it and transmitted it. He refused to tell me who issued the complaint, and he refused to say anything whatsoever about the complaint itself. I pointed out to him that, unable to discuss the complaint with either Mrs. Helsingforth or with him, it was impossible for me to defend myself or even know what I was accused of. He raised his arms skyward. He could do nothing about it. Problems inside the laboratories didn't concern him. Throughout this meeting Mr. Barrow was as soft, as viscous and as hard as an octopus.

From that day on I was double careful in the lab. I treated the women and the A's with flawless courtesy, and I sidestepped Grabel without actually doing anything wrong. Furthermore, I began to keep the records that I've mentioned.

On March 15, when I thought Grabel had almost been neutralized by my efforts, I received a second memo from the castle:

Dr. Martinelli:
> You have failed to heed my recommendations of Jan. 26th, and your conduct with regard to female co-workers and A's in your laboratory has changed only superficially, if at all. For the second time, I am asking you to change your attitude.
>
> Hilda Helsingforth

I was horror-struck, but, once over my moment of stupor, I realized it was no longer possible to remain passive. I sent Mr. Barrow a report on the personnel in my lab. I was ashamed to admit it: The report was a monument of injustice. Certainly, I didn't lie; all the facts were true. But the light in which they were conveyed, out of perspective and out of context, the synthesis that I made, was a flagrant inequity. It lambasted Grabel—by far, very far, my best researcher. I had only one complaint with Grabel, but it's precisely the one that I couldn't utter: Grabel wants my job; he's quite capable of handling it, and, with the aid of A's and women, he's trying to eliminate me by any means.

I was going to turn in my report to the administrator—in person. When he understood what it was about, the oily Mr. Barrow retched and considered me with a look of revulsion mingled with a touch of panic. He didn't know, he said, if he was permitted to accept a message of this type from me and, still less, if he should transmit it. I told him that this dilemma was his concern, and walked out, leaving him astonished by my "arrogance." That's how he was to characterize my conduct later on.

Hilda Helsingforth nevertheless received my report, for, a week later, Mr. Barrow handed me the following memo from her:

Dr. Martinelli:

You have complained about your co-workers and your co-workers have complained about you. Obviously, there is a very bad situation here, one which doubtless explains the meager results your research has yielded up to now.

Hilda Helsingforth

Hilda Helsingforth's memo had been handed to me at the evening meal in the cafeteria, and I didn't open it until Dave was in bed. I had the feeling that the blood was draining away from my head. I had to sit down. My legs wouldn't stop trembling, and I watched them tremble with a feeling of shame. After a moment I managed to get to my feet. I reached the kitchenette and drank a whole glass of whisky. Since my arrival in Blueville I had been drinking only in medicinal doses, and all this alcohol, instead of reviving me, knocked me senseless. I went on sitting there motionless, in a kind of lugubrious stupor, and I tried vainly to gather my wits. I then slipped back into the feeling of basic unintelligibility and merciless cruelty that Blueville had always given me. Only this time I wasn't in the grips of diffuse anguish but real panic. The note that I'd just read could mean only one thing: It had prepared me for receiving, in the coming week, my letter of dismissal. I was therefore condemned to death. Dave, too, within a time scarcely more remote. Abruptly, I felt a wave of nausea that gave me a foretaste of death. I only had time to rush to the toilet. I threw up everything, whisky and supper. When it was over I caught sight of my reflection in the mirror. It couldn't be called pallor. My skin was a blue verging on green. In that instant I understood the meaning of the expression "to go into a blue funk," and, curiously enough, I burst out laughing.

From that moment on I felt better.

Before going to bed I took a strong dose of tranquilizers, I fell asleep like a log, and in the morning when I woke up I realized that I couldn't live the days to come at the fever pitch of the day before. There was madness in that situation, and, if I accepted it, I was going to lose my balance. In a few seconds the die was cast. I decided to hand in my resignation.

No doubt about it, I was signing my own death warrant, but I preferred to do it of my own accord rather than feel myself being pushed into it by degrees. As soon as my mind was made up, as soon as I'd killed all hope within myself—and not a moment before—I regained my courage.

I wrote my letter of resignation at once and handed it to Mr. Barrow after breakfast. Unfortunately, he didn't open it in front of me. I would have enjoyed seeing his reaction.

I could hardly wait to do the next thing that came into my mind. I ran to my lab, called for Dr. Grabel, shut myself up with him in my office and, without mincing words, abandoned myself to the most delicious rage of my life. For half an hour I battered him furiously under my reproach and my invective. He tried to react, insinuating that this scene would cost me my job. But I cut him off at once. I announced my resignation triumphantly and, once again, submerged him with my grievances, not letting him get a word in edgeways. He looked at me, pale, silent. What struck me most of all, for it was totally unexpected, was reading in his eyes a kind of sympathy and, even, respect.

5

Hilda Helsingforth's reaction reached me on April 3:

> Dr. Martinelli:
> The contract that you signed binds you to the Helsingforth Company for two years and, while it entitles the company to discharge you at any time, it does not give you the right to resign—unless you wish to cede to the company the monthly payments that we have blocked on your account with us.
> Hilda Helsingforth

I almost shouted with joy on reading that note. My resignation had been refused, and Hilda Helsingforth had stepped down from her pedestal. I no longer faced a sadistic and all-powerful god but a greedy boss who talked contracts and money.

I sensed my advantage, and I exploited it at once. On April 4, I wrote the following letter to Mr. Barrow:

> Dear Mr. Barrow:
> Mrs. Helsingforth is right. The poor results achieved by my laboratory up to now can be ascribed to the strained relations that have arisen between myself and the A's.

As far as I am concerned, my resignation is still effective and I am willing, in order to regain my freedom, to give up the sums owed to me by the Helsingforth Company.

Sincerely yours,
Dr. Martinelli

It should be noted that this letter didn't go all out. I only blamed the A's and didn't mention the women, who actually gave me just as many problems in the lab. My silence on this point was a tactical move: I didn't want to fight more than one enemy at a time.

Hilda Helsingforth replied on April 15:

Dr. Martinelli:

I have noted the fact that you offer your resignation in writing for the second time. I now have the right, on the day when you are separated, not to give you the severance pay provided for in your contract.

Meanwhile, I ask you to continue the assignment for which you were recruited.

Hilda Helsingforth

As I'd done previously, I waited until I was at my place, alone, before opening the envelope. I was afraid of having pushed my luck. I breathed a sigh of relief and began to laugh derisively. Yes, derisively. I found the writer's efforts to regain her little terror tactics ("the day when you are separated") crude, insecure and unconvincing. The idea that I might be worried about severance pay when they were driving me out of the protected zone!

I had the feeling that I'd emerged victoriously from this exchange of letters with Hilda Helsingforth. And I got keen pleasure from this, but it didn't last long. Happiness isn't the kind of plant that can grow in Blueville. And actually, from the look of it, this joust of letter-writing hadn't helped matters.

In the lab everything was still just as bad. And the research was making no headway.

I had too little hope. I'd told no one that Anita had informed me she would visit this coming Saturday. Yet Mrs. Pierce had guessed it. Am I really that transparent? Were her eyes able to read Anita's letter (crumpled, then uncrumpled) through the fabric of my suit and the leather of my wallet?

Of course, if Mrs. Pierce was aware of Anita's visit, everyone in Blueville must know about it, including the single women and the A's. For Mrs. Pierce was the only P.M. wife who had managed to establish social relations with the higher castes. Possessed by her insatiable curiosity, she had accepted no silence or icy looks or snubs from them. She overwhelmed them with her friendliness, disconcerted them with her intuition and disturbed them with her prophecies.

Her hunting ground was the cafeteria. Her tray full, she never sat at a P.M.'s table—not even her husband's. She was sure of seeing us whenever she wanted and put us aside for an evening tidbit. In the cafeteria, turning her bird face and hawk eyes right and left, she picked out her future victims and swooped down unexpectedly on an A's or single women's table where she saw an empty seat. She made herself at home, overpowered her neighbors and talked endlessly. As she knew everything about us, she interested, she amused, she perturbed.

She also amazed with her talents. She was a graphologist, physiognomist, palmist. She knew every name and first name. There was nothing she didn't know about everyone's age, worries, tastes and weaknesses. To Dr. Grabel, she could talk about his collector's passion, which she knew all about, God knows how, because he wasn't in the least talkative. She went after Mrs. Barrow and conquered her in less than a week. Mr. Barrow held out for a month, then he fell into her hands. "I can't get hold of him, Ralph, he's slimy." Nevertheless, she finally learned how to handle him: vanity. Mr. Barrow's vanity was enormous, hypertrophic, pathologic. I watched Mrs. Pierce in action; it was an unforgettable sight. Hopping toward him on her little heron legs, she came up to Mr. Barrow with an ecstatic look and, as soon as she was in range, flooded him with compliments. He lapped it up; he swallowed the most outrageous flattery, hook, line and sinker. I got her along and said to her, "Joan, you aren't stingy with that stuff—you're dishing it out with a ladle!" She laughed, with her quick, sharp laugh that was so much like a seagull's cry. "No, Ralph, I'm laying it on with a trowel. With Mr. Barrow, you've always got to lay it on with a trowel."

Wednesday night, as I went past the windows of the Pierces' barracks, someone inside tapped on the glass. I raised my head, saw nothing, but I was used to Joan Pierce's signal and went inside.

She was alone, standing before the window. She put a finger to her lips, gestured to me to be seated, which I did. She had her field glasses glued to her eyes, and, as the drapes were drawn, I wondered what she could see, when I discerned, above the lenses, two little circles that she had cut, but not completely, in the material, enabling her to see without being seen. I suppose that when she wasn't in action she kept the two little flaps in place with Scotch tape.

I waited a good five minutes, but I wasn't bored. I like Joan Pierce as much as it is possible to like a woman without loving her. From that standpoint I had nothing to worry about—she didn't exist. She was devoid of any kind of charm, shape, sensuality or, even, sex. But, her body aside, I had a great affection for her, and I also enjoyed her affection for me, the way that she had of grabbing me and, most of all, the fact that each time she gestured to me it was to tell me something new. In that hermit existence at Blueville, where nothing ever happened—except work for the time being and anguish for the future—a piece of news was priceless.

I waited and she kept me waiting, like a great performer, sure of her audience, who didn't spare the stage effects.

Okay. I was ripe. And she was ready. She detached the field glasses from her eyes, put one finger back on her mouth, headed toward a corner of the room, got down on her knees and began to manipulate the wallboard, which I couldn't see, for her back was turned to me. When finally she came hopping back, she looked like a smiling hawk and let out several of her super-shrill laugh-cries. She sat facing me in a rocker and rocked fast, which unnerved me, for if I watched her too long she was going to make me sick.

"Ralph, you can speak freely. I've disconnected my bugging. Since Anita is coming to see you on Saturday, you really ought to find and disconnect yours, Ralph, particularly in your room. There's no need having Mr. Barrow enjoy your fun!"

Here there was a new gull's cry and frantic rocking in the rocker. I lowered my eyes and smiled with an embarrassed look.

"Stop, Ralph!" she cried, laughing. "Stop putting on that innocent act!"

"You stop that rocking. I can't stand it."

"Oh, I'm sorry, Ralph. I forgot."

She became motionless. I looked at her.

"And how did you know that Anita was coming?"

"Monday, when you got her letter."

"You recognized her writing on an envelope?"

"No, of course not. You're forgetting that you receive your mail at the lab. I saw the face you made at lunchtime."

I said, a bit ruffled, "I didn't know my face was that easy to read."

"It isn't, Ralph, don't worry. Just for me, who knows the context."

"What *context*?"

She laughed. "Is it absolutely necessary for me to spell it out? Well, let's say . . . growing eagerness for female company"— how nicely put!—"and anxiety with regard to your future relations with Anita."

"And what has changed in this context?"

"Starting Monday, the eagerness became feverish"— laugh—"and you went through phases of hope and discouragement. In addition, you do much less talking about Dave and you're hardly concerned about him anymore."

"I might have been thinking about another woman."

Several seagull laughs.

"But you've been thinking about it, Ralph! Don't try to kid me, you big hypocrite. But you figure the other women are inaccessible and you've classified them as dreams."

I fell silent. So she had guessed about Pussy, God only knows how, since it never crossed my mind for a second that Stien . . . No, no, he wasn't that type.

I was dumfounded by her clairvoyance, and even before I had considered my action, as rational as that of any savage consulting his witch doctor, I asked her, "Joan, in your opinion, is Anita going to come?"

She wasn't laughing anymore. She looked at me in a kindly way with her piercing eyes.

"Very probably. And you mustn't be angry with her if she's failed to show up two or three times. Or if she's inclined to see less and less of you. No, Ralph, don't make that face. Anita isn't doing as she pleases. Most of all, she's headed someplace where you can't follow her. She's worked hard, she's made tremendous sacrifices and now she has a terrific career. She isn't going to give all that up for you."

I said in a toneless voice, "So it's me that she's going to give up."

"Not at all. You're staying in Blueville, stuck in Blueville like a wife at home. And she's the big man, always on the go, off on a whirlwind of big business. She's thinking of you. But she isn't here."

"Don't you think she'd come more often if she loved me more?"

A laugh like a seagull cry.

"That, Ralph, is reasoning that I'd qualify as feminine. Anita has compartmentalized her life. Like a man—two pigeonholes. In the bigger one, her career. In the other, you."

"Really charming."

"Be a little sincere, Ralph. You aren't madly in love with Anita. You have all kinds of other dreams about other people."

Once again I had those mingled feelings about Joan. I admired her, but she got on my nerves. She saw everything, she knew everything and, the Lord only knows, she never let you forget it. It didn't matter whose toes she stepped on, the secrecy that she violated and the sensibilities that she offended.

I was haughtily silent, but my haughtiness failed to impress her. She found it funny. She was strengthened by the affection which she had for me and which I returned to her. And sure of this strength, she plunged ahead. The woman was an expansionist.

She gave me goose flesh and made me uneasy. If this kept up, there wouldn't be an inch of my consciousness left for me to feel safe in.

She laughed. "I remind you that Anita is quite fond of you."

There were short, sharp laughs. A whole flock of seagulls taking wing.

"Something I can understand furthermore," she said, searching me with her beak and her keen eyes. "You're a handsome fellow, Ralph, in a small package. Please, don't give me that frightened look! I'm not propositioning you. Anyway, what would you do with a big skeleton like me? You, most of all, who likes well-upholstered women." (How did she know that?) "And then, you know, I don't exactly shine for my sexiness. No, no." (She laughed.) "Poor Reginald." (Reginald, that's her husband). "I derive pleasure mainly through my eyes, Ralph."

I was dumfounded by the ease with which Joan Pierce handled taboo subjects. And I understood her exceptional social success at Blueville. She was straightforward, she said anything under the sun, she had no complexes. And the fact that she had none tended to free you from your own. Take me, for example. I had always been very embarrassed—especially when I was younger—about my shortness. And I admired the fact that Joan could make an allusion to my size without irritating me, that she even joked about it (my "small package"!) and that her joke went over—wrapped in a compliment. What's more, the joke went over quite well. A little arrow that sticks in your skin always leaves a scar, even if, at the moment, you hardly feel it. I was going to be angry with Joan, I sensed it.

What's more, it was me who was embarrassed, and to disguise my embarrassment I said, "What were you looking at when I came in, Joan?"

"Fascinating things," she replied with a little laugh. "Did you know, Ralph, that homosexuality has become an institution with our militiawomen?"

"I suspected as much."

"Well, now I'm sure of it. Poor militiawomen. Actually, that isn't what interests me. It's the fact that there's a sniper among them."

"A *sniper?*"

"And how! You see, they couldn't have put them through a very rigorous screening. This girl uses a gadget that betrays a certain nostalgia for the male anatomy."

"Do you mean a vibrator?"

Several laughs like seagull cries.

"Oh, no! It isn't a vibrator! It's bigger, much bigger, more complete and more sophisticated. I'm not going to describe it to you. I hope someday I'll be able to show it to you. It's quite amazing." She laughed hysterically.

I broke in on her. "Just who is this militiawoman? Do I know her?"

"Unfortunately, you don't, Ralph. And it isn't Pussy. Don't lie. I'm aware of the weakness you've had for that tramp since you put her elbow back in place. When you stopped here that night while you were looking for Dave, you seemed completely intoxicated. Lord only knows what's so fascinating about an elbow!"

Her kindly hawk eyes searched mine, and then it was my turn to laugh. For in addition to her marvelous attributes, Mrs. Pierce was cheerful. She disarmed all problems of their potential seriousness. At Blueville, that was invaluable.

I told her so and her face clouded over at once.

"No, Ralph, you're wrong. My cheerfulness is a defense. I'm as worried as you could be. Even more, because I think that I can foretell more than you. I find you quite carefree."

"Me—carefree?"

"Oh, I know you worry plenty about Dave and, in second place, about Anita. But believe me, Ralph, you should untangle yourself from your personal life a little and think more about the future of the P.M.s in Blueville. There are things I don't like. There are things that frighten me, too."

"Example?"

"Example: You were delighted when Hilda Helsingforth turned down your resignation—right? Okay. I understand you. But what does that actually mean? That you're a prisoner. That they're determined, physically, to keep you from leaving. Frankly, Ralph, if you packed your suitcase and Dave's and if you showed up tomorrow at the sentry booth, do you think that they'd let you through?"

I looked at her and then, all of a sudden, while my eyes were attached to hers, I saw with her the scene that she had just evoked. I saw it with her clairvoyant eyes, and I had the absolute certainty that the militiawomen would forbid me from going past the gate. I also understood that I'd always known it. But when you've been free so long, servitude takes some learning.

Joan followed all my thoughts one by one. She resumed: "Do you know what Stien calls Blueville? A deluxe concentration camp. And that's just about it: good food, heated swimming pool, lounges, horseback riding. But a system of barbed-wire fences, a machine gun on a lookout tower, a curfew, listening devices everywhere, the telephone monitored, the mail opened. I forgot: neither radio nor TV. And every now and then a few odd newspapers. Ralph, do you think it's just for fun that I go poking my nose in every corner? I want to be informed, that's all. It's vital to be informed, when things are being kept secret from you."

She spoke vehemently, passionately. And I discovered a Joan that I hadn't known: responsible, serious-minded. Up to now I'd admired her gifts, but the clownish, tattletale side of her had misled me. This woman was, in reality, a rock. My esteem for her went up sharply.

"Joan," I said after a moment, "thank you for speaking to me in confidence. On the other hand, if you're telling me all this, I'm aware that there's a reason. So, go on, talk."

Joan was a good actress. When you expected her to speak, she was silent. Or rather, she made a silence felt. At once it was as if a little red light had been turned on and had begun to flash: watch out, I'm silent, what I'm about to say is important.

"Get some results, Ralph," she finally said. "Find your vaccine. And be quick about it. You can't imagine how important it is."

"But I *can* imagine," I said, a bit ruffled.

Nothing stopped her. She went over my pique, she charged, she knocked down my fences, she trampled my territory.

"No one would ever know it. Your lab couldn't be running worse! There's a war between the castes. You spend more time fighting than working."

I was wounded, furious. She really went too far. My private life—okay. But couldn't she stay away from the exercise of my profession? My lab was none of her business. I didn't want her coming around sticking her beak in there!

I put my hands into my pockets and scowled. Raising my voice, I said, "Was it Reginald who supplied you with this information on my lab?"

I should have kept quiet. I'd just given her a *casus belli* to pursue her invasion.

"No, sir!" she replied with a sharp cry of triumph. "Reginald didn't tell me anything. Reginald is an unwavering supporter of Dr. Martinelli! Reginald is one of those people who die in silence rather than talk!" She got her second wind. "But I know. I know—it doesn't matter how—that you're hated by the women and the A's in your lab. And with good reason! And that you also hate them. That's just great! Really fine! Excellent conditions for research!"

With all my lines breached, I could do nothing but counter-attack feebly.

"Naturally you would have turned the other cheek and made my lab into a real paradise."

"Of course, Ralph," she answered with crushing calm. "And that's just what you've got to make it into now. At least, if you want to achieve results. The rejection of your resignation puts you in a position of strength. Exploit that, Ralph. But gently. Along the lines of compromise and fairness."

She was right. I hadn't thought about capitalizing on my position of strength and especially, I had to admit, not along those lines. Joan was a genius! Her astuteness overwhelmed me, and I was so speechless that all I could do was pull the torn pieces of my pride around me and beat a retreat.

I gave her a little smile, half sickly, half friendly. I straightened my position and said to her, "And after that, General, do you have other instructions to give me?"

"Oh, yes," she replied quite matter-of-factly. "All this is nothing. I've got something really sensational to show you."

She had been carefully hatching this dramatic turn since the beginning. She moved away on her stilts, snatched her big black purse off the table and came back to me, clutching it in her claws. Was she going to pull out one of her dolls or a rabbit, like a magician? Or a flock of doves?

No. Much more simply, a magazine that she brandished at the length of her skinny arm.

"This, Ralph, is priceless! It's one of the issues of *New Era* that they neglected to let us have. And with good reason! I salvaged it yesterday, not without trouble, from Mr. Barrow's wastebasket. Fortunately, I've got keen eyes. All the same, it wasn't easy—opening my handbag, going up to it, stooping— and at the same time buttering up the great man, who was strutting up and down the room telling me about his career. There it is. Read it, Ralph. Don't say anything to anyone and give it back to me."

"But this issue is from Thursday!"

"There, you see—it's just come out. Barely a week ago. And, most of all, it features a long article entitled 'Law and Order.' Read it. You'll see, you'll get some new insights into the outside world."

"Thanks, Joan," I said, folding the magazine and hiding it as best I could under my jacket.

I gave her a friendly wave and started to leave, but she called me back, her sharp eyes buried in mine.

"And, Ralph, one last thing. In the cafeteria, do stop looking at Mrs. Barrow so much. They're going to notice it."

New Era, which I carried under my jacket like a thief, had been founded shortly after President Bedford took office and was supposed to reflect White House views. I waited until Dave went to bed, then I locked the door of the barracks, drew the curtains in my room and, not without a certain feverishness and the pleasant feeling of doing something forbidden, began to read "Law and Order."

The article was rather long but of the utmost interest, particularly because it emanated from Deborah Grimm, whose famous sentence on sexual intercourse I have already mentioned. I had to admit it—there was something enticing about a long article from that pen. To be sure, I wasn't disappointed; it exceeded my every expectation.

Deborah Grimm began by revealing the mortal uneasiness felt by the Bedford Administration when the epidemic, having ravaged the police force—particularly exposed since it was in daily contact with the population—had posed the question of maintaining law and order. Certainly, female militia had been formed at once, but there were only a handful of them, with little experience. So it was expected that criminality would go skyrocketing—particularly those robberies that had made the streets of large American cities as unsafe as certain quarters of London in the Middle Ages.

No such thing happened. By an unprecedented irony, the statistics on robberies, rapes and murders decreased as the strength of the police dwindled. "In its forecasts"—I quote Deborah Grimm—"the Administration had overlooked an important factor. The vice from which the underworld lived— gambling, drugs and prostitution—were almost exclusively male vices."

So the epidemic inflicted a mortal blow on the rackets to which those vices gave rise. While it led to the gradual extinction of male clientele, the epidemic also wreaked havoc among pimps, drug pushers and owners of gambling joints. The channels of organized vice were dying at both ends.

In New York, the hundreds of prostitutes who had flourished in midtown Manhattan found themselves overnight *"with no pimp and with no customer."*

There were, however, some "shadows in that picture." Those prostitutes who had been not victims but accomplices of male vice tried to set up other rackets and, to some extent, managed to do so. Among the women who had been "contaminated by their companion" there was still considerable demand for drugs, and the pushers tried to reorganize the networks that brought narcotics from the Far East to the United States.

Immediately, the female militia went into action against these suppliers of poison. Despite scanty police training, they scored major successes over the female underworld, which itself had scarcely been broken in. Allowance must be made in these successes for "an attribute not always found in the male policemen who had preceded them: incorruptibility."[1] It wasn't just drugs. In other fields, the ingenuity of crime also found ways of operating. As we all know, the Bedford Administration closed the porno bookstores, under penalty of stiff prison sentences, banned the manufacture and sale of erotic objects

[1]According to Anita, to whom I later spoke about this article, this remark was overly optimistic. Once in contact with organized crime, the female militia began losing as much in moral rigor as they were gaining in experience.

and those, in particular, intended for women. This law doubtless had beneficial effects on public morality, but it also created
great demand, particularly for items of a phallic character, "and
this despite the fact, now scientifically proven,[2] that female
orgasm comes from friction on the clitoris and not from the
intromission of the penis into the vagina" (sic).

No doubt this reflects—and I quote—"engrained habits and
ancient superstitions in a sex that wound up attributing magic
power to the symbol of its oppression."

Whatever the case may be, the female underworld wasn't
long in finding a source of enormous profit in the clandestine
manufacture of phallic gadgets, some of which, highly sophisticated, were soon selling for a king's ransom on the black
market.

The militia, continued Deborah Grimm, had recently
searched the basement of a rubber factory, finding an item
folded and packed so that it took up little space in a box. The
label gave it the harmless designation of "Superdoll." But once
inflated by one of those foot pumps sold with rubber rafts,
Superdoll took on the appearance and almost the consistency of
a good-sized naked man equipped with a phallus at rest. On the
back of this man, between the shoulder blades (thus within easy
reach of the female user, who was supposed to hug him), there
was a panel of buttons controlling the hardness and the
additional inflation of the phallus, its operation as two-speed
vibrator and the emission, by intermittent spurts, of a warm and
lubricating fluid.

Superdoll went for eight hundred dollars—factory price—and
could be bought by mail order, with credit terms available. The
survey revealed that a group of clandestine middlewomen had
muscled into the regular Superdoll sales channels and was
offering home delivery of the item at a thousand dollars apiece.
These hucksters must have stockpiled the item by means of
mass mail-order purchases, for, as soon as the factory was shut
down, Superdolls appeared on the market, offered door to door,
at the price of two thousand dollars cash, with no guarantee of
replacement parts.

While the manufacturer and saleswomen of this "repugnant

[2]I did not consider this "fact" to be "scientifically proven" (Dr. Martinelli).

gadget" (sic) were prosecuted, this did not hold true for the users, whose names and addresses were on file—at least, those women who had bought Superdoll by mail. As far as the users were concerned, the Attorney General considered that an immoral act, not a crime, was involved, since *"this act could not lead to untoward consequences in social terms."*[3]

On the other hand, the Attorney General took a more severe attitude toward acts that implied "the presence and participation of a whole man." In this category, those P.M.s were to be exempted who, owing to their scientific or economic importance, had been placed in zones of protection and could be considered harmless, since they were under constant surveillance. The S.P.M.s (self-protected men) were no problem either. In general, these were millionaires who, at the outbreak of the epidemic, had taken refuge on their estates and had set up their self-protection there by firing male employees or by demanding that they submit to the Ablationist initiation.

There was one other group that soon raised serious problems for the militia—"the stags," as they came to be known in police jargon.

I couldn't finish Deborah Grimm's study; the light in my room went out. Curiously enough, it made me feel as guilty as a twelve-year-old boy caught reading a forbidden book. It took me a second or two to realize that I hadn't been punished but that it was ten o'clock and I had been surprised by the camp curfew. I undressed in the darkness, which was pierced at regular intervals, despite the thickness of the curtains, by the searchlight from the lookout tower. When I'd put on my pajamas I stuffed the magazine under my pillow, and briefly lit my flashlight (it was my last battery and I was saving it) in order to set my alarm for 5:30 A.M.

I couldn't sleep. I had read Deborah Grimm's article with the utmost discomfort. I was horrified by the fanatical and repressive character of the society that she described.

I had not only gotten confirmation that the P.M.s were actually prisoners rendered "harmless" by strict surveillance, but it was now clear that, in the outside world, the image of men

[3]I assume that Deborah Grimm was referring to pregnancy in these terms (Dr. Martinelli).

appeared to be totally negative, and relations between the two sexes held so suspicious that even simulating them became an offense.

The effect made on me by the article didn't deter me from wondering about the identity of the militiawoman Joan Pierce had termed "a sniper" and who was using a gadget that, I supposed, couldn't have been much different from the Superdoll. Joan had asserted that it wasn't Pussy, but I wondered if I should believe her and if Joan's statement wasn't aimed at discouraging my daydreams. At any rate, she hadn't succeeded in doing so—at least, as far as my nocturnal dreaming was concerned. This particular night, dreams troubled me until dawn, and terrifying situations (Reverend Ruth Jettison forcing me to drink *Caladium seguinum*) alternated with erotic situations where my partner was sometimes Anita, sometimes a woman who managed to look like Pussy, Jackie and Mrs. Barrow all at the same time.

I was startled when my alarm rang and sat up, soaked with sweat. I took a shower, pulled on my thick bathrobe and, with curtains open, sat at my table. I had a good hour to finish Deborah Grimm's long article before Dave woke up.

My turbulent night must have refreshed me anyway, because I felt much more optimistic that morning. I realized that Deborah Grimm's study was obviously an admission of defeat and that the new taboos were, in fact, difficult to enforce. Encouraged by this realization, I resumed my reading with a lighter heart and even managed to laugh at certain passages. Although Deborah Grimm lacked the least sense of humor, the contrast between her sustained, highly moral tone and the enormities she took for granted sometimes had a comic effect. But on me the effect was one of mingled indignation and disgust.

As earlier, I give only a summary of Deborah Grimm's article, with only her most memorable sentences quoted verbatim.

The "stags," continued Deborah Grimm, were young men who had left their jobs in the cities with the spread of the epidemic and who now roamed the countryside, living off the land. At the beginning they had joined together to form bands, but having recruited their members indiscriminately, they themselves were struck by Encephalitis 16 and wiped out. The survivors had learned their lesson from the experience and lived alone, only approaching women and wearers of the green rosette, "usually for the purpose of robbing them."[4]

The stags, who were hunted by the militiawomen, eked out a precarious existence in rural areas. From their number the female underworld recruited the male prostitutes that it supplied to satisfy the appetites of its wealthy women customers. Suppression proved difficult from the outset, owing to the fact that the stags were dispersed over the countryside in a large number of private houses that rented out one or two rooms to tourists for the night. The price they asked for these rooms (always luxurious) was so exorbitant that no forewarned person would ever dream of paying it.

Appearances were as perfect as they were deceptive. The stag, dressed in a white jacket decorated with a green rosette, worked as a barman or bellhop and refused all gratuities, no matter what service was demanded of him. Thus the crime of prostitution could not be proven, since the stag, always impeccable, never appeared in a compromising situation. He simply offered no resistance to the advances of the female guests.

In order to prosecute these houses and their owners, the female customers had to testify that they'd had relations with the stags. So it was decided to give them impunity within certain limits. In most cases, furthermore, wealthy middle-aged widows were involved.

Having contracted "inveterate heterosexual habits in the course of long experience" and having passed the age where they might normally be able to satisfy those habits, the women felt intoxicated with their new freedom and with the power that their money gave them. Sexually exploited in their youth, then deserted by men because of their age, the women had the chance to turn the tables on the former dominating sex and let themselves be carried away "by a true sexual addiction." Some of the women would make the rounds of a single state all in one month, sleeping in a different house every night. So it was quite easy to spot these houses by trailing the women without arresting them.

If these women, at the time of their arrest, showed them-

---

[4]This generalization was deliberate calumny, I found out afterward.

selves willing to cooperate and to make confessions that would make it possible to indict the female pimps and the stags, then leniency could be shown. Generally speaking, after paying a fairly large fine, these wretched women were hospitalized at their own expense in a clinic, "where fresh and wholesome nurses speedily managed to re-educate their instincts by means of suitable exercises" (sic).

The panderers who put the stags on the market, on the other hand, were sentenced to prison terms ranging from two to five years. And the stags, unlike female prostitutes of the past in cultures dominated by men, were meted severe sentences. The courts held that, although these men had undeniably been exploited in economic terms, "it was impossible to overlook their domination, or what they felt as such, during sexual intercourse." For this reason they were sentenced to an average of ten years. They could nevertheless have their terms shortened by a year if they agreed to the Ablationist initiation. But these men were so hardened and "their incurable sexist pride" such that, so far, none of them had agreed to an early release on this proviso.

The middle-aged widows or single women of whom we have spoken had husbands and lovers. So they could cite as an excuse "the habits that these relations had engendered." But what about the teenaged girls and the deviations that had been observed among them? In the high schools, colleges and universities, daily courses in sexual education had been instituted. They demonstrated women's historical oppression by men over the centuries, the relationship of master to slave that, necessarily, involved all kinds of relations with him, the sadistic, brutalizing character of his embrace, the dangers of pregnancy and venereal disease and, finally, his irrelevance to the female's pleasure, since that resided in the clitoris. In spite of the surveillance under which the teenagers were placed and notwithstanding the fact that they never saw boys their own age, as the latter lived in hiding in the country, a goodly number of the girls sought and provoked—by force if necessary—the contacts against which they had been warned.

This didn't involve stags or a secluded house out in the woods (the rates of which would furthermore be prohibitive for teen-aged girls). These crimes were perpetrated in urban areas, daily "and I should say almost under our very eyes."

Next, Deborah Grimm went on, came a case that, unfortunately, was not an isolated instance but one that she quoted at greater length, owing to its sociological significance. It involved a certain Mr. B., retired clergyman, age seventy-five and residing in Dallas. As his car had broken down, he was returning to his domicile on foot when he was attacked by two teenagers. At gunpoint, these girls, who were sisters, forced him into a car and drove him to an isolated suburban house, belonging to an aunt who had gone away on a long trip. What took place next was told by B. as he replied to the questions of the woman lawyer defending him at his trial.

THE DEFENSE FOR B: Will you tell what happened when Maggie and Betsy led you into this house?

B: Is it absolutely necessary for me to answer that question?

JUDGE ANNE WILKINS: Yes, you must. Don't forget that you're here as an accomplice, not a witness. It's in your own interest to help the court establish the truth in this sorry business.

B: I'll try, Your Honor. (A pause.) Maggie and Betsy led me into the bedroom and, while threatening me with their guns, ordered me to disrobe.

JUDGE: Did you obey?

B: I had no choice.

JUDGE: Answer yes or no.

B: Yes.

THE DEFENSE: What did they do next?

B: They tied me to the bed.

THE DEFENSE: On your belly or on your back?

B: On my back.

THE DEFENSE: Were you bound hand and foot?

B: Yes.

THE DEFENSE: What happened then?

B: They abused me.

JUDGE: Speak up.

B: They abused me.

THE DEFENSE: How?

B: Maggie handled me, causing an erection, and then sat on top of me, facing me.

THE DEFENSE: Then what?

B: Well, Betsy struck me in the face and cursed at me.

THE DEFENSE: Why?

B: She didn't understand that I wasn't in a position to have a second erection right away.

THE DEFENSE: What did you do?

B: I tried to explain to her that, on account of my age, it was impossible.

THE DEFENSE: Did she accept your explanation?

B: No. She was very naïve.

JUDGE: What do you mean by that?

B: Betsy thought that men could have erections at will.

THE DEFENSE: What happened next?

B: Betsy went out to buy something to eat. And as my nose was bleeding, Maggie took care of me and tried to cheer me up. She also loosened my bonds. Just then Betsy came back with food and a dog collar.

JUDGE: Do you mean an ecclesiastical collar?

B: No. A real dog collar, with a fairly long leather leash.

THE DEFENSE: Then what happened?

B: She put the dog collar around my neck. She untied my bonds and, holding the leash in one hand and her revolver in the other, led me into the kitchenette. There she forced me to get down on all fours under the table.

THE DEFENSE: Then what?

B: They ate.

THE DEFENSE: Were they dressed?

B: No. They were both naked.

THE DEFENSE: Did they feed you?

B: No. Betsy was against it. At one point, Betsy gave me a kick under the table and asked me in a threatening tone of voice if I were now ready to have an erection. Again, I explained to her that, having been beaten, humiliated and starved to boot, it would be impossible for me.

THE DEFENSE: What happened next?

B: The two girls argued. Betsy wanted to beat me black and

blue until I "understood." But Maggie was against it. She claimed that better results could be had by tenderness. Fortunately, she won the argument.

THE DEFENSE: What happened then?

B: The two girls made me sit at the table but without removing my dog collar, and they gave me something to eat and drink.

THE DEFENSE: What kind of drink?

B: Whisky.

THE DEFENSE: Did you drink a lot of it?

B: I'm afraid so—more than I should have. I was a mass of nerves.

JUDGE: How much whisky?

B: Half a bottle.

THE DEFENSE: What happened next?

B: After drinking, Betsy asked me to caress her.

JUDGE: Where did that take place?

B: As I've said, in the kitchenette. Betsy pulled me by the leash until I was up against her legs. She was waving a revolver.

THE DEFENSE: What did you do?

B: I obeyed.

THE DEFENSE: Then what?

B: After a while Betsy noticed that I had an erection. She made me sit down and sat on my lap.

JUDGE: Was she a virgin?

B: I couldn't say. I was a little drunk.

THE DEFENSE FOR BETSY: I wish to point out that this erection was entirely spontaneous.

THE DEFENSE FOR B: Objection, Your Honor. B. was tied up with a chain, threatened with a revolver. He'd been beaten and cursed and they'd made him drink.

JUDGE: Objection overruled.

THE DEFENSE FOR BETSY: I wish to submit to the jury that, by the accused's own admission, there was no handling on Betsy's part and that B.'s erection resulted from the shameful caresses that he perpetrated on the person of a minor.

THE DEFENSE FOR B: After being ordered to do so and under the threat of a gun.

THE DEFENSE FOR BETSY: Was that threat present in B.'s mind when he had his erection? I say it wasn't.

THE DEFENSE FOR B: I say it was. The general context here is one of terror and threat arising from a kidnapping. There's been technical rape.

THE DEFENSE FOR BETSY: I contest the fact that there can be technical rape when an "entire man" is involved. The erection is, in itself, a phenomenon of aggression.

THE DEFENSE FOR B: Don't forget that we're talking about an entire man tied to a kitchen chair with a leash and threatened with a revolver.

THE DEFENSE FOR BETSY: That, of course, was an erotic setting. It couldn't have displeased B., and it didn't prevent local aggression by the phallus. On top of this, B. spent two weeks in that house, allegedly confined by the two sisters. Who would believe that a vigorous man like B. never found a chance to escape?

THE DEFENSE FOR B: He was tied at all times.

THE DEFENSE FOR BETSY: Come, now! If he had stopped having erections, Betsy and Maggie would have set him free.

I shall break off the excerpts from that scandalous trial here, Deborah Grimm continued. I nevertheless point out that the jury refused to charge these two girls with kidnapping, rape and unlawful confinement. Notwithstanding this, the girls were found guilty of immoral conduct and sentenced to one year in a house of detention for minors. For his part, Mr. B. received a prison term of five years.

I have no doubts, Deborah Grimm went on, as to the equity of the verdict with regard to this sad specimen of humanity. But the sanction administered to the teenagers strikes me as unsuitable. The sentence errs by its excessive severity. Kidnappings and rapes of elderly men have had a tendency to increase in the jungle of the big cities, "usually followed by the mutilation of the victims." These assaults are blameworthy, of course, if we see them in social terms. Nevertheless, they show that teenaged girls are coming back to the teachings that we have inculcated in them. "By a reaction that is basically healthy though brutal in its expression," they throw their guilt on their partners and demonstrate their repentence by destroying the temptation to which they have yielded. Thus, these girls are not entirely bad and call for re-education rather than repressive detention. And I should say that, nowadays, the trend is toward this type of sanction.

As to "entire men" in their old age, who are being assaulted more and more, they pose a completely different problem. For reasons of security, they have requested (without consenting to the Ablationist initiation) permission to wear in public the green rosette with the gilded letter of the A's. But the A's are violently opposed to this. The secretary-general of the Federal Association of A's (FAA) has pointed out that, while the elderly men withstand the epidemic better because of the slowing of their spermatogenesis, they do not, however, enjoy total immunity like the A's and would therefore represent a danger of contagion against which the other "entire men" must continue to be warned. The solution, the FAA secretary-general declared, was obvious: FAA would remain open to all entire men seeking access (regardless of age) to the Ablationist initiation and to all the social, moral and prophylactic benefits that it entailed.

This appeal fell on deaf ears. It is estimated that barely 10 percent of American "entire men past" the age of seventy-five agreed to join the A's. According to the study made by a Harvard psychologist, it appeared that male pride was deeply rooted in these old phallocrats and that it delighted them to retain, if only in theory, a potency that a great many younger men had, by their own volition, surrendered. One old black, aged eighty-nine, said during an interview, "I prefer to die an entire man!" "Don't you know," asked the woman conducting the interview, "that without the green insignia of the A's, you run the risk, living in the cities, of being kidnapped, raped and murdered?" "Might as well go that way as any other," the old black answered with an obscene grin.

Naturally, that case involved a very primitive male individual, but the women interviewers concluded that the motivation was the same in elderly men of the white race having received a higher education: Every case involved "sexist pride and a secret desire for aggression and domination over the individuals of our sex."

The elderly men, Deborah Grimm concluded, actually represented a greater danger than the stags, for the latter lived a precarious existence in remote parts of the countryside and were accessible only to a handful of wealthy women. Thus, the question was whether "in the name of the outmoded concept of individual freedom," elderly entire men would be allowed to raise havoc with urban female adolescents, or if, in the general interest, it would be decided to use restraint with regard to them and compell them by decree to join the Ablationist ranks.

My reading done, I realized that there was still lots of time before Dave woke up. I reread the article from beginning to end. But that still wasn't enough. I went back for a third time over certain passages—particularly over B.'s cross-examination and the evaluation of the "equitable" verdict that sentenced him to five years' imprisonment. After which I hunted up the passage where Deborah Grimm described the teaching that was dispensed daily to girls in educational institutions. Finally, I went back over the last paragraph and I weighed every line of it—particularly those that came out against "the outmoded concept of individual freedom."

Actually, Joan Pierce was right. I'd been most irresponsible in concerning myself with my little personal worries. I'd been living in Blueville in a state of selfish myopia, not seeing any farther than the barbed-wire fence. Joan Pierce had predicted that Deborah Grimm's article would shed some light on the situation. Light! Lightning was more like it. And what I saw dimly was almost more frightening than what I'd imagined.

To think that a week before I'd almost felt reassured when my resignation had been turned down! How I'd clutched at the straw! How readily I'd resigned myself to being deprived of newspapers and information, to being kept like a child in ignorance, not being able to control my own life, wrapping myself up blindly in Dave, in Anita, in my little circle of friends at Blueville, in my dreams and my frustrations.

I'd just awakened myself, and the awakening was quite terrifying. Compared to the outside shadows, Blueville was almost an oasis. You were stifled there, certainly, but at least you might live. You were watched around the clock, but you ran no risk of being assaulted when you stepped out of your house. Nor were you thrown in prison to punish you for being kidnapped. The word "protected man" took on a somewhat less ironic sense when you knew what was happening outside the protective enclosure. Hell, for "entire" men, was not, as I'd imagined, as Stien himself had thought, inside the barbed-wire fence; it was outside.

6

My conversation with Joan Pierce took place on Wednesday evening. The next day, Thursday, I decided to confront the female co-workers of my lab. Obviously, there would have to be a general showdown in order for me to overcome the crisis, but I didn't want to have it out with the whole staff. That would have raised too many problems for me. So I divided up the difficulty: first, the women; then, Dr. Grabel; finally, the rest of the A's. In other words, I set myself up three hurdles of decreasing severity, assuming that I cleared the first one successfully. I figured that, if I could rally the women to my side, I would be robbing Dr. Grabel of his most influential supporters.

I didn't use the room in the lab where we ordinarily showed films and held small gatherings. I wanted to give the meeting a more familiar tone. I had six chairs brought into my office and, instead of placing them in front of me, arranged them in a circle, my intention being to give up the dominant position that sitting at my desk would have given me and to be seated among my female co-workers, on an equal basis. Once this was done, I called them in one after another over the intercom.

The women came in one by one, looking rather troubled, it seemed to me, and exchanging quizzical, if not actually uneasy, looks among themselves, although, in reality, they had nothing to fear from me in view of their superior social status. I think that this little tremor must also be considered a remnant of the "engrained habits" that Deborah Grimm deplored in her article. In spite of the indoctrination that they'd received, the women couldn't help seeing me as a boss, and a masculine boss at that, a doubly dominating person.

Although my ultimate aim was to win them over, at first I did nothing along those lines. Quite to the contrary, looking unconcerned, I greeted them with that kind of cold, meticulous politeness that I despise in others because you can suspect all sorts of things behind it. I'd always treated the women this way, since the first letter in which Hilda Helsingforth criticized my relations with them. I went on. It was my intention, first of all, to put the women through a fairly unpleasant quarter hour. That would make them more appreciative of my subsequent gentleness.

My female laboratory assistants took seats in the circle and I sat in the middle of them. That gave rise to some embarrassment and discomfort. We weren't separated by the barrier of my desk. I was in contact. And for them—what contact! With sexual enemy number one! With the sexist! With the phallocrat! With the inferior and demonic creature! But at the same time, I suppose, a somewhat fascinating creature for women socially condemned to frequent only A's.

From the outset I attacked. I pulled out of my pocket the counter-complaint that I'd sent to Mr. Barrow following the complaint that had been made about me and read the women the criticism that pertained to them. Certainly, as I've already said, I had spared them in this document, my aim having been to concentrate my fire on Dr. Grabel. Finally, however, I called them to task for a number of professional errors, actually rather minor but very well substantiated, as every detail about times, days and names was given in my report.

When I finished—and I had the feeling that I'd told nothing new—I let a silence grow heavy and then said, "Is there anyone who wishes to dispute the facts that I've just cited?"

A silence, then Lia Burage replied in a calm voice, "As far as I'm concerned, I don't deny the facts."

The tone of her voice suggested that there were other things she disputed. But before giving her the floor I wanted to cover my rear.

"Is there anyone else who wishes to present observations?"

And I looked at the women around me one by one. They shook their heads without a word. I took my time. I wanted to fathom these opaque faces.

The average age of these five women fell somewhere between thirty and forty. None of them was ugly, none was stupid, none was lazy. Mrs. Lia Burage and Elizabeth Crawford, the two endowed with the best minds, were also (what an injustice for the others) the two with the best figures. Naturally, being a damned phallocrat, I sometimes employed the old names. They aren't used nowadays and are forbidden by an unwritten law suppressing Mr., Miss and Mrs. as being unduly sexualized. Since the beginning of the modern age one must say, "Crawford," "Burage," "Martinelli."

Actually, I didn't always use Miss or Mrs. I allowed for subtle differences. For Crawford I would say, "Crawford." She was a widow and she had removed the wedding band from her finger. But Lia Burage, less conventional—or, perhaps, more attached to her husband's memory—kept her ring. When I spoke to her, deliberately violating the unwritten law, I would call her *Mrs.* Burage. She never criticized what Mr. Barrow pointed out as being a "lack of taste" on my part. But, then, why the devil did people call Barrow Mr. Barrow? What was the meaning of that misplaced insistence on a sex which, in his case, had been twice removed?

"Mrs. Burage," I said, turning to her, "I believe you have something to say, haven't you?"

"Yes, Doctor."

Her eyes and the tone of her voice were correct and cold. I sensed that she was going to pay me back, with interest, for my icy politeness. I waited. I was not without a certain secret affinity for Lia Burage. First of all, on account of that wedding band she'd been brave enough to keep and then because her chestnut hair reminded me of Anita. The same milky complexion, the same undeniably feminine shape. Yet her eyes weren't green but blue. A pure blue that didn't need to play at being sincere, nor to hide behind fluttering lashes. Quite to the contrary. Her eyes sought yours like a sword, crossing your blade, then thrusting home.

"I'm not disputing the errors," she said curtly, "only their seriousness."

All right. The time had come for me to play it fair and square too. The night before I'd made up my mind not to slip back into the unfairness of my written report.

"Right," I replied. "You're quite right. They aren't too serious. Under other circumstances, I'd never mention them to you."

Big eyes opened wide in the circle that we formed and, biggest of all, Lia Burage's. While she was preparing to duel fiercely with me, she saw me advancing toward her with my guard down, my breast exposed. A reaction that did credit to her: She withheld her blow.

Crawford relieved her: "In that case," she said, "I don't understand."

"What don't you understand?" I asked calmly.

"That you felt the need to make a written report about trifles."

Elizabeth Crawford was a little dark-haired woman, frisky, capricious, less serious than Lia Burage. But her professional qualifications were matchless. She had every right, as far as she was concerned, to talk about trifles. I wasn't going to argue about the word.

With a show of serenity, I explained that I had received two memos, one on top of the other, from Hilda Helsingforth criticizing my attitude with regard to the women and A's in the lab; that I'd learned from Mr. Barrow that a written complaint against me had been filed with him. But I hadn't been able to find out from him either the name of the person who'd lodged the complaint or what it was that I'd done wrong.

There was no bitterness in my voice. I wasn't recriminating. I was stating the facts. Nothing but the facts. My desk was bugged without a doubt.

With that I fell silent, running my gaze around the circle. My silence compelled Lia Burage to speak once more. But she didn't do so with a light heart. I could see that in her blue eyes.

"So you've written your own report as a kind of revenge?"

"That doesn't seem to fit the facts. Everyone knows that I'm particularly vulnerable here. I'd say that I wrote my report in self-defense."

A silence.

"Doctor," continued Mrs. Burage, "wouldn't it have been simpler to tell us what you had against us rather than write to Mr. Barrow?"

"You're right, Mrs. Burage. It would have been simpler, more normal, more friendly and, if I dare say so, more honorable. And that's why it's surprising that the person who accused me lodged his complaints with Mr. Barrow instead of coming straight to me with them."

Lia Burage blushed deeply. Her complexion, like her eyes, made her unsuited for hiding emotions. And I sensed a certain embarrassment in the circle of eyes that converged on me.

Crawford then gave the accusation a helping hand, but without brutality, with even a kind of restraint, I should almost say, with friendliness.

"Doctor, I must say, you didn't give the impression of being very accessible."

"I must say"—that struck me funny. Perhaps the time had come to turn on that famous Latin charm. I didn't really like that too much. It was a bit whorish to my way of thinking, but, after all, wasn't acting like a whore the weapon of the weak?

I gave Crawford my most suave smile.

"Do you mean that I'm abrupt, arrogant, authoritarian?"

"A bit like that," replied Crawford.

I laughed and, impulsive woman that she was, Crawford laughed, too. Except on Lia Burage's lips, there were smiles all around. That's what made the atmosphere relaxed: a statue fallen from its pedestal. The massacre of the father. All of this, metaphorically, of course. But there's nothing more nourishing for the soul than an image.

Except for Lia Burage. Her blue eyes weren't going to let go of me so fast. She said without batting an eyelash, "If I may take the liberty of saying so, Doctor, you're also terribly unfair."

The smiles stopped at once, and I understood three things: first, that Lia Burage was alluding to the position in which I kept Dr. Grabel; second, that Lia Burage was basically a loyal, courageous woman; third, that precisely because of these attributes, she played the part of the dominant animal among the lab women. If I won her to my cause, I'm sure that she would show me the same loyalty and the same courage.

"Do you mean that I'm unfair to Dr. Grabel?"

"I think you don't want to recognize his merits."

A silence.

"You're all wrong. I do recognize them. Dr. Grabel is a very intelligent man and a very good research worker. If I leave, he'll be perfectly qualified to replace me."

Astonishment. Silence. Exchange of glances.

"In that case," Lia Burage finally said, and she left her sentence in suspense.

But no sentence was ever less in need of being completed. I said in a conciliatory tone, "Put yourself in my position, Mrs. Burage. I'm not Jesus Christ. How can I give a worker a promotion, even if he deserves it, when he's turned in a report against me?"

That's when there was a cry—what the people in the theater call *"cri de coeur,"* a revealing sentence uttered vehemently all at one swoop.

"But Dr. Grabel never wrote that report!" Lia Burage said. Her shoulders quivered, her bosom rose, her hair was thrown back. A superb sight. I looked at her and I made a mental note to savor that picture later on. But for the moment I asked coolly, "How do you know?"

"Because it was me!"

I wasn't expecting the first outcry and still less the second. I was confused. And my absurd blindness suddenly became obvious. How could I have imagined that an ordinary A like Dr. Grabel could afford to turn in a report to Mr. Barrow intended for Hilda Helsingforth? Only a woman, strengthened by her caste superiority, and writing to a woman over the head of a castrate, could have that audacity. Only she could have denounced to the high authorities the evil ways of a lab head who, though a boss in technological terms, was nevertheless just a P.M.

There was nothing I could do about it. After all, could a Soviet general in World War II have been surprised that a political commissar had written to the party to criticize his conduct?

I remained silent. And I asked myself a few questions. Lia Burage obviously had an influence over her colleagues, something which I had explained by her charisma and her intellectual qualities. But couldn't that influence be attributed to semi-official duties of the type that I've just mentioned? By any chance was Lia Burage working in my lab as Hilda Helsingforth's eyes and ears? Or, at any rate, the safest repository of trust and orthodoxy?

I looked at her and said in a neutral tone of voice, "May I ask you a question? Have you seen the counter-report that I sent to Mr. Barrow?"

"Of course," replied Lia Burage, as it were taken for granted.

"Just you or all of you?"

"All of us."

"And the A's, too?"

This naïve question touched off amused smiles in the circle.

"Why, of course not!" replied Burage.

All right. I made a note of it. In the hierarchy of the new era the A's weren't as close to the women as I'd thought.

"You were luckier than I, Mrs. Burage," I said tartly. "I haven't read the report that you turned in to Mr. Barrow on me."

"That's only natural," she replied, calmly staring at me with her blue eyes.

I was on the verge of anger, but I remembered the bugging device and restrained myself.

"It isn't as natural as all that," I said with a hint of harshness in my voice all the same. "If I don't know what I've done wrong, how can I correct myself?"

"All you had to do was ask us," Lia Burage answered.

"I'm asking you," I said bravely.

To think that, at the start of this meeting, I'd thought that I was going to put them through a rough session. And there I was, after ten minutes of conversation, bound hand and foot at the stake, exposed to their arrows. Me who, in the former world, had never managed to get the upper hand over a woman—at least, not over the ones that I loved! I got ready for the worst.

A silence. A busy consultation of eyes. It was Lia Burage who struck me with the first tomahawk.

"We feel that you don't have a proper attitude toward us."

"Proper!" I replied indignantly. "I *am* polite."

"It's a false, superficial politeness," Crawford said. "Actually, you're unfriendly—except today."

"Contemptuous," added (ex-Mrs.) Morrison.

"And most of all," said (ex-Miss) Jones, "you're practically indecent."

"Me—*indecent*?"

"And you're not even aware of it!" exclaimed (ex-Miss) Mason. "You really act like a hardened phallocrat. You're imbued with your male superiority. You stick sex everywhere."

Was I going to be a new Orpheus, torn to pieces by these maenads?

"For example?" I asked in a stifled voice.

"I won't give you one. I'll give you several," Lia Burage answered, her blue eyes staring at mine. "You make distinctions among us that are aimed at dividing us. You call Crawford Crawford, Morrison Morrison. But you call me Mrs. Burage. Why?"

I thought I had a reply for that. I said calmly, "I noticed that Crawford and Morrison had removed their wedding rings, whereas you had kept yours on. I thought that you might be a little old-fashioned, and as I'm old-fashioned myself, I used the old designation with you."

This explanation had results that were unexpected and, for me, humiliating: It cheered them up. They laughed—all except for Lia Burage. Looking at me, half amused, half condescending. And Crawford, always capricious, said in a mocking tone, but a mockery without malice, "He doesn't understand anything!"

This relaxation didn't please Mrs. Burage. She went "tsk-tsk" with her tongue while looking at Crawford and resumed in a serious tone. "The fact that women remove their wedding rings doesn't have the importance that you attach to it, Doctor. I've kept mine on because my finger has become thicker."

There were new laughs that Burage repressed at once. Calm restored, I tried to defend myself. "Is that the indecency?"

"No," answered Burage. "It's a lack of taste. Mr. Barrow told you so, but you didn't pay any attention."

"Why *Mr.* Barrow, in this case? Isn't it old-fashioned?"

"Mr. Barrow is the administrator. And then it hardly matters. Mr. Barrow is an A."

Logic that left me aghast. When I gathered my wits I resumed. "Let's discuss my alleged indecency."

"It's not alleged," Burage replied. "It's real. On January fifth you grabbed Jones's hand to show her how to do a correct preparation."

At this recollection (ex-Miss) Jones, a blonde, blushed and lowered her eyes in embarrassment, while compassionate eyes converged on her.

"And I shouldn't have done that?" I asked, bewildered.

"No."

"But I had to show her."

"Yes. Verbally. Without touching her."

"But I had no ulterior motive!"

Burage looked at me with her transparent eyes that showed every virtue.

"Doctor, you didn't have an ulterior motive *consciously*. But Jones was right in complaining. And I did my duty by conveying her complaint."

Trying to give my face the most neuter and least masculine expression possible, I looked at that virgin on whom the touch of my hand had produced such an effect. I had the feeling, all at once, that this new era was a kind of return to Victorianism. At least in the initial phase of intersexual relations. Because there was no doubt about the final phase.

"I'm sorry, Jones."

"Oh, it's nothing," replied Jones, turning scarlet. "It's forgotten."

My humility had a good effect on them all—except on Burage. I thought she'd understand that I wasn't so repentant. She went on, stern as a judge: "Doctor, I've also spotted more subtle indencency in you. The minute you think you can do it, you use your voice, your eyes, your smile, for seductive purposes."

"I thought you considered me arrogant!"

She was triumphant: "We do! Sometimes you're arrogant, aggressive, dominating, which is the brutal type of sexism. And sometimes you use charm, which is the disguised type."

"Can you give me an example of charm?"

"Just now, with Crawford. And when you asked her if she found you abrupt and authoritative."

I had only one way out: innocence.

"Crawford, have you interpreted my attitude the way Burage has?"

She laughed. "Yes, Doctor. And I found it very funny."

"You didn't *just* find it funny," Burage said with a squashing glance.

And Crawford went silent, shamefaced, biting her lips. Decidedly, nothing escaped Burage's blue eyes.

"You even use charm on me," Burage continued accusingly. "A moment ago when I told you that Dr. Grabel hadn't written that report, you looked me up and down lewdly like a mere sex object."

I was losing my patience—and my temper. I felt like releasing an enormous vulgarity in Burage's direction, the maximum obscenity. No, I couldn't lose sight of my goal, which was to make peace, at any cost, with these neo-Puritans.

"You're wrong, Burage," I said in a voice in which I stifled the deep and scandalous resonances. "You spoke with vehemence and I thought vehemence was very becoming in you."

"You aren't supposed to pay attention to my physique."

"How can I help it? I see you. You aren't a ghost."

"You can see me without looking at me that way. Dr. Grabel never looks at me like that."

I wanted to gnash my teeth, but I controlled myself.

"Perhaps Dr. Grabel's aesthetic sense isn't as finely developed as mine."

"Do you mean that you admire me?" she asked accusingly, her prying blue eyes staring at mine.

I was stymied by the turn that the dispute had taken.

"Before answering you," I said, "I'd like to make one remark. In general, I'm very much alive to the beauty of people. For example, I admire Jespersen. But that doesn't mean I'm homosexual."

"Be honest, Doctor. You don't look at Jespersen the way you've just looked at me."

I dodged again. "How have I looked at you?"

"So that I'd understand that you found me pleasing."

"Not at all," I said. "I looked at you with admiration, it's true, but it was an overall admiration. It applied to your intellectual being as well as your physical appearance."

"And that," Burage replied with the utmost contempt and turning to her companions as if to conclude her demonstration, "is the kind of hypocritical, lying compliment that men used to make to women in the past. They pretended to refer to the women's minds and, actually, they only had designs on their bodies."

"What are you talking about?" I asked vehemently. "Is my wife Anita a mere sex object for me? Did I marry an idiot for her pretty body? A doll for her beautiful elegance? Or did I marry a very intelligent, well-educated woman who, as you all know, has always followed her career away from me?"

Burage hadn't been expecting this outburst. She was too honest to ignore it. She remained silent. She looked at me. I detected a certain perplexity in her eyes.

I went on: "I'd like to explain, as a doctor and as a man, that it's impossible to eliminate every trace of sexuality from professional relations between men and women. As far as I'm concerned, I've always reduced it to its minimal dose. I've never chased my nurses or female lab assistants. I've never gone out with them. I've never invited them for dinner."

Burage became tougher. "Doctor, the look that you gave me a minute ago didn't have any minimal dose of sexuality. Besides, where sexist aggression is concerned, I don't know what a minimal dose is."

"Couldn't we put an end to this argument?" asked Crawford. "It's becoming too personal."

Crawford wanted to get revenge on Burage. Actually, however, she was right. I tried to persuade Burage that there hadn't been lust in my admiration for her, and she was trying to convince me of the opposite. Obviously there was some ambiguity in this.

Burage, in turn, became aware of it and fell silent. But she was silent, if I may say so, with strength, with dignity, without going back on what she'd said, without making concessions.

Laboriously, I took the floor again and, to save face, I constructed a false symmetry.

"At any rate, thanks, this discussion has been very useful.

I've told you what, to my eyes, was wrong. You've told me what, to your eyes, was wrong. All of us are going to keep those things in mind."

"There's still Dr. Grabel," said Burage sharply.

I could always count on her for not forgetting a thing.

"As to Dr. Grabel," I replied serenely, "there's been an unfortunate error on my part. I'd thought he had turned in the report that Burage wrote. This misunderstanding has been cleared up, so I've got nothing against Dr. Grabel."

And why I shouldn't have had a grudge against Burage God only knows! But all of us there, myself included, took it for granted.

With royal obliviousness, Burage accepted her complete impunity. But that didn't make her turn me loose. She pursued me, her sword at the small of my back.

"What do you plan to do with Dr. Grabel?"

"Give him an assignment on a level with Dr. Pierce's."

She inclined her head and, if I guessed correctly, I received a good mark from her. And from Crawford a parting arrow: "Doctor," she said with a malicious smile, "can I ask you a question? Since your report on us is already a month old, why have you waited until today to talk to us about it?"

I also gave her a smile. I made it brief and, I trust, without apparent sexism and replied, "Here's why. Some time ago I got a memo from Hilda Helsingforth telling me that, in her opinion, the meager results we'd had until that time were due to my disagreement with the women and the A's in the lab. I learned my lesson from that letter and handed in my resignation."

I looked at them and, in particular, at Burage. Obviously she hadn't known about it.[1] She might have been a confidential agent, but they didn't confide everything to her.

"In fact," I said, "I've given my resignation twice. And Hilda Helsingforth has refused it twice. I've reached the conclusion that Hilda Helsingforth feels that I can improve my relations with the women and the A's. And that's what I've tried to do today."

[1]She did know. Grabel had told her. But I didn't find out about that until long afterward. (Dr. Martinelli).

I paused and added: "The future will tell if I've succeeded."

This speech, which, from the point of view of the concealed listening device, was unassailable, had a certain effect on the women. I could tell. My speech had been, almost without my knowing it, very clever. Throughout the meeting I'd let myself be placed in a position of weakness, and only at the end had I tempered the victory of those facing me, revealing to them my strong point.

I felt this unconscious cleverness. I wanted to finish on that note and got to my feet. Salutations. Exit the ex-weaker sex. Farewell, ex-objects that have become subjects. Why must your emancipation go through my degradation? Where is true equality?

I sat down at my desk. As always in Blueville, I had a feeling of unreality. Actually, I wasn't shocked that my assistants had helped my self-criticism. That wasn't the problem. I knew a good many big bosses in medicine whose departments would have run better if they'd agreed to this practice.

No, what plunged me into deep unease was the type of grievance they had with me: a smile, a look, the contact of a hand, so many crimes. I would never get used to that fanatic counter-sexuality.

And, most of all, I was astonished. How malleable people were! How quickly they let themselves be molded. Millions of Germans, at Hitler's word, believed that the Jews were evil! Millions of Americans approved of the barbaric raids on Hanoi! And now women . . . It was beyond belief! It hadn't taken more than six months to instill in those intelligent lab assistants the phraseology of the day and the ideas that it transmitted.

I thought that I'd have trouble making peace with Dr. Grabel. I didn't. All the hard feelings that he'd had for me vanished in a wink in the joy of his promotion. All in one swoop I reconciled myself with every member of his caste.

There was profound solidarity among the A's. To offend one was to offend all. Those in the lab had believed that I was contemptuous of them. Now they felt reborn and harnessed themselves to their tasks with a new fervor. When an A is satisfied, he's a real workhorse. His only interest, his sole pleasure, his sole vice is work. Give him a job that he likes, the chance of a promotion, a good salary, and he'll toil under the yoke like a real ox. Not a step out of the furrow, hours and hours in the harness, enormous endurance and exemplary docility.

At the same time I enhanced Lia Burage's administrative powers and with very good results. Her scientific background was fairly meager, but her influence over the three castes was enormous. Burage is our cement.

But, unlike what happened with Grabel, my personal relations with Burage are a bit uncertain. As I had been denied the right to look at her, smile at her and, of course, touch her—even at arm's length—I made up for all these denials by daydreams that the reader can imagine. Oh, yes, I'd reached that point! Just like adolescence! At night Lia Burage joined Pussy, Jackie and Mrs. Barrow in my secret gardens. But in the daytime I behaved, as soon as she came up to me, with an irreproachable neutrality, my gaze dull, my eyes half closed, my back bent, my voice stifled, my bodily attitudes retiring and, in my movements, some kind of modest spinelessness that I'd copied from the A's. It was the height of hypocrisy since, while I was doing my best to look asexual, I inhaled, my nostrils palpitating, her delicious odor. When she left me I would straighten up and feel like whinnying.

For her part, Burage sorely tried my nerves. I noticed it with a bit of panic. With men, her grip on herself relaxed, she couldn't quite control her conduct. Three or four times in a single day she would change her attitude toward me. In public, of course, she was coldness personified. I'm referring to our private meetings, in my office. Today, for example, I've had four different Burages. In the morning (features drawn, tired look, dark-blue rings around her light-blue eyes) a sullen, monosyllabic Burage. At 11:00 A.M., a Burage immersed in the day's problems, busy, active and, with me, direct and even friendly. At four o'clock, God knows why, a block of ice. And late this afternoon, in my office, an argument. The bugging device in my office must end up in her office, otherwise she'd take greater precautions.

It began with an administrative quarrel and ended with a

husband-and-wife squabble. I'd committed a new crime! At three o'clock I met Crawford in a corridor and smiled at her. Useless to deny it—she saw me! Reply: I smile at Dr. Grabel, so why not at Crawford? You're the sexist, Burage. You see ulterior motives everywhere.

Here, always irreproachable with regard to my bodily posture, I allow myself some teasing. Resounding professional praise of Crawford, coupled with particularly insistent praise of her even temper. Conclusion: Crawford has a redeeming feature; she gives me a change of porcupines.

Burage's aggressiveness is redoubled and becomes provocation. Her blue eyes sparkling, her bosom heaving, tossing her chestnut mane (which reminds me so much of Anita), Burage marches straight up to me and takes me to task. I'm a damned hypocrite! If I think that she falls for my smirks, I'm mistaken! She sees through my game. I haven't changed deep down—still just as arrogant! An inveterate phallocrat! I've simply changed my tactics. I pretend that I'm an angel to be more seductive.

Seduce who (laugh)? You? Crawford? That Jones? It's really too stupid. Write your report. I don't give a damn. So long, porcupine. I don't even want to argue with you any more. I slam the door as I leave.

My anger is, of course, false, but there is nothing in our relationship that isn't false. That's the paradox: Owing to the dominant counter-sexuality, everything between us is sexualized. There's nothing innocent any more, no attitude, no movement, no look. Even an averted look becomes suspect. And, finally, in our quarrels, Burage and I talk only of sex. She starts it by mentioning my phallus, if only to condemn it. That's all she ever talks about! Why should she reduce me to this single function? I'm not defined by the presence, in my anatomy, of a reproductive organ. I'm also a neurologist, a research worker, a loving parent—and a disappointed husband.

On Saturday, Mrs. Pierce's demi-prophecy proved untrue. At noon when, to my mind, only a few hours separated me from her, Anita telephoned. My heart was in my mouth. She was sorry, but it was *absolutely* impossible for her to come that night. On the other hand, it was *absolutely* certain that she would come on Wednesday. A silence. Wednesday? I asked incredulously. In the middle of the week? Yes, Wednesday. I couldn't get any explanation out of her for this odd date, and I hung up, despondent. That very night, in search of solace, I told Joan Pierce about this conversation, but I couldn't get the slightest commentary. Wednesday? asked Joan Pierce. Two looks followed: the first, quick as lightning; the second, pitiful and serious.

The weekend couldn't have been worse. During our horseback ride I scarcely paid attention to Pussy, and I didn't back up Stien, who, wearing that Tyrolean hat from which his long white hair emerged, led the two militiawomen into a conversation. I stayed off to the side on Chouchka, forlorn and mute. I didn't even wake up when Jackie—yes, that's right, Jackie—quite unexpectedly gave me a look and a half smile. I was fed up with that incomprehensible sex.

On my return, Dave had a second, though milder, fit of hostility. He didn't like my Sunday cavalcades. He must have feared that, splitting the skull of one militiawoman with my big saber and slinging the other one across my saddle, I might gallop across into nearby Canada, deserting my son at Blueville. But this time I was so disgusted with everything—and even with him—that I treated his sullenness with an indifference that was almost unfeigned and with very good results: He stopped sulking almost at once. Better still, the next night I wasn't awakened by a scream at 2:00 A.M. with a nightmare of guilt. A good lesson. I'll remember it.

Luckily, on Monday, I didn't have time to think too much about myself. In the morning mail there was something new, and at Blueville something new—when it comes from the outside—produces a mighty effect. It was a letter worded as follows:

Dear Dr. Martinelli:
In view of the havoc raised by the epidemic among the male population of the United States and the country's need to renew its population, the Federal Sperm Bank, set up in Washington, D.C., on May 2, has given us your name and address as an important person living in a protected zone in Vermont and a possible donor of sperm.

If you agree, a sample-taking team will stop at Blueville at 7:00
P.M. on June 3.

This letter was signed Dr. F. B. Mulberry, who called himself
the Montpelier correspondent of the Federal Sperm Bank. The
letter was mimeographed, only my name having been typed.

I concluded that I might not be the only one in Blueville to
have received this joke, and I spoke of it to Stien and Jespersen
in cautious terms. Have you received a letter signed Mulberry?
An approach that I also used with Pierce and Smith but with
negative responses, whereas Stien and Jespersen (the former
quite worried) acquiesced and agreed to meet that same night at
my place. Why my place? Because, in anticipation of Anita's
visit, I'd looked for and found the monitoring device in my
room, and, like Joan Pierce, I could disconnect it at will.

Stien sat on my bed, his hat on his head (despite his
abundant white hair and the very mild temperature), and Jess
took a seat on the second of my chairs. A long silence. Stien
grumbled, spoke—partly in Yiddish, partly in German, partly in
English—and as I pointed out to him that he was almost
incomprehensible, he glanced at me, from under his pugnacious brows, through the many folds of his eyelids, with
unfriendly gray-blue eyes, as though he held me responsible for
Mulberry's letter.

"Well, we've made it," he finally exploded in rapid though
Germanized English. "Here we are back in that old eugenic
crap! Just like the Nazi period! I should have expected it, after
that stinking questionnaire about my ancestors when I got
here. Ralph, always watch out for people who ask about your
forefathers. They're either racists or eugenists! And they're
both just as bad."

"You're exaggerating," Jespersen said. "Eugenism isn't so
terrible. For instance, sterilizing defective individuals strikes me
as highly justifiable."

"You don't know anything about it, chemist!" Stien bellowed. "First of all, sterilization is ineffective, as dominant
defects reappear by mutation. And recessive defects can be
transmitted by healthy people. Most of all, sterilization opens
the door for all kinds of abuses. Did you know that in the state

of California, where emasculation of criminals convicted of sexual offenses was authorized—well before Bedford—two judges ordered the castration of one hundred and one inmates? They were homosexuals and exhibitionists."

"How do you know all that, Stien?" asked Jess, as if he were surprised that a biologist might know the laws of the state of California.

Stien shrugged, knitted up his brows and replied with contained rage, "Because I'm a dirty Jew, with a long nose and big ears, so I can spot injustice a long way off."

Having spoken, he half turned his back to Jess, as if he refused to see him. I looked at him. His face was a network of wrinkles. His eyes disappeared in the pouches of his eyelids, and, around his drooping, tense mouth, two bitter lines joined his pugnacious chin.

"Come now, Stien," I said, "let's not lose our heads. For the moment they aren't castrating us—just collecting our sperm. It's exactly the opposite."

What made me say that? Stien looked my way, concentrating his contempt on me.

"Ralph," he said in a smothered voice, "you don't think. This isn't just the opposite—it's exactly the same. Castration and selection are the front and back of eugenism. What does a breeder do when he wants to improve the race? He castrates most of the males and picks one or two of them as studs. Selection is based on castration."

"If you allow me to say this," said Jess, "selection doesn't yield bad results—particularly, for horses."

Stien raised his arms skyward and, in the vehemence of his movement, rose from my bed:

"*Aber Mensch!* We aren't horses! We're men! We're free beings! No one has the right to treat us like cattle! No one has the right to say, We're going to make this one into an ox. And we'll take the sperm out of that guy and use it to inseminate our cows! *Donnerwetter, Mensch!* I'm no bull! I'm a man. And I'm not going to give one centiliter of my semen so they can fertilize God knows how many dumb broads twenty years after I die!"

"Twenty years after you die?" asked Jess, dumfounded, and as Stien still refused to look at him, he turned to me.

"Maybe not twenty years after his death," I replied, "but in any case ten or fifteen years after it's collected. There's no problem—it keeps very well."

"Then it's already been done?" asked Jess.

I looked at him. Good-looking Jess. A symphony of pastel shades in which the dominant ones were the blond of his hair, the pink of his cheeks, the azure of his eyes. But a specialist rather limited to his specialty.

"Nowaday, it seems that we have a federal sperm bank," I said. "Before there were private banks. They preserve your sperm at the temperature of liquid nitrogen in exchange for a fee of twenty dollars a year."

"But what for?" asked Jespersen, raising his brows.

"Well, suppose you've had a vasectomy done on yourself and you still want to keep the option of procreation."

"But in that case, why get a vasectomy?" Jess asked, smiling.

"It's a matter of principles, I think. There were men who considered it their responsibility to have themselves sterilized and not the women with whom they had relations. And the men kept the sperm, which they could no longer produce, in a sperm bank, in case their wives wanted to be fertilized."

"Idiots!" shouted Stien. "Damned idiots!" He stood up, gnashing his teeth, and, as he didn't know what to do with his rage, he sat back down and grumbled, "How clever! Stockpiled sperm and a sterile penis!"

Jess looked at him but, receiving no invitation to join the conversation from that side, turned back to me. "Personally," he said, "I think it's pretty generous of those men. Why force women to take the pill? Why shouldn't it be up to the man to make intercourse sterile?"

"But it isn't at all the same," I replied. "A woman can always stop taking the pill. Vasectomy is really reversible only twenty-five percent of the time. It's mutilation and we're not sure that it isn't dangerous."

"Madness! Madness!" said Stien. "Don't talk to me about these American imbecilities! At any rate, nowadays, there's no more problem about vasectomy. They castrate people at the drop of a hat." (I concluded from this remark that Joan Pierce had shown him Deborah Grimm's article and that he'd remembered what it said about elderly "entire men.") "That isn't the problem. The problem is—do we agree to being reduced to the role of studs?"

A silence.

"Before answering," I said, "let me think it over for a minute, so that at least you won't accuse me of saying things rashly."

Stien reacted to that remark in an unexpected way. He smiled at me with a look of approval, as if he were evaluating my reply with a connoisseur's eye.

I got to my feet and I headed toward the window. I separated the double curtains a bit. It was dark. There was nothing to see except the single women's barracks facing me, twenty yards away, dimly lighted. Burage slept there. I even knew where her window was.

Actually, I didn't do any thinking. I had it all thought out. I just wanted to give myself a moment's respite, to get some room. Of the three of us, Stien was by far the best informed, the richest in varied experience and the wisest. But I didn't want him pushing me around. Oh, he didn't do it knowingly, but the result was the same. With him, conversation tended to become a monologue, and soliloquy degenerated into a prosecutor's summation. Stien had a mania for accusation, for indignant denunciation, for vehement contempt. It wasn't aimed at us when he started out, but, as he had us within easy reach, we would wind up catching it.

Having scored this point, I went back to my seat and said, "It strikes me that the main question is: Are they really going to give us a choice? Are we free to refuse? It would appear that we are, since Mulberry says in his letter 'if you agree.' But I see, just after that, he makes an appointment for us with a collection team—as if he were sure we'd agree."

"Quite right," Stien said.

"Thanks for your approval, Stien," I said with a hint of sarcasm. "I've got only one way of making sure they're giving me an alternative and that is by saying no. And as this refusal could be considered unpatriotic, I'll say that it's a question of principle. I'm going to claim that I find self-manipulation disgusting and that, on the other hand, I refuse to be handled by a male nurse. I'll say that, no matter what the purpose, it amounts to homosexuality."

"Not bad," replied Stien, and his face, wrinkled like an old elephant, wrinkled itself even more. He shook his head right and left and looked at me with a sly smile. "Not bad, only I've gone you one better. I'm going to say that I intend to remain faithful to Jewish law and that I put this kind of manipulation in the same category with the sin of Onan, Genesis, Chapter thirty-eight."

I looked at him and shook my head. "That's not so great. They're going to say that your seed won't be spilled on the ground and soiled but, on the contrary, will be hoarded preciously for future fertilizations."

"They won't raise any objection at all, Ralph. Religion is a bastion, and they wouldn't dare attack it."

A silence. We looked at Jess and Jess blushed. He said, not without bravery, "I intend to agree."

To my great amazement, Stien didn't bellow and didn't even demand an explanation. What's more, neither did I, except that my eyes did the demanding for me. Jess stared at me with his limpid eyes.

"I don't want to look like I'm judging you or criticizing you, but, as Ralph said, I consider a refusal as unpatriotic."

"I didn't take the responsibility for that opinion," I said hastily. "I attributed it to the authorities."

"I understood," Jess replied, "that you didn't agree with them. Well, I do."

I remained silent and so did Stien. I didn't feel like explaining to Jess that, basically, he was right, but not in this particular instance. Because the administration that governed us couldn't be trusted—especially not where we're concerned! Let tyranny and highhandedness take over and, after treating us like breeding animals, they could decide tomorrow to turn us into A's. I didn't say anything about all that. I didn't know if Joan Pierce had lent Deborah Grimm's article to Jess. I didn't think so. She must have distrusted his naïveté, just as I did. Perhaps, too, his conformism.

"It's time to reward spying," Stien said.

Out of kindness for Jess, whom he had wanted to humiliate minutes before, he put an end to the argument. "To reward spying"—an expression that we owed to Stien—meant that, after a confidential talk, I was to reconnect the bugging device and give it a half hour of inoffensive conversation with a concomitant consumption of whisky—at least, for my two companions. We did this in case anyone had noticed Jess or Stien entering my quarters and was wondering why they'd left no audible record. Of course, in this case, there would still be a time gap in the bugging, something that could have been picked up. But how can you live without taking chances?

Once Jess and Stien had left, I put on my pajamas and walked up and down in my bedroom. After a while I stopped before the window and, as I'd already done that night, I raised a corner of the curtain. Across the way, locked up in a bedroom like mine, Burage either slept or didn't sleep. Between us, scarcely twenty yards and a formidable taboo. Our connection—for me, at any rate—would have been suicide.

And yet, on June 3, when my refusal was rejected, as I was sure it would be, a sampling team would come to collect my semen. In a year, in ten years, that semen would fertilize some Ohio or Alabama women selected by computer because their traits complemented mine. Babies would be born from this remote-control insemination, remote both in space and time. These babies would be raised in state nurseries, without knowing their parents or even their mothers, freed for other duties. What a fine race we were going to have! How pure it would all be! Our culture's latest find: people permanently broken of the sex instinct.

I heard Dave stirring in his room. I stopped, held my breath and listened. No, nothing. Poor Dave. He was twelve. He didn't know that he'd already become obsolete.

7

Anita arrived Wednesday evening, just as I was getting ready to go to the cafeteria with Dave. She was pale, tired, tense. She gave me a quick kiss, gave Dave a distant wave, declared to nobody in particular that she was starving to death but that, first, she had to take a bath and change. With that, she shut herself up in the bathroom with her suitcase.

Our reunion hadn't lasted more than three minutes. Not much, after one and a half months apart. I phoned Mr. Barrow to ask him if I could bring Anita to the cafeteria. Of course, Doctor, he answered with his suave, hard voice, Kate and I will be delighted to have her at our table (a pause) with you, naturally (he said that fast and rather carelessly). Dave, I presume, will be happier at the table with his little friends (*and how!* whispered Dave, who had grabbed the receiver).

With that I hung up and waited, and Dave waited, both sitting, both silent. Now and then our eyes met and he averted his at once. I knew exactly what was going on inside him. He'd already sensed how much this first contact had disappointed me, he'd felt sorry for me, he'd gotten even.

Anita must have been reborn, like Venus, on contact with the water. A little pause in the doorway of the bedroom, intended for general admiration. Marvelous dark auburn hair curling over her strong, graceful neck, barely a suggestion of lipstick and a little touch of makeup around her green eyes, a single jewel, but one of quality: a snug-fitting necklace made of gold, which emphasized her milky complexion; and, enhancing everything by its sobriety, a very simple black dress, which she filled quite nicely and which must have cost a fortune. And there she was in front of us, sure of herself, with a way of carrying her head that I'd never seen, as if the importance of her position had heightened the awareness of her beauty.

I paid her a compliment without warmth. And Dave kept still. She went beyond that mitigated welcome. She was hungry, she declared with a proud look, as if her hunger was more valuable than ours, and, majestically, she led us toward the cafeteria, walking so fast that Dave and I could hardly keep up.

Obviously, at the castle cafeteria, where she arrived a few strides ahead of us, she created quite a stir, the room being crowded. Everyone there knew who Martinelli was (and I'm speaking of her, not me), her lofty position; everyone knew how rare her appearances were. Barrow got to his feet and drew close, pushing his paunch before him, his polished skull bent forward, his face gleaming with respect. As he was very tall and Anita was of medium height, he became oval before her. He rounded himself; he coiled up and surrounded her with his oily amiability.

Anita received these homages graciously. Democratically, she accepted a tray, which was then filled by the counter-woman, and while I fell in step behind her she reached the reserved table, smiling left and right with the gracefulness of a lady politician. Dave left us and I found myself seated between Anita and Kate Barrow. I didn't need to worry about conversation. Mr. Barrow had eyes and tongue only for my wife. Mrs. Barrow didn't dare speak to me or see me. At any rate, Anita was the honored guest. I was just the one who followed and didn't count.

Yet I would have liked for Anita to speak to me and smile at me from time to time, if only to keep me from losing face. She did nothing of the kind, perhaps because, in spite of everything, she felt embarrassed by the embarrassment that my presence at her side created, perhaps also because she was stuck in that kind of formal, pointless conversation in which Barrow had trapped her. So I tried detachment, even distraction, and let my vague looks wander around the cafeteria, enough, at any rate, to notice that Dave wasn't having a good time with his "little friends."

Mrs. Pierce, seated at an A's table, never missed a crumb of the situation, searching Anita with beak and eyes and throwing me a quick smile of sympathy, none of which prevented her from submerging Dr. Grabel on her right in a flood of words. To my left, at a nearby table, Crawford and Burage sat down. While pretending to be absorbed in the remarks they were exchanging and not looking at us, they actually never took their eyes off us. At one point I intercepted a sweeping glance from Burage to Martinelli (I'm speaking of Anita, of course) that wasn't exactly benevolent.

In the middle of the meal, to my grand surprise, an abrupt change came over Anita, a change imperceptible for the others but not for me, who knew her well. Her features grew taut and a little tic made her upper lip jump every now and again—in her, a sign of great inner tension despite her considerable aplomb and the apparently faultless attention she was paying to Barrow's inane remarks.

Obviously, we made a scandalous couple. Much more so than the married P.M.s, since people had grown accustomed to them and the indecency of their relations were confined, if I may say so, within the walls of Blueville. But Anita came from the outside. And the fact that she was so close to President Sarah Bedford, the fact that, despite this, she seemed to have made the long trip from Washington to Blueville in order to sleep with a P.M. added to the tremor of disapproval. I sensed this tremor in the looks (or missing looks) from the single women and A's.

Moreover, that was why Mr. Barrow wouldn't talk to me and wouldn't even see me. Of the couple's two components, I was the more sexualized object at Blueville, the one that created scandal—in former times, the equivalent of a call girl exhibited in public by a Secretary of State. Clearly, my presence at Mr. Barrow's table at Anita's side was perceived by him, by the A's, by the single women, as lack of taste, one that was tolerated but deplorable. As to Kate Barrow, she was in agony, all the more so because she knew—as I did—her own secret thoughts. Seated at that narrow table where I couldn't make a move without touching her elbow, or stretch my legs without bumping into hers, she was burning up. She was experiencing all the feelings of attraction and repulsion that a sensual and chaste male Puritan would have when driven by necessity into the company of a loose woman. Under everyone's eyes—what's more, under the eyes of her adipose spouse—she was paralyzed with terror at the thought of betraying so much as an infinitesimal degree of specific interest in me. So the poor woman made up her mind to stare at her plate and, whenever she raised her eyes, to stare at her husband. No tub of fat, no machine for dispensing verbal bureaucracy at the table will ever receive more attention!

I was infinitely relieved when I found myself alone in my room with Anita. Dave had gone to bed. Not a word was exchanged, and while Anita undressed, gritting her teeth, I typed a note inviting her (as I hadn't disconnected the bugging device) to an inoffensive meeting, ending with a good night. I handed her the sheet of paper. She read it, frowning, and from the look of her—she was in a horrid mood—I saw that we were going to have trouble, in the next few minutes, carrying on the most commonplace of conversations.

However, we somehow managed to do it, though grudgingly on her part. Anita kept on lapsing into silences from which it was a struggle to extricate her. She avoided my eyes. She half turned her back on me. She pulled on a pair of pajamas—Anita, who had always slept nude with me. Finally, I disconnected the bug and there I was in bed with a block of ice that I couldn't even undress. She remained insensible to my caresses, and she was so stiff, so tense and so cold that, after a few minutes, she'd reduced me to impotence. That's all I had to show for over a month of waiting—a miserable failure.

I got out of bed in a fit of anger. Naked as I was, I paced up and down in the room, frustrated, furious, and I said in a stifled voice, trembling with rage, "I shouldn't have bothered to disconnect the bug. Mr. Barrow would have found it most enlightening. Nice going. Now you're right in line. You've internalized the taboo."

"I haven't internalized anything at all," replied Anita in a toneless voice, her hands clasped over the nape of her neck, her eyes fixed on the ceiling. "Naturally, since you haven't been able to perform tonight, you're blaming it all on me."

"Like a dirty phallocrat!"

"I didn't say that," she replied with exasperating calm, and her eyes roved all around the room without meeting mine.

"But you thought it."

"I didn't think anything of the kind," she said with the same inexorable coldness. "And, I'll say it again, it's not my fault if you don't want me any more."

I strode over to the bed, completely beside myself, and I said to her, stifling my voice because of Dave, "How do you expect me to want a woman who doesn't even take off her pajama top when she has intercourse?"

"All you had to do was ask me," she replied with an insincerity so blatant that it left me dumfounded. "There!" she added, unbuttoning her pajama top and removing it with military precision. Having said this, she lay down again on her back, rigid, her arms at her sides, as though she were at attention.

She said to me, "I obeyed. Are you happy?"

"I don't give a damn about your obedience," I answered and, snatching up her pajama top, I flung it in her face.

"Thanks for the elegant gesture."

"It's only natural! What can you expect from a sexist? A dominator! Arrogant! Brutal!"

"I didn't say that! Stop putting words in my mouth that I haven't said."

"But haven't you been thinking them? Go ahead, deny it. This is what they've made you into with a six months' bombardment of propaganda. A frigid woman."

"I'm not frigid," she replied angrily. "It isn't my fault if you can't get an erection."

"An erection! On a board!"

She looked at me, her eyes blazing. "I'm not a board, far from it. I've got very definite reasons for reassuring you on that point."

"Oh, because it's better with other men in Washington? With 'entire men' that have one foot in the grave? With your girl friend? Or with a Superdoll?"

"Ralph," she answered, all at once regaining her composure and measuring me coldly. "You are the limit!"

After provocation, contempt.

"Do you mean that I typify the sexist such as they've trained you to see him?"

"The scene that you've just made is the best training I need."

"At last! Finally the blindfold has been lifted. Finally you see Ralph Martinelli for what he is. For ten years he'd been there and you'd never noticed his cloven hooves!"

She made no reply to this, and I felt a great silence, a final silence coming, the silence that can't even be cut with a knife.

I put my pajamas back on, as I was starting to get cold, and pulled on my bathrobe. I tried to think, but my mind was a ball of fire. At that moment I hated Anita, and my hatred carried me away for a few seconds.

There's always been an undertow in me after a surge of anger. I sat on the edge of the bed, looked at her and took her hand. I expected her to pull it back, but no, she wasn't going to make that effort. She let me have it—inert. My fingers closed on dead fingers that belonged to no one. And that, once more, was provocation. There'd been open violence—the pajama top flung in her face. But there was also surreptitious violence—the hand that let itself be held while rejecting you. Actually, that hand was a symbol. A minute before, when I'd gotten into bed with her, Anita—while looking as though she were yielding— had refused me. The pajama top, the passivity, the bottled-up ill will—they were all so many sly rejections.

All right. I wasn't going to do the same thing by rejecting, with violence, this hand that didn't want mine. I set it down gently on the sheet. It was now or never to apply my behavior therapy. I got up and began pacing up and down again but this time calmly, without clenched fists in the pockets of my bathrobe. I didn't want to hate Anita. And I didn't want to become a misogynist either. If there was one lesson I'd learned it was this: Never go after the wrong enemy. The enemy wasn't Anita or her sex. In the whirlwind, in the confusion of the moment, there was that solid rock to which I clung—my affection for Anita. I would have sworn to it: It wasn't true. Anita couldn't have become somebody else. I'd just told her so. I didn't believe in the cloven hooves that grew all of a sudden on people that we love.

I replayed the film of the evening, from Anita's arrival to the moment that I was living just then. I finally saw the chain of events. And there was light.

I sat down beside her on the bed but without holding her hand, and I said softly, "Anita, are you going to leave me?"

A long silence.

"Yes."

"That's why you came on a Wednesday?"

"Yes."

"You didn't want to write to me? You wanted to tell me to my face?"

"Yes."

I didn't resume at once. It took me a while to control my voice.

"Well, I appreciate that. You didn't pick the easy way out."

"I wanted to explain . . ."

I was almost incredulous. I couldn't believe that a part of my life was leaving me. And I asked her the first, most anxious of my questions: "Are you leaving me for good?"

"I don't know."

A silence. I said with a toneless voice, "Does this decision come from you?"

"Of course not." Then she went on, in the most passionate tone of voice: "Ralph, listen. In the six weeks that I haven't seen you, this was the program. On Monday each week I went in to meet Bedford and ask her if it was all right if I spent the next weekend at Blueville. She would tell me with a suave smile, 'Of course not, Anita,' and she'd add a remark, half in jest, half in earnest, of this type: 'In other words, it's like a drug—you can't go without it.'"

"Oh, no!"

"That's not the half of it. Friday night rolls around and I get a call at my apartment from Bedford's secretary. She tells me something has come up, Martinelli, the President is expecting you at Camp David to work over the weekend."

"That's awful! Why does she do that? Out of jealousy?"

"Oh, no, thank God, she doesn't feel that way about me. Bedford does it out of conviction."

"Do you share that conviction?"

"Not at all."

I said to her with a taut little smile, "You've changed."

"No," she answered heatedly, "I haven't changed. Women's liberation is one thing. And hatred of men is another. Hatred of men is psychopathic plain and simple. I've never gone along with that madness."

"Except right now."

I'd said that involuntarily and already regretted it. Anita looked at me and said, "I'm sorry, Ralph. I was cold. I didn't know how to tell you that I was leaving you."

I placed my hand over hers. "Forget that stupid remark. Go on. You were telling me how your weekends had been sabotaged. You called it off three times, so I gather that the business about Camp David happened three times."

She tightened her lips.

"With variations and increasingly evident hostility on Bedford's part. And my loss of influence was Deborah Grimm's gain. Apparently I just wasn't in the 'line' any more. I felt myself becoming a 'traitor.'"

"What about last weekend?"

"Last weekend was the big decision. On Friday Bedford called me into her office. She was all sugar and honey when she told me that she'd appointed me U.S. ambassador to France."

"But that's a big promotion, Anita."

"Yes and no. The assignment ahead of me is an important one, it's true, but at the same time I know they're trying to get rid of me."

"Is that out of spite?"

"That's only part of it. I quote Bedford: 'Anita, once you're set up over there, you'll be making only a few quick trips back and forth between Paris and Washington. A pause. And no more Blueville. You have to cut out that business once and for all.'"

"I'm dumfounded. Did you ask her why?"

"Of course. Here's what she answered: 'I consider that a woman diplomat who's married and who feels an attachment for her husband is a security risk.'"

"That's what they used to say, not so long ago, about homosexual diplomats."

"I didn't remind her of that. I asked for twenty-four hours to think it over and then, on Saturday, I told her that I'd accepted. On condition that I break the news to you myself. She did everything to make me call off this last trip, but I wouldn't give up. She's the one who made it for Wednesday. I leave day after tomorrow for Paris."

In a quavering voice I said, "Why, Anita, that's blackmail. You should have refused."

It was Anita's turn to look at me, then avert her eyes and tell me in a low, weary voice, "Ralph, you live in Blueville. You don't realize the kind of regime that we're living under." And, as if I hadn't disconnected the bugging device, she lowered her voice still more in speaking these words. She went on: "If I'd refused, I would have been blacklisted and I'd have had a tough time finding a job."

"You?"

She bowed her head. "Yes, me."

"In that case," I said hastily, "you could have come to live with me in Blueville. There are married P.M.s here."

"Bedford thought of that possibility. She hinted that it would mean your having to leave Blueville."

I lifted my arms skyward. "But how could she do such a thing? Blueville is a private firm. And I'm doing essential work in Blueville."

"Your work doesn't interest Bedford in the slightest."

I looked at her. I was thunderstruck. "How do you know?"

"When I came here, I was asked to bring a report back to the White House. A status report on the work of Stienemeier and Jespersen, to be handed to me in a sealed envelope by Mr. Barrow. Never your work. Listen, Ralph, is there any logical reason why Bedford should be interested in the survival of men?"

A silence. This remark was too important. I'd think it over the next day. For the moment I was in a big hurry.

"I can't believe that Helsingforth isn't interested in my work. I offered her my resignation and she turned it down."

"I know, I know," Anita said with a sigh. "Turning down your resignation is part of the bargaining that went on two weekends in a row."

"Do you mean that it was Bedford who told Helsingforth to turn it down?"

"Yes, through me and in these terms: 'Anita, if you want Helsingforth to turn down Dr. Martinelli's resignation, telephone her on my behalf. Just don't go there.' And that was two weeks ago."

A long silence, and I resumed, breathlessly: "I can't believe that Helsingforth didn't have something to say in the matter! After all, if I come up with a vaccine against Encephalitis 16, the Helsingforth Company will make a fortune selling the stuff."

Anita shrugged her shoulders. "There's no guarantee that she could sell it. We're going through a time of economic crisis. Things could be worse, but even so companies are going out of business every day. Helsingforth is three quarters ruined. There's hardly anything left of the pharmaceutical empire that her husband had founded. Without the subsidies that Bedford gives her, Helsingforth would have to shut down Blueville."

"Do you mean that Bedford controls Helsingforth by her subsidies?"

"In a way, yes. But it isn't that simple. The two women have close ties. Helsingforth financed Sherman's campaign to a large extent. Perhaps she also knows a thing or two about Bedford—especially about her relations with Sherman."

A silence. I looked at her. I tried to grasp a situation that couldn't be grasped.

"If I understand correctly, by going to Paris you're protecting me from Bedford, but you aren't protecting me from Helsingforth. Helsingforth still has leeway for a decision."

"Yes," Anita replied, "that's about the size of it."

Thinking it over, I was astonished at using an expression like "you're protecting me" so casually in speaking to Anita. Two weeks before, when I'd handed in my resignation, I'd been proud of my courage, proud of having "compelled" Helsingforth to turn it down. What childish impertinence! Actually, I was just an insolent boy that hadn't gotten a whipping because he was "protected." It dawned on me in that very second: I had only the illusion of free will. They'd made me into a puppet whose strings were pulled by three women: Bedford, Helsingforth, Anita. Of these three women, only one was benevolent—the one who was leaving in order "to protect me."

Just then I hardly felt grief over Anita's leaving. I received another, more terrible shock—humiliation. Under my arms, down my back, in my hair, sweat began to trickle. The odor of it, in that confined space, bothered me. I was afraid it might bother Anita too. I got up, removed my bathrobe and made my way to the bathroom. I took a shower. Then I rubbed myself with eau de Cologne. By the odd way the bottle moved, I realized that my hands were shaking.

When I came back from the bathroom Anita suggested reconnecting the bug so as to do over the showdown we'd just had. I acquiesced. It was prudent, as Stien said, to "reward spying."

Although we'd worked out the script for this "act" before-hand, I was struck by the ambiguity. Every now and then Anita seemed almost more sincere than she had in our earlier, confidential scene—particularly when she told me, "I'm not going to remind you who I am, Ralph. A career woman, first and foremost. And, to my mind, this implies no home, no husband, no child."

"No husband?" I asked, hoping to enter into the spirit of her game.

"No," Anita replied with a note of harshness that struck me as unfeigned. "No husband in the traditional sense of the word. Have you already forgotten our compact, Ralph? Actually, by mutual consent, we had destroyed the basis of the marriage while outwardly maintaining the legal bond."

At another point Anita seemed to be telling me about her future assignment with more ardor than the scenario required.

"I've reached a summit, Ralph. It's exhausting but, at the same time, it's exciting to be among the three or four people close to Sarah Bedford. I've learned, Ralph. I've learned tre-mendously. And I tell you with all modesty—I'm sure I can handle the job that's been given to me."

I don't quite remember what I answered—probably some-thing like: You're sacrificing your husband for your career. Actually, it's a stupid thing to say. Many a man has sacrificed his wife for his career, not by deserting her so much as by excluding her from his life. Yet, as I was attempting to play my role in this pseudo-showdown, I looked at Anita and thought: It isn't just Bedford's dictatorship and blackmail. It isn't just the need to protect me. There's something else, something tossed onto this side of the scale, something that makes the side where I am awfully light. It's lifetime ambition.

At last the moment had come to bring the curtain down on our little theatrical production. As we'd arranged, I offered Anita a divorce. She refused. To her eyes it was "as outmoded as marriage." We agreed that we would retain a fraternal affection for each other. But the fleshly bond was broken permanently. Anita wouldn't come to see me at Blueville any more. We'd write to each other.

With that I disconnected the bug and scarcely had the time to get back into bed when Anita threw herself into my arms, warm and palpitating. She was after a return match, I thought. Not me. I was humiliated by my dependence and the deceit to which we'd been driven. Despite all that, I reacted in the way she wanted. My body seemed to be capable of making its own decisions.

This tumult calmed, I still didn't feel calm. I lay resting on my back, in the dark, my eyes wide open. I was doubly angry with Anita—first because she'd refused, then because she'd yielded. To my mind, the sadness of our farewell didn't call for this lovemaking.

When doubt sets in, it keeps gnawing away at you. I was now wondering about Anita's motives in coming to tell me about our separation. Was the contact she wanted face to face—or body to body? Everything seemed to indicate that she hadn't wanted to make this last big trip for nothing. I also marveled at the way she handled her body—either a block of ice or a furnace. But always in control of herself and the situation.

What's more, her tension, her nervousness were gone. At my side lay an entirely new woman—a relaxed mind in a satisfied body. And satisfied with my collaboration. We mustn't let the good things in life slip past (without overdoing them), even if the collaborator goes out of your life at daybreak.

I must have dozed off a few seconds. When I awoke, I was

alone in bed. I heard noise in the kitchenette and, getting up, I found Anita there, dressed in nothing but her pajama top, seated at the little white table, greedily devouring a large can of tuna she'd come across in my refrigerator.

"Sit down, Ralph," she said, inviting me to my own table. "I went ahead and opened it. Want some?" she added almost grudgingly.

"No, I'm not hungry."

"Well, I am," she said, vastly relieved at not having to share it with me. "Where does this tuna come from?"

"From the canteen. I suppose they want to get us used to contributing to our upkeep, even though they withhold a large amount from our pay for meals."

But Anita wasn't concerned about what happened in Blueville. She was only interested in what was going to happen in Paris. To explain the great part she was about to play there, she began discoursing (with her mouth full) about the international situation.

What she said was enormously interesting to me. In the newspapers that we received at Blueville, there was nothing, absolutely nothing about what was going on beyond our borders. You would have thought that the heads of the foreign departments of the big newspapers had died, along with their correspondents, and that the major wire services had gone out of business. A total blackout.

And an intentional blackout, Anita told me, for the situation in the nation had never been so serious. Since the outbreak of the epidemic, the sailors, soldiers and airmen that the Pentagon maintained at great expense in hundreds of bases all over the globe had begun dying at such a rate and in such proportions that they'd had to repatriate all the servicemen in order to keep their equipment from falling into the hands of the indigenous populations. Despite this, the government had been forced to abandon planes, cannons, tanks and, unfortunately, highly sophisticated atomic bombs stored in Thailand. Everyone was wondering if our former allies hadn't sold the bombs to the Chinese.

The political consequences of this withdrawal had been incalculable: All the foreign governments actively supported by the State Department—particularly in Southeast Asia and Latin America—had fallen in the weeks that followed. Nationalist regimes had replaced them at once. These regimes weren't all Communist, not by a long shot. But they all shared a common attitude—resentment and distrust of the United States.

On top of this, the Bedford regime was viewed abroad—beginning with neighboring Canada—with uneasiness and disfavor and its dictatorial character often denounced. In the Canadian press, which had remained free, Bedford's antimale sexism was compared, in veiled terms, to Nazi racism. Although they were forbidden in the United States, thousands of copies of the Canadian newspapers most critical of Bedford were being smuggled across the border at different places and were circulating clandestinely in the United States.

For the White House, the situation in Europe was even more disturbing. The epidemic had reached them later and they had fought against its spread earlier. Very soon, Europe isolated itself from the United States by a *cordon sanitaire.* At the same time, the United States had to repatriate the forces that it kept in Germany. Thus, the European nations had found themselves alone in a dramatic confrontation with the U.S.S.R. Terrified at first, they eventually settled down, working out a very profitable *modus vivendi* for Europe which, dominated by a sort of Franco-German condominium, was conquering almost the entire Soviet and Eastern European market.

Anita emphasized an important point: France was the only European country that still had a man as President. His name was Emmanuel Defromont. He would be eighty-eight years old in a month. Naturally, we Americans found him a bit on the old side. But, in times of crisis, France always liked to put elderly men in command. When Clemenceau took power in 1917, he was seventy-six. Pétain became head of state at eighty-four, and De Gaulle stepped down at seventy-nine. Gerontophilia, Anita stressed, was one of France's most constant political traditions.

When the epidemic broke out in France, it coincided with the presidential elections, and Defromont was elected on the strength of political experience and age. Hardly had he been elected when he dissolved the Chamber of Deputies and set up new elections. But he wouldn't allow the representatives to choose their own substitutes. He left that to the voters from each electoral district. That way, in each district, there were two representatives completely independent of each other, one male and the other female, the latter generally representing a more conservative line than the former. The wily Defromont was banking on this result. He knew quite well that he had only a narrow voting margin in the Chamber and he hoped that, as the males died out, his majority (becoming increasingly female) would grow larger. Defromont was fully aware of the fact that the cult of the father had remained engrained in Frenchwomen since De Gaulle.

Everything went just the way he'd planned. Head of a presidential regime and backed by an unconditional majority, Defromont eventually gained as many powers as Bedford. But he didn't use them in the same way. He didn't touch individual freedoms and respected, in particular, freedom of the press. The newspapers dragged him through the mud, however, unfairly criticizing everything that he did, including the Draconian (but quite effective) measures that he'd taken to stem the spread of the epidemic in France.

Physically, Defromont was tall, broad-shouldered, majestic, his hair white and wavy, with a snowy beard. Actually, he looked like God or, at any rate, like the image we have of him. But he was also very French, having a marked liking for good food, fine wines, women, quotations from classical writers and speech-making. Yet he loved all that with moderation, and he made this moderation the yardstick for his views. Hence, his pronounced antipathy for Bedford.

For Defromont, the American President represented crowning immoderation and the height of excess. In private, he always recalled that time in Bedford's career when she'd marched down 14th Street in Washington with a sign proclaiming that she was a lesbian. It wasn't that Defromont, a clever Hellenist, nourished any hostility toward homosexuals; on the contrary, he'd abolished the ordinance of 1945, which, in France, made it possible to persecute them. But he found it extremely bad taste to run around proclaiming one's sexual choices in the street. "Just imagine, Constance," he said to his wife, "just imagine Napoleon parading down the streets of his hometown carrying a sign that said, 'I love blow jobs!' Even the Corsicans wouldn't have taken him seriously!"

We learned these details from Mme. Defromont's maid. This agent's name was Agnes. She was of the utmost service to us, but, as time went on, she became attached to the old fellow, confessed everything, went over to his side and gave us tons of false information.

When it was found that, statistically, France had suffered proportionately far fewer losses of male life than the United States since the outbreak of Encephalitis 16 and even fewer than the other European countries, Defromont—without waiting for the end of the epidemic—began saying that he'd saved France and, not satisfied with looking like God, he eventually became convinced that he *was* God, although retaining his sense of humor and his gift for history. Clever with that, Anita said. Defromont "sold" a certain image of France to all her neighbors, and he managed to convince them of his country's superiority in all matters. Even the Germans had now been convinced and followed his footsteps. In short, what was good for France was good for Europe! And if things went on at the rate they were going, Defromont (by dint of his style) would succeed in making a European Europe under the aegis of France (a prospect that wasn't very heartening for us).

So there was already a latent conflict between us and Defromont. Strangely enough, it erupted over Cuba.

When the epidemic began to wreak havoc among U.S. troops, Bedford withdrew them from Guantánamo, the base in Cuba the United States had obtained at the beginning of the century, after occupying the island militarily for four years. This withdrawal, Bedford emphasized, was temporary, not implying any decision on the part of the U.S. to give up its rights. But Fidel Castro didn't see it that way, of course. He'd been demanding the return of this portion of his territory since 1959, and, as soon as the base was abandoned, he had it occupied by the revolutionary armed forces. Bedford protested that he was violating the treaty of 1903 and that, at the very least, the base had to remain demilitarized.

Fidel Castro replied with a speech given on the Plaza de la

Revolucíon in Havana, at the foot of the column dedicated to the memory of José Martí. He said that he was quite familiar with the "monster" (he was referring to the United States) although he hadn't lived, like José Martí, "in its entrails"; accordingly, he was quite familiar with its rapaciousness. He emphasized that it was quite possible to change Presidents every four years in the United States, put in a man with blond hair instead of a man with dark hair, a tall one instead of a short one, that you could even change his sex (laughter), but there was one thing that couldn't be changed: *"El imperialismo yanqui!"* (Tremendous ovation.)

Fidel Castro, who, on that day, felt very tired, having just recovered from the flu, spoke only four hours. His conclusion was firm and clever: In reoccupying Guantánamo, he had merely reestablished Cuba's sovereignty over a trace of Cuban soil. But, at the same time, he announced (not without solemnity) that, henceforth, the base at Guantánamo would not be rented or loaned to any foreign power, even if it were a friend of Cuba.

This promise, which answered our concerns, was aimed at the U.S.S.R. and was intended to reassure the Pentagon, but the Pentagon didn't take anyone's word, not even its own. It urged Bedford to make reprisals against the Cuban leader. And Bedford might not have made them if (unfortunately for the doves in her Cabinet) one of our agents in Havana hadn't managed to send us a tape recording of Castro's speech.

Bedford had listened to it and a simultaneous interpretation. As Cuba was an island, it was more easily protected than the rest of Latin America against the epidemic, and judging by the clamor of the crowd at Havana, it was obvious that great masses of men remained there. The screaming of these enraged males had a disastrous effect on Bedford. She was terrified by Castro's voice, by the hypervirility that it gave off; what's more, she was horrified by the joke he'd made on her sex and the hearty laughs with which it was met by that gathering of phallocrats. So she gave the go-ahead signal on the Pentagon's plan for bombing Cuba "to get them to negotiate in earnest."

"I tried to show her," Anita said, "the stupidity of that move, but it was no use. After all, Guantánamo was Cuban and we hadn't done anything when China had reoccupied Formosa. Once more, we would be accused of sparing big countries and attacking small ones. But after hearing the voices of Castro and the Cubans, Bedford fell prey to an antimale hysteria that I could no longer control. She overrode my advice with all the consequences that I'd foreseen. The U.S. Air Force lost half its pilots. Havana became a martyr city, Fidel Castro a hero, and the whole world protested, except England, which was afraid that Spain might use the precedent of Guantánamo to take back Gibraltar—something that Spain actually did afterward, without firing a shot."

The most vehement of the protests against the bombing of Havana was Defromont's. Although he was a visceral anti-Communist, he had a fondness for Castro. Under that Marxist crust, Defromont saw a fellow Latin persecuted by the Anglo-Saxons, just as Joan of Arc had been by the English and De Gaulle by the Americans. On top of that, Defromont had kept a certain freshness of emotion. He liked to express himself, and he had the talent to do it. In contrast with American Presidents, who generally avail themselves of a brain trust in writing their speeches, French Presidents are traditionally hard-working, loaded with culture and overflowing with eloquence. Defromont wrote his speeches by hand. He committed them to memory and gave them with overwhelming majesty, surrounded by lightning like Moses in the Sinai. His advanced age had in no way detracted from his pungency, and he delivered a scathing diatribe against Bedford, one that was reprinted verbatim in newspapers all over the world, including those that pretended to condemn it. As everyone knows, when an American President gets an international slap in the face, his closest allies secretly delight in it.

But, after all, a speech is only a speech, and the affair wouldn't have gone further than an exchange of nasty letters between diplomats if someone in the Pentagon hadn't made an astonishing move. It must be said in their defense that the Pentagon generals had been living in despair and frustration since the outbreak of the epidemic. They had at their disposal the most sophisticated weaponry in the world and would soon have no one left to operate it. The strength of the three branches of the armed forces was dwindling with each passing day, and the generals themselves were dying twice as fast as the civilians—perhaps, ventured Anita, because not being busy any more, their spermatogenesis was more active.

One thing, at any rate, is certain: It was absolutely without the consent of and unbeknownst to President Bedford, the Secretary of Defense and the three chiefs of staff of the Pentagon that an Air Force general ordered a mini-raid on Havana by three planes, in the course of which the French embassy was destroyed by a laser bomb and the ambassador killed.

From France, Defromont unleashed thunder and lightning. He gave a second diatribe against the United States in which he spoke of a "barbarous attack," "war crimes," "premeditated murder." Rather cleverly, however—or perhaps because he'd been well informed—he didn't try to blame Bedford for the second bombing and confined himself to demanding apologies, reparations and punishment of those who were guilty.

My advice, Anita said, was to give satisfaction to the terrible old man. After all, as Cuban antiaircraft had gunned down all three planes, the men who'd flown the mission were already dead and, as for the ones who'd given the orders, they probably wouldn't be long in joining the pilots in the Hereafter, as the Pentagon grew increasingly depopulated with each passing day.

Once again, Bedford didn't take my advice. As a woman, she was afraid of making herself a laughingstock by admitting that one of her military men had gone over her head and waged a personal war against France. In vain, I pointed out to her that, since Truman's time, no American President had managed to get himself obeyed completely by his generals and that all the embassies in the world were perfectly aware of this little weakness in our Executive. Bedford preferred to cover the Pentagon and got herself bogged down in childish fibs: The second bombing had taken place as a "protective reaction" to prevent a raid by Castro's air force on Miami. Furthermore, the French embassy had, in all probability, been destroyed by a spent SAM missile that had missed its target. Thereupon, with a forced laugh, she'd offered her "regrets."

Defromont gave a third speech in which he'd denounced

disdainfully the White House's preposterous version, a speech that exceeded the two earlier ones in virulence. But, this time, he didn't confine himself to speaking. He recalled his ambassador, made it known to the U.S. ambassador in Paris that his presence in that capital was no longer desirable, imposed a visa on American visitors in France, nationalized those French companies whose capital was in U.S. hands, and closed American centers in French territory. Judging by the speed with which these two last measures were carried out, Defromont must have been planning them for a long time—the first one for reasons of economic independence, the second because our cultural centers in France had been disseminating Deborah Grimm's ideology—rather tactlessly, it must be said. We were aware—from one of Agnes's reports—that her philosophy "turned the old man's stomach."

With that, another agent of ours, one in Ottawa, managed to get us photocopies of letters exchanged by Defromont and the Prime Minister of Canada. The letters left us stupefied.

The name of the Canadian Premier, of French-Canadian ancestry, was Colette Lagrafeuille. In his first letter Defromont confided to her that, in the past, he had known a young Frenchwoman by that name, with whom he had unfortunately lost touch, and that he'd tried vainly to find her again, that he cherished her memory and that for this reason and on the basis of her name alone, the Canadian Premier already meant a great deal to him—besides, of course, the long-standing, historic bonds that connected France and the province of Quebec, which was the birthplace of the lady to whom he was writing. Coming from such a famous and venerable statesman, these words greatly touched the Premier, and despite the enormous age difference (or perhaps because of it) a correspondence sprang up in which, imperceptibly, Defromont slipped from confidence to compliment, from compliment to suggestion and from suggestion to counsel.

This warm contact bore its fruits: When the bombing of the French embassy in Havana occurred, Lagrafeuille unhesitatingly fell in line with the protesters, sided with Defromont in his subsequent quarrel with Bedford and began by refusing to extradite American "stags" who were taking refuge on her territory in ever-increasing numbers. On this occasion I learned from Anita that, contrary to Deborah Grimm's biased statements, the stags weren't all corrupt men—far from it. Actually, they were young men who had merely taken refuge in the country to escape the ravages of the urban epidemic.

In short, Anita went on, the situation outside was disastrous. In Latin America and Asia, we'd lost our bases, our protected governments, our raw materials and our markets. China had recovered Taiwan, and Japan was drawing closer to China, the latter having settled its differences with the U.S.S.R. As to Europe, under Defromont's influence it had isolated itself from us and was tightening its bonds. Still worse, at our borders Canada, chafing more than ever over the issue of her independence, was showing us obvious ill will.

"This is the background," Anita concluded, "of my ambassadorship in Paris with Defromont. Bedford has finally taken the course that I recommended and, considering that Defromont was one of the keys to the situation, I was assigned the task of making peace with him . . ."

Abruptly, in the middle of the sentence, Anita closed her eyes and fell asleep. I asked her a question, but she didn't answer. The light didn't seem to bother her. Her face, in the brilliance of the lamp, was relaxed and her breathing serene. And those were the last words and the last image that I would have of Anita. She'd warned me that she was leaving the next morning at 6:00 A.M., that she wouldn't even stay for breakfast, that we wouldn't have time to talk again.

I experienced mingled feelings. And, most of all, immense relief. I understood why the news from abroad had vanished from our newspapers. The collective hysteria that we were living at Blueville was a local phenomenon, a kind of witch hunt extended to a whole sex, one more manifestation of our tendency toward Manicheism. Throughout our history we have always chosen to incarnate the principle of evil, turning it into a scapegoat and persecuting it. Now, under the reign of Bedford and her clique, the devil became men. But this madness hadn't really gone beyond our borders. Bedford hadn't been able to spread it.

At the same time, I was indulging in rather painful reflections on my personal destiny. I'd have preferred Anita to leave me in some other way than with a report on the top-level political deals she'd gotten herself into. I'd have preferred a simpler goodbye, a few words more at my level. Perhaps I wasn't precisely her husband, but I'd been her friend. Six years of close ties could have ended on a more human note.

I had indeed seen her quiver a moment before—not with emotion but with impatience at the thought of the great role that she would play with Defromont. I had no trouble imagining that she was vibrating with the desire to charm the older charmer and meet his cunning halfway. She slept beside me, but actually she wasn't there any more. She was totally wrapped up in the more exciting future. As to me, there was no use hiding it from myself: I'd already fallen into the trash cans of her biography.

To sleep, I took a tranquilizer. The next morning, when the first siren woke me, I found no sign of Anita. She'd gone away without saying goodbye. It was easier that way, I had to admit. Once again I admired the way she simplified her life.

My head was heavy. I had a bitter taste in my mouth and a disgust for living that a cold shower couldn't remedy. I shaved and went back to dress in my room. I looked at that room as if I'd never seen it before. It was as empty as it could be.

I was ready well ahead of my usual schedule, but, strangely enough, Dave was ready too. Together, we headed down the path to the cafeteria. Between the barracks we walked abreast of each other, a yard apart and, as usual, without speaking. It was warm. The sky was low and overcast, and the sun wouldn't come out.

A hundred yards from the castle—I later realized that it had taken him all that time to make up his mind—Dave said, "Has she left?"

"Yes. Very early this morning."

A silence. I looked at his delicate face and the big dark lashes lowered against his cheek.

"Is she going to come back?" he asked hoarsely.

I was dumfounded by his question and by the intuition that it implied. The uneasiness in his voice didn't reflect his own feelings. He didn't like Anita. I glanced at him, but he didn't lift his eyes. He walked on, his profile motionless, a yard from me, lengthening his stride to keep up with me.

"No," I answered after a while.

No reaction. Not a look. Not a flutter of lashes. And having said this "no," everything seemed even more negative, including the suffocating layer of clouds that weighed heavily on our heads.

We were twenty yards from the castle. I hadn't seen Dave shorten the distance separating us. And all at once, slipping into my right hand, I felt his hand, small and warm. I squeezed. I didn't look at Dave. It was useless; he wouldn't have said anything. I adjusted my stride to his. We walked on together.

8

Anita left me in my sleep at 6:00 A.M. on Thursday. Two hours later, at the second blast of the siren, I was at the lab. And that's when there was a happening, the importance of which I sensed without fully grasping its implications. I found the following note on my desk:

BE CAREFUL. THIS MORNING, BETWEEN 7:25 AND 7:30 A.M., THE BUGGING DEVICE IN YOUR ROOM WAS CHECKED OR CHANGED. BURN THIS.

THE PORCUPINE

The note was printed in capital letters, but, at first sight, I knew who'd written it. "The Porcupine" was the nickname that I gave Burage during our quarrels. And Burage's room, in the single women's barracks, faced mine. That morning, earlier than usual, I'd left my quarters at 7:20 A.M. I'd been ahead of my usual schedule—that's why I noticed the time. Just as I left my quarters someone must have reported my departure to the technician of the monitoring department. From her window Burage had observed her arrival, her presence in my room and the length of time she stayed, useful information in determining the importance of what the technician might have done.

Not much, in all likelihood, since her stay lasted only five minutes. But I would have to make sure of that, since I'd been advised to do so. For the key to my quarters there was no problem—the cleaning department had a duplicate.

If this note was from Burage, I arrived at a conclusion, which, all things considered, was hardly astonishing. Burage had a key to my office at the lab. Arriving at the cafeteria a few minutes after me, she must have left more quickly, written her warning, placed it on my desk and locked the door behind her.

One thing astonished me: Why write to me instead of speaking to me? Because of the bug in my office? But Burage had never seemed to fear it. Whenever she came looking for a fight, she never in any way concealed the personal note that she injected in our relations. If Burage—supposing that it had been her—had run risks to warn me, they were limited risks. At any rate, not many minutes could have elapsed between her arrival at the laboratory and mine, and from her office she could have watched the door of mine to be certain that no third party had a third key (a highly unlikely hypothesis).

There was still the motive. Why would Burage, who acted in the lab like a woman trusted by the authorities in Blueville, have betrayed her bosses to warn me?

The simplest, most romantic and most stereotyped answer was that she loved me. I wasn't conceited enough to believe that. But I know that Burage was interested in me. Certainly, her interest wasn't strong enough to make her betray her side. She wasn't the type. Not at all. I didn't know how to back up this hunch, but I sensed Burage's total loyalty to the choices that she had made.

Then, was that warning a trap? Why would Burage set a trap for me? Since our big showdown and, to a great extent, thanks to her, the team had grown closer knit. The lab was running; we were making progress in our research. And between Burage and me, there was more than the physical complicity that I've described. There were solid bonds, born out of our work.

My first impulse was to call Burage, to show her the note and ask her for an explanation. I thought better of it. There were two things I had to check.

That morning, when I left the lab at noon, I stopped off at my place. I locked my bedroom door, drew my curtains, got down on my knees beside my bed and, without touching anything, ran my eyes as closely as I could over the piece of wallboard that I usually removed in order to disconnect the bug. It was attached by a nylon thread glued partly on the removable section, partly on the continuous wallboard. Certainly, I could foil the trap and glue the thread back on after having removed the panel. But there might be a second trap concealed under the first. What's more, I was almost sure that the schedule of my visits would henceforth be recorded, and I wanted to avoid turning Mr. Barrow's suspicions into certainties.

At any rate, one point seemed sure: The person who'd written me the note was telling the truth: The monitoring department had stopped off in my bedroom.

Never had an afternoon seemed longer than that one, separating me from an appointment I'd made with Joan Pierce for that evening. Finally, there I was. She was delighted. She swooped down on me as she would on some prey. With her beak and her talons, she got ready to poke through me and extract from my head all the news about Anita and the world that it might hold even (who could tell?) without my knowing it. But I stopped her with a wave. Without saying a word, I handed her the warning that I'd received that morning. It was a complete mystery to her, for I'd never spoken to her about the Porcupine. She read it, and as soon as she was finished I handed her (still without speaking) an office memo signed "Burage," which I'd brought from the lab. Among her many talents, all of which focused on knowing everything about her fellow mortals, was graphology. She threw herself on the two documents and devoured them.

"Why, of course, it's the same person," she said at once in her rapid way. "She hasn't even tried to disguise her handwriting. She's confined herself to printing capital letters. But, at any rate, as the capitals of her cursive script are printed, that's no disguise. Look at the initial 'B' in the office memo: 'Bacterial colonies for Dr. Martinelli.' It's the same 'B,' and it's highly characteristic. The transversal bar goes way out to the right of the second down stroke. That's a sign of an energetic, dynamic personality. Sit down, Ralph. Why the Porcupine?"

I told her. She burst out laughing, threatening me with a scolding finger, but made no other comment. I told her how my own bug had been boobytrapped and I asked her if I could trust Burage.

"Absolutely," she replied. And transfixing me with her keen eyes, she added, "You're making progress, Ralph. At last, you're coming out of your personal cocoon. And you're becoming cautious."

I let that remark and its implications go by. I went on: "Why should I trust Burage to that point? You're basing what you've said solely on that analysis of handwriting, aren't you?"

"No."

The "no" came quickly, decisively. But Joan Pierce wouldn't say any more about it. Right away she began questioning me. I left out my personal relations with my visitor of the night, but, aside from that, I told her everything about the international situation, just as Anita had described it to me. Joan Pierce listened to me with an excitement that she could barely control. Her eyes sparkled, her breathing grew rapid, her hands opened and closed in her lap. The minute I stopped, she would ask questions. Her speech was clipped, fast, tense. And while I spoke, she made a continual, mechanical movement with her fingers, as though she were storing up greedily all the data that I gave her.

When I finished she got to her feet excitedly and, parading her tall, skinny frame around the room, said with pent-up eagerness, "That's excellent! It confirms all the little bits of information we were able to gather!"

I was struck by that "we." Pierce watched me out of the corner of her eye as she walked and caught my surprise. She followed up with "Yes, all that confirms everything Reginald and I have been thinking"—a remark that baffled me, as I was well aware that Joan left "poor Reginald," as she used to say, completely out of matters that intrigued her. That "we" didn't refer to the Pierce couple, I was sure of it. She stopped and looked at me.

"Ralph, one question."

"All the questions that you want, but, please, stop that pacing up and down—and, Joan, not the rocking chair either!"

Pierce sat down on a chair with a quick laugh.

"Still feeling funny, Ralph? Well, that's just what I meant to ask you: How do you feel now that Anita's left?"

"Pretty good."

"What do you mean—'pretty good'?"

"I admit that it really bothered me at the time. But I felt liberated afterward. And why shouldn't I tell you so? Tonight I feel immensely relieved at the idea that I won't have to wait for her any more."

A silence. Her bright and prying eyes fastened themselves on my face.

"Ralph, one more question. Has Anita left you for keeps?"

"As far as I'm concerned, yes."

"Do you mean that even if she came back to you in a year or two . . ."

"No. I'd never agree to her coming back. You see, Joan, I realized something this morning: I don't think much of Anita any more."

A silence. Joan said, her sharp eyes planted into mine, "Are you angry at her because she's putting her career ahead of you?"

"Oh, no! I could understand that very well. No, what I find fault with about Anita is that she goes on working for a tyranny and, what's worse, for a tyranny whose ideology she doesn't even approve of. Oh, I know the excuse she gives herself. Staying at Bedford's side, she's trying to limit the damage. But that's the excuse every opportunist uses. The fact is, Anita's basically cynical. She's repudiating her whole philosophy of life. Why? For an ambassador's post!"

Pierce straightened up and, with both hands in her lap, looked at me.

"At last!" she said. Her hands fluttered over her shoulders. "At last, Ralph, the blindfold has fallen from your eyes! At last you see the situation for what it really is!"

I raised my brows. "But, whenever we've talked, you've always defended Anita."

"That was all put on. I wasn't going to get into a quarrel with you! I wanted you to find out for yourself. And now you've done it. You've turned the corner. You've gotten out of Anita's clutches. It was an awful stain on your reputation, let me tell you. And you've washed it out." She went on triumphantly: "I've always had confidence in you, Ralph. I've always said that one of these days you'd see through her. Nice going, Ralph. Finally, we're going to be able to work with you!"

Again, I noticed that "we." I also noticed that, this time, Pierce didn't bother to camouflage it.

She leaned forward and said rapidly, "Listen, Ralph, you've been here twenty minutes. That means that with the bug connected again, we're going to have to make chitchat for another twenty minutes. It's too much. And I'm still running the risk that somebody noticed the time when you entered my place and let the monitoring service know right away. If that were the case, they couldn't help but notice the blank section on the tape and my bug, which is also boobytrapped." She resumed: "Ralph, time is flying. I'm going to ask two things of you: From now on, don't take any action without consulting me."

"Action? What do you mean by that?"

"For example, writing a letter of refusal to the Federal Sperm Bank."

"What? You know about that?"

"Of course."

"I haven't said anything about it to you."

"Nothing secret. I simply heard about it through Mutsch, who got it from Stien."

A pause.

"Is Mutsch one of the people that I can trust?"

Pierce shook her head from left to right.

"Mutsch herself is entirely trustworthy, Ralph. Unfortunately, she's given herself away and they've got her under close watch."

"She's given herself away?"

Pierce laughed, her sharp little laugh so much like the cry of a sea gull.

"Oh, Ralph, you're not cut out for living under a dictatorship! Do you remember when I stopped you from contradicting Ruth Jettison? Mutsch went ahead and did it."

"Yes, certainly. I remember. Mutsch was terrific!"

"Mutsch was terrific, but she fell into a trap. Ruth Jettison's phony sermon reeked of provocation. It was intended to get Blueville's resisters out into the open."

I was stunned. I felt completely lost. Had I really understood anything of what was going on in Blueville? It looked as though I'd made one mistake after another—mistakes in judgment, interpretation, behavior. My resignations, for instance, that I was so proud of!"

I went on: "How did I do the wrong thing in turning down the Federal Sperm Bank?"

Pierce gave a quick smile. "You haven't done anything wrong. You've done something foolhardy."

I said, a bit offended, "To hear you, foolhardiness is my main trait."

"Not exactly. You just don't think things over enough."

Thanks. A little oil after all that vinegar.

"But . . .?"

"You're too spontaneous."

"And that's a fault?"

"It's a fault *here.*"

"And was my letter of refusal a mistake?"

"Not a mistake in itself, Ralph. But a tactical error. Don't forget that fighting means exposing yourself. You mustn't fight over a minor point—above all, when it's a point on which you don't stand a chance of winning."

Since I didn't "think things over enough," I thought things over. And it all came to me in a flash. She was right. Deep down, I'd never believed that Mulberry would buy my objections. Stien hadn't believed his would work either. I could have sworn to it. We'd been acting like children, the two of us. We had put up token resistance. How futile it had been to fight! How stupid! I looked at her. "Then Jespersen was the only realist among the three of us?"

Pierce's face grew gloomy. Her lips were pressed together, her hands tightened.

"Oh, Jespersen!"

She didn't say any more about it, but she'd said enough. I received this new warning in amazement. She got to her feet.

"Excuse me, Ralph. I'm a bit pressed for time."

"But you had two things to tell me. And you've only told me one of them."

She looked at me with a little smile and I thought, it's impossible. I look as though I'm asking her for instructions. By any chance was I already part of "we"?

"When you've got a little more to tell me, Ralph, don't come here. Go through the Porcupine."

I couldn't believe my ears, and I said, "Burage?"

"Use her nickname since only the three of us know it."

"But, Joan, there's a bugging problem in my office at the lab, too."

She smiled. "Let me tell you, that bug has never existed."

Friday morning at eight o'clock I found Dr. Mulberry's reply on my desk. It was what I'd expected. Yet it contained a surprising detail, one that might have shocked me if I hadn't managed to retain a few shreds of my sense of humor, even in Blueville.

> Dear Dr. Martinelli,
>
> I can easily eliminate the objections that you have raised on moral grounds. The team we are sending to Blueville will be made up of a driver and a female sample-taker. You need only deal with her. In this way, there will be no automanipulation or homosexuality.
>
> I'm counting on you not to raise further objections to something that each male citizen should see as a patriotic duty having absolute priority.
>
> I expect a note by return mail from you confirming your acceptance.
>
> Sincerely yours, etc.

I suppose that it was better to laugh than to feel humiliated. And thrown into the bargain, what was I to think of the "sample-taker" who would be having such brief, intimate relations with me? Was she a nurse? Had she received *ad hoc* training? Had she volunteered for this very special assignment? Or, on the contrary, had she been compelled to perform it in the name of a "patriotic duty having absolute priority"?

I called Burage into my office, knowing beforehand what she

was going to advise me to do. But I hoped to capitalize on the talk to ask her some questions.

There she was, responding at once to the intercom, despite the fact that she was above me in the chain of command and doubly so: by virtue of the status of women in the new era and also by virtue of our new relationship within "we."

She certainly didn't look as though she believed in her superiority. There she was, pleasingly small, well rounded and modest, noiselessly closing the door behind her and awaiting my "instructions," a file folder under her arm as a pretext for seeing me.

I handed her Mulberry's letter and, while she read it, as a lock of hair that I'd have liked to touch fell over her eye, I looked at her with new eyes. I noticed mace-shaped earrings that I couldn't remember seeing before. In spite of her dark auburn hair, which, like Anita's, was opulent, Burage didn't resemble my ex-wife. Her eyes weren't green but blue. Her nose wasn't aquiline but round. Her chin was round, too, but firm. I feared that, up to then, I'd paid too much attention to her features and not enough to her expression. That day, for the first time, in the light of "we," I made an effort to "see" Burage without taking her physical attraction into account. And what struck me just then in that face wasn't its intelligence. In her forehead, in her cheekbones, in the line of her jaw, in the expression of her eyes, in the curl of her lips—as sensual and enticing as they were—I read undeniable vigor. All right. I had to make up my mind to go beyond the prejudices of our society and henceforth associate the idea of femininity with the idea of strength.

Burage handed back the letter and said impassively, "The fact that they've got a female sample-taker proves that they've already run into P.M.s with the same objections as yours."

"Do you know Stien's objections?"

"Of course. And I also know Mulberry's reply. Stien got it yesterday. I'll summarize it for you: 'Dear Professor Stienemeier, according to the rabbis that we have consulted, you are sticking to the letter of Chapter thirty-eight of Genesis and are overlooking the spirit of it. The sin of Onan was voluntary sterility. The operation that our department has in mind will, on the contrary, increase your fertility, and, since you are married, the manipulation can be done by your wife. The female sample-taker need only come in to collect the semen in the test tubes.'''

A silence. It seemed to me that all this could have been said in another way—who knows, even with a bit of a smile. After all, the absurd isn't necessarily Kafkaesque—it can also be funny. I mean, the idea of consulting rabbis! No, Burage, her file folder under her arm, her arms crossed waist high, looked at me without seeing me, and not one of her features moved. I felt myself being overcome by her coldness little by little, and I said, my brow lifted, "And now?"

"And now you'll say yes by return mail to that appeal from the fatherland."

She said that without batting an eyelash, without even seeming to perceive the irony of the expression.

"What about Stien?"

"Rita will advise him to agree."

"'Rita'?"

"That's the name we've given to our mutual friend."

I looked at her. No doubt about it, I was in "we." Was that the reason why I found myself suddenly with this block of ice? To make me understand, once and for all, that she was in command?

I resumed after a moment: "Burage, I'd like to ask you a few questions."

She looked at her watch and replied curtly, "I've got five minutes. After that, we'd better talk about this file."

"I'll make it brief. Where does the bug in my office end up?"

"In mine."

A little silence followed to enable me to recuperate.

"So you can erase the tape?"

"When and where I want."

"Second question: How does it happen that Barrow and Company trusts you?"

"I've been an activist in Women's Lib for a long time."

I jumped. "You're a Women's Libber?"

"You didn't think I was the type?"

"No, as a matter of fact."

A silence and I resumed: "Perhaps I'm stupid, but I don't understand any more."

"It's quite simple: I'm a Women's Libber, but I'm absolutely against anti-male sexism, the war of the sexes and the taboo on marriage."

"But that's Anita's position!"

Burage frowned, her blue eyes blazed, and she said with immense contempt, "There's a big difference. I'm fighting Bedford. Your ex-wife is serving her."

"Yes, I know. I realized that," I replied after a moment.

"A little late."

Rather severe, that Burage.

"True. As Rita says, I had trouble getting out of my personal cocoon."

I allowed myself a little laugh that she didn't echo. She resumed: "So that everything is clear for you, Doctor, I'd like to explain: I'm a Libber, but I'm against Women's Lib as Bedford sees it, and I'm very much against Bedford as a dictator."

"Well, I agree, as you must know."

"I'm pleased about that," she replied coldly. "Everything is going to become much easier."

I went on after a moment: "Are you ready to talk to me about 'we'?"

"Why? You know our aim."

"I'd like to talk about people."

She said curtly, "In Blueville, you'll deal only with Rita and myself."

I looked at her. This was much as to say that the cells of the clandestine movement had been rigidly partitioned so that the destruction of one might not bring on the destruction of all.

I resumed: "Of us three—are you the leader?"

"Yes. But you still have the right to express your point of view."

I already sensed that this right was purely theoretical.

"One more question, Burage: Let's say that Bedford's been neutralized. What's the ultimate goal of the movement?"

"To reestablish the *status quo ante*, except with regard to the condition of women."

"Why such a modest goal?"

"To have the broadest base possible."

"And is it broad?"

"It's growing every day. Even in Congress."

Now there was something that could give me a little hope. So the docility of the Congress "widows" was no longer as unconditional as it had been. But what could Congress actually do? Impeach the President? To be sure, that had already happened in our history. On the other hand, when the President was a dictator, did it stand to reason that he would let himself be judged without using force against his judges?

"Just one more minute," said Burage.

That Burage really treated me highhandedly. And still with the file folder under her arm, that cold, impersonal look. A model employee who was dictating her orders to me.

"One final question, Burage: From now on, will your behavior with me always be the way it is today?"

"Yes."

Her eyes transparent, her tone neutral, her attitude self-effacing.

"So no more quarrels?"

"No."

I smiled. "I'm going to miss them." No response to my smile. I said rather awkwardly, "No more quarrels? Why?"

Feelings that I couldn't unravel softened her gaze.

"Quarrels aren't necessary any more, Doctor, since I trust you now and can openly express my feelings."

"Your feelings for me?" I asked, raising my brows.

"Please," she said curtly. "No hypocrisy. Don't pretend that you aren't aware of them."

I remained speechless.

"Must I spell them out?" she asked aggressively.

I didn't feel like speaking, but if I had felt like it, she wouldn't have given me the time.

"All right, Doctor, I want you," she said with extreme coldness.

I was flabbergasted. I wouldn't say that I blushed—but almost. And incredible as it seemed, I lowered my eyes!

Burage's reaction was unexpected. She laughed.

"Doctor," she said, "you are funny! You may have come out

of your personal cocoon, but you still haven't emerged from your phallocrat cocoon! Admit it, you're almost shocked because a woman took the initiative of telling a man that she wanted him. You'd rather have kept that male prerogative."

"No, as a matter of fact, I was more startled than anything else. You understand, it was the first time. But, all the same, it's very nice to hear something like that. Especially when the feeling is mutual."

Anger hardened Burage's blue eyes, and she said with murderous irony, "Oh, so you want me?"

"You know perfectly well."

Another laugh, only this time very close to a sneer.

"But it's very different with you, Doctor. You're like a stallion in a corral. You want all the mares that have been penned up with you! Mrs. Barrow! Crawford! Pussy! Me!"

Nobody was going to great pains to spare my dignity that day. For Dr. Mulberry I was a bull in an insemination center, and for Burage a stallion in a pasture. It was my day for animal comparisons.

I wasn't going to deny the facts. It was obvious that my least little look in Blueville had been watched, caught, weighed; that "Rita" and the "Porcupine" had commented on them. Well, that's the price Puritan societies must pay; the people in them are only interested in sex.

"Well, when someone is polygamous in thought only," I said, "he can afford to be selective. But there's one remark that I'd like to make."

The derisive laughter was over now. Burage's face became serious once more and she looked at me in apparent serenity. Yet I thought, judging by the very, very slight quivering of her earrings, that she had sensed what I was going to tell her.

"Burage," I said, "if the stallion, as you say, could get out of his corral, I know which mare he'd choose."

She didn't flutter her lashes and replied coldly, "Does that hot air come from the book of sexist seduction?"

"Not at all."

A silence. She considered me with her transparent eyes, not speaking. Then her look changed. I sensed that she believed me and that a wave of emotion had passed over her. But it all happened in a second. Her face hardened again, and when she spoke, her words burst on her lips, one after another, with a force that amazed me.

"Listen, Doctor, let's get this straight once and for all. As long as we're together inside the Blueville compound, there won't be anything. Do you understand—nothing. Not so much as a kiss, not a hand touching another hand, no brushing up against me, no looks." She added, "For the time being, we have a job to do, that's all."

On the morning of June 3 Burage chose a slack time to give me her instructions. She had listened to the bimonthly report on our research that I'd recorded and then given to her on tape. She found it overly optimistic—not in itself but tactically. I should stay well within our actual progress in reports intended for Mr. Barrow. I objected that I wasn't the only one who could analyze our findings. Dr. Grabel also . . .

Burage interrupted me. "No danger. Dr. Grabel won't talk."

I looked at her. Was Dr. Grabel one of "we"? He was an A! It was unbelievable.

I resumed: "If I have to do my report over from scratch, I'd at least like to know your tactical reason."

"Well, we don't know how Helsingforth is going to react when the vaccine becomes ready for use. It's going to raise problems for her. After all, you must admit that the vaccine doesn't quite fit the Bedford line. We'd like to keep one jump ahead of Bedford so she doesn't make a move that catches us napping."

That reminded me of something Anita had confided to me: When she returned from Blueville, she brought back to Bedford a sealed envelope containing reports on the work of Stien and Jespersen that Barrow had entrusted to her. Never my reports.

I told that to Burage. She seemed struck by it. And what struck her wasn't so much the White House's apathy for my research (it was to be expected) as the keen interest shown in the "projects" of my colleagues.

Burage drew a deep breath. "Doctor, it's absolutely necessary that you find out what Stien is doing."

I frowned. "You're raising a touchy question there. Stien and I have both been sworn to secrecy."

"By whom?"

"Helsingforth."

"Does that commit you?" asked Burage disdainfully.

"Not since I've joined you people. But Stien doesn't know what your aims are. He's not going to understand my curiosity. Perhaps he'll even find it suspect."

"If he refused to give you the information, is he the kind who'd write up a report on you?"

"Oh, no! The thought of it would horrify him!"

"Well, then, Doctor, go ahead, we haven't got time to waste with scruples."

Burage looked as if she meant business. While she spoke she kept an enormous distance between us. In her two capacities: model employee and political leader. I felt as if I was talking to a dummy behind the glass of a show window, glass half an inch thick. Except, however, you don't see a dummy breathe. And Burage breathed, a very perceptible phenomenon owing to the fullness of her bosom. Another familiar sign: the little quivering of her earrings. Burage, your earrings have gone over to my side. They betrayed you to my profit. My profit! That's saying a lot. But it was nice, all the same, to sense a fire smoldering under the dust of that volcano.

Stien, whom I'd arranged to meet at Pierce's after lunch that same day, came in very distrustfully. Despite the sun, which was actually quite weak, he kept on his old-fashioned black overcoat (it was very long; I suspected that it dated back to the Second World War) in Johnny's room, where Pierce received us. He also retained his greenish, bullet-riddled Tyrolean hat through which his long white locks escaped and a thick, red woolen scarf knitted by Mutsch. And I found him muffled up that way, sitting—or, rather, lying—in Joan Pierce's rocking chair, rocking furiously and cursing both the grippe that had laid him low and the weakness of my remedies. Buried under his hat, his scarf riding up to his ears, he looked like a big turtle that barely pokes its wrinkled head and its suspicious little eyes outside its shell, ready to pull everything back in at the slightest alarm.

Naturally, I took all the precautions in the world. My request was preceded by a highly sophisticated *captatio benevolentiae*. It wasn't vain curiosity on my part. And, still less, personal curiosity (Pierce threw me an uneasy glance; she found that I'd said enough about it) but after all, when you lived in conditions like ours ("prison camp inmates," as he'd put it himself), and when you were deprived of the right to inform yourself, any information that one of us might have and might pass on to the others became priceless, etc.

Stien let me talk without saying a word, his little blue eyes lurking in the folds of his eyelids and glancing quickly and angrily—now at Joan Pierce, then at me, then back to Joan. He rocked with frenzy, something that added to my uneasiness, and he knew it—he knew my idiosyncrasies. The more I spoke, the more he buried himself in his muffler and his hat, his neck sinking into his shoulders, retracted from head to foot. His keen eyes, disappearing and reappearing in the folds of his eyelids, stalked me without the tiniest glimmer of sympathy. The further I went, the more I sensed that I was heading toward defeat.

"Have you finished?" Stien asked, stopping the rocker.

"Yes."

"Well, listen."

Thereupon, he sneezed, took out his handkerchief and, between two sneezes, vehemently denounced physicians: a caste of pretentious ignoramuses who fooled around with heart transplants when they didn't even know how to prevent or cure the grippe.

Again, he blew his nose with an ostentatious, contemptuous noise, coughed, wiped his mouth and launched into a speech in which I was placed totally under indictment: my ethics, my very being, my conduct, my rashness, my—and I quote—"coarse and insatiable libido," my congenital imprudence, the inability I'd revealed (once again) to keep a promise or a secret—in short, my "incorrigible irresponsibility."

Although I was used to this kind of rhetoric and, with Stien, I always made allowances for chronic irritability and theatrics, this time I thought he was overdoing it, especially in front of Joan (who was reduced to silence by her amazement). I was hunting for my most caustic retort when, all of a sudden, getting up from the rocker with a sprightliness that his sprawling pause had never led me to expect, Stien bellowed, "Short and sweet, my answer is no, no and no!"

After this crescendo on the final "no," he gave me an abrupt smile and an enormous wink, strode rapidly to the little typewriter on which Joan Pierce was typing notes for her husband, sat down, pressed a few keys diligently, stood up again and, without looking at us, without a word of apology for Joan, whose page he'd just ruined, he turned his back on us and went away. The door slammed, and we saw him go by under the window, his hat pulled halfway down over his forehead and his muffler riding up to his eyes.

Pierce hopped over to the typewriter on her stilts and I followed her.

"Joan," I said, "if you've got a pair of scissors, will you . . ."

I motioned her to cut off the line that Stien had just written. She obeyed without a word. Although the text must have been obscure to her—it was an abridged reference to an issue of a monthly biology publication—I wasn't going to explain anything aloud. I was going to heed Stien's precautions, even if they seemed excessive. Perhaps he'd realized, as Joan Pierce maintained, that he was more closely watched than anyone, owing to Mutsch's clash with Ruth Jettison. Clearly, he no longer trusted even Pierce's disconnected bug.

I knew I could find the monthly in the castle's science library, and for the first time that afternoon, I waited impatiently to rush over there, once my day at the lab was over.

There were no call slips for periodicals. You could either consult them there or take one issue home, providing you left a green card on the shelf, showing your name and the date on which the periodical was borrowed. Obviously, I chose the first method, I found the reference with no trouble and I read the study that it designated, standing before a lectern without making notes. I had suspected as much: It was an article written by Stien himself two years earlier. It was quite short, about ten pages, but fascinating for me, for us—in the context of Blueville and the nation. I digested everything by scanning and I reread it more slowly and more closely, so that I would omit nothing the next morning when I made my report to Burage.

When I left the library I ran into Mr. Barrow. The expression "ran into" isn't the most fitting: It supposes something hard, rigid. But Mr. Barrow was flaccid and spongy. He didn't touch you; he sucked you in. He ensnared you with his oily eyes, his thick flabby lips, his nose that hung like a trunk. Slimy and metallic at the same time, his voice clung to your skin like molasses. His absolutely bare skull was as greasy as if he'd rubbed it with wax, and he loomed up before me in the corridor leading to the cafeteria, impassable and gelatinous. I might have tried to get through that jellyfish, but what would I look like when I reached the other side? I stopped, as if at the edge of a huge puddle of oil in a garage. Obviously, Mr. Barrow had something to tell me. And as soon as I became motionless, he said to me, without a preface, in a chaste and hushed murmur, "Dr. Martinelli, I presume you haven't forgotten that Dr. Mulberry's team should be coming to Blueville this evening. I thought it wise to ask him to schedule their arrival for an hour later than originally decided, so as to give their movements around the camp maximum discretion. For the same reasons, I decided that the operation should be done at each person's quarters and that you were to be treated last" (how I love that euphemism!) "in your quarters at nine o'clock. At that hour, if my memory serves me" (mainly, he relied on his bug, for I'd never told him anything of the sort), "Dave is asleep. I want to be sure," he continued with a frightened look, "that everything goes on as decently as possible. And I'm counting on you" (he said this with an air of authority) "to welcome Dr. Mulberry's team, which" (here he raised his voice) "is carrying out a very ticklish assignment in a patriotic spirit that deserves our respect."

"Certainly, Mr. Barrow," I replied in the best Bluevillese tone of voice.

Mr. Barrow added nothing. He had said everything, with all the bureaucratic inflections that the situation demanded. Furthermore, he didn't have to say goodbye to me but, rather, to let me pass in that narrow corridor, pulling in his paunch so that nothing of me would graze him. I also stepped aside in passing. I didn't want to burst him inadvertently and see his viscosity spread over the floor. There. I was around him. I moved away, relieved. Strange. Just from listening to him I already felt slimy.

9

Nine o'clock. Dave was in bed. There I was, on the job, so to speak, and with nothing to do, strolling around my bedroom, ashamed and at the same time curious. What I feared just then wasn't the act itself—which could be called medical if need be—but the preliminary social contact with the operator and her personality. Because any nurse that would accept such an assignment out of a feeling of duty and patriotism was the kind of girl that made my blood run cold.

My fears were unfounded. At ten after nine, a pick-up truck stopped in front of my barracks. I rushed to open the door, for fear that my visitors would wake Dave with their knocking, and I found myself in the presence of a robust woman in her thirties who said to me in a raucous voice, "Dr. Martinelli? Attaboy, that's the spirit. You're in a hurry. Were you waiting behind the door?"

She turned to someone I couldn't see and shouted to him, "Ricardo, bring the kit. The customer's in a hurry!"

"Not so loud," I said. "My son's asleep in the next room."

"Okay," she said. "I can behave. The kid—how old is he?"

"Eleven," I replied, taking her arm and leading her into my bedroom.

"Too young," she said with a little smile.

She went ahead of me and, in passing, she gave my lower abdomen a little caress, as if it were the most natural thing in the world, an act of pure courtesy taken for granted from a female guest.

"Ricardo!" she shouted raucously, turning back toward the threshold she'd just crossed.

"Shh! My son's asleep."

"Oh, that's right! Well, Ricardo," she said, scarcely lowering her voice, "are you bringing that kit—or what? No way we can get to work," she said with a wink and a laugh.

Nothing about my visitor bore even a distant resemblance to the medical profession. She was wearing a ton of makeup. Her dark eyes were studded with false eyelashes thick as bushes, her pancake base ocher, her lips crimson. Not exactly beautiful. Her features were thick, her nose large, her cheekbones broad, her forehead small. But all this saved her from being commonplace by an immense mouth that almost went from one ear to the other with full, voluptuous lips, a splendid set of teeth and a pink tongue that was revealed whenever she spoke and which seemed abnormally agile and voluminous.

"How about it, Ricardo? Is that thing coming?" she shouted hoarsely and went back to the door, waggling her hips.

Just at that moment Ricardo appeared. He was a Latin American of short stature, with delicate features, a thin black mustache, a white cap on his head; on his back a white jacket, decorated with the green rosette with the gilded letter of the A's; on his nose sunglasses and over his face as a whole, a melancholy air. He set the kit down on my desk and threw the woman an inquiring glance.

"That's Ricardo," the woman said, coming back my way and giving me a glance, to which I paid no attention, so she followed it up at once with a smile that spread the corners of her lips. That mouth was quite fascinating, both for its grandiose proportions and for the beauty of the lips, teeth and tongue. What's more, while her eyes—despite the false lashes and paint that lined them—appeared rather insignificant, her mouth was expressive, constantly in movement, the tongue going and coming, the lips contracting and relaxing, the teeth showing themselves and hiding.

"You can call me Bess," she continued, pointing her right thumb in the direction of her left breast.

"Hi, Bess. Hi, Ricardo."

"Buenas noches, señor," Ricardo said, looking at me with irreparable sadness. He spoke Spanish, the way blacks once spoke pidgin English—a bit of folklore to please the gringo.

"Hi, Doc," said Bess, who was slow in joining this courteous exchange.

Ricardo looked at Bess a second time, humbly and inquiringly, and Bess turned to me.

"Dearie," she asked, "want Ricardo to stay?"

I looked at her, disconcerted, but there was nothing to be read in her eyes. Fortunately, she smiled and I understood.

"No, no," I replied abruptly.

"Everyone's got his own thing," Bess said with an air of impartiality. "No harm in asking. Go wait in the car, Ricardo."

Ricardo slumped, his face sank and, without moving, he glanced at Bess with the look of a dog turned out of the house because its paws were dirty.

"You hear, Ricardo?" Bess snapped but with a smile that convinced me at once that she actually felt a certain degree of affection for Ricardo.

Ricardo felt it all right, still refusing to budge, seemingly on the verge of tears. I intervened.

"Ricardo needn't sit out there in the truck all by himself. He can wait in my kitchenette with a glass of bourbon."

"Bourbon? You got some?" asked Bess, making a violent movement of inhaling and suction with her enormous mouth.

"Do you want some?"

"Never before work!" Bess replied, drawing back her thick lips virtuously.

I moved forward, took Ricardo by the arm and led him into the kitchen. He seemed agreeably surprised, both by my short stature and my amiability. His face relaxed when he saw the whisky being poured. He took off his dark glasses as if they might interefere with his drinking. I saw his eyes. They were darkened by broad circles, and even the bourbon couldn't quite take away their forlorn look.

I left him. In my room, Bess was unpacking her kit, accompanying her movements, which were altogether medical, with lots of unnecessary swinging of buttocks, hips and breasts.

"You're a good guy, Doc," she said with a big smile that opened down to her gullet as if, out of gratitude, she were about to swallow me.

"Ricardo doesn't look too happy," I said, coming back to her, fascinated by the beauty of the gapping maw.

"He's got no cause to be," Bess answered. "Those dirty bitches played a lousy trick on him. Ricardo, he's a Puerto Rican. They bring him in by the thousands, you know" (no, I didn't know), "because they need somebody to do the heavy work. And those bitches gave him a story that this *caladium* stuff only had temporary effects. The poor son of a bitch fell for it and drank the stuff. And now that he knows he's frigid for good, he won't stop crying over his cock."

I made it clear to her by gestures that my room was bugged.

"I don't give a shit," she said. "Poor Ricardo. He's got a wife and a houseful of kids back home. And he sends them all his bread. I'm the one who sends the money orders, because he don't know how to write. He says he's never gonna go back to his wife, seeing as how he'd lose his honor with her if she found out he couldn't do it any more."

"Honey," she continued, "you should get into your pajamas. You'll feel more relaxed."

"But that will slow you up," I replied.

Bess laughed and I never took my eyes off her mouth. I'd never seen anything so big and so beautiful. Another laugh.

"You're nice, you know. *Qué delicadeza!* Like Ricardo says. Don't worry," she resumed with another laugh. "I've got plenty of time, seeing as how I'm workin' for science now!" (She laughed.) "Three in one night—what's that mean for me? I can't say I'm overworked!"

I began to undress. Bess emanated a vulgarity that I found agreeable; it came so naturally for her.

"Overworked," Bess resumed, frowning, "that's not exactly the word I was looking for. There's another one. Wait, I got it. Somethin' with sex in it."

"Sexploited?" I asked.

"Oh, so you know it, too?" Bess said, looking at me with

respect. "That sociologist broad who retrained me, she never stopped telling me: 'Bess, you've been sexploited by men.' Finally, I asked her, 'Excuse me, but what do you mean—sexploited?' 'It means you've been exploited sexually by men.' Oh, Doc, I couldn't believe my ears! 'Me?' I sez. 'Me—sexploited by men?' 'Why, of course, Bess,' she sez. 'I'm sorry,' I sez, 'but there's a mistake. It's me who was sexploiting them! Boy, did I ever make them cough up, those guys, for a quickie that I wouldn't even call work!'"

She laughed and, although I knew that the woman sociologist had been right in theory, the laughter from her wide mouth was so contagious that we were both laughing like old pals, while she did her "work."

Then came the "quickie," which, I supposed, amply rewarded the bugging device.

In the kitchenette, I poured Bess a shot of burbon, a small dose for me and a second glass for Ricardo, who looked at me with somber, doleful eyes.

"You," said Bess to Ricardo, placing her hand flat over his glass, "you hurry up and stick these test tubes in the freezer and then you can get drunk!"

Ricardo obeyed and Bess exclaimed, "My badge! Where the hell did I put my badge?"

"What badge?"

"The badge those broads gave me at the gate of the camp. They kept my I.D. card. And one of them warned me, no badge and you don't get back out. Ricardo!" she shouted, seeing him reappear.

"I've got mine," Ricardo replied, wrapped up in his sadness.

"Well, what about mine? I gave it to you!"

"No, you didn't," Ricardo said, his mustache sad, resigned in advance to inequity.

And, as a matter of fact, she hadn't given it to him, for they found the badge. It had fallen out of Bess's pocket onto my bed when she'd bent over me.

"See you next week," Bess said, having tossed the bourbon down her wide gullet at a single gulp.

"You're coming back?" I asked in amazement.

"And how!" Bess answered. "Didn't you know? This won't be my last 'visit.' And you know what I mean by that."

The following morning I awoke as usual at 6:30—a good thirty minutes before the first siren. I remained in bed, mulling things over. I'd often get good ideas for the lab that way. At times, too, I would slip into sex fantasies. No need to describe those daydreams. We all know that they offer the reward of making anything seem possible.

That morning I was thinking about Ricardo, about the rather unscrupulous methods of recruiting labor under the Bedford Administration, and from Ricardo I moved on to Bess, to her astonishing physique, to the pleasure I got from meeting her. I was thinking of social pleasure. Blueville was so stifling that a person like Bess, so completely spontaneous, brought in a whiff of fresh air. Yes, that's what I said—fresh air.

Then I moved on to Anita, but in a much more detached way—not like an episode in my private life, not like a case. I recalled the path she'd been traveling for ten years. That path had changed. She had, no doubt, "arrived," but not in the same condition as she'd started. And right then and there I understood why, in our films, relationships between men are often convincing, whereas female characters are so pale and weak. Women are stuck in their coital, maternal or decorative function, to exist only as females of the species. Accordingly, they no longer have any possibility of developing or of becoming interesting. Anita, however, had evolved. She'd fought with real situations and had made a number of decisions that altered her being, decisions that had corrupted her to some extent. It was a long jump from the Anita that I'd known ten years before to the cunning, cynical politician that she'd become. To be sure, I didn't approve. But I acknowledged it as a fact. Anita was a person who lacked neither dimension nor weight.

I had a great deal to say to Burage that day. So as not to attract attention with overly long confabs, it was arranged that I should make my reports to her, not all in one swoop but in little batches. Burage had the impression that our relations intrigued Crawford and that she tended to spy on us.

I used chronological order and told her, first of all, about Stien and his subterfuge for informing us, but she'd already heard about it from Rita and broke in impatiently.

"What's he up to?"

"He's making clones."

"How do you spell that?"

"C-l-o-n-e-s."

"What's that?"

"Animals whose birth is the result of technology and not sexual intercourse."

"And are there such things?"

"Yes, in oviparous animals. You take an unfertilized frog's egg and you remove its nucleus, which bears female chromosomes. You replace this nucleus with an intestinal cell taken from a tadpole. If it works, you get a second tadpole that is an exact copy of the first or—if you like—its double."

"Why—its double?"

"Burage, you and I are a mixture of mommy chromosomes and daddy chromosomes. But the second tadpole is going to have the same male and female chromosomes as the first tadpole from which the intestinal cell was taken. And of course he will be of the same sex. You recall that the egg of the frog was enucleated and no longer had chromosomes."

"What's the use of having a tadpole that's the double of another tadpole?"

"The practical use?"

"Yes."

"None. But if we move from oviparous to viviparous animals, then it starts to become worthwhile. For instance, let's say you have a bull that's extraordinary for the amount and quality of its meat. It can be very profitable to get identical copies of that bull without having to cross him with a cow."

Burage looked at me. She tossed back her dark auburn hair; her earrings (a simple club-shaped metal plate) quivered, and her bosom rose. She's burning, I thought. She sensed the truth about Stien's research. She said, "A second bull, identical to the first one, obtained without stud—isn't that it?"

"Yes."

She knitted up her brows. "Or a second cow, identical to the first one, without even the remote presence of a bull—in other words, without insemination."

"Yes."

"Let's not use the example of a cow," Burage continued in a voice vibrating with restrained sarcasm. "Let's use a woman."

I entered into her game.

"Let's take Bedford, for example."

"Yes," Burage replied, her eyes sparkling, "let's take Bedford! What happens?"

"Well, first let's select one of the cleaning women at the White House, a black woman, of course. We'll pick one who's young, healthy and strong. We take an ovule from her and we enucleate it. We insert, in this denucleated ovule, a cell taken from Bedford's intestine and when the cell begins to proliferate, we put it back into the black woman's uterus."

"That's perfect!" Burage said, clenching her fist so hard that her knuckles turned white. "Why didn't we think of that sooner? The black woman isn't the mother, of course. The black woman is a mere carrier. The black woman is a kind of prenatal wet nurse. She's going to give the fetus her warmth and her blood. She's going to carry it nine months and she's going to have the 'thrill' of giving birth! But the baby won't be hers. Genetically, the baby will be purely Bedford."

"Yes, Burage. And what's more, the baby will be Bedford's double, a female double, of course, born only of herself, without pregnancy and without delivery."

"And without any male participation! Doctor," Burage went on furiously, "your sex might just as well die out! Without you, we'll have parthenogenetic babies that blacks will bear instead of us!"

She was beside herself, I could see that clearly. Her cheeks were flushed, her lips trembled, her fists were clenched. She came up to me, her eyes shining, and said to be in an abrupt way that allowed no reply, "Doctor, give me your hand."

Dumfounded, I held my hand out to her. She covered it with her own, brought it to her mouth and bit the second joint of the index finger.

"There," she said in a low voice, "I wanted to do that much at least."

Then she released my hand and pivoted sharply on her heels, tossing back over her shoulder, "I'll be here at quarter to twelve," and, with her hair sweeping over her shoulders like a horse's mane, she dashed out of my office.

I was alone. I looked at my hand. Burage hadn't really bitten me. She'd left the marks of her teeth in my flesh. Unfortunately, it didn't last. The saliva had already dried up and, gradually, the marks faded away, except at either end. As they were the sharpest, the two canines had made the deepest marks. Two small round dents, a bit on the reddish side. I'd keep them a little longer.

When she came back at quarter to twelve, she had gone from the inner fire to the glacial phase. First, she settled an administrative question that she seemed to have her heart set on, then—right afterward—she questioned me about the visit of the sample-taking team. At first, my replies hardly seemed to interest her—except when she heard that the sampling was to be repeated every week. Then the interview changed into an interrogation. She wanted to know all about Bess and Ricardo, where they came from, their behavior, their weakness for bourbon. Next, she had me start my account over again right from scratch, exploring every detail, weighing each word, criticizing me accusingly for my omissions (ah, you see—you hadn't told me about the badge!), coming back a third time over the dialogue, complaining that it was incomplete, skimpy, badly told, that I was leaving out the tone—Doctor, you've got acting ability, don't forget! Now's the time to use it. So, harried, pestered, rushed, I performed. I didn't recount the incident; I acted it out. I imitated Ricardo, his forlorn look and his thick Spanish accent. I imitated Bess, her good-natured vitality, her vulgar accent, and in the course of the game more details came back to me that I recounted with gusto and pleasure.

I'd finished. Transformation in sight. Burage's brows knitted themselves, her blue eyes turned bluer, her earrings quivered, her lips grew taut.

"In short," she said, "you had lots of fun."

"What?" I asked in amazement. "But you're the one . . ."

"Nice going," she resumed, gritting her teeth. "What a nice time you had! And you describe it all with such smugness."

"But you're the one who kept after me for the details!"

"I didn't ask for that many! At any rate, I've got to admit it, you gave me enough of them. You're quite a poet, Doctor, where whores are concerned! What a description! That enormous mouth! That 'natural' way of doing things! And let's not overlook the ineffable charm of her vulgarity!"

"Now, Burage, it was you who asked me to liven up the story."

"You didn't need to liven it up! It flowed from your head, from your heart. Not to mention other organs! Nice going, Doctor. From now on you'll know what to do with your Wednesday nights."

"But Bess didn't tell me she was coming back next Wednesday."

"In that case, it's just great! She'll come every week. But will it be Wednesday? Will she come on Thursday? Will she come on Friday? Uncertainty in the certainty? An enjoyable habit and a little suspense! What could be better?"

"Hey, wait a minute, you were the one—"

"And you call her Bess!"

"That's the only name she gave me."

"Never mind that! She had plenty of time to give you the rest of her life history. You're really making progress with your vulgarity."

"Burage, you forget that it was you, yourself, who advised me . . ."

"Are you sorry now that I did? Just think, Doctor, you would have missed this historical monument—the biggest mouth in the United States. Because, if I understand you right, it's the dimensions of the mouth that excite you."

"No, I never said that!" I answered, involuntarily looking at her mouth.

"I beg your pardon, Doctor! You did say that. On your list of preferences, first comes the mouth, then vulgarity."

"Burage, this is absurd."

"Oh, please," she said, tears of rage welling up in her eyes, "don't give me that stupid look!"

She turned her back to me and left, her hair streaming in the wind, resisting at the last second a desperate urge to slam my door as she left.

I was making progress, I thought. I was dephallocratizing myself. The proof—I didn't look at this scene with the amused superiority that it would have prompted in me before. I had made a realization: Men called women illogical but, actually, women's logic was different from theirs. Burage's was quite understandable—the objective and intensive interrogation was the group, "we." What had followed was she and me. To be frank, would I have liked it if some man came around every week and manipulated her? I shouldn't have sung the praises of vulgarity; I should have kept that oral lyricism to myself. Perhaps the only thing "female" about that scene was the suddenness, the speed and the verbal brio of the attack. I'd been overwhelmed before I knew what hit me.

I was getting ready to leave my office for the cafeteria when Burage reappeared. Her face was smooth and calm. She must have washed her face and brushed her hair. I looked at her warily. Was she going to nip the second joint of my index finger or pounce on me again, scratching and clawing?

Neither one. We were now being objective.

"Doctor, one more thing on the clones. Have the experiments already gone from oviparous animals to viviparous ones?"

"Probably. Stien is using mice."

"How do you know?"

Again, the interrogation.

"You know how absent-minded he is. The other day he stuck his hand into his overcoat pocket—probably to get his handkerchief—and pulled out a mouse. Naturally, I can't swear that the mouse was a clone."

"All the same, Doctor, taking an ovule, enucleating it, inserting an intestinal cell in it, monitoring the proliferation and transplanting it at just the right time in a uterus—that's a long, slow process and extremely complicated."

I shrugged. I had no intention of reassuring her. I wasn't reassured myself.

"The experimental stage is always complicated. They don't

find shortcuts until later on, when they begin working on an industrial scale."

"Industrial scale!"

I looked at her. Was I, in spite of everything, getting a little stung by her stings? Now I felt like giving her a talking to.

"What do you think, Burage? Who do you suppose finances Stien's work? Do you think this kind of research is disinterested?"

"The mass production of parthenogenetic babies! You can't mean it, Doctor!"

I kept silent. She looked at me with her blue eyes whose expression could change so quickly. But for the moment they were pensive and focused.

"Jespersen!" she said finally. "We've absolutely got to know what Jespersen is doing!"

I didn't know how to interpret this, and, as she said nothing, I ventured, "Do you want me to ask him?"

"Oh, no," she said, "not you, anybody but you! That would be much too dangerous!"

I was having lunch at the cafeteria, Dave at my side, when the P.A. system began to broadcast the switchboard operator's voice: "Dr. Martinelli . . . Dr. Martinelli . . . Dr. Martinelli." The conversation died out and all eyes, with varying degrees of candor, converged on me.

When she would call us to the phone, something that hardly ever happened any more, the switchboard operator got on your nerves by repeating your name over and over, in an impersonal and monotonous voice. Dr. Martinelli . . . Dr. Martinelli . . . Dr. Martinelli . . . Her voice was greatly amplified by the loudspeakers, and in the long, deserted corridor where I was, its echo preceded me from one speaker to the next: an insistent, lugubrious litany, as if the Lord were calling me to his court to answer for my sins. Dr. Martinelli . . . Dr. Martinelli . . . Dr. Martinelli . . . That powerful, disembodied voice, falling from on high, must have resounded throughout the whole castle, pursuing me wherever I might hide—in the library, in the lounges, in the pool, in the underground gym.

It had become increasingly difficult to make outside calls in

Blueville. You had to make a written request the day before to Mr. Barrow, and most of the time they would tell you the next morning that there was no one at the number you wanted. Whether it was true or false, you had no way of finding out. As to incoming calls (except for those from Anita to say she wasn't coming) it had been four months since anybody at Blueville had received one.

Dr. Martinelli . . . Dr. Martinelli . . . Dr. Martinelli . . . It wouldn't stop. My name was going to be repeated over and over throughout the immense building until I showed up. I had the depressing feeling of being hunted.

The two public telephones—now almost useless—were located in a little hallway that came before the men's room. They weren't booths—just two phones side by side on the wall. I went to the first and lifted the receiver.

"Dr. Martinelli speaking."

"Dr. Martinelli," replied the switchboard operator's voice, "please report to Mr. Barrow's office at once."

Why at once? And why was Barrow sending for me in the middle of lunch? What did he have to say that couldn't wait?

I didn't need to knock on Mr. Barrow's door—it was open. And, strangely, Mr. Barrow stood waiting for me in the doorway, he who was so fond of receiving you seated massively behind his desk in his pomp and glory. True, he was standing, somewhat withdrawn, and because it was the only thing that projected into the corridor, I caught sight of his paunch first. I hurried my steps. And Mr. Barrow's face appeared. It was convulsed—well, as much as fatty magma can be convulsed. But it was clear enough for me: his jowls shook. Without a word, as if he didn't trust his voice, he stood aside to let me by. But he didn't stand aside as you might expect by moving back into his office but came entirely out of it so that once inside I half turned to him, thinking that he was going to follow me. But not at all.

"Dr. Martinelli," he said in an almost inaudible voice.

I looked at him. His globular eyes spun around in their sockets like panic-stricken animals and sweat ran over his gleaming skull.

"Dr. Martinelli," he said in a breathless voice that was choppy and indistinct. "The phone is off the hook on my desk. This is confidential. I'll leave you alone."

And he closed the door on me. I was alone! In Mr. Barrow's office! In the Holy of Holies! That which he never left without locking with two locks as complicated as those on a safe. Alas, I wasn't Joan Pierce. I didn't have her nerves. I did little more than glance into the wastebasket—empty. Actually, it wasn't until later on that I would remember that glance. At the time, I wasn't aware of it. Mr. Barrow's fright had contaminated me. My heart thudded against my ribs. I was fascinated by the receiver that I saw, off the hook all right, on the huge mahogany desk. I headed over to it, picked it up still sticky with Mr. Barrow's sweat, and I was so disgusted by this that I took the time to wipe it with my handkerchief before bringing it to my ear.

"Dr. Martinelli speaking."

"One moment, Doctor," the switchboard operator said. "I'll get your party back on the line."

Nothing. Not a sound. The phone was dead. An interminable wait. My legs were weak. I wasn't going to go so far as to sit on Mr. Barrow's big, black, vinyl armchair, but I sat on his desk, something that was even more irreverent in a way, as I afterward realized. At the time, my head was empty, my temples pounded, and I noticed that the hand now holding the receiver was also perspiring.

I must have gotten used to the silence in those few seconds, for I jumped when it was broken. A voice burst into the phone, strong, hard, authoritarian. That first instant, I couldn't tell if it was a man or a woman. Mainly, I was struck by its volume. It resounded in my head as if it were taking over.

"Dr. Martinelli?"

"Yes."

"Are you in Mr. Barrow's office?"

"Yes."

"Are you alone?"

"Yes."

A pause.

"I'm Hilda Helsingforth. Chouchka will be saddled and waiting for you in her stall at exactly two P.M. You mount her and report to the checkpoint. The guards have been informed and a militiawoman will escort you. Over and out."

She hung up. I hadn't had time to say a word. And,

furthermore, I wouldn't have been able to open my mouth. My lips were stuck together. In one swoop, my saliva had dried up. I got to my feet. I leaned on the desk with both hands for a few seconds. When I went out I saw no further sign of Mr. Barrow.

I headed for the men's room. Fortunately, it was empty. I turned on the cold water and slapped my cheeks hard with both wet hands. I dried myself and took a few deep breaths, pacing back and forth. Every time I went past the mirror, I took a quick glance at myself. But I saw that I still was too pale to go back into the cafeteria.

10

When I rode up to the checkpoint on Chouchka, the sentinel handed me my badge, under the eyes of the guards, who were watching us intently through one of the barracks windows. Ten yards away, her body molded in a blue-green uniform, carbine slung across her back, a pistol at her hip—Jackie waited. She sat on a dappled gray gelding, a sorry specimen that, like the rest of the horses, inspired repulsion in Chouchka. The mare's ears folded back, and I immediately drew in the reins to prevent her from acting up. I was astonished by Jackie's presence. Just the day before I'd learned through "we" that Pussy had been discharged from Blueville. I'd expected to see her partner go the same way after all those forbidden discussions with Stien, Jess and myself. But no, there she was, in the flesh, on a mission that she must have known to be important, judging by her impassive look. And I felt sure that Jackie was the only one who knew where she was taking me. I was well aware, as I rode by, that the guards found it strange for me to be going out by myself.

"You go the usual way, Doctor," Jackie said as soon as I'd pocketed the badge. "I'll ride behind you."

She'd spoken in a loud, authoritarian voice without favoring me with a smile.

The usual way, I supposed, was the trail used for our Sunday rides on horseback. I started off, painfully aware of being a prisoner pushed ahead of an armed escort. Oh, no, I don't want to dramatize. My departure from the cafeteria had been public and noticed. I didn't think that my personal security would be at stake in the immediate future. That didn't prevent Jackie from being behind me, armed to the teeth. I didn't even have a pen-knife to defend myself. We were alone and we were going deep into a forest where, on our previous rides, we'd never met a living soul.

What's more, that June day was lugubrious. It had rained for two days and two nights without let-up, and, although the rain had stopped at noon, the break in the weather that followed didn't live up to its name. The sky was lined with big black clouds that crept over the tops of the fir trees, just asking to be burst. The path (thank God, it was sand and gravel) held up under Chouchka's hooves, but a latticework of inex-haustible streams had eroded and gullied it as they ran down-hill—at times cutting across the trail. Each time, Chouchka, who didn't like water, sidestepped, breaking the rhythm of her trot. I decided to walk her without Jackie reacting behind me. Besides, the trail now climbed the wooded hillside at a steeper angle.

Walking my horse had another advantage: It gave me time to total up my relations with Jackie. A meager harvest. At the time of the Jespersen incident when, after dismounting, I'd gone up to her, my head at the height of her boots, she had felt (I believed) the vibrations of the short, unexpected and powerful desire I'd had for her just then. On the next ride she had broken in roughly on the ambiguous "showdown" I'd had with Pussy. And then, on the Sunday that had followed the phone call in which, for the last time, Anita called off her trip, Jackie had given me a look and a half smile, both of them friendly and very cleverly concealed from the eyes of those present.

But did that mean I could really trust her? If Pussy had been fired, didn't it stand to reason that, of the two girls, Jackie, not Pussy, had given Mr. Barrow a truthful account of the Jespersen incident? Her services as an informer had, no doubt, merited her the trust for the assignment that she was carrying out with me. In which case, hadn't the smile and wink of the previous Sunday been a trap? I couldn't get myself to believe it. The girl didn't have the transparent eyes of a liar. On the contrary, her eyes were full of things. And when someone is so well upholstered, with the straightforward energy of that square face to top it off, they just don't take naturally to double-dealing. At least, I didn't think so. Or I didn't want to think so, which amounted to the same thing.

There we were, around the bend that screened us from Blueville. It seemed to me that the time was ripe to probe my enemy's defenses. I brought Chouchka to a halt and half turned in my saddle, leaning on the mare's croup with my right hand. I gave Jackie time to catch up to me. That didn't take more than two seconds, but I didn't need any more time to run my eyes over her and take inventory while she was moving toward me. A beautiful, healthy girl with sloping shoulders, a deep bosom, plump cheeks, blond hair cut short and eyes that I'd thought blue but were gray, a color that I found striking at the time, possibly because of the dark sky and the stormy light.

In a voice that tried hard to be natural, I said to her, "Where are you taking me?"

"Keep going, Doctor," she replied harshly. "You've got no business asking me questions."

I looked at her. A mask for a face. Nothing to be read there. Just then, Chouchka, who no longer felt my reins, whipped around suddenly and, her ears flattened, made a lunge at the gelding that I was just able to prevent in time. But that was enough for the gelding to turn in his tracks and start galloping away downhill, Jackie barely able to stop him.

I waited. When Jackie came back to me, breathless, one blond lock falling over her ear, her face was flushed and her eyes flashed. She shouted at me in anger, "If Chouchka pulls another stunt like that, I'm going to open fire!"

"At Chouchka or me?" I asked insolently.

"Doctor," she screamed, beside herself, "you've got no business asking me questions!"

I roared back, "Well, I'm going to ask you one whether you like it or not! Why did you pick a gelding? You know perfectly well that Chouchka hates them!"

"I didn't pick him," Jackie answered more calmly. "They gave him to me all saddled."

At the same time, she gathered up the reins in her left hand and, with the fingers of her right hand, leaning her head forward, she replaced the blond lock that had escaped from her service cap. It was a gesture that I followed mechanically at first but that moved me all of a sudden. It seemed so feminine in a situation that was so unfeminine.

Jackie caught my look and, I think, my emotion as well, for she lowered her eyes and a silence settled over us, one that was not at all unfriendly, for a full second.

"Keep moving, Doctor," she said, making a visible effort at regaining her military demeanor. "We've got a long way ahead of us."

That "long way" was an indiscretion that must have violated her orders and an indiscretion, I thought, calculated to reassure me. I circled Chouchka around and started her at a walk up the right trail, if I may use the term "right" for a trail I'd never taken. Of course, it might have been a trick: Jackie wanted to lull me into a sense of false security in order to render me more docile. Not being able to come up with the answer to this, I consulted my instincts, but, as usual, they only supplied me with hunches that contradicted one another.

Up to there it had been the "usual way" taken when we went on our group rides except, on this day, the streams had gullied it and the tall firs lining the way shook themselves above us at the slightest breeze. I was pleased with myself for having worn my raincoat, and, hunting for my gloves in my pockets, I found something that had lain there rumpled, wrinkled, forgotten for months—my golf cap. I pulled it on. I wanted to keep my head dry and also to have the pleasure of remembering a little bit of my past. Brief pleasure. Memories came surging back and my spirits sank.

Could I have said no to Hilda Helsingforth's order that afternoon? Absolutely not. The danger of losing everything had been too great. And there I was, a hostage or prisoner, escorted to an unknown destination, an armed militiawomen at my back. The future didn't belong to me, not even the very near future.

The trail grew less steep and, if for no other reason than to escape all those gloomy thoughts, I began to trot. Good old Chouchka. The one unquestionably friendly presence in that forlorn landscape. Aside from the sandy, sodden trail, running endlessly through the fir trees, there was nothing but a leaden sky and a wan light coming from someplace or other. The only sound, when the wind died down, was the soft thud of my mare's four hooves, repeated in a muffled echo behind me—and never out of time—by the gelding's hooves. That idiot of a horse was trotting in step, like a soldier.

I reached the fork in the roads famous for Jespersen's mad gallop and, sure enough, I started up the trail to the left. An order rang out behind me: "To the right, Doctor!"

To the right! The taboo trail! Jespersen's "flight"! Pussy's shot! I reined Chouchka in and faced her.

"Did you say to the right?"

Jackie drew closer, beautiful and stern, looking taller than she really was, the barrel of her carbine sticking up behind her shoulder. She halted her gelding a good distance from Chouchka and said harshly, "You heard me!"

I stared at her. "We're not allowed to take that trail," I said, my lips taut.

"Today you are."

"Who says?"

"Me."

A brief pause to think things over, and I made a decision that relieved me. I refused to obey.

"No, thanks. I'm not going."

Jackie looked at me. She was so amazed by my recalcitrance that she forgot to be angry.

"What?" she asked, incredulous.

"I won't go up that trail."

"Why not?"

"It's forbidden."

Then it was her turn to stare at me.

"Doctor, I just finished telling you that today, as an exception . . ."

She didn't end her sentence; but she'd spoken patiently, as if she were addressing an obstinate child. I noticed that her eyes were more worried than irritated. There she was in a fine mess, my girl soldier. The parcel was rebelling—it refused to be delivered to the addressee. What was she going to do? Threaten me? That hadn't worked too well a minute before.

I gauged her confusion by her silence. It reassured me. The situation became quite clear: Jackie had orders to hand over the parcel intact. She hadn't been ordered to destroy it en route.

But I pushed my advantage—just a little.

"Thanks," I said. "I don't feel like getting shot at."

"Me—shoot at you?" she asked incredulously.

"Pussy shot at Jespersen all right."

"Pussy got frightened and, anyway, that wasn't the same. Jespersen was breaking the rules. With you, now, you're obeying an order."

"But maybe that order is a trap."

"A trap?"

"I go down that path and you shoot me. Then you claim that I was trying to escape."

Saying these words, I stared at her accusingly. I was employing provocation, I knew this quite well. I suspected her sincerity, even though—inside—I no longer doubted her.

"Doctor!" she said indignantly.

She blushed. Not with anger this time but with mortification. And as she had that kind of transparent skin through which the blood can be seen clearly, the crimson spread in a broad wave from her forehead to her cheekbones and from her cheekbones to her round neck that emerged from her tunic.

"Doctor," she resumed vehemently, "I'm not in the S.S.!"

I was rather surprised by that. I hadn't thought that the young militiawomen was so well endowed with historical knowledge.

"Well," I said, "if you want to reassure me, just trot on ahead of me. I'll follow you."

"I can't do that," she replied at once. "That would be wrong."

And as I said nothing and kept a stony face, she added, "Please, Doctor."

I looked into her eyes. They were a beautiful deep gray that was underlined (although she had blond hair) by thick dark lashes. That "please" was really an entreaty, not a formal clause. She'd spoken in a low voice.

I went on: "Will you guarantee my personal safety?"

She didn't avert her eyes, and the look that replied to mine was straightforward.

"As long as you're with me, yes."

An ambiguous reply with which I had to be content. Besides, Chouchka was impatient. Her rather bulging eyes fixed on the gelding. My horse had grown restless during this conversation and I'd have to wheel her around two or three times to thwart her aggressive impulses.

"All right," I said, "I trust you."

And as the "forbidden trail" was a straight, level stretch, I started down it and began to gallop. Chouchka seemed happy about this release. With alacrity, she dug her four shoes into the trail, throwing up water and sand. The gelding followed.

Five minutes later I came back to a walk. We were starting down a steep descent and, at the end of the drop, an obstacle confronted us. The trail was cut by a sheet of murky water that flowed down from a small valley. It was out of the question to jump it. If the current and depth permitted, the only solution was fording it.

Jackie caught up to me. "We've got to cross," she said decisively.

I shook my head. "Not before we've sounded it."

I dismounted. I tied Chouchka to the supple branch of a fir tree, sought and found in the underbrush a fallen limb, trimmed it to make it lighter and, moving out until the water was halfway up my boots, I drove in my sounding rod as far out as I could reach. It was just possible, I thought. There were strong eddies, but the afternoon's clear spell had worked in our favor. The current was not overly swift and we were in no danger of being carried away.

I turned around. Jackie, having dropped her reins over the gelding's neck and withers, was engrossed in an unexpected activity—she was writing in a small notebook. At the same time, she raised her eyes and, without saying a word, beckoned me closer. When I came up to her knees, she handed me the pad—without releasing it, however—and I read: *H. H. knows all about the Jespersen incident.*

I bowed my head, also in silence; then I moved away. I went over to untie Chouchka and got into the saddle, amazed. Jackie had, of her own accord, given me three bits of information that were of the utmost importance to me: 1) She had written; she hadn't talked—i.e., she thought that we could be monitored by a long-range electronic listening device. I asked myself the question: Was that how H. H. "knew all about" the Jespersen incident? 2) She had given me confirmation of something that I'd already suspected but hadn't wanted to believe: I was being taken to Hilda Helsingforth. 3) Most of all, she was warning me in the event that H. H. should question me about the Jespersen affair.

There could be no more doubt about it: I had an ally in Jackie.

As I'd expected, Chouchka made lots of trouble. She capered and pranced without wanting to get her hooves wet. Jackie forced her gelding out into the current first. The idea worked. Chouchka plunged in. While we were crossing one behind the other, the water almost up to the horses' bellies, I saw Jackie throw the tiny shreds of her message into the current. I looked at her straight back and her strong blond neck. I was overwhelmed by a surge of gratitude.

When we emerged from the stream, Jackie waited for me to pass her and ride ahead once again. She kept her eyes lowered, and everything about her suggested that I should remain silent. I followed that mute order. But after a hundred yards or so, Chouchka walking up a steep grade, I turned halfway round in my saddle and looked at her. Her resolute gray eyes met mine. No, sex had nothing to do with that exchange, unless at a diffuse, vestigial level. I was being offered a pact of friendship. I was flustered, upset. I saw Jackie with new eyes. Even the weapon that she carried no longer had the same meaning. For the first time since I'd been in Blueville, the initials used to designate me were justified—I was a "protected man."

I turned around again on my horse and Jackie nodded to me. In a vast clearing on a gentle slope, a cabin made of logs. Fifty yards away, a woodshed. Farther on, a stable, where we unsaddled the horses, each in a stall.

"Come on," Jackie said.

As she walked abreast of me this time, I threw her a sidelong glance. Impassive again but worried. There was something bothering her; I could read it in her eyes. And her nervousness, precisely because it was restrained, heightened mine.

The cabin wasn't as modest as I'd thought. Moving ahead over the field—Jackie behind me—I discovered a rather long building: a covered pool, judging by its glass roof. It was built with tropical wood. In short, a simple little thing that must have cost a fortune.

We entered a little hallway cluttered with boots and overcoats where I left my raincoat. Then Jackie pushed open a glass door. We walked along the narrow side of the pool, and at the far end we came to another door that Jackie opened before me.

"Wait here," she said in a loud voice, as if she were speaking to nobody in particular. "Helsingforth will be right out."

With that, she pivoted on her heels. Regretfully, I watched the nape of her blond neck, her solid shoulders and even her weapons, now friendly, as they moved away.

I went in. A wide, rectangular picture window framed a mountain landscape obscured by a driving rain and patches of white mist. I couldn't see a thing. A copper hood gleamed vaguely, but in the fireplace facing the picture window there were no flames, only some embers amid the ashes. In that light, as far as I could tell, the ceiling and walls were paneled with reddish wood. Beside the fireplace I made out a huge couch that lost itself in a shadowy corner.

I closed the door behind me and took a few hesitant steps in the direction of the picture window. Big dark clouds over the forest, white fog in the hollows, crepuscular light. The mountains didn't look very inviting. Things were much better on my side of the windowpane. The room wasn't cold, but it gave off an atmosphere that chilled me. I had the feeling that the things behind me were watching me malevolently. An illusion, of course. But telling myself this over and over didn't do any good—I still had the same feeling. A glance around. With its wood paneling, its copper hood over the hearth (that was the only thing I could see clearly), it was a rather inviting little room. But I felt unwelcome there. It was odd, distressing and paralyzing the way I had the feeling of being followed everywhere by hostile eyes. I gave myself a shake. I straightened up, stuck both hands in my pockets and paced back and forth in the room. Very weak light. But recalling the tone and the contents of Helsingforth's letters, I didn't even dare look for a switch to turn on the lights. It looked as though the room was bristling with prohibitions and taboos aimed at me. I felt that I had no rights—not even the right of being there.

The wait went on and on, to demoralize me. It was a worn-out old trick but one that worked, I realized frantically. Well, I was going to beat that trick. I was going to think about something else. I decided to get the fire going again. I'd be able to see the place at any rate. I moved two blackened pieces of firewood that had lost contact and, squatting, stirred up the embers with a bellows.

The flames shot up and a voice snapped behind my back, "Leave that fire alone! Nobody told you to start it going!"

I rose. A lamp was lighted dazzlingly. I blinked. At the farthermost end of the couch, leaning against the wood paneling and swathed in a great russet shawl from which her bare feet emerged, I saw a twenty-year-old girl. If ever a physiognomy belonged to the "weaker sex" it was that one. With her long, slender neck, her delicate features, her lackluster eyes and her halo of wispy blond hair, she seemed the soul of fragile femininity. But there was nothing angelic about the expression on that face. The physique was reassuring, not the eyes.

"Excuse this intrusion," I said. "It was so dark, I didn't see that you were here."

A little insulting laugh. "I'm well aware of that. It was most enlightening to watch you. Thinking that you were alone, you strolled around this room like you owned the place. You looked like a bantam rooster strutting around with his hackles up. Every move you made showed the arrogance, egotism and bad breeding of the male. It was comical and repugnant all at the same time."

I was astonished by the brutality of this attack. When I

recovered my voice I replied harshly, "If you find my presence repugnant, I don't see why you sent for me."

"I didn't send for you."

"Aren't you Hilda Helsingforth?"

"Of course not," she answered with contempt. "I'll have you know that I want nothing to do with a P.M. I've done everything possible to stop you from coming here, and you're here against my will."

She spat this in my face like a cat, panting with rage, her back braced against the wood paneling, hatred coming out of her eyes. I turned my back on her and headed for the glass door.

"Where are you going?" she demanded.

"I'm going to wait for Helsingforth in the pool."

"You'd better just be going *period*!" she cried in a strident voice. "Take my advice! You don't know what you're in for!"

I didn't reply. I closed the door behind me. I really didn't know what I was in for, but I did know that I wasn't going to stay in the same room with that madwoman another second. As a matter of fact, I was quite shaken. I decided to walk around the pool to calm down. I took a few deep breaths, removed my hands from my pockets and, not without some effort, tried to relax.

"Strutting," as the girl in the shawl had said, I'd reached the great picture window at the southern wall when a door slammed at the other end and in strode a woman whose size astonished me. She had a riding crop in her hand and wore jodhpurs, boots and a turtleneck sweater. She stopped short when she spotted me and planted herself there in an odd pause. The woman's Herculean body faced me, but, her face turned to the left, she showed me only her right profile and looked at me out of the corner of one eye, like a bird.

"What are you doing here?" she asked accusingly.

I'd had enough of this terrorism. I reacted with "You ought to know. You're the one who sent for me."

She withered me with a glance but still, I noticed, with a single eye.

"Don't pretend that you didn't understand my question. What are you doing here, in my pool?"

The tone implied that I was unworthy of setting foot there.

"The person in the living room didn't appreciate my being there."

"What *person?*" she asked haughtily. "There's only one person here—me."

If the girl in the shawl didn't belong to the human race, where did I belong?

"Come along," she said. "I'm going to look into this."

And, with great strides, swinging her whip at arm's length, she headed toward the living room. I followed her.

An unexpected sight. The girl with the wispy hair was stretched out prone, her face buried in the upholstery of the couch. She was sobbing.

"What is it, Audrey?" asked Helsingforth.

"This man," Audrey replied, straightening up and pointing an accusing finger my way, "tried to rape me."

I cried out indignantly, "That's a lie!"

Everything about Audrey—her eyes, her sobs, her pose, her nudity—was false. She looked like a third-rate actress that some director was trying vainly to fit a role. As the victim of a rape she just didn't make it.

"Audrey," Helsingforth said coolly, "stop sniveling and tell me what happened."

But Helsingforth was also a bad actress. She overdid the impassive note.

"This monster . . ." Audrey said.

It was enough to set your teeth on edge. It was all so faked—the words, the intonation.

"This monster," Audrey resumed, "pounced on me the minute he got into the room. Fortunately, I managed to break away from him, seize the gun and give him notice that he was to leave."

"Give him notice!" That was really too much. I broke in: "That's a tissue of lies."

Unfortunately, I said it instead of shouting it. That wasn't at all convincing. I was starting to be a bad actor myself. Perhaps because I'd caught it from my mediocre partners.

Helsingforth turned her right profile to me, brandished her riding crop and just as if she were threatening an unruly dog with being punished, she said without raising her voice, "Have you finished?"

"You see?" Audrey said, still sobbing. "He tore my panties and my bra!"

She pointed to the evidence strewn over the couch. Among the exhibits was the revolver that had driven me off. I noted with relief that Helsingforth seized the weapon, locked it up in the drawer of a small table, pocketed the key and resumed a firm stance before Audrey. As her great height and broad back prevented me from seeing my "victim," I took a step sideways but remained at a distance. I was almost sure that Helsingforth wouldn't hesitate to strike me if I opened my mouth again.

"In your opinion," asked Helsingforth with crushing calm, "why did Martinelli tear your bra straps?"

"Well, I suppose, to see my breasts," Audrey answered, lowering her eyes.

Helsingforth laughed and pointed an enormous finger toward Audrey's frail torso.

"You flatter yourself, my dear. You've got nothing to see."

She laughed. For once, she was being natural. Nastiness suited her better than impassiveness. She made an unexpected move: She snatched up the bra from the couch, brought it to her nose and sniffed it.

"Just as I thought. You're lying," she said threateningly.

"Hilda!"

"You're lying, you little tramp. That bra doesn't even smell of sweat. A woman perspires when she's being raped. First of all, because she's frightened. Then, because she's struggling. You're lying and you're lying to me! You had the nerve to set yourself against Martinelli's visit, and when I went around you you tried to sabotage it. Okay. I'm going to teach you to be a rebel. Since you're nude, we're going to take advantage of that."

"No, no!" Audrey cried, wide-eyed with fear, cringing away.

Helsingforth leaned over and, with a quick, incredibly brutal movement, seized her by one foot, turned her over on her belly, slid her down until both legs stuck out over the couch. She then pinned them between her riding boots and, three times, without haste, with perfect calm and a force that terrified me, struck her buttocks with the whip. Three red welts appeared. Audrey let out a cry, just one, and strangely enough she didn't sob any more; she whined in a subdued voice, as if she were afraid of making too much noise.

Helsingforth seized her by an arm, threw her off the couch and sat down, her legs splayed out. She said abruptly, "Boots!"

Audrey, naked and sniveling, straightened up to pull them off. It wasn't easy. She lacked strength, and every part of her was trembling. But at the same time she was overflowing with zeal and humility, as if this servile task pleased her.

"Martinelli," Helsingforth said, turning her Jupiterlike profile my way and staring at me with her dark eye, "you're in a fine mess."

"Me?"

"You heard Audrey. She accuses you of rape."

I replied, forcing myself to remain calm, "You know perfectly well that it isn't true."

"It isn't true as far as my relations with Audrey are concerned. But that doesn't make it untrue with regard to my relations with you."

"I don't understand."

"Sweater!" Helsingforth said to Audrey, and she added menacingly, "And cut out that moaning. You're making me sick."

Audrey fell silent.

"Martinelli," resumed Helsingforth as soon as her head emerged from the sweater, "you still don't understand the situation very well. Around here, the truth is what I say is true. Think it over. If I decide to corroborate what Audrey says, what court will acquit you?"

"But that would be perjury!"

"So what?" she said, raising her brow.

I was silent. Was this a threat that I should take seriously, or just a sadistic little joke in passing?

Just then, doubtless delighted at the idea of seeing me put in jail, Audrey let out a little bird cry and, bending her neck, placed a tender kiss on Helsingforth's forearm. She drew back at once, placed her large foot on the girl's bare breast and, with a snap action of her foot, pushed her away. Audrey went sprawling on the floor and sat up at once without betraying the slightest trace of anger or resentment.

"You're crazy," Helsingforth said sneeringly. "Stop your fawning and keep your tenderness for yourself. I don't want any of it. I've already told you so."

While shrugging out of her bra, she added curtly, "Pants."

Just then I turned away and looked at the fire in the fireplace. There must have been some hesitation on Audrey's part, for Helsingforth repeated the order impatiently. And from pants they must have gone to panties, since I heard Helsingforth say sarcastically, "Take it easy! You don't have to tear them. Nobody's going to believe that I was raped!"

A silence. The floorboards creaked. I supposed that Helsingforth had gotten to her feet.

"I'm going to take a swim," she said with a certain pomp, as if it were an important act the world should know about. "Audrey, give the stopwatch to Martinelli. As for you, go get dressed and make me some tea."

Audrey didn't turn over the stopwatch to me with her own hands. She set it down on the table with a venomous look.

When I stepped into the indoor pool, Helsingforth, standing, nude and monumental, on the apron, waved for me to go around to her right. I must admit that it occurred that she might be one-eyed, for her left cheek remained hidden constantly by the mass of her black hair she pulled over to that side. No, she wasn't one-eyed. At that very instant I caught sight of her left eye—dark and shining—and no nicer than her right.

At my signal she catapulted into the water. I started the stopwatch and looked at her. The woman was a superb athlete. She swam so fast that she created a kind of hollow in front of her face that made it almost unnecessary for her to turn her head a quarter of the way to the side. But, most of all, I was impressed by her heroic dimensions (she couldn't have stood less than six foot two) and by her musculature, which, though well coated, suggested great strength. While I followed her progress, the thought occurred to me that, if women went on being the dominant sex in our society, it was possible that the sports they practiced might, in a few generations, alter their morphology and make women—interms of size, weight and muscles—the larger member of the couple (that is, if there still were any couples).

Helsingforth had said eight lengths. On the eighth, I stopped the timer as soon as her fingers touched the mosaic tile. She was dissatisfied with her time, accused me of having clocked her wrong and, her brows knitted up, emerged from the water, streaming, grabbed two towels and threw one to me without so much as a look my way, saying curtly, "Dry my back."

After a second's hesitation, I complied. If I had to have an altercation with her, I'd better not have it over some minor point. And, apparently, she took herself for the queen. Was it because of her millions? Or her physical strength, which I was touching just then (my eyes were at the level of her collarbones) and which I found frightening, because I knew that she wouldn't think twice about using it on me. I made a mental note to hide—at any cost—the fear that she inspired in me. This decision, as I would later realize, was unwise. It was like that instinct that prompts women never to show fear of the strength of certain men so as not to awaken the brute in them.

My towel went back and forth, and I realized with astonishment that I was enjoying this monumental drying. The texture of her skin was so fine, the forms so beautiful and, despite their power, so undeniably feminine that I continued this pampering longer than was necessary. Oddly enough, neither Helsingforth's ferocity nor her great dimensions could intimidate me in this domain.

"That's enough," Helsingforth said, and, without turning around, she reached out to get the towel and threw it over her shoulder. I saw her lean to one side to dry her hair with the second towel. I also turned my back on her and moved away.

"Martinelli," she asked, "what do you think of me?"

I faced her. She had planted herself before me in that strange pose that I'd already noticed, body facing me and head in profile or, rather, three quarters turned, looking at me out of the corners of both eyes.

"Do you mean—physically?"

"Yes."

Nothing could surprise me any more. I'd been her dryer.

Now I'd become her mirror. I looked that giant Narcissus up and down and replied, "Exceptional."

"What do you mean—exceptional?"

"I mean, your size, your beauty and your proportions."

She threw me a suspicious glance. "What's wrong with my proportions?"

"Nothing's wrong with them."

"Well, why do you say they're exceptional?"

"Well, your pelvic girdle is smaller than your scapular arch."

"Doctor, no mumbo-jumbo. Just say that in plain English."

"Your shoulders are broader than your hips."

"And that's exceptional?"

"Yes, in a woman."

She scowled. She had no trouble looking down at me and said in an Olympian tone of voice, "Doctor, you're behind the times. The traditional ideas of masculinity and femininity are completely outmoded."

Well, now, didn't I know that? They'd been drumming it into my head long enough. How could I have forgotten the new Gospel? Besides, wasn't it obvious? No more heterochromosomes XX! No more ovaries or ovules, or secretion of estrogens! And, of course, no more tubes, uterus or vagina! All over, the vulvar slit and the clitoris! Finished, menstruation! Gone, breasts, nursing and pregnancy! And no more difference, either, in the heartbeat! And even supposing that I had taken the liberty of making a most inoffensive remark at this point—namely, that the pubic hair of the beautiful athlete facing me was very classically triangular and not, like mine, diamond-shaped—I would have been accused at once of heresy and the most reprehensible deviationism.

I availed myself of the weapon of the weak: I kept still. I allowed Helsingforth the "feminine" privilege of the last word.

There are times, in the lives of people, when words have the power to change events; when we find, to our amazement, that verbal delirium has replaced scientific truth. I was living one of those times and I sensed the utter futility of rowing against the tide. The error was too great. I had to wait until the magic of formulas had blown over. Meanwhile, I had to admit that the superwoman who loomed up before me with her enormous boobs was built exactly like me and governed by the same physiological laws. Well, why not admit it? Why not also admit that, while being like her, I was, precisely because I was a male, ineffably inferior. What's a little contradiction anyhow? After what I'd been through I wasn't going to worry about logic.

"Martinelli," Helsingforth said, "go wait for me in the living room. I'll meet you there."

Finally! I was going to find out what she wanted of me. I left her, and, out of the corner of my eye, I saw her reach the door that led to the bathroom.

11

What strikes me today, when I recall the scene that followed, is the artificial and unconvincing quality lent to it by Helsingforth. Even her words had a false ring. They were stiff and affected as though she had prepared her lines in advance. Through and through, her attitude reflected a kind of cold sadism that, when put to the test, failed to give her the moment of pleasure she'd expected from it. She was a paranoid persecutor, no doubt about it! But her cruelty lacked the spontaneous quality of violent emotion. It was rather a system and a fairly laborious system at that.

Furthermore, as I've already noted, she overdid it. All her mannerisms were exaggerated. For instance, when I stepped into the living room, I saw on a small, low table a teapot, toast, butter, jam—and a single cup. I wasn't invited.

As deliberate boorishness, it belonged in the same category with her custom of omitting the complimentary close at the end of her letters. It was so heavy-handed that it missed its mark.

Another example: Helsingforth coming from the kitchen finally appeared in the living room. She didn't come in—she made an entrance. She "strutted" around in a silky, iridescent bathrobe beneath which she was quite clearly nude. Without so much as a glance my way, she sat down in the only armchair and said to me, the way you'd nudge your dog, "Sit!"

That was a bit too much. It was childish. And what I felt just then wasn't humiliation but a kind of amused contempt. It seemed to me that Helsingforth could have been a little more subtle in her dirty tricks. I even had to make a serious effort to remind myself just how dangerous she was and how vulnerable I was.

Okay. I sat down on a stool and, staring at the toast—I'd just realized that I was hungry—waited.

Silence. She drank. I suppose she was trying to give the impression that, in her, this was a sacred function, like all her functions: The whole world stopped and watched her. Frankly, it didn't work—I didn't fall for it.

After all, in Blueville, I'd had dealings with genuine people: Pierce, Burage, Stien, Grabel. Even Mr. Barrow was authentic in a sense: He believed in his bureaucracy. And then the camp's lookout tower, the barbed-wire fences, the labs and the complicated social life with its castes, its bugging and its clandestine life—these were solid and real. But here everything was fake. The cabin, to begin with. From a distance, it looked like a log cabin in the woods, like so many others in Vermont. But when you went inside you found a pool with a marble rim. And in that movie-studio scenery, what was Helsingforth supposed to be? A Grecian heroine? A sacred monster? No, the only thing impressive about her was her measurements. Take away the height, the musculature—and what was left? A ruthless businesswoman, an ill-bred millionairess and a third-rate actress.

I sat on my stool, silent, deferential, my eyes lowered, but that was just a pretense. Inside, I was sneering. I was looking down at my companion. I was degrading her. I was dragging her through the mud. That Helsingforth was a big fake. A run-of-the-mill sadico-paranoiac who took herself for Nero because she spanked her sweetheart. Basically, despite her grand airs, she was vulgarity personified. No style. No finesse.

It even reached the point (and this was reckless) where I forgot that she held my life in her hands. And not just my life. As soon as I came into contact with her, I rephallocratized myself. I wallowed in sadistic reveries that weren't always in the best taste. For example: I get to my feet, seize her stool, smash it over her head and, taking advantage of her loss of consciousness, rape her.

Just at that very instant my rape victim set down her cup on the tray and looked at me, a glance that—from her—I would qualify as benign. Neutral voice. Velvet gloves. Christ, was she a rotten actress! How she overdid it! How she telegraphed her punches! As if I couldn't imagine the ferocious follow-up after that sickeningly sweet beginning!

"How's your lab doing?"

"Very well."

She thwarted me at once. "Too well." She went on: "I've received a report that mentions an excessive intimacy between you and Burage."

I replied in a neutral voice, "Burage has important administrative duties. I see her frequently, and our relations have improved a great deal."

A pause. She stuck her nose back into her cup and took it out again to tell me harshly, "I've received other reports about you, mentioning an ambiguous attitude toward Friedman and Mrs. Barrow."

"Friedman?"

"The militiawoman you call Pussy."

After a moment I replied, "Ambiguous isn't the right word. My attitude is proper, but I can't deny an involuntary attraction for the persons you've mentioned."

Helsingforth considered me with icy eyes. And, after it was too late, I asked myself why I'd made that idiotic confession. Perhaps because, having denied the charge about Burage, I'd tried to get the other two off the hook. No, it wasn't that. The real reason was that Helsingforth's third-rate acting had exasperated me and I was playing my part any old way. In a style that wasn't my own. Once again I realized: You can't play a scene right with someone who's acting badly!

"I hope, Doctor," Helsingforth said accusingly, "that you're aware of the seriousness of what you've just said."

But when it came to seriousness, her own was hardly

convincing. I replied, "I'm aware of it. On the other hand, I suppose that you expect me to give you frank answers."

I was trying to get out of it any way I could. And it wasn't going very well.

She paused dramatically and said, without raising her voice, "Well now, Doctor, what are we doing about your resignation?"

So that was it! I could see it coming a mile away. And, to boot, as if she was asking me for my opinion. That sadistic little affectation was clumsy and stupid. But it had its effect on me. My mouth went dry. I had trouble getting my lips unstuck, and when I spoke it was with a toneless voice.

"Has anything new developed that could make you reconsider your decision to keep me on?"

"There is something," she answered with such badly done impassiveness that I knew at once there was another blow coming. She went on: "In October the Bedford Administration won't renew the subsidy for your research."

As blows went, that one fell wide of the mark. First of all, because it had been foreseeable. Second, because my research would be over by October. And even before.

I told her so.

She said nothing, and then she put on a little act for me that was clearly a trick. In slow motion she poured herself a second cup of tea, put two lumps of sugar in and stirred with her spoon. That took a minute. Deep suspense. I watched the flames with a patient look.

Having kept me, so she thought, on tenterhooks this way, she said with that pseudo-impassive look, "Whether you finish or not, it's highly unlikely that I'll be allowed to put your vaccine into production."

I'd known that, too. Helsingforth wasn't telling me anything. She was simply confirming what I knew. And I showed neither surprise nor indignation. Her bomb hadn't gone off. I kept silent.

It was a pity that I didn't consider it wise to lift my eyes and look at her, but I thought that she had been disconcerted by my insensibility. She resumed after a moment and in a tone of voice that struck me—this time because it seemed natural: "Believe me, I'm not happy at the thought of losing this huge market. As far as I'm concerned, all I ask is to put your vaccine on the market. But the way things are right now, it seems out of the question."

She'd almost sounded human when she spoke to me about her money troubles.

I kept quiet, my eyes lowered, and I asked myself a few questions. If she was convinced that she couldn't market my vaccine, what was stopping her from firing me right then and there? And if she intended to do so, why didn't she do it by mail? What was the sense of this meeting?

I was bristling, all my senses alerted. I was awaiting the follow-up. And the follow-up came, quite unexpectedly.

"Martinelli, you've confessed an 'involuntary attraction' for Friedman and for Mrs. Barrow."

"I've done nothing reprehensible—neither in word nor deed."

"There have been looks."

"Yes, but the looks themselves have stopped."

"I know."

She considered me with her right eye and, I think, her left eye, too—despite the camouflage of her hair.

"And do you also feel an 'involuntary attraction' for me?" she asked.

So that was it! I was flabbergasted. Well, I was glad I'd decided, right from the start, to act like a shy maiden and keep my eyes lowered. Because this time the powder wasn't damp. The bomb went off! And I was really amazed. I felt like a typist who'd just been propositioned by her boss.

I had absolutely no idea of what to answer, and quite at random I said, "I'm a little hungry. Can I have a piece of toast?"

It wasn't such a bad idea, after all. If she wanted to go to bed with me, the least she could do was feed me.

"You can," she said reluctantly.

I leaned over. I didn't content myself with taking a slice of toast—I buttered it. And without undue haste I brought it to my lips.

"You owe me an answer," she said impatiently.

"I can't make up my mind to give it to you."

"Why?"

"It could incriminate me. You've just chalked up a few miserable looks at Pussy and Mrs. Barrow as crimes."

"I'm the judge around here," replied Helsingforth.

If my fate and the fate of my vaccine weren't at stake, I might have been grateful for her cynicism. At least, things were out in the open. She didn't believe a word of the prevailing orthodoxy.

Under her gaze I sensed that I couldn't stall any longer. I set down the half-eaten slice of toast on the table and said, "There is the attraction you've spoken about, but it's being checked by fear."

"Explain that," she said with an impassive air.

"You started this talk by letting me know that you might discharge me at any time. I'd like you to reconsider that remark."

"Why?"

"So you won't think that my actions are prompted by fear."

A look. She was trying to make up her mind about understanding. Haughty brows. A pout. Very bad mimicry of disdainful incredulity. With that, she laughed. Loudly, at the top of her voice. A contemptuous laugh. Insulting, provocative. From deep down—ha! ha! ha!—with the utmost contempt. And it didn't work, of course. She misplaced her treacherous laugh; it didn't ring true, completely out of tune with her voice. My ear was offended, not me.

Not to mention that she dragged out her ha! ha! ha! too much. Happy laughter is always long; nasty laughter is always short. Hers was doubly false—in its ring and its length.

"Martinelli," she continued with her most contemptuous look, "you're not too bright. If you think I'm going to guarantee your stay in Blueville in exchange for your 'services,' you've got another think coming. You aren't in a position to bargain anything whatsoever. If you give in, you'll get nothing from me—not even a promise of keeping you on."

"If you give in!" she'd said that without a smile. Despite the dangers that I ran, I began to be amused by this great deployment of force aimed at getting me to sleep with her. After all, I might not have gained anything. But I certainly had nothing to lose.

I made up my mind to counterattack this old trouper.

"May I ask you something?" I said politely.

"Yes."

"A few minutes ago, when I was drying your back at the side of the pool, you could feel, couldn't you . . ."

I left my sentence hanging in midair, and I gave her a smile—a bit on the whorish side—one for which I would have reproached myself if it hadn't been necessary.

"Well, of course," she replied as if it were taken for granted.

"In that case, don't you think this blackmail about my resignation is a bit superfluous?"

"Yes," she answered, "if just having you were enough for me. But that isn't enough. I also want to subdue you."

Good Lord, "subdue" me! Like Julius Caesar subdued Gaul! How she overdid things! All for a little copulation!

I was going to try to get around this enormous wasp.

"Subdue me?" I asked with an agreeable smile. "I don't see how that's possible. In view of the fact that I want you, there's some ambiguity in the situation. If I decided to sleep with you, you'd never know what had prompted my decision—desire or fear."

I saw from her look that she didn't like that at all, being caught in the nets of rather subtle reasoning. She got out of it as best she could by smashing everything.

"You know, Martinelli," she said brutally, "if there's one thing I don't care a rap about it's your Italian cleverness!"

I didn't get time to answer. A bolt of lightning illuminated the room with a blinding white light. There was a clap of thunder nearby, very hard and very loud, and in the kitchen someone screamed.

"Audrey!" cried Helsingforth.

She leaped from her armchair with a heavy agility, jerked open the kitchen door and, a second later, reappeared, carrying Audrey in her arms.

"Doctor!" she cried anxiously. "Has she been hit?"

As she spoke she lay her down on the enormous couch. I went up and leaned over.

"Don't touch me!" Audrey cried, throwing open her eyes and staring at me with revulsion.

"It's nothing," I said with a little laugh. "Her reaction proves it."

But Helsingforth wasn't laughing. She sat on the couch, leaning her broad back against the cedar paneling, lifted Audrey's body with surprising tenderness, placing the girl's head and torso on her lap and, supporting her slender neck in the crook of her arm, stroked Audrey's hair with her broad hand. At the same time she heaped on Audrey a string of tender, indistinct words that sounded like a muted purring and roaring all at the same time.

I couldn't believe my eyes. Or my ears. I'd had mistaken ideas about paranoiacs. I'd thought that the hypertrophy of the ego, together with persecutory sadism, prevented them from being able to love. What an error! My own eyes had confirmed the fact: Whiplashes didn't stop tender feelings.

I admit that I'd never seen the relationship of those two women in this light. And I began to feel a bit embarrassed about being there. Seeing the little sadistic games was all right, but I didn't want to intrude on an intimate relationship.

I made a decision: I'd slip away.

As I moved toward the door, Helsingforth lifted her head, as though surprised to see me there.

"I'm leaving for Washington tomorrow," she said absently. "I'll be back in a week."

It was over. She'd simply erased me out of the landscape. She hadn't said anything as polite as a "goodbye." But I interpreted her phrase as both taking leave of me for the present and arranging to see me in the future.

With the door of the deluxe cabin closed behind me, I inhaled a good mouthful of air—and swallowed some water. It was raining cats and dogs, but, strangely enough, the sky was lighter than during my meeting with Helsingforth. I ran to the stables in the rain. The gelding was already saddled, and, in Chouchka's stall, I was relieved to find an average human being in the person of Jackie.

"You can speak without danger," Jackie said, tossing me a natural, straightforward smile which, after all I'd been through, had the effect of a ray of sunshine. She added, "Don't worry, the storm makes any kind of bugging impossible. And, besides,

Helsingforth has other fish to fry just now. I started saddling your Chouchka at the first bolt of lightning. I was sure of what would happen. Audrey has a phobia about lightning, and that brings the maternal instinct gushing out of Helsingforth, and then there's a lot of kissing and hugging."

"Do you know them so well?"

Jackie laughed. "I bring the happy couple their supplies twice a week. By jeep and, when the jeep can't get through, on horseback."

She unfastened a transparent blue raincoat from her saddle. She buttoned it tightly over her uniform and pulled the hood over her service cap. She was charming like that, and, what's more, my militiawoman had changed. While she cinched her gelding's girth, I detected a kind of happy anticipation in her sparkling eyes, her quick movements, her warm smiles.

"Saddle up!" she said with an effervescent little laugh. "You'll ride ahead of me as long as we're in sight of the house, Doctor. Afterward, that won't be necessary."

I pulled my golf cap down over my ears and buttoned the collar of my raincoat right up to my Adam's apple, without illusions about its watertightness. I sensed beforehand the icy little streams that it would let down my back. More practical by far was the militiawoman's hood, which gathered under her chin by means of a drawstring and revealed only the pink oval of her face and her gray eyes, where an inexplicable joy seemed to dance. Her foot in the stirrup, she threw me a final sparkling look before heaving herself up into the saddle.

Once we were past the gate, she overtook me and trotted abreast of me, without speaking now but constantly turning my way her hooded, rain-blurred face in which I saw, moving in a confused vision, the pink of her cheeks, the gray of her eyes, the white of her teeth. Jackie was posting. Whenever she lifted her posterior from the saddle to accompany the undulation of the horse, she brought her pelvis forward, arching her back and drawing in her buttocks, a movement that, by its energy, repetition and rhythm, seemed to mime the act of love.

We reached the sandy trail. We had more room there than on the trail that wound its way among the cedars. And, most of all, a long stretch over flat ground lay before us. The rain was coming down in sheets, lightning blinded us at times, and the dull rumbling of thunder endlessly reverberated through the mountains in a kind of paroxysm that was both soothing and exciting at the same time.

Jackie turned to me and, her mouth full of rain, cried with alacrity, "Gallop, Doctor?"

"Sure!"

At the end of the level stretch, we eased back into a trot to take a hairpin curve. After rounding the bend, we came to an abrupt slope gullied by the rain where we were forced to bring the horses to a walk.

Under the blue hood Jackie's pink face, lashed by the rain and wind, turned to me constantly with a gaiety that I found pleasant even if I didn't share it. My problematic future at Blueville weighed on my mind. I was watching Chouchka closely, for the rain had gouged ruts in the sandy trail and Chouchka kept sidestepping, at times coming close to the gelding that this proximity frightened, at other times bringing us too near the sheer drop at the edge of the trail.

It was with relief that I saw us reach the bottom of the valley. As a matter of fact, I didn't see it. The mist that had accumulated there kept it concealed from me, and it wasn't until the last second, when I was right on top of it, that I saw it.

Amazement. The stream that we'd forded in coming was enormously swollen and its muddy waters were so swift that we would have been swept away, horses and all, if we'd been fool enough to attempt the crossing.

I looked at Jackie. "Well, what do we do now?"

"I don't know," Jackie replied good-naturedly. "Wait."

She smiled. She blinked to defend her eyes against the stinging rain, but, between her half-closed lids, her gray eyes had lost none of their gaiety.

"Wait?" I said. "Wait in this downpour for the rain to stop?"

"What do you suggest?" she asked with the same merry, mischievous look. "Come now, Doctor," she added, laughing, "don't take it so tragically."

"Oh, you think this is funny, eh?"

She laughed. "What I find funny is that you haven't anticipated all this happening. But I have!" she went on in the same restrained jubilation.

"But this isn't the only crossing, is it?"

"Yes, it is!" she replied triumphantly. "I know these woods. I've made enough patrols here."

"Well," I asked impatiently, "have you made up your mind?"

She was looking at me with feigned seriousness.

"To tell you the truth, Doctor, there are only two possibilities: Either we spend the night in the rain or we go back to Helsingforth's."

"I'll take the rain," I answered glumly.

"That's the spirit, Doctor! After all, what's a night out in the storm? You've got warm clothes, a good raincoat, a golf cap . . ."

"I'm not thinking about myself," I replied, irritated at seeing how lightly she took it all. "I'm thinking about Dave. He's going to be worried."

"Doctor," she said, laughing even harder, "I see where you get your reputation for being a mother hen. Come now, Dave has a lot less to complain about than you. He's nice and dry! And he isn't facing the prospect of going without his meal!"

"You don't know Dave. He's going to panic if he doesn't see me come back. He's very sensitive."

"So are you," she said with an entirely different tone and look. "Thank God there's nothing tough-looking about you."

She wheeled her gelding around and told me over her shoulder, "Come on, we're not going to stay here. Our horses will get cold."

She went trotting back up the slope we'd just come down, and I pushed Chouchka abreast of her. I had water trickling down my back, my hands turning blue and my feet frozen in my boots. The sky was dark, and although the storm continued its rumblings a long way off, the rain hadn't stopped—far from it. Without a sudden let-up or violent downpour, the rain fell with that maddening regularity that can go on for hours or days. Furthermore, I was ravenously hungry. I could only think about that slice of toast I'd grubbed from Helsingforth and had only half eaten.

The slope became steep again. Chouchka was struggling. I walked her. Jackie did the same and threw me an amused look out of the corner of her eyes.

"How's it going?"

"Not so good."

"In other words, Doctor, you're not the rugged type."

"No."

"You're forgetting your duty, Doctor. You should get off your horse and build me a lean-to out of logs, if for no other reason than to protect my beautiful fair complexion from the elements."

"Don't count on it."

"Come now, Doctor, put a little will in your work. In two hours' time you'll have a nice roof over my head!" She laughed again. "We go to the left, Doctor."

"Where does that trail lead, do you know?"

"I haven't got the faintest idea."

Obviously, she was pulling my leg, since she'd just told me that she knew the woods like the palm of her hand from having patrolled them many times. I said nothing. Besides, even if I'd wanted to say something, I couldn't have. Jackie never stopped. It didn't seem to matter to her what she said. She was expounding, in a mocking way, on the theme of the anti-hero. What struck me wasn't her words so much as her cheerfulness. Jackie radiated animal joy. I felt sure that the blood was coursing faster through her vigorous body, that the rain and cold were incapable of penetrating it and that, under her clothes, her skin was warm and velvety.

We came out into a vast clearing and, with her riding crop, Jackie pointed to a large brown spot, barely visible in the rain and mist, at the far end.

"Do you see that?" she asked.

"No, not very well. What is it?"

She laughed. "A hut, Doctor. You won't have to build it."

"You've been there before?"

"It's our command post when we patrol the woods. Helsingforth lent it to us. Actually, that was her first Walden. You're going to be able to eat, sleep and, most of all," she added with friendly smile, "let your son know you're safe."

I was touched that she'd thought about Dave, and I returned her smile with interest. Thereupon, she began to gallop. I followed suit, and in less than a minute we were at the hut. She rode around it. I followed her, and I saw stalls for the horses under a shed roof.

"Doctor," Jackie said, "leave your horse saddled in her stall. I'll take care of it. I'm going to give her a good brushing and mine, too. Meanwhile, the key is under a rock in front of the door. Make a big fire in the fireplace and see what's in the refrigerator. But wait till I get back before you use the phone."

Although I later realized the slight paradox in the situation, I was grateful to Jackie for assigning me the domestic chores. I was frozen, and the mere idea of making a fire warmed me up.

Once the flames were jumping high, I inventoried the refrigerator. I found there butter, eggs and bacon, which made my mouth water just to see them, and in a cupboard tea, salted crackers and canned pineapple. There was more than enough. When my woman soldier showed up I was setting the table while the eggs were sputtering in the frying pan with a delicious smell of bacon that filled the hut and whetted my appetite.

Jackie scarcely had time to wash her hands and there we were, seated face to face, the flames roasting one side of our faces while we ate greedily without a word, but in an atmosphere of relaxation and complicity, trading happy looks: two healthy animals who got on well together, hitched to the same rack, and who were going to share the same stall. My feet were becoming warm again inside my boots. A pleasant warmth was spreading through my belly, and I was dead-tired, with that kind of fatigue that is, perhaps, the most exquisite pleasure—especially when you've eaten your fill.

"What about Dave, Doctor?" Jackie asked mockingly, setting down her teacup. "Have you forgotten him?"

"You told me to wait for you before using the phone," I answered with a mixture of insincerity and remorse.

She got to her feet, and, standing beside a small desk, picked up the receiver and dialed a number.

"Hello," she said, "this is Lieutenant Davidson. Would you transfer me to Mr. Barrow?"

She had spoken in a harsh voice, reminding me of the old Jackie.

A fairly long wait. And while she was listening, with the receiver to her ear, I had ample time to look her over. Her blond hair, cut/in bangs, was tossed back, neither long nor short—practical. Her skin was sunburned, her eyes gray, with the beginning of the crow's-feet that sportswomen develop, broad cheekbones, a solid jaw and, emanating from this straightforward physiognomy, a look of common sense and balance that I found very attractive after my encounter with those two madwomen.

There. She'd gotten Mr. Barrow and she was explaining the situation to him. She didn't speak to him like a higher-up but more like an equal who was slightly lower in the chain of command. True, Barrow was an A and, as I'd just learned to my amazement (I knew nothing about insignia), Jackie was a lieutenant.

When she asked Barrow to let Dave know that I wasn't going to be there, I broke in.

"Would you please tell Dave to spend the night at the Pierces'? They have a bed."

She transmitted this to Barrow with the tone of someone who is used to giving orders and hung up immediately.

"And now," I asked, "are you going to call Helsingforth?"

She laughed. "Nobody has the right to call Helsingforth."

"Not even Barrow?"

"Not even Barrow." Looking at me with laughing eyes, she added, "Relax, Doctor. Helsingforth isn't going to disturb us in the middle of the night."

She said "us" without the slightest embarrassment. I was the one who was embarrassed.

"What does your rank signify?" I asked, sitting down on the bed and leaning my back against the wooden partition. "Do you command the militiawomen at Blueville?"

"Yes. I took over just a short time ago."

"In that case, how is that you're the one who handles Helsingforth's supplies?

"I've been handling her supplies since the time I was an ordinary militiawoman. And when I was commissioned an officer, I received orders to volunteer to go on doing the same work."

"Orders from whom? From Helsingforth?"

She smiled. "The milita isn't under Helsingforth. The section that I command was assigned to Blueville by the state of Vermont. My leaders are in Montpelier."

"And are they the ones who ordered you to keep on supplying Helsingforth?"

"No," she replied, looking me in the eyes. "It was 'we.'"

I was dumfounded. I stared at her and remained silent. It was a mistake, I realized that too late. I should have asked her what "we" was. My silence betrayed me.

She laughed, grabbed a chair and straddled it in front of me, leaning her forearms on the back rest.

"Listen, Doctor," she said, "before you start asking me innocent questions about 'we,' I'll tell you how 'we' recruited me. And, first of all, if you're interested, I'm going to tell you who I am. I'd just received a master's degree in sociology when the epidemic broke out. As you can well imagine, they didn't need sociologists any more. And, believe me, I was awfully glad to be recruited by the militia. No need to tell you that my degree was worthless. But I'd gone out for sports, I'm a good shot and I was in Women's Lib."

"You were in Women's Lib?"

"I'm in Women's Lib, Doctor. Or, to be more precise, I'm ninety percent in agreement with the movement. And in disagreement with the rest."

"And what's the remaining ten percent?"

"Come on, Doctor," she replied with a laugh. "I'm not going to write you a report."

I returned her smile. "Aren't you a sociologist?"

"Well, basically, I'm of the opinion that we mustn't mistake our enemy. Men aren't the enemy—even if they often play a negative role with regard to women. We mustn't confuse the actor who plays a part with the one who writes the script."

"And who did write the script?"

"The misogynic culture that we inherited."

"Bedford would tell you that men are the ones who founded that culture."

"Oh, Doctor, that was so long ago! We just can't accuse men of a second original sin. Besides, I happen to be fond of men."

And saying this, she looked at me with her gray eyes in such a direct and clear way that I felt a little shiver run down my spine.

"You aren't very orthodox," I said, pursuing the conversation in order to hide my excitement.

"I'm going to shock you. Some days I even wonder if women really do liberate themselves through work."

"Now, wait, that happens to be true!"

"Mainly, it's true for the thinkers in the liberation movement. They're lawyers, doctors, reporters. In other words, an elite. But do you think it's very 'liberating' for a woman to be working on an assembly line with a foreman looking over her shoulder? Or, for that matter, for a militiawoman?"

"You're not too crazy about your job, are you, Lieutenant?"

"It makes me sick. The day before yesterday I read in *New Era* that the military profession was one of the most noble and most important of women's conquests! Frankly, this is one conquest I'd gladly have left for men. Being a militiawoman is stultifying. Endless routine! Not to mention the danger."

"The danger?"

She replied curtly, "We sometimes come under fire."

"When?"

"Out on patrol. But, up to now, never at the camp."

"Who attacks you?"

"We've got two types of adversaries: gangs of looters and anti-Bedford guerrillas."

I looked at her wide-eyed. "Are there anti-Bedford guerrillas?"

"Lots and well armed—especially here. They use Canada as a sanctuary."

"Men?"

"Mostly women and a few men."

"That's marvelous!"

"I think so, too. But you won't see them. They'll never attack Blueville."

"Why not?"

"Because you're there."

I looked at her in amazement.

"Doctor," she said, looking at me gravely, "you don't seem to realize that your research represents a great hope for thousands of people."

I had a lump in my throat, and for a few seconds I was incapable of opening my mouth.

"Jackie," I said after a while, "you were going to tell me how you were recruited by 'we.'"

She laughed, got to her feet, lit a cigarette and took a few steps around the room. I looked at her. There was something contradictory about her silhouette and bearing. Her uniform, her boots, the way her heels struck the floor, the way she threw her shoulders back—that was all masculine and military. But her undulating hips and under the tunic her breasts were clearly outlined (all the more so because she stood straight). There was the same ambiguity about her face. The features might have been masculine, but the skin was smooth and fine, the pupils constantly animated, the face infinitely more mobile than a man's.

"Doctor," she resumed with a look of gaiety, mockery and complicity (the effect of which was to make me open my ears), "about four weeks ago Rita, whose room faces mine, informed me at ten A.M. that the militiawomen's barracks were going to be searched from top to bottom by experts brought in from Montpelier. Rita suggested that I entrust to her any 'forbidden object' that I might have in my possession. Which I did and rightly so. An hour later, they went over my room with a fine-tooth comb. Doctor, do you have any idea of what this object is?"

"Yes, I think so."

She began laughing without embarrassment, went up to the fire, warmed each heel of her boots in turn.

"Any other questions, Doctor?"

"Yes, do you know why 'we' gave you the order to handle Helsingforth's supplies yourself?"

A silence. I noticed that she'd hesitated before replying, and when she did reply the answer was brief.

"'We' thinks that, since Anita left for Paris, your life depends solely on Helsingforth."

With that, silence. She wouldn't say any more about it, and she changed the subject.

"Furthermore, it's highly enlightening to be around Helsingforth and Audrey. As enlightening as what goes on, with the official blessing, in the militiawomen's barracks. You know, Doctor," she continued, coming back to her firm stance before me but without sitting, "I wonder if it's really worthwhile eliminating men. I've noticed that within the female sex, a second sex has been reconstituted, and couples are formed—

with all problems that couples face, including the one about who's going to do the dishes and which of the two is going to dominate the other—the 'strong one' or the 'weak one'?"

"I suppose it's Audrey that does the dishes."

"There's no doubt on that score. Audrey has the status of a domestic slave, but it isn't certain that she's 'dominated.'"

A silence again. Then Jackie threw her cigarette into the fire with a decided look, left the room and returned with her carbine that she stood in the corner the wall formed with a little night table. Having done this, she checked methodically to see that the doors, windows and shutters were closed. The rain continued to beat on the shingled roof. I followed Jackie with my eyes.

"A little room, Doctor?" asked Jackie, sitting beside me on the bed. She turned toward me, eyes shining with amusement.

"Doctor," she asked, "you aren't in any doubt about the nature of the forbidden object that Rita hid for me, are you?"

"No, as a matter of fact, I'm not."

"On the other hand, what you don't know is that I've given it an identity. Yes," she went on happily, "that's the power of the imagination for you. I've actually managed to endow that object with a personality of its own. Well, Doctor, aren't you going to ask me the name I've given it?"

"I'm not going to ask you, but you look as though you'd love to tell me."

She laughed. "Right!" She went on: "Well, should I tell you?"

"If you want to."

She considered me with enormous mischievousness, her lips puffed out with restrained laughter, and a jubilant flame danced in her eyes.

"Well, Doctor, I've named it Ralph!"

With that, she made merry over my expression and laughed endlessly. While she rocked back and forth, shaking the bed and herself with gales of mirth, her eyes were stalking me. And with perfect naturalness, when her laughter subsided, she placed her hand on my thigh and left it there, without taking her eyes off me. Gradually, her face became serious again, her eyes changed and, I suppose, mine did, too.

"All right," she said as if she'd made up her mind. And with her toes, she removed her boots and sent them flying one after the other across the room. Then, rapidly, she unbuckled her belt, rolled it around the revolver and tossed the whole thing onto the bed behind her.

Although I was carried away by the contagion of desire, I wasn't blind to the irony of the situation. It was clear from the military accouterments strewn around the room and the virile haste with which they'd been shed that the soldier had come home from the wars—home to me.

12

As soon as we got into Blueville, I went over to the Pierces' to pick up Dave. He was still sleeping, and I noticed that "Rita," although she was alone with me—Pierce and John had gone off for a swim before breakfast—made no attempt to disconnect the bug and talk to me in confidence. And yet, obviously, she was eaten up with curiosity. Her hawk eyes searched me, and while I woke Dave with the usual precautions she moved around me, sniffing me like a hunting dog, and when I was leaving she gave me a smile and a wink full of hints. I was worried. If she could guess the kind of night I'd had just from my scent, it behooved me to take a shower.

I did even better: I took a bath and, what's more, I nearly fell asleep in my warm tub. Dave reminded me that they didn't serve breakfast after 9:00 A.M., but discreet and tactful as usual, he didn't ask me any questions while I shaved and dressed. There I was, very presentable, I thought—my night of debauchery washed away, Anglo-Saxon-style, by soap and water—and on the way to the castle I had a man-to-man conversation with Dave, who was most attentive. I told him, *sotto voce*, that I couldn't tell him anything—except with regard to the swollen-river incident, which I dramatized, and the hut in the woods, which I described. I was afraid that he might sulk, but not at all.

The long dark lashes on his pale cheeks quivered with interest in my story.

In the cafeteria, avoiding Stien's table (he threw me an unfriendly glance when I came in), I picked the one where Rita was sitting with Pierce and John. I didn't feel like talking, and I was counting on Rita to keep the conversation going, which she did marvelously. While searching the room with her keen eyes, she warded off the looks which, on that morning, had a tendency to converge on me. As for me, I kept my nose in my teacup, aside from one brief glance at the table where Burage sat with Crawford. At the table and not at Burage herself, because I remembered all too well Helsingforth's disturbing question about our relations. I would have liked to have been a woman just then, to know how to see without looking, something women can do so well.

Leaving the cafeteria, I bumped into Mr. Barrow in the corridor. His naked, gleaming skull bent my way, he was—strangely enough—the first to say hello and, what's more, he said it with a kind of oily complicity, while his globular eyes were fixed on mine like suckers to pump them of any information that they might hold. I made my eyes as vacant as I could while, with a voice that was neutral, factual and conscientious, I informed him that I wouldn't be going horseback riding with Stien and Jespersen, as there was an experiment in progress at the lab I wanted to watch. Whatever you wish, Dr. Martinelli, he said with a slow and unctuous smile that spilled over into his jowls, humiliating me for some unknown reason. He added with his suave, hard voice: "It goes without saying that the Sunday horseback rides aren't compulsory. After all, everyone has the right to be a little tired now and then." On these ambiguous words, he moved away, waddling his fat hips but with a surprising agility, as if his thick legs were bouncing against the floor like soccer balls.

Dave whinnied like a colt when I told him that, aside from a visit or two at the lab and a siesta, I was going to spend the day with him—at the pool or on the tennis court? It's up to you. Both! he answered enthusiastically.

I hoped that I'd measure up on the court; and three hours of riding, the day before and that morning, hadn't done my backside any good, and the night I'd spent had left me a little weak in the knees.

At the lab, where I went right after breakfast, I'd scarcely opened the door when Dr. Grabel came to meet me. Although it was a Sunday, it didn't surprise me to see him, in view of the importance of the experiment in progress. In his long, bladelike face topped by a balding, oblong skull, his dark eyes, small and piercing, shone with excitement and he stooped his tall, lean body to tell me in a vibrant voice, "I think we've got it!"

It was quite clear for me, though apparently inexplicit, but we had to deal with the bugging. Without a word, I went past Grabel and strode down to the room where we kept our experimental animals under lock and key.

A glance was enough. The control dog—inoculated but not vaccinated—was dead. But the three vaccinated and inoculated dogs couldn't have been more alive. And, as we approached them, overflowing with gratitude for our visit, they yapped excitedly and wagged their tails frantically. I went up to their cages and patted them one after another. What desperate kindness, what inexplicable love I saw shining in our victims' beautiful brown eyes—so ingenuous, so frank, so unlike man's eyes.

"Have they eaten?" I asked, turning to Grabel.

"Food and water. And when I walked them, not the slightest loss of balance. No disturbances. They're completely euphoric."

I'd been expecting these results and I was infinitely pleased with them—or, rather, I would have been pleased with them if the thought of what was coming next hadn't filled me with anguish. I'd learned through Burage that there was no bug in the kennels.

"Dr. Grabel, I don't think it's necessary for me to remind you: only Smith, Pierce and Burage are to be informed. The others mustn't know about the experiment."

"Every precaution has been taken," Grabel said. "As you can see, there are no markings on the cages of the vaccinated dogs."

I remained silent and rightfully so. I'd always known that

someday, I would have to inoculate myself, after taking the vaccine, with the Encephalitis 16 virus. I also knew that after all the experiments, which had cost our poor dogs their lives, my chances of recovery were excellent, provided no errors were made with the dosage and that the reaction of men to the vaccine was as good as a dog's reaction—which was probable but not proven. In short, I'd been weighing all of this— including the margin of error—for a long time. But up till this point I'd had only an abstract idea of this final experiment, in which I must stake my life on the success of our research. For those last few minutes it hadn't been abstract any more. The moment I'd been dreading had come, I was touching it, I was living it.

"Are we doing another experiment with the dogs?" Grabel asked, as if he'd heard my silence.

I replied in a toneless voice, "No, we're pressed for time. We're going on to the next phase."

Something quite unexpected happened then: Grabel smiled. That smile was doubly surprising: It was rather inappropriate, and Grabel seldom smiled. I must admit that, given the state of mind I was in, his reaction left me aghast. After all, the "next phase" was me. And after me, the lab's P.M.s: Pierce and Smith. And certainly not Dr. Grabel, on whom the vaccine couldn't have been conclusive, since he already enjoyed immunity as an A. So Grabel had no cause for concern. He didn't run the risks of contamination that were involved in the daily handling of viral strains. That's why I couldn't figure out his laughter and the look of expectancy I'd just discerned on his face.

I remained silent. I distrusted my reactions—especially, where they concerned Grabel, with whom my relations had become quite good, after having been so poor.

I had another reason for sparing him. On several occasions Burage had insinuated (without actually saying it) that Dr. Grabel wasn't a stranger to "we" and that, at any rate, "we" trusted him implicitly. This was, furthermore, an unfathomable mystery to me. That an A might be sympathetic to an anti-Bedford movement baffled me. Wasn't it obvious that the defeat of Bedfordism would destroy the privileges of the A caste without giving them back what they'd lost?

I looked at Grabel and I said to him wryly, "The prospects aren't brilliant for me, you know. The next phase won't exactly be any picnic."

Grabel greeted this veiled rebuff serenely, I'd almost say merrily.

"I suspect as much," he said, accompanying these words with a little chuckle.

Then he added with a tactlessness that I'd qualify as staggering: "So what? The sooner the better."

Monday morning Burage was waiting for me in my office, her face serious, her look meaningful.

I've got some news for you," she said bluntly.

"Good news?"

"Good and bad. First, Rita's bug has been boobytrapped just like yours. From now on, you'll have only one contact: me," she said with a certain satisfaction. "Second, Rita was able to get together with Stien . . ."

"Where? Her bug is boobytrapped."

"In an undetermined place," Burage replied curtly, tossing her dark auburn hair with an imperious look, but at the same time her blue eyes (the expression of which changed so fast) told me to see in her reply caution, not distrust. "And believe me," she continued, "it wasn't easy, even for Rita, to get through that old crocodile's hide. But it was worth the trouble. Rita found Stien very much aware of the dangers that his research poses for your sex. And, at the very least, he isn't going to rush matters."

"I'm deeply relieved."

"Don't celebrate so fast," Burage replied, her earrings trembling against her neck. "The next part isn't so great. After putting out feelers on him, we've decided not to contact Jespersen. It looks as if he's fallen completely into the Bedfordist mold. Does that surprise you?"

"Not really. He showed a very orthodox attitude when we were asked to give sperm."

"Yes, I remember. You viewed his position with great generosity at the time. Not me. Jespersen is one of those people who confuse servility to the Administration with a sense of duty."

Silence.

"On the other hand," she resumed, "we've managed to have an extremely valuable contact with someone from his lab."

"Someone?"

"It doesn't matter whether it's a male or a female," she said rapidly. "Doctor, have you tasted the Ablationists' drug?"

"*Caladium seguinum?* Certainly not. Not even in an infinitesimal dose. It's a viscous, greenish liquid with a highly disagreeable smell."

"And taste, according to what I've been told. Well, the Jespersen project is aimed at remedying that."

I raised my brows. "Remedying what?"

"The appearance, odor and taste of *Caladium seguinum.*"

"You mean that Jespersen is trying to make them more acceptable?"

"Better than acceptable—imperceptible. The aim of Jespersen's project is to make *Caladium seguinum* a liquid as colorless and odorless as water. And just as insipid."

A second or two went by before I understood all the implications in that undertaking. And when I understood them, I was speechless.

"Well, what do you say to that, Doctor?" Burage asked, pressing her lips together. "Is it clear enough? The Bedford Administration is carrying out one of the plans cherished by the Nazis: castrating men without their knowing it."

I thought of poor Ricardo right away and I told Burage about him.

"Of course," she said harshly, "but from now on they won't even need to lie to Latin American labor. And do you think Bedford and her clique will stop at foreign workers?"

With a chuckle that rang false in my own ears, I replied, "I won't have the nerve to drink a glass of water any more."

"A glass of water!" Burage exclaimed. "When *Caladium seguinum* is clear, odorless and tasteless, it can be mixed into any food."

I looked at my hands clenched the desk. The more I thought

about it, the more outrageous the plan seemed. I'd always found it scandalous that the California penal code accepted castration as one of the sanctions for sex crimes. And that was a sentence pronounced openly after a public trial. But this surreptitious means of sterilization would allow the Bedford Administration (and any local administrations for that matter) secretly to wipe out virility. Once more my fears had proven well founded. Bedford's anti-male sexism was a kind of racism and, like all racism—if ever it got into power—must lead to criminal manipulation of the human being.

"And to think that it's a man of science, a distinguished chemist who's lending a hand in these schemes," I said, wringing my hands. "How far has Jespersen gone with it? Do you know? Is he almost done?"

Burage permitted herself a half smile, and a flame danced in her blue eyes.

"Jespersen has been held up by a series of untoward incidents."

A silence fell and I said, "That's a very dangerous business."

"Very. But courage isn't the prerogative of your sex."

I'd been informed. The "we" contact in Jespersen's lab was a woman.

Burage looked at her watch. "We've been talking for ten minutes. That's too much. I'll come back to see you early this afternoon. Oh, one other thing, Doctor. You're going to lose a good lab assistant."

"Who?"

"Crawford."

I opened my eyes wide and said angrily, "What has she done to make Helsingforth fire her?"

Burage's blue eyes became bluer. "Helsingforth wasn't the one who fired her. It's us—liquidating her."

I stared at her in amazement. "Do you mean *physically*?"

"Doctor, who do you take us for? We'll just content ourselves with hiding an incriminating object in her room the day before the search."

"And how will you know when there's going to be a search?"

Burage said nothing.

"What kind of object?"

"You know perfectly well."

It really didn't matter. It wasn't the means that bothered me; it was the end result. Crawford was an excellent lab assistant and, what's more—and, well, a lot more—I loved to see her walk around the lab. Oh, I didn't smile at her any more. I was too afraid of Burage's ire. But I was going to miss her.

I was wrong in letting my mind wander with Burage there. She read my thoughts, one after the other, on my face, and just from the way she tossed her flamboyant hair I expected the worst.

"Do you have any objections, Doctor?"

"None," I replied in a cowardly way. "But I'd still like to know what Crawford's done."

"Oh, nothing!" Burage answered with devastating irony. "Except send to you-know-who a little report on you and me."

I looked at her. So she already knew all about my meeting with Helsingforth. Jackie, to whom I'd told the story the night before, hadn't wasted any time in contacting her.

Burage resumed. "Don't you believe it? Wasn't Helsingforth's question about our relations enough? Do you need more proof? You never noticed that Crawford was spying on us?"

I would have been lying if I'd said no. I therefore decided to say nothing. But my silence was going to spare me from what came next, quite to the contrary. Burage, showing her claws, swooped down on me.

"Doctor," she said, her bosom heaving and her eyes aflame. (My eyes photographed her that way, magnificent, at the height of animal fury, and my lust, which had picked a bad time, took over. I was scarcely listening to her. I had an overpowering urge to grab her in my arms.) "Doctor," Burage said in a low, vibrant voice, "you've got a particularly hypocritical way of keeping quiet! That way you don't have to admit that bitch's guilt! Or ask me what prompted her to turn in the report! Because, naturally, you're innocent as a lamb in all this. You never noticed anything was going on. You just gave the party in question one of your seductive smiles every now and then."

"You're being unfair, Burage," I said without too much conviction. "The smiles had stopped."

"You're so two-faced!" Burage hissed, taking a step toward

me as if she were about to spring at me. "You really have all the shortcomings, Doctor, not to mention—and I quote one of your friends—your 'coarse and insatiable libido.'"

"Thanks for the quote," I replied, tight-lipped. "Give Stien my thanks. And thank Rita for having passed it on to you."

"And you can also thank Crawford for giving you such pleasant times when you used to go into her lair to check her preparations. Oh, that's right, no more smiles from you—not even a look!" (So she'd been watching me!) "But that warm voice, Doctor, those enveloping gestures, your Latin charm! And that bitch—arching her back to show off her bosom and letting a lock of dirty hair hang down over her eyes for dramatic effect."

"Stop!" I said, raising my hands. "I confess! I liked Crawford! But her hair wasn't dirty!"

"Wait!" Burage exclaimed with unfeigned indignation. "You dare admit it? What repugnant cynicism!"

"Come now, Burage, you've got to make up your mind. I'm a hypocrite if I deny it and a cynic when I admit it."

"You're both!" she said with restrained fury.

But this time I cut her off before she went any further.

"Let me ask you a question, Burage, before you tear me apart. If Crawford liked me, it's because she liked men. In that case, why not recruit her for "we"?

"I'd thought of it, don't worry," Burage replied more calmly, with a note of regret. "Unfortunately, Crawford is one of those inconsistent people whose body thinks one thing while their head thinks another. Crawford is a Women's Lib bigot, a narrow-minded Bedfordist. If she'd gone to bed with you, she would have enjoyed it—and then she'd have turned you in."

There was no way of proving that hypothesis, but, mulling it over, I thought it must be true.

"And now what's going to happen to her?" I asked.

"Do you mean when they find the Superdoll in her closet? Don't worry, Doctor, nothing really serious. Mrs. Barrow will send her to the rehabilitation center. There, she'll be taught that, as the vagina is only weakly innervated, the female orgasm is one hundred percent clitoral, and the male's penis has nothing to do with her pleasure."

I knew that refrain. I'd read it in Deborah Grimm's weighty prose. But what struck me was the change in Burage. As if the idea of Crawford going far away had cheered her up, I suddenly had a new person in front of me: gay, exhilarated, playful.

"What do you think about this, Doctor?"

"Me? I'm no gynecologist, and this is a very controversial question."

"You have an opinion, haven't you?"

"Oh, an opinion! There's another opinion for every research worker. Believe me, Burage, anyone who claims to know the truth about female orgasm is an unmitigated charlatan."

"Come, Doctor, don't be so modest," Burage said, tossing her dark auburn hair and staring at me with gleaming eyes that were half excited, half mocking. "You must have your opinion on the problem. Let me guess! As an inveterate phallocrat, you must set great store by vaginal orgasm."

"There's Kegel," I said defensively.

"Who's Kegel?"

"A gynecologist."

"And what has this gynecologist had to say?"

"He got the idea of treating women with bladder trouble by using exercises aimed at strengthening the muscles that surround the vagina."

"Did it work?"

"It worked beyond all expectations. His patients not only recovered but they soon noticed that they were achieving orgasm for the first time."

"And what do you conclude from that?"

"That the pubo-coccygeal muscles play a major part in female orgasm and that they are strongly stimulated by the pressure and friction of the penis inside the vagina."

"The pressure and friction of the penis. That's so well put! You're a poet, Doctor," she said mockingly.

But, at the same time, inexplicably, she blushed to the roots of her hair, turned her back to me quickly—her hair sweeping across her collar—and she said to me in an arrogant, authoritarian tone of voice over her shoulder, "I'll be back to see you early this afternoon. I've got to let you know about two decisions that concern you."

At lunch I noticed that Stien continued to snub me. He wouldn't favor me with a look and, what hurt me still more, I'd become transparent for Mutsch as well. God knows what interpretation they'd given to my absence on Saturday and my refusal, Sunday, to participate in the horseback riding. Compensation: Dave, at my side, was quite happy. He threw me knowing looks, an accomplice and an admirer at the same time. Obviously, he was happy to have a father who—in Blueville—could get past the barbed-wire fence and spend a night in the woods under mysterious circumstances.

My eyes lowered to the level of her hip, I watched Burage trot my way and take a seat with her tray at an empty table, where she didn't stay alone very long, for, my eyelids still halfway down, I saw a belly squeezed into blue pants that I recognized as Crawford's. A quick glance like the beam of a lighted bell buoy: My observation was confirmed. And what's more, that female Judas was smiling in the friendliest way at the co-worker she'd denounced.

Dave left me to meet his little tennis friends—notably, Joan Smith, aged eleven and a half, whom he prefers to all the rest because she's a girl and she's "soft." I watched this budding phallocrat move away.

Once the last meager mouthful had been swallowed, I also left the cafeteria and forced myself, just as I was heading for the exit, to make a friendly little wave at Jespersen, who'd just come in, svelte and handsome; but now I knew what lurked behind that likable wrapper. A second later I gave exactly the same wave—aren't appearances deceiving?—to Rita, who smiled at me with her gleaming eyes while she hopped, tray in hand, alongside a tall, gawky woman with dark hair. I immediately wondered if that could be the contact for "we" in Jespersen's lab.

I met two people in the long corridor that led to the exit: Mr. Barrow, who, from a distance, I saw bouncing my way on his thick, rubber legs and who, two paces away, stopped, bent his oily skull toward me and whispered to me in confidence that the sample-taking team would come at nine o'clock that night and he hoped I'd give them a proper welcome. I told him he could rest assured on this score, and I must admit that I turned around to follow him with my gaze, so astonished was I by his gait. The cafeteria door finally swallowed his huge buttocks and I went on. I wasn't alone very long. At the other end of the corridor appeared Mrs. Barrow. As soon as I saw her, I lowered my eyes modestly, as behooved a P.M. aware of his double inferiority—as a man and an "entire man"—in a world where everything, including the weak innervation of vaginas, reminded him that he was superfluous. But just as I half closed my lids, keeping in my field of vision the lower half of Mrs. Barrow, who was undulating agreeably my way, I had to straighten up, square my shoulders, lengthen my strides—in short, I began "strutting," as that awful Audrey would say. My body didn't know how to lie. It lied so little as I was about to pass Mrs. Barrow that I raised my eyelids, contemplating the person before me, and was amply rewarded, for I got a look right back and a smile so explicit that there wouldn't have been any need to top them off with a grazing of Mrs. Barrow's hand against mine just as she went past me.

Thanks, Mrs. Barrow. In all probability, nothing would come of these signals from one ship to another in the Blueville night and, anyway, I was old-fashioned. Adultery wasn't my forte; it was nothing but a game to cheer people up without serious ulterior motive. Just before the look and the smile, you'd turned your head, looking behind you mischievously to make sure of being alone. A little monkey business, nothing more. For a split second you'd raised the lid of that stifling orthodoxy. And now you felt better and so did I, who was beginning to wonder how far the female complicities of "we" extended and if you weren't particularly well placed to inform the Porcupine about the dates of searches.

With my presence and my voice, I encouraged Dave's exploits on the tennis court for a few minutes and then went back to the lab. A disagreeable surprise was awaiting me there. I'd had Grabel prepare three doses of vaccine for Smith, Pierce and myself that afternoon, and I found only two. I called Burage on the intercom. She came in so quickly that she must have been at her desk waiting for my call.

"Burage," I said as soon as she'd closed my door, "you're the only one besides me to have a key to my office. And I've just found that the third dose of vaccine is missing."

"Oh, please!" Burage exclaimed with a forced gaiety. "Don't look at me like a policeman. It doesn't suit you at all. There's no mystery. I'm the one who disposed of the third dose."

I couldn't believe my ears. "You've disposed of it?"

"Right."

"Without my authorization? Without consulting me? What's this world coming to? I'm beginning to wonder if I still head this lab."

"Come now, Doctor, don't lose your temper. Nobody's disputing the fact that you head the scientific end of the lab."

"Burage, give me back that vaccine at once."

"That's impossible," she replied quite serenely. "It's already been used."

"*Used!*" I exclaimed, raising my arms skyward. "By whom?"

"I'll tell you who in a few minutes."

"Don't you know that it's very dangerous? That we still can't guarantee the safety of this vaccine?"

"The person who has used it is perfectly aware of that and has volunteered to serve as a guinea pig."

"Burage, the person's name! I demand that name at once! This is extremely serious! Things are going on behind my back in this lab, things I find quite awful."

The expression in Burage's eyes changed and became serious. "Sit down, Doctor. Anyway," she said in a tense voice, "I planned to tell you everything. I'm sorry this was all bungled so that you noticed the missing dose before I could speak to you about it. Actually, the dose that's missing is one of a number of decisions 'we' has made with regard to you."

I raised my brows and said curtly, "Well, I'd be curious to know what they are!"

"They have to do with the lab and—" saying this required an effort—"your private life as well."

"Oh, that's just fine!" I exclaimed, placing both hands flat on the desk and straightening up. "Now 'we' is running my professional life and my private life! And they're making decisions without my knowledge. I'm not even allowed to participate in discussions about me!"

"There aren't any men at the council meetings of 'we,'" Burage replied evenly.

"This is getting better all the time," I said sarcastically. "This is how you respect democracy and the equality of the sexes! I thought the aim of 'we' was to restore the *status quo ante*, except with regard to the condition of women."

"No, Doctor," answered Burage, staring gravely into my eyes. "I told you that when I wasn't really sure of you. The truth is different. 'We' wants the end of Bedfordism but not the abolition of female power."

I gaped at her. "Do you mean that once Bedford is beaten and 'we' takes over, men still won't be allowed in governing bodies?"

"No, not in the initial stages." She went on emphatically, "Listen, Doctor, and please don't be so shocked. Try to understand us. Bedford discredited Women's Lib with her excesses and her anti-male terror. But history shows that this kind of terror always leads to a backlash. After Bedford, the pendulum will, in all likelihood, swing the other way. We want to prevent that. We want to avoid a misogynic reaction that would put the condition of women back where it was a century ago. That's why we're organizing now to keep women in power after Bedford."

I looked at her. "All the same, Burage," I said with a lump in my throat, "you lied to me."

Burage's reaction was surprising. She smiled, came up to the desk and put her hand on mine, then withdrew it and looked at me affectionately.

"That's true," she replied with an almost tender smile. "But there was nothing personal about this deceit, Ralph. It had nothing to do with us. It was due to general orders from 'we.' We've got to be very reassuring, very conservative with new contacts."

I reflected: It was entirely probable that a misogynic backlash would come after Bedford. But that female power was the best party to ward off this danger, I wasn't so sure. But I'm inclined to let the future straighten itself out all alone. I'm not a maximalist. I've been too close to death. That there were Women's Libbers who repudiated hatred of marriage, men and babies and who were struggling with all their might to destroy Bedfordist fanaticism represented quite a step in the right direction.

"Well, Doctor, what do you think about it?"

I looked at Burage. I neither tried to hide my thoughts nor express them rashly. After all, I owed a lot to "we," including the prospect of survival.

"Well," I replied, "I think there's a lack of balance in the solution that 'we' is contemplating for the future, but everything will work out in the end. The main thing is that you don't hate males."

Burage laughed. "Ralph, your answer smacks of Italian finesse."

"And your remark is colored by a certain racism," I replied tartly.

I'm not ashamed of my Italian ancestors—far from it. But I don't like people unearthing them over and over again to pay them tribute for my shortcomings or my qualities.

The intercom lit up. I pressed the button down. It was Grabel. He reminded me that I had intended to take a look at the dogs. As I knew that, out of prudence, Burage liked to break up our meetings, I got to my feet at once, and I arranged to meet her in half an hour.

I found Grabel in the *ad hoc* room walking one of the three inoculated dogs on a leash to observe their gait. As I hadn't seen him since the preceding day, I asked him how he was and, to my great surprise, he replied to this innocent question in detail.

"Well, not so bad. I had quite a nasty headache, some reactions of dizziness, but nothing serious, and since this morning I've talked incoherently twice."

The fact that he felt the need to tell me about talking incoherently astonished me. I looked at him. His long, blade-like face wasn't different from the way it usually was: free of lines and without color. On the other hand, there was a certain tension in his eyes and a certain nervousness around his thin lips. Was this the effect of overwork? I was inclined to believe it. In the lab, Grabel did the work of two men.

"What if you took a rest?"

"Oh, no!" he exclaimed. "Idleness will only intensify my anxieties. I'd rather go on working."

He gave a little laugh with "my anxieties," as if they were taken for granted, and I wondered what anxieties he meant and why he spoke of them as if they were of no consequence. Were people supposed to be "anxious" when they were A's? Or was Grabel living in a semi-depressive state where he could accommodate everything while finding it all oppressive? I was surprised because I'd always thought that Grabel had more drive, was more dynamic than any of the A's who worked with us in the lab.

After seeing that the three dogs were still in good health, I left Grabel and went back to my office. I didn't have to call Burage; she was sitting there. She stared at me with concern.

"Are you angry, Doctor?"

"Because you'd concealed the ultimate goals of 'we'?"

"No. For all the little nasty cracks I made."

"Which ones?"

"All of them."

"I can't say that you tried very hard to spare my feelings."

"Oh, then you admit you do have feelings!"

"Yes. You can add that shortcoming to your list."

"Sorry, Doctor. I'm committing the same offense. I'm not usually so pugnacious."

She sat down on the other side of my desk, threw back her dark auburn hair and said, earrings quivering against her milky neck, "You know, it's hard living so far and yet so near . . ."

She left her sentence in suspense.

"It's not much fun for me either."

She straightened up on her chair, and a dangerous little light made her eyes blue.

"It's not the same for you. You've got your rewards. For instance, a little hut in the woods . . . ?"

"Where did you get that information?"

"Do you confirm it?" asked Burage, her pupils dilating.

"Yes."

"I got it from Rita. But it's only a hypothesis. 'I have the impression,' Rita said, 'that our little stud spent a rather wild night in his hut.'"

"Thanks for the 'little stud.' In particular, thanks for the 'little.' You have a knack for quoting snide remarks."

"Do you admit the 'wild night'?"

"And thanks, too, for the trap you've laid for me. I took your remorse for the real thing."

"In other words, Doctor," she hissed, 'you're the husband of every woman . . .'"

"You're all wrong," I said. "I'm no Don Juan. I never deceived Eileen."

As I couldn't say as much for Anita, I kept quiet. Burage sensed my reticence at once; I read that in her stormy eyes. And all of a sudden I realized what I was doing: I was justifying my private life to a woman who was neither my fiancée nor my wife. Once again I'd let myself be maneuvered. Burage had been contemptuous of my accusations, and she'd succeeded in foisting hers on me, putting me on the defensive. I got to my feet in a temper. I turned my back on her and looked out the window.

There wasn't much to cheer you up outside. Barracks, barbed-wire fences, a lookout tower and, between the barracks, what had once been a green field but which the snow, then the constant rain, all the comings and goings, had transformed into a muddy road. Gray skies, low clouds, mild temperature. I felt as if I was living in grayish cotton.

I turned around and told her, "Burage, please, let's drop the subject."

A burning look. "It's all so easy! Especially when you think that, on top of everything, you're going to have a visitor tonight."

"What visitor?"

"The biggest mouth in the United States!"

I jumped.

"When did you find that out?"

"This morning."

She'd heard about it before me! And from whom? From a switchboard operator? But did the switchboard operator also know the dates of the searches? I didn't think so. Everything seemed to indicate that Mrs. Barrow was the antenna of "we" within the Blueville administration.

I looked at my watch.

"Five minutes already, Burage. What if we moved on to serious business?"

She gave a tic at "serious," but she said nothing.

I saw by her breathing, her lowered eyes and the stiffening of her neck that she was trying to regain control of herself. I kept quiet.

When she raised her eyelids her blue eyes seemed worried.

"Doctor," she resumed after a moment, "you aren't going to like what I have to tell you about the decisions of 'we' with regard to you."

"Okay, I'll try to control myself."

She looked at me dubiously.

"At any rate," she said with a rather forced smile, "I'm here to absorb the shock."

"Is it that bad?"

"It isn't bad at all. But you're going to have trouble accepting these arrangements."

A silence.

"Shall I start in?" she resumed with obvious embarrassment.

"Yes, yes, of course," I answered with impatience.

In a hushed voice that quavered a little she said, "There have been two decisions on the vaccine. First, 'we' doesn't want you to be the first to use the vaccine. Second, if the vaccine turns out to be safe, 'we' forbids you to inoculate yourself with the Encephalitis 16 virus."

"Why, that's almost unbelievable!" I exclaimed, getting to my feet when I finally regained my voice. "Do you realize what 'we' is asking of me? A shameful violation of the rules of medical ethics! They're asking me—the head of the project—to make someone else run the risk of testing the results!"

"Sit down, Doctor," said Burage, "and listen to me. 'We' is perfectly aware that you're being asked to violate the usual rules of medical ethics. But the situation isn't usual. Your research is being subsidized by an Administration that has no desire to see your work brought to a successful conclusion. Up to now that subsidy has provided the Administration with an alibi, and, furthermore, they're preparing to cancel the subsidy. Under these conditions, 'we' thinks that our only hope of manufacturing this vaccine lies in smuggling it out of Blueville and into Canada. You're the only one who can do that."

"Anybody can do that! Pierce! Smith! Grabel!"

"You're wrong. All three have a major handicap—they're unknown. And who would have faith in a vaccine that's presented by an unknown doctor who's entered Canada without a passport? On the other hand, your name alone would be enough to open every door. The Martinelli report has been translated into every language on earth, and you're not only known by specialists but by the public at large. If you gave a press conference on Canadian TV, it would have a tremendous impact in Canada, the United States, all over the world."

"All right. There's a lot to be said for your scenario. But do you think I'm going to ask my co-workers to run the risks of the vaccine for me? And on the first inoculation?"

"You'll be running lots of other risks when you escape from here!"

"Oh, so it's all been decided! Without appeal! I'm going to escape! Tell me, Burage, is there still one decision, one single decision that 'we' is willing to let me take?"

"Come now, Ralph. Swallow your pride and be a little realistic. When the vaccine is tested on men, what else will you be able to do but escape? Do you expect to go to your good, humane, charming Helsingforth and tell her, Here it is, the vaccine is ready; it's up to you to manufacture it? Come on, you've got some imagination. What decision would she make? Only one—to put the vaccine in some safe place and start bargaining with Bedford to make her pay a stiff price for its destruction. That's what your vaccine will be good for! Something to be bartered in a big money deal. As for you, they'll shut your mouth one way or another. For example, they'll accuse you of raping Audrey."

"Helsingforth could also decide to produce the vaccine overseas."

"She can do it, providing that she defies Bedford, but 'we' doesn't call this a good answer."

"What do you call a good answer?"

Burage moved forward quickly, bent over, put her hands over

one of mine and said passionately, "Ralph, there's one thing that you've got to realize. Your vaccine is a political act. It's going to bring Bedford down. You'll strike from Canada. That's a friendly country for us."

"I'm going to *strike*?"

"Yes. On Canadian TV. You've got only one thing to tell them: the truth. That'll be enough. Your revelations will give the United States Congress the opportunity it's been waiting for to impeach President Bedford."

She took her hands away. I looked at her and waited quite a while before speaking.

"If I understand rightly," I said slowly, "'we' doesn't want me to run the risk of testing the vaccine because they're holding me in reserve for another kind of battle."

"Yes, that's it. You've summed it up perfectly."

I kept still. Burage remained standing, red-faced and tense.

"Look," I said after a moment, "how can I ask my co-workers to shoulder my responsibilities for me?"

"You won't have to ask them, Doctor. We've done it for you. They've agreed."

I roared, "What! Behind my back?"

"Not so loud, Doctor. Crawford hasn't left yet."

"That's outrageous! You simply bypassed me!"

Several times Burage shushed me, her finger to her lips. The telltale on the intercom lit up. Habit prevailed over my indignation: I pressed the button.

"Dr. Martinelli," said Pierce's voice.

"Yes?"

"Would you please come right away? We're worried. Dr. Grabel has just been taken ill."

Burage turned pale, both hands moving to her cheeks.

"The vaccine!" she said in a scarcely audible voice.

"What?" I asked, amazed. "What's that you say?"

"Dr. Grabel vaccinated himself this morning."

"You're crazy!" I said, getting to my feet. "Why would Grabel have vaccinated himself? What good would that do him? He's an A!"

"Dr. Grabel isn't an A," Burage replied in a low, panting

voice. 'We' supplied him with forged A papers before he applied for Blueville.''

To my immense relief I saw at a glance that Grabel had only fainted and not even completely. Pierce had been wrong because he was a virologist without great clinical experience. There was nothing that even remotely resembled the carus coma or even, in the initial stage, the deep stupor that characterizes E-16. His face wasn't inert. The eyelids fluttered, his lips moved, his body shuddered, his head moved alternately right and left. Besides, Grabel hadn't lost complete control of his body, since he remained seated—collapsed would be more accurate—on a chair.

"Did he fall?" I asked.

"No," answered Pierce. "He complained of dizziness and visual disturbances. He sat down and lost consciousness."

"Help me," I said. "We're going to stretch him out on the floor."

Once Grabel was flat on his back, I loosened his tie and massaged the upper part of his chest. Then a hand offered me a jar of alcohol. I poured it generously into my cupped hands and continued the massage. Grabel opened his eyes and said in a weak, faraway voice, "Thanks."

"He's coming to," said a female voice behind my back.

I looked at Pierce, and just as I was about to make a comment on the vaccine I saw Crawford. I remembered just in time. We were "in her lair," and she was the one who'd handed me the jar of alcohol.

"I'll take over for a while," Pierce said.

I got to my feet and looked at Crawford. "This happened in your office?"

"Yes," she replied and, at once, as Burage had so rightly observed, she arched her back and thrust her bosom out. How odd. I must have perceived the effect this trick produced on me, but I hadn't, strictly speaking, noticed it.

I was now quite reassured about Grabel, and for once (it was to be the last time) I had a good chance to look at Crawford. Calumny, Burage! Her hair wasn't dirty. But it was true that, at will, she made her hair into a provocative screen in front of her beautiful dark eyes. What a shame to lose this girl.

"How did it happen, Crawford?"

"Dr. Pierce has already told you that," interrupted a stern voice.

I didn't even have to turn my head. I recognized the claws. It was my lioness tossing her mane.

But Crawford wasn't going to let her little role be usurped. Undulating from head to toe, she gave me the same account Dr. Pierce had given me—only more so.

Burage broke in again. "Dr. Grabel has completely regained consciousness."

I turned around.

"And his color," Pierce said.

Pierce himself was absolutely colorless. His hair was a dull blond, his eyes faded, his lashes white. As he bent over the stricken man his round, soft and shapeless face made a striking contrast with Grabel's bladelike face.

Grabel kept on blinking, then managed to focus his vision on me and said in a weak and toneless voice, "Perhaps the dose is off."

Burage's eyes pointed out Crawford to me, sending an anxious message. I said hastily, "Don't try to talk. Rest. Crawford, would you please go and get my stethoscope?"

"Yes, Doctor," Crawford said with zeal.

She went out, followed immediately by Burage, who, apparently, didn't intend to leave her alone in my office. Pierce closed the door carefully behind him.

"I hadn't seen Crawford," Grabel said in a voice that was growing firmer.

He was coming out of his adynamia and, from second to second, his consciousness was reconquering broad zones of his brain. I watched him in a knowing way, but I made no comments. I didn't know if the bug there ended up in Burage's office.

Crawford, vibrant and undulating, returned with the stethoscope and made a point of touching my hand as she gave it to me. I kept my eyes lowered like a maiden. I got down on one knee. While I listened, in that position, to Grabel's heart, Burage entered with a cup of coffee.

I played the game: "Have you already had this type of syncope, Grabel?" I asked professionally.

Grabel smiled at me. "Yes, it's happened to me before."

I resumed, with the tone of a rude consultation. "You should look after yourself. Don't overwork. Go to bed early. Get some exercise." I added with a smile, "And easy on the coffee."

This little medical joke relaxed the atmosphere. Pierce and I helped Grabel into his chair, his eyes shining gratefully, and he took little sips from the cup that Burage administered to him.

That afternoon I wouldn't find out about the decisions of "we" concerning my private life, for I thought it necessary to have a meeting at once with Pierce and Smith in my office. Grabel (completely recovered, it seemed to me) came in afterward. Burage wasn't present, but she must have been listening in from her room.

The most remarkable feature of our conversation was that no one mentioned the fact that Grabel wasn't an A. I didn't want to admit to Pierce and Smith that I hadn't known and hadn't been told Grabel would be the first to be vaccinated.

I gave the conference a purely technical note. The vaccine had been prepared from pus attenuated by aging, and it was hard to tell, after a single experiment made on a man, if the attenuation left something to be desired, if the dose was too strong quantitatively, or if antiseptics shouldn't be mixed into the preparation. There was nothing exact about the solution we agreed on. The thrust of the matter was that we were groping and that we decided to play it safe, so alarming had Grabel's reaction seemed to us. We were going to prepare a new vaccine on the basis of older strains and test both its safety and efficiency on the dogs.

Throughout our little conference I looked at Smith more than I had ever done before. I'd suspected for quite some time that Grabel was involved in "we" and that Pierce, in this regard, could only be influenced by his wife's strong personality. But I'd never expected any complicity by Smith with an anti-Bedfordian movement. This complicity existed, however, since he knew about Grabel's vaccination and his false identity.

That was what astonished me. Everything about Smith, starting with his name, was perfectly ordinary. Although he was full of those useful traits without which no society can function for more than a week, he was self-effacing and timid; his insignificance was reflected in his physical appearance. From this point of view he had one of those faces that can be forgotten even if you've seen it a hundred times. What's more, he was one of those bachelors who gradually become rooted in solitude. He hardly spoke, seldom smiled, played no sport. He blushed when Burage spoke to him, and Burage claimed Smith hadn't married because he'd never worked up the courage to propose to a woman. And that was the paradox of it all. There he was, thrown suddenly into the dangers of a clandestine conspiracy and ready to fight (him—a loner) so that married couples might again be possible.

When the conference ended I let Smith and Pierce go, but I detained Grabel and said to him, "Thanks. You risked your life in my place."

He smiled and his long, austere face brightened.

"No need to thank me. As you know, I was originally recruited by 'we' to get you out of here."

I nodded, even though that 'to get you out of here' astonished me. I hadn't known that my ouster had been premeditated to that degree.

Grabel went on elliptically, "When 'we' decided to work with you, I had to find some way of being useful."

"Come now, you've been very useful in the lab—and you still are!"

"No more than Smith or Pierce," Grabel said with a modesty that, strangely enough, seemed genuine. He added, "At any rate, because I was officially an A 'we' thought I had a great advantage for testing the vaccine without Barrow knowing it."

I looked at him, raising my brows. "What advantage? I don't understand."

"Well," he replied, "if the test had gone wrong, it would have been easier to conceal the cause of my death and, consequently, the test itself. Nobody would have suspected an A of testing the Encephalitis 16 vaccine."

I was flabbergasted, both by the cunning of "we" and by the

quiet courage of Grabel, who had agreed to be "useful," even after his death.

The silence continued. I looked at Grabel. I'd have liked to shake his hand, but I shrank from how theatrical the gesture would have seemed for us. Finally, I gave him a little pat on the back and said, "I was very relieved when you opened your eyes."

"So was I!" he replied with a little laugh.

I laughed, too. I'd never believed Grabel capable of humor. And there, while we were looking at each other, laughing, a current of friendship, unexpected and warm, went between us.

As soon as Grabel left I felt weariness dropping on my shoulders. I also felt ravenous hunger and I looked at my watch. It was time to go back to the cafeteria. They didn't serve after seven o'clock. I locked my office and went by Burage's to drop off the key. She had a duplicate, but she insisted—and rightly so, I believe—on keeping both of them at night. She was always the last one out of the lab, and, before leaving, she would stretch a nylon thread across the lock in order to know if my door had been opened while I was away. The next day she would be there inevitably at 7:00 A.M. to open the place for the two cleaning women, and she wouldn't leave until they were gone.

"Good night, Burage," I said, dropping my key into the palm of her hand. "See you tomorrow."

"See you tomorrow," she replied with a troubled look.

I suppose that she'd been summoning up her courage to let me in on "we's" decisions about my private life and was very disappointed to have to carry forward her effort to the following day.

Once the meager supper was out of the way and Dave was in bed, I listened for Bess's delivery truck to come driving up.

It was odd the way everything in Blueville became a routine. With Ricardo seated in my kitchenette in front of a glass of bourbon, I didn't even bat an eyelash any more when Bess announced—and she used to say it each time—that she was going to give me a "first-class ticket to paradise."

I must admit that my conception of paradise was both less intense and less brief. Which isn't to say that I scorn life's enjoyable moments, as minor as they may be. Something that Bess praised me for afterward.

"At least, you're a regular man," she said, smiling at me with her broad mouth that was wholesome, sparkling. "You don't make things complicated. But take the old crab, for instance! The minute he sees me he makes a face! You'd think I was insulting him! Even though I didn't think up the idea of sperm banks. Up till now, in that department, I've squandered the stuff." She laughed. "I'd never have thought of saving it. A crazy idea, those banks! Don't get me wrong—I'm not saying anything against them. Seeing as how, just now, I'm making a living in the service of science. That's right! The old guy ought to understand that. As one colleague to another. His wife, too. And what takes the cake, she does the work instead of me! And besides getting me mad, she's mad at me! Because I see her husband's pecker. I got to see the thing if I'm going to collect his 'savings.' No, aside from you, I don't get any consideration. You take that big Swedish guy, for example, he's even worse. Doc, that guy's a character. He looks down at me. Not a word! Like I wasn't there. And once I start in, he's like a corpse. It takes forever!"

When we rejoined Ricardo in the kitchenette, he had both elbows on the table in front of his empty glass and he was crying.

"Jesus!" exclaimed Bess. "Where'd I ever get a driver like this from? As soon as I'm gone five minutes he starts bawling!"

"It isn't that, Miss Bess," Ricardo said, tears streaming down his cheeks. "It's because I heard the doctor. That's what reminded me of it."

"You shouldn't be listening, little rascal," said Bess, sitting beside him and putting her arm around his shoulders. "Doc, give him another one and don't forget me. This poor boy," she said, taking Ricardo's handkerchief from his pants pocket and drying his eyes, "he just can't get over it. Still taking it hard that his thing is soft!"

Thereupon she laughed and Ricardo said with dignity, "Don't make jokes about it. Señor," he said, turning to me as someone more apt to understand him, "when I made love to my wife in Puerto Rico, I used to come so loud that I'd wake up the whole building! Then, what did those neighbor ladies do? They'd shake their husbands and they'd say, 'You hear? It's Ricardo! And you go on sleeping, lazybones!' Señor, I'd done everybody a favor," Ricardo concluded proudly. The tears ran over his cheeks.

"Stop thinking about it," said Bess, taking his head into the hollow of her shoulder. "Maybe when the epidemic is over they'll be able to graft a pair of balls on you from some guy who got killed in a car accident. That's possible, right, doc?"

"Basically, there's no reason why it couldn't be done."

"*Gringo* balls?" Ricardo asked sneeringly. "What am I supposed to do with those?"

"Talk polite," Bess said, giving him a little slap on the cheek. "Doc's a gringo."

"Doc ain't no gringo—his name's Martinelli," Ricardo said through his tears, giving me a collusive smile that was childlike and charming.

"Go on, drink," Bess said, seizing Ricardo's glass and sticking it between his lips.

He drank. He drank in little sips but greedily and steadily, as if he were getting drunk. When the glass was drained, scarcely had Bess set his head down on the table when he closed his eyes and was asleep like a baby.

"Well, here I go again," she said. "I'm still in shape to do the return trip behind the wheel. Talk about a driver!" she continued, raising the shoulder on which Richardo's head rested.

She went on: "Don't expect to see me next week, Doc. I won't be coming. And the week after, do you know when I'm coming back? On a Sunday! Would you believe it? I read it in my orders, in black and white! I got to work on Sunday! The Lord's day! It's a disgrace. I know nowadays science is everything. But even so! Wouldn't you say—science or no science—it's a sin? Sex on Sundays. I've never done that! I don't go to church, no, I sleep! That's my way of observing the sabbath."

With that, she drank, then set the glass down gently and looked at Ricardo's head on her shoulder.

"He's a burden, this little guy," she said without the slightest bitterness. "A millstone around my neck. He gets me down with his crying, and most of the time it's me that winds up doing his work. But I'd never have the heart to turn in a report on him. Never. He'd lose his job. And then what'd become of his wife and all his kids in Puerto Rico? Not to mention him. He gets me down making me feel sorry for him. You gotta understand, Doc, poor guys like Ricardo, the really poor guys, what fun do they get out of life, aside from their cocks?"

Having said this, she tilted her wide face, vulgar and heavily made up, and looked at Ricardo. She looked at him indulgently, tenderly, and with her right hand she patted his cheek.

13

At my office I found a great to-do that morning over our decisions from the previous day, but it was a muffled to-do. Within the lab we had, so to speak, set up a second lab, the results of which were to be hidden from the first. At any rate, I was very busy and worried, and it wasn't until 11:45 that I could receive Burage. I saw by the circles under her eyes that she'd slept badly, too. I told her to sit down.

"We don't have much time," I said, throwing a glance at my watch. "Go ahead, Burage. I'm ready for the worst."

"Doctor, would it bother you to sit down instead of jumping around that way behind your desk?"

"I'm not jumping around," I said curtly. "You're quite nervous."

"It's you that's making me nervous. Please, sit down!"

"It's unbelievable," I said harshly. "It seems we've reached the point where, right in my own office, I'm supposed to sit and stand when told to do so."

"Doctor!" Burage said vehemently.

We looked at each other, embarrassed by this childish behavior. We were really getting off to a fine start! If this was the way we were beginning, how would we finish?

"Well," I said, forcing myself to smile, "I'm going to give you proof of my good will."

I sat down, but naturally she wouldn't acknowledge my concession. Instead of that, she fell silent and looked with annoyance at my fingers, which were drumming on the desk. I stuffed both my hands into my pockets and leaned back in my chair, my legs splayed out in front of me. I looked at her, tight-lipped. I made up my mind to keep quiet.

"Do you think you're making this any easier?" Burage asked with irritation.

"I'm listening to you. What more do you want?"

"I want you to drop your arrogant attitude."

"Yes, sir!" I answered in military fashion.

I sat up in my chair, squared my shoulders and looked straight ahead, my face frozen, my eyes inexpressive.

"Ralph," she said in a voice that broke, "stop clowning!"

I was about to argue about the word "clowning" when—fortunately—I looked at her. I didn't believe my eyes. She was on the verge of crying.

I got halfway out of my chair.

"Burage!" I said in a completely different tone of voice.

"Remain seated, Ralph! Whatever you do, just don't touch me!"

How had she known that I was going to take her in my arms? I sat down again. And at that second, our eyes meeting, I felt the full force of the bond that had sprung up between us. Could I leave her—even to escape? I said much more gently, "Is is that hard to say?"

"Yes, hard enough."

"Do you want me to help you?"

"Yes."

"What's it all about?"

"Helsingforth."

"Oh," I said.

Incredible as that may seem, I'd almost forgotten about her.

"Well," I asked, "what about Helsingforth?"

"'We' thinks that when she comes back she won't have forgotten her plans about you."

"What plans?"

"You know perfectly well."

As a matter of fact, I did. Although I'd done everything not to remember them.

"So?"

"'We' thinks that you should give in to her."

I remained thunderstruck for an instant, then I rose and, not knowing what to do with my hands, grabbed the back of my chair and squeezed it with all my might.

"'We' can think what it pleases," I finally said in a voice stifled by rage. "But I have this to tell you: I won't allow myself to be turned into a pimp by anyone. Not even by 'we.'"

"Doctor, please sit down!"

"And it's you, Burage, passing on these instructions!"

"Let me explain."

"There's nothing to explain."

"Yes, there is. This decision . . ."

"This 'decision'!" I sneered.

". . . was the focal point of a very thorough discussion. We voted to approve it."

"Nice going! And you, of course, voted for it!"

"Yes, Ralph," Burage said, meeting my eyes, "I voted for it."

I looked at her. That last reply had brought me to my senses. I was growing calmer by degrees.

"Do you realize what 'we' is asking of me? To become the sex toy of a paranoiac! Because she is a paranoiac, in case you didn't know."

"'We' knows it better than you," replied Burage testily. "'We' made an in-depth study of Helsingforth's psychological profile. 'We' knows exactly what she is. Bedford has given Helsingforth a free hand as far as you are concerned and Helsingforth—" she hesitated and resumed, with a grimace of disgust—"is going to act out her fantasies. She has three aims," she continued, making an effort to regain the methodical tone of her ordinary reports. "To make you pay for your letters of resignation by humiliating you. To use you as a sex toy. To use you as a means of torturing Audrey."

"A brilliant analysis!" I said sarcastically. "And you ask me to agree! Yet you know what happens to a toy when we grow tired of it."

Burage looked me square in the eyes and said, separating each word, "Helsingforth will break you in any event, whether you agree or not."

"Why agree in that case?"

But this logic failed to impress Burage. She said calmly, "You don't understand. It's purely a question of time. According to the study made of Helsingforth's character, 'we' is convinced that if you refuse, Helsingforth will retaliate *immediately*." She emphasized the word.

"What can she do? Fire me?"

Burage looked at me, shaking her head, and replied elliptically, "Worse. Much worse."

She didn't need to say more. I believed her. I snapped, "I fail to see how I'd be changing the situation by agreeing to Helsingforth's propositions."

"I told you how: You'd be stalling for time."

"And what's the advantage of that? In a month the problem would crop up again in the same terms."

"A month! It would be just marvelous if we had a month ahead of us."

"Why?"

"To settle the problem of your escape."

I resumed after an instant. "I'm no Tarzan, but it doesn't strike me that it would be so hard to escape from Blueville with Canada nearby."

"Don't be so sure. The border is closely watched. And in your case there's added difficulty."

"What's that?"

"Dave."

"Now, wait a minute!" I exclaimed, sitting back down and placing my hands flat on the desk and jumping to my feet again. "You've even thought of Dave!"

"'We' knows you, Ralph."

I replied sarcastically, "No doubt they've made an in-depth study on my psychological profile!"

"At any rate," said Burage curtly, "'we' knows what it can ask of you and what it can't ask of you."

That remark made me blink even before I'd grasped its implications. I would ponder it afterward with amazement. First, shock; then, understanding. Logically, it should have been the other way around.

"Oh, that's excellent!" I said, clenching my teeth. "What

tact! What delicacy! 'We' knows what it can ask of me. Like prostituting myself to Helsingforth!"

Burage turned red, her bosom heaved and she answered with abrupt anger, "That's quite enough, Doctor! Stop this acting! There won't be any prostitution. Helsingforth won't give you any money and it won't bother you to have sex with a woman that you find beautiful."

"I find her beautiful?"

"That's what you told Jackie."

It was horrible! They told each other everything! My every word was collected, repeated, labeled and filed carefully in a drawer for future use.

"But that doesn't mean that . . ."

"Ralph, you're a damned hypocrite! When you protest against the idea of having sex with Helsingforth, it's your phallocratic pride that's making you do it. You've got to be the one who takes the initiative, even if it's only an illusion! Your male pride's been wounded. It's an insult to your machismo, that's all."

I snapped, "You're mixing up your Latins, Burage. Machismo is Spanish."

"It's all the same!" she answered, jumping up and shaking her hair and earrings furiously. "You're one of those Latins who're always in rut! A tomcat! Any female cat looks good to you! An alley cat, like Bess, or a tigress in her cage. It's all the same to you if there's a grotesque difference in size between you and your mate! You even think you can make a mountain like Helsingforth say 'uncle' with the tip of your phallus! You're a sexist, Doctor! An inveterate sexist and nothing will ever change you!"

I looked at her and kept still. Oh, Burage, Burage, here we are back in the old rut, the racist denunciation of my ancestry, when that's just what you like about me, the verbal aggression as a substitute for intercourse and unfathomable insincerity (no, I won't call it feminine) of your grievances. Yes or no, Burage, wasn't it against my will, expressed in writing, that they forced the "alley cat" on me? Did Jackie let me have even the illusion of making the advances? Am I happy about being mixed up with that pair of vipers in their deluxe cabin? As to my "sexist pride," oh, no, don't believe that! That's no more than a memory! I don't claim to conquer anyone with the tip of my phallus. (What an expression!) I accept my protected-man status as best I can. And my feeling is that it will be some time before it ends. To tell the truth, I don't even want to be around to see the end. My only ambition is to make it—alive and entire—from Bedford's hateful matriarchy to the liberal matriarchy of "we."

But why should I tell her all that? She knew it as well as I did. She and I always knew what ran beneath our words. I preferred changing the subject.

"Burage," I said after a while, looking her in the eyes, "you realize what's going to happen when I leave with the vaccines. There will be an investigation, interrogations. You'll be implicated."

"Not just me," Burage replied quite coolly but without sitting down again. "Pierce, Smith, Grabel. They'll probably suspect us of being accomplices."

"You might not have known that my reports to Barrow were underestimating the progress of our research."

"And not know about your experiments? When I was in charge of the dogs?"

I thought it over. "Before escaping, I might make up a report, one that's completely accurate—except for the chronology of the experiments. And you might be able to hand over the report to Barrow on the very day of my escape. It would be your alibi. For you and the team."

"Yes," she replied, nodding her head. "It's an idea."

With that, she looked at me enigmatically. And she fell silent.

I went on after a moment: "When does 'we' plan to have me escape?"

Her face hardened and she answered, "As soon as possible."

At the time I didn't know what to make of her look, and, as the prolonged silence embarrassed me, I thought I'd get out of it with a joke.

"Well, you'll soon be rid of a nasty tomcat," I said.

But, clearly, it had been the wrong move. She winced as if

she'd been slapped. She turned pale. I saw her eyelids flutter and tears fill her eyes. She turned her back on me and, without a word, she headed for the door.

"Burage!" I said, getting to my feet.

She went out. She wasn't even going to slam the door. Oh, no, I know my Burage all right. Unable to master her emotions, at least she controlled her nerves. The door closed gently and noiselessly. Like a page being turned.

I remained standing behind my desk, my hands empty at the end of my arms. I felt very much alone.

Almost a week had gone by since my tumultuous meeting on June 9 with Burage. Which isn't to say that my conversations with her had ended—far from it. The day after the storm, she asked me curtly to describe Bess and Ricardo's visit in all its details. Which I did, at first wondering if this wasn't masochistic curiosity on her part. No, the attention with which she listened to me and the searching questions that she asked me afterward convinced me that it was an official inquiry and that all the information she got out of me would be turned over to "we."

On Friday, the 12th, there was a search in the single women's barracks, and on Saturday morning I found a laconic note on my desk from Barrow informing me that my assistant Crawford had—and I quote—"left on a study trip." Would I like to have her replaced? asked Barrow.

I played the game in my reply. I claimed to be surprised by this abrupt departure. I protested it (though with moderation), regretted that Crawford hadn't let me know about it and hoped that she would come back. But, given the advanced state of my research, I did not deem it worthwhile replacing her.

There were two reasons for this that I kept to myself. First, because I felt that, in all likelihood, the hypocritically proposed replacement would not be made. And then because, if there were the possibility of a replacement, I preferred not to alter the makeup of a close-knit team by bringing in a woman who was unknown (in every sense of the term). With Crawford gone, we might not have to fear any more spying.

Having couched my reply to Barrow in administrative terms that were clear only to him, and as my intercom wasn't working, I went to show my letter to Burage in her office. Since my escape had ceased to be a remote possibility and had become a priority plan, Burage—although still just as energetic—had lost her gaiety and her color. And, that morning, somewhat surprised, somewhat stung as well, I noticed— along with her bright complexion and her happy eyes—a certain effervescence of her whole being. I told myself bitterly that women were incomprehensible since this one, who had seemed to thirst for my company, was already reconciled to my leaving. With that, she read my letter, a playful smile on her lips (I'm sure that Crawford's leaving didn't plunge her into gloom). My eyes wandered around the spartan little room, hardly bigger than a closet, and fell—just above her flamboyant hair—on a very gaudy wall calendar that I'd always seen there. But what I noticed that day surprised me. The date of Sunday, June 28, had been circled with a red pencil.

Burage had eyes everywhere—on her shoulders, her collarbones, the nape of her neck and on the top of her head. Just then, while she was bent over my letter savoring its bureaucratic fine points, she picked up both my surprise and the direction of my gaze, turned around and understood. At once she blushed (what can you do with that milky complexion?), betrayed her embarrassment by the effort she made to repress it, commented hurriedly on my memo to Barrow, spoke too much and too fast and, finally, with no apparent motive, got to her feet to screen the calendar from my view.

As a male—hence, subaltern—member of 'we,' I felt obliged to keep somewhat in the background. I therefore asked Burage no questions. But I asked myself one: What was important enough about Sunday, June 28, to make Burage put a circle around that date?

An hour later I returned to Burage's office to ask for some information. I was so lost in thought that I was already in the middle of the room when, raising my eyes, I realized that Burage wasn't there. I was going to leave. I changed my mind. There was something different. The gaudy calendar, the sole

note of color in that austere room, was missing. And I didn't
have to go very far to find it: There it was, lying flat on Burage's
desk. I went over and examined it. The circle around the 28 had
been erased. You could even see (by looking closer) little shreds
of rubber and paper (and closer still) the imprint of the circle
made in the paper by the point of the pencil, while traces of
graphite remained.

All right. I wouldn't raise any questions about that, either. I
was even going to try to forget about it. After all, it was only
one little mystery in the basic unintelligibility of Blueville.
Furthermore, it was Saturday, the day Helsingforth had set for
her return. The thought of this, while I was heading to the
cafeteria for lunch, took away my appetite.

Dave had gone ahead of me and was already seated at a table
with his little friends, beside his favorite, Joan Smith, whose
lack of angularity was indeed quite remarkable.

To my astonishment, while I was looking for a table, my
meagerly filled tray in hand, Mutsch beckoned to me from a
distance to sit at her table. I found a seat there, between Stien
and her, which she had apparently been saving for me. The
inexplicable snubbing had ended. There I was—back in their
good graces. Under its amiable white bangs, Mutsch's round
face poured torrents of affection on me, and Stien himself gave
a few friendly grunts my way, while complaining indignantly
about the bad weather. To hear him, you might have gotten the
idea that the weather itself was racist. Despite his abundant
white hair (and because of the drafts, he explained) Stien had
kept his hat on and, around his neck, the woolen scarf knitted
by his wife—in my opinion, crudely knitted but, of course, it's
the context that counts. And the context, that day above all,
touched me. I envied that old couple whose union had lasted,
unchanging, forty years. My thoughts becoming gloomy, I
wondered sadly, when one of the two died, what would become
of the other, and if that one could go on after this mutilation in a
half-life. At this point I changed suddenly into Stien, and I saw
Mutsch lying, stiff and pale, on her deathbed and me on my
knees, desperate at losing such a good, maternal wife.

This vision thrust itself on me so vividly that it brought a
lump to my throat, and I jumped when a warm and dimpled

hand—the dead woman's!—came to rest over my hand and when a voice whispered in my ear, Come on, Ralph. Don't pull that gloomy face. There may not be any phone call today.

No, she wasn't wrong. I'd been lying to myself in attributing my anguish to her death. I looked at her. Absurd, my imagination. Past sixty, Mutsch was in perfect physical shape, her cheeks fresh and her eyes bright. The lump in my throat wasn't her death; it was the anticipation of Helsingforth's voice in the receiver.

I smiled at Mutsch and, immediately afterward, at Stien, for the old fellow was jealous. He wasn't at all pleased that his "little treasure," as he called her in German, put her hand over mine. What's more, she'd withdrawn it at once and, for my part, after my smile, I kept still. The cafeteria must have been heavily bugged. Besides, how could I interpret Mutsch's remark? I was willing to bet that she didn't know and that nobody from "we" had told her who'd phoned at lunchtime last Saturday. It was probable that she had seen, from the look on my face when I'd come back to the table, how much that phone call had upset me and she'd drawn her own conclusions. But if that were the case, why snub me that way all week long? And why this reconciliation now?

Leaving the cafeteria, I met Mr. Barrow in the corridor. All these encounters in that same place weren't simply a coincidence. In his office he had a closed-circuit television on which he watched the cafeteria door. In any case, there he was, out of his lair and coming at me noiselessly on thick crepe soles.

There he was, shiny, greasy, oily. Oh, no doubt about it, you wouldn't have any trouble writing a gloomy poem or horror movie about Barrow. When that big whitish blob moved toward me, I always had the feeling that he was going to phagocytize me. By the way in which he was heading my way, floating on his pseudopods—his huge, shapeless body filling the narrow corridor—I wondered if, throwing his cytoplasm to the right and left of my person, he weren't about to surround me, drown me in his fat and digest me. Nevertheless, when he was a good yard and a half away—prophylactic distance—he stopped, as if he were afraid of being contaminated by the bacillus of virility if he came any closer. Furthermore, I knew how much he feared physical contact with his fellows, even with his authentic fellows, the A's. And when I saw him stop that way, his glaucous eyes asking me not to close the gap between us and his jowls already puffed up with long-winded phrases, he made me think of an octopus rather than an amoeba. I couldn't bear the way in which his globular eyes ran their suckers over me, looking for a crack through which they might pump my mind. Paralysis overwhelmed me. I felt like a fly tied up in sticky threads.

"Dr. Martinelli," said Mr. Barrow—and that did it; his voice trapped me; I sank into the molasses—"I've had a phone call from Helsingforth informing me that it will be impossible for her—" he didn't mind delays—"to come to Blueville this weekend." Helsingforth, he continued with that pseudo-prudent way of expressing himself that went so well with bombast, hinted that it was quite probable that she wouldn't be able to come the following week either. Particularly urgent matters were keeping her in Washington, where she must have a series of meetings with the Secretary of Health, Education and Welfare. He didn't say HEW. He wasn't one for abbreviations; he even had a way of making things longer.

Thereupon, Mr. Barrow added with a smile that shook his jowls like jello: "I thought you'd like to know about it." Then he fell silent, his eyes like accomplices.

While he loomed over me and swamped me from all sides with his mass I realized that, hidden in the air of importance with which he spoke to me, there was a servile attitude mingled with resentment. Mr. Barrow bowed before the favorite of the moment but awaited the fall. Thanks for letting me know, Mr. Barrow, I said. And I noted that, at once, he twitched. Even for saying "thank you" there was a bureaucratic style. And my sentence offended him because it was so short.

Yet never had a "thank you" been more sincere, Helsingforth's "urgent matters" gave me a week's respite, perhaps two. That's when you can actually feel the value of each passing hour. I'd had the same feeling two years before when an operation (just a minor one) that I had to undergo was delayed for three weeks. I savored each day of that unexpected reprieve. I also told myself that Helsingforth's absence was buying us time for our plans, without danger and without humiliation. Both would be coming soon enough.

On Sunday I went horseback riding with Jess and Stien, a little to relax after a feverish week at the lab, a lot to see Jackie again. Disappointment. I caught sight of her in front of the guardhouse, elegant and martial, supervising the distribution of badges by the girl sentinel and the pickup of three P.M.'s by two mounted militiawomen to whom she gave her instructions, on foot, in a clipped, well-articulated manner. Her chin lifted, service cap over one ear and hands on her hips, she spoke domineeringly to her subordinates. I couldn't make out what she was saying, but, from a distance, I admired her silhouette. And I was disappointed—she wasn't coming, since she had delegated her powers. And furthermore, not a look my way. Not a single one. Not the slightest. Apparently the soldier's return had been forgotten. That night in the woods, among other nights, didn't count. Oh, how fickle soldiers can be! I felt like a girl who'd been thrown over.

As for the vaccine, everything was going ahead (despite some groping) as planned. Our new preparation, made up on the basis of older strains, was tried successfully on the dogs. And on the 18th, without asking Burage's opinion, I decided to vaccinate myself. I did develop some symptoms but really minor ones that in no way resembled Grabel's alarming reaction. On the 19th, Smith and Pierce vaccinated themselves in turn. Burage heard through Pierce that I'd made myself into a guinea pig the day before, and I got a severe reprimand. I defended myself. What else could we have done? Vaccinate Grabel *again*? Would the experiment have been conclusive with him immunized by the first vaccine? As a matter of fact, Grabel is out of the running. And he can't even be inoculated with the virus to check the effectiveness of the first vaccine, since we've given up on that preparation, having found it too dangerous. In fact, I was wrong, very wrong, to tell him that, for three days later, on the 22nd, Pierce informed me that he had successfully carried out a self-inoculation on orders from "we." That he was the one to tell me and not Burage was damned clever. Because I couldn't exactly attack a man who'd just risked his life to prove the effectiveness of our second vaccine.

But I called Burage right away and I gave her a piece of my mind. Burage astonished me. She was overflowing with gaiety, with enthusiasm. She thrust aside my reproach in the most off-handed way, and, full of eagerness, she immediately went to a counterattack.

"Doctor, you have a serious shortcoming for an underground fighter. By nature, you're undisciplined. You pay no attention to orders. You do things *por la libre*, according to whim."

That phrase sent me into a rage. It was Iberian and I didn't see why—in addition to my supposed Italian faults—I should also bear the failings attributed to Spain.

"You shouldn't say that," I said in a ruffled tone. "Up to now I've never refused to follow instructions from 'we.'"

"Except for the vaccine. And as for the rest," Burage added with an exasperating smile, "what patience and persuasion we had to use!"

"You don't really expect a scientist to obey without understanding, do you?"

Burage tossed her dark auburn hair.

"Leave your damned science out of this! We're dealing with a war, not research. We can't keep explaining things all the time. You ought to sense that. But, instead, you demand privileges!"

"What privileges?"

"Of understanding the whys and wherefores of an order at all times. If every fighter in an underground army made the same demands as you, the struggle would become impossible."

I replied without amenity, "Thanks anyway for being so patient."

"Don't thank me—that's going to stop. From now on I'm going to transmit orders from 'we' without a word of explanation."

I looked at her with mingled feelings.

"I suppose all this is just a long preface to some new demand."

"Exactly." She looked at me, half amused, half impertinent, and said, "'We' has given you the order to grow a mustache."

"Burage!"

I threw up both hands in astonishment, and just then I thought: She's going to say that it's an Italian gesture. I brought my hands back down onto the desk, but, unfortunately, too hard, much too hard, and I smacked the blotter. That's just some more dramatics! I could read it in her eyes.

"That isn't serious."

"It's very serious," Burage answered. "Don't think for a minute that I'm going to stand for it. Or waste my time playing games with you. Not when I have so little time to enjoy your company."

She said this in a mocking tone that left me speechless and, in a split second, filled me with uncertainty and bitterness. On the spot, I forgot about that stupid mustache business. I was thinking only about Burage. The bond between us couldn't have been as strong as I'd imagined if she took our separation so lightly.

Of course, I'd known it before, but I'd learned it even more since coming to Blueville. What made no sense was that people spent half their lives either wanting or dreading what was going to happen the next day. Hustled without respite from due date to due date, they went from one wait to the next, losing their ability to enjoy the present.

I've often thought that if our imagination of the future were localized in one precise spot in the brain, neurosurgery might fix it so that this spot was less irrigated than the others. Our daily anxiety would be diminished, including the supreme anxiety—of death. Since I'd been in Blueville, I'd literally done nothing but wait: for the replies to my letters of resignation; through endless weeks for Anita's visit; since the beginning of my stay, for the success of our research; for three weeks, another phone call from Helsingforth; and, simultaneously, the day of my escape.

At least, if I were expected to plan the escape, that would have kept my mind occupied. No, I had to wait, ignorant and passive, for an attempt whose every detail, right down to the date, had been planned by "we." Never had an escape been less heroic and less venturesome. I had the feeling of having about as much power of decision as a package being readied for smuggling. The only difference—and it wasn't in my favor—was that a package doesn't suffer states of anxiety.

Burage disconcerted me. She gave me instructions, for the

vaccines I was to carry away, that led me to believe the day of my escape was near. Strangely enough, as the time went by and the day drew closer, she became happier and happier. As though what lay in store for her at Blueville after my departure—the suspicion, the interrogation and, who could tell, even the torture—was going to be an uninterrupted series of pleasures. At the same time, I didn't recognize her any more: The serious, knowing, responsible Burage, the kingpin of the lab, the practical mind whose systematic way of doing things I appreciated, that tireless worker, the first to arrive, the last one to leave, seemed to have made way for a sixteen-year-old girl who did nothing all day but laugh, joke and sing (true, under her breath and still getting her work done).

Questions got nothing out of her. Why was she so happy? Because she was relieved, she answered, laughing, at the idea of getting rid of me soon! Thereupon, she laughed some more and started in on my mustache. She made jokes *ad infinitum*: I looked like a foreign adventurer, a wop, a gigolo. I was straight out of a 1930ish gangster film with Paul Muni or George Raft, or I looked like somebody running for President in some Latin American country or simply a waiter in an Italian restaurant. My sexiness had increased 80 percent "on the vulgar side, mind you, but I know that isn't likely to bother you." Furthermore, she herself wasn't totally insensible to it. When I left, I'd have to kiss her on the mouth. That way, she'd find out what it was that had made the women of the 1930s shiver.

Something else was new—and fairly disturbing. While she claimed to be relieved at seeing me go, she was now doing something with me that she had never done up to then, except once: She was being provocative. The nipping of my index finger had long remained the one exception in an attitude of rigid distance. She had warned me as soon as she'd confessed her feelings: not a hand that touches another, not a grazing contact, not a look.

That was all over now. As soon as Burage entered my office, she stared at me with dilated eyes and began—while talking shop—a sort of dance. I couldn't keep track any more of all the mane tossings, the neck bending, the torso twisting. And her voice! Her voice that became hoarse, husky, "fascinating."

Burage revolved around me, she inhaled me, she gave out a little gurgling laugh that resembled cooing. It even reached the point where she would put her hand next to mine on the desk and, without paying attention, glue her arm against mine. Yesterday, with a document in her hand, she stationed herself right behind me, set the paper down on my desk and, reading it with me, forgetting about her body in the heat of reading, leaned her bosom against my shoulder. I even had the impression—I felt her breath so close—that she was going to kiss the nape of my neck. No, a brake must have operated just in time. But I heard the change in her breathing rate and, what's more, I felt it distinctly at the level of my collarbone. I diagnosed it as a temporary tachycardia with erotic motives. Furthermore, I was able to make the same diagnosis about myself almost at once.

I knew this was happening, but I didn't claim to understand it. I failed to see the connection, if there were any connection between my leaving and Burage's gaiety, or, more surprising still, between her amorous effervescence and our separation. On the other hand, Burage's abnormal behavior had a beneficial effect: by occupying my mind enough to take it off my anxiety. I noticed that of late, in the course of sleepless nights, I was thinking more about Burage than Helsingforth's phone call.

But it came all right. Miracles just don't happen. On Sunday, June 28, at 1:00 P.M., in the cafeteria, the switchboard operator's voice exploded in the loudspeaker and began its interminable call: Dr. Martinelli, Dr. Martinelli, Dr. Martinelli . . . I hated the powerful, disembodied voice that fell on me like a sentence, while the room grew hushed and everyone's eyes converged on me. At least I thought they did because, for my part, I wasn't looking at anybody, aside from Dave. I patted him on the shoulder and managed to smile at him with an assurance that I was far from having. To the best of my ability, I played the role of the heroic father he had assigned to me. But as soon as I turned on my heels to go away, I felt as lonely as a Christian thrown to the lions. The switchboard operator continued her monotonous litany and would continue it until I picked up the receiver. I remembered the sinister effect that call had produced on me four weeks earlier. And this memory superimposed itself on the fear that I already felt and made my blood run even colder. I zigzagged among the tables of the cafeteria, staring straight ahead. I felt as if I was being pursued, not like Cain by the eyes of God but, what was worse, by my own name. Each time that it came back, I felt a little more hunted.

There was something inhuman in that endless repetition and in the indifferent nature of the voice calling me. I could sense that it was only the instrument of destiny, that I and my fate were foreign to it. No hate or love or impatience. Simply by calling me the voice plunged me into anonymity. I had the impression that the dead lined up at the gates of hell must be called in the same way.

Dr. Martinelli . . . Dr. Martinelli . . . Dr. Martinelli . . . The loudspeakers in the corridor were taking over and, in there, because it reverberated from one end of the narrow corridor to the other, the sound took on an almost menacing volume. I was relieved with I saw Mr. Barrow standing in the doorway of his office, gesturing to me to hurry. I quickened my pace. I reached him. He drew back from the door but not fast enough: Entering the room, I bumped my elbow against his paunch. He gave a little asexual cry. I murmured a word of apology and, at the same time, threw a professional glance at his abdomen, as if I had expected to see it burst like an abscess.

The receiver wasn't lying on the desk but in the cradle of the telephone, and I wondered why it had been absolutely necessary that Helsingforth send for me instead of leaving the message with the administrator. As she did nothing aimlessly (and her aims were generally malevolent), I supposed that she enjoyed the idea of worrying Mr. Barrow by circumventing him.

I picked up the receiver, and the switchboard operator's voice left the loudspeaker to come into my ear.

"Dr. Martinelli?"

"Yes."

"I'll connect you with your party."

A long silence. Out of the corner of my eye I saw Mr. Barrow bent double, his oily skull forward, close the door of his office with exaggerated discretion.

"Dr. Martinelli," Helsingforth's voice said.

Those two words resounded like the blow of a fist on the desk. Helsingforth got going as soon as I said yes. Why did that woman's voice have to be ten times louder, more authoritarian and more brutal than the voice of the most hardened phallocrat? I glanced at my watch. Taking into account the length of the journey, she wasn't even allowing me half an hour to get ready.

A dismal trail on Chouchka under a uniformly gray sky and behind me Jackie, who, for an hour and a half, from the foot of the lookout tower to Helsingforth's deluxe cabin, granted me no word, no look, no smile. I turned around in the saddle several times. I asked her innocuous questions twice. She answered in monosyllables. And having done this, her beautiful gray eyes—which, God knows why, still seemed to be green, possibly because of the very thick dark lashes that bordered them—remained fixed on her gelding's mane.

Once again, I experienced a feeling that I'd always had, very much amplified by my present anxiety. When a woman didn't pay any attention to me, I had the impression she was abandoning me. No, it was not conceit. It was something entirely different—the frustration of an emotional need. And what disturbed me even more, when I turned around one last time to my escort on the next to last bend before the corral, I saw that her face wasn't really impassive. Little lines stretched her eyes, joined her brows, pulled down her lips. At last I saw her true state of mind: She was worried. And the fact that my bodyguard, armed to the teeth, was so lacking in confidence didn't make me any more confident.

We reached the goal.

"Leave Chouchka, Doctor," Jackie said as I was preparing to unsaddle the mare. Then, leaving the gelding in his stall, Jackie came into mine, carefully closing the door behind her, and said in an indifferent voice, "Chouchka may have lost a shoe. Do you want to hold her? I'm going to take a look."

I grabbed Chouchka by the reins of both sides of the bridle. Jackie stopped, tapped the shoe, saying, "Easy, easy," raised the left foreleg, threw a quick glance at the undamaged, gleaming shoe and, suddenly, extending her hand, tapped me on the left knee and said, "Relax, relax." Strangely enough, this gesture did anything but reassure me. That Jackie deemed it necessary only heightened my uneasiness.

I moved out of the stall. I had a hundred yards of field to cover. The grass had shot up with the rains. Green and dense, it reached my hips on both sides of the narrow trail, which had become overgrown with ankle-deep grass during Helsingforth's absence. My heart was pounding and beads of sweat formed in the hollows of my hands. Yet the stupid power of minor annoyances, even at times of stress, is great. I noticed with irritation that I was going to get my feet wet.

14

When I came in, she was in the pool, nude. No sign of Audrey. Helsingforth had her back turned to me—and what a back! Her statuesque, bronzed body cut through the transparent water, leaving a frothy wake. She reached the satyr that spouted into a basin at the far end of the pool, turned around and came back to me, emerged from the water two yards from the apron where I'd come to a stop, plastered her hair over left cheek and, turning three quarters of the way to me, contemplated me in silence. I marveled at how she could be at my feet yet still look down at me.

Finally, she said curtly, "Don't just stand there. Get undressed and come in for a swim."

I stripped, with an outward show of willingness. Meanwhile, doubtless to embarrass me, she never took her eyes off me, weighing and underweighing me, like a horse that she was buying. I should say a pony, given the difference in our proportions. I got through it fairly well, I believe. At any rate, without shame. I couldn't believe that it was humiliating for a man to undress in front of a woman, as her dark and contemptuous eyes tried to convince me.

"Your prudishness is ridiculous," she said. "Take off your underpants."

"I was waiting for you to ask me."

The way I'd said it, the remark was one of those slight insolences which, on my last visit, I'd discovered to be the best weapon of the weak. Just go far enough to offend but not far enough to touch off a punitive reaction. A tyrant can't get angry at everything—it's impossible.

"You're growing a mustache," Helsingforth said with a pout. "That doesn't suit you. It's a mistake."

I didn't answer this. I dove in and when I came up a few yards away I stayed on the surface by treading water.

"Is that all you can do?" asked Helsingforth sternly.

"I swim a little."

"Well, then, swim!"

I obeyed. I used the crawl up to the satyr's basin and I came back to her, without driving myself but making an effort at style. When I stopped, my face turned to Helsingforth, she said, "It could be worse. Your kick is rotten, but your arms are right."

For once, for the first time, she'd spoken just about normally, without contempt, without aggressiveness, with an obvious desire to humiliate. Technique had prevailed over sadism.

I was dumfounded by it, and she must have noticed my astonishment, for, at once, surprised at having become almost human, she knitted up her brows and said brutally, "Let's get out."

Actually, I wasn't sorry to be done with it; no swim had ever given me less pleasure. On the apron, without a word, with just a simple gesture of handing me her orange towel and turning her back to me, Helsingforth reminded me of my duties as drier. I performed them and, as on the previous time, not without agitation.

My eyes came up to her collarbone and I was struck, once again, by the harmony of her proportions, by the fine texture of her skin. Her muscles were big but well coated, and she was indeed a woman, magnified in every way like a statue but not desexed by this enlargement; quite to the contrary, all the characteristic curves, the small of the back, the breasts, the belly, the thighs, were magnified, hypersexualized and, hence, even very attractive.

I had nothing against that body. The personality that inhabited it was disturbed, but for the moment I didn't hear Helsingforth's voice. I didn't see her cold eyes. I could almost forget the power she held over me.

Furthermore, she gave me a respite. She was motionless, mute, her eyes closed, her vigorous arms dropping along her body, one leg relaxed, all her weight resting on the other, which made her hip swell out. This pause completed the illusion. I was up against a gigantic idol, not made of stone but of flesh, an idol inhabited by a mind. Emboldened by her immobility, I moved around her. I took up a firm stance in front of her and rubbed her shoulders, glancing furtively at her impassive face, the right eye closed, the left eye and cheek concealed by the flood of hair whose regular waves seemed sculpted in marble. I saw all this with foreshortening, since my eyes came up to the level of her chest, and in order to reach the powerful, muscular neck, round as a tower, I had to raise my arms. My orange towel moved down to her huge breasts, firm and erect, and my drying became lighter, for I was afraid that Helsingforth might awake from her petrification. But nothing happened, and I went down farther, stooping even more until I got down on one knee to work on her legs.

"That'll do, Martinelli," Helsingforth said in a hoarse voice, as if, in a few minutes, she had lost the habit of speaking.

I got to my feet again and, giving myself room, I handed her the towel, meeting her right eye whose gaze still hadn't regained its ferocity.

"Get the fire going again," she told me curtly, and, tossing her towel over her shoulder and turning her back to me, she reached the other end of the pool and disappeared through the glass door of the living room.

I suppose she'd carried the towel away to prevent me from using it and, hence, from getting dressed again. I also suppose that the fire she wanted me to get going was the one closest to me, for I noticed that, in addition to two hot-air ducts, there were two fireplaces in the great glassed-in hall. One was across from the pool, in the middle of the wall dividing it from the house proper; the other, three yards away from me, in the rest area, to the left of the all-glass wall of the house. In front of this one I saw a low table, a wicker armchair and oak stools.

I added some kindling to the embers. I piled up pieces of firewood and pumped the bellows. Relieved, I saw flames shoot up. Despite the room temperature, I had begun to feel chilled. I warmed myself front and back and was already dry when I saw through the glass door that Helsingforth had reappeared, nude and majestic, taking big strides. Audrey followed, her thin arms encumbered by a tray laden with the famous silver teapot, toast and—I couldn't believe my eyes—two cups.

Audrey was dressed in a white turn-of-the-century dress, with an officer's collar and a chignon. She resembled the idea that I had of Nora in *A Doll's House.* Her face was drawn and tears coursed down her cheeks.

When the two women reached the lounge, I concealed from Audrey the most insufferable part of my nudity by turning to face the fire, but I watched the scene over my shoulder.

"Sit down, Doctor," Helsingforth said. "This stool is made of oak, so it's not likely to give under your weight. And you, Audrey, stop crying. I wouldn't want your tears landing in my cup. The doctor is different. The doctor likes everything about a woman, including her wetness. If he wants to catch your secretions in his cup, that's his business. Put that over there. And don't try to make me feel sorry for you by rubbing your little arms with that suffering look. Even fully loaded the tray doesn't weigh more than ten pounds. Doctor, your modesty is absurd. Turn around and sit down. Audrey wants to say hello. Audrey, say hello to your friend. You owe him that much. He almost raped you."

"Hello, Martinelli," Audrey said in her sweet, breathless, musical voice, throwing me a look of hatred.

"Now, that was hardly affectionate!" Helsingforth resumed with a little laugh that resembled a whiplash. "Come on, Audrey, start over. I want my toys to get on well together."

I don't want to go back into the theatrical, artificial character of Helsingforth monologues. The woman was a rotten actress, and what she said almost never rang true. But I noticed that, in the area of petty cruelty, she had a certain talent. "I want my toys to get on well together" was rather clever. True, it left me quite cold. But Helsingforth's slave winced.

"Hello, Martinelli," Audrey said without improving her look a great deal.

"Are you jealous, Audrey?" Helsingforth resumed, raising

her right brow. "And who says you're allowed to be? Do you have some rights over me? Answer, you little vermin!"

"No," Audrey answered, tears streaming down her cheeks. "I don't have any."

"That's the spirit! From now on, Audrey, you'll give Martinelli a nice smile."

"I'll try," Audrey replied in a toneless voice.

"Try! I advise you to do so. Also try to take him for his proper worth. You don't realize—the doctor is a rare object. A deluxe object. Especially now that the stags have a tendency to be political."

I cocked my ears: data from "we" confirmed.

"Help yourself, Audrey," Helsingforth went on, sitting down in the wicker chaise lounge.

Nudity must have been usual for her. She wasn't embarrassed in the least. Quite to the contrary, her movements were marked by perfect ease.

She resumed: "And serve the doctor, too. We must feed him before demanding an effort of him. Audrey, if you spill so much as a single drop of tea on the table, I'm getting up and giving you a slap."

"I'm sorry," Audrey said, her delicate face blurred by tears.

"I detest your apologies. And your humbleness. You have the soul of a slave, Audrey. You crawl at my feet like a dog, your tongue hanging, always ready to lick me. You should model yourself after the doctor. Now he never crawls. He's handed me his resignation twice. And that means that he's jeopardized his life three times. And do you know why he's going to have sex with me? Because he's afraid? No! Because he hopes," she said sarcastically, throwing me a ferociously ironic look, "that it's going to give him time to develop his vaccine and save the human race."

And there it was: the right psychological moment to break my silence. I enveloped Helsingforth's body with a look that I myself would term impudent and I said in a tone of voice loaded with insinuation, "You've oversimplified my motives. You're in a better position than anyone to know that I'm not walking to my funeral."

Helsingforth laughed. And I noticed once more that her

laugh had something of a sneer to it. She never laughed with you but at you.

"Do you hear, Audrey? The doctor is Italian. He's a poet by nature. Audrey? Do you think you're a poet because you like to dress up in disguises?"

Audrey gave a violent shudder and her face was convulsed. "But you, yourself, Hilda . . ." she said with a look that touched me.

"Proof that my tastes change," Helsingforth said. "Actually, I'm starting to get fed up with your masquerades. Those old clothes are stupid, you ought to understand that. They do nothing but make you ridiculous on top of all your other faults."

Helsingforth squared her shoulders, caught her breath, and her eyes bulged slightly. I knew that sigh: She'd found another topic.

"And what do you hope to prove with that white dress, Audrey? That you're a virgin? So what? That's nothing to be proud of. Doctor," she continued, as if she were giving me her slave, "does Audrey please you?"

"No," I answered prudently.

Helsingforth laughed. "And what would she need to please you?"

"A few more pounds."

"Do you hear that, Audrey? The doctor thinks you're too skinny. And you are skinny—skinny, virgin and depraved."

"Hilda!"

"And what's more, stupid," Helsingforth continued, warming up to the task. "Stupid enough to take the ravings of a Ruth Jettison for gospel! To the point where you've never tried anything else in life but your fawning and bootlicking. Listen to me, Audrey: I serve Bedford because she serves my interests, but I don't give a damn for her dogma. I'll get my pleasure with anyone I please."

"But, Hilda," said Audrey, pitiful and shocked, "you know quite well that pleasure—"

"Stupid little bigot, shut up!" Helsingforth roared. "Your ignorance is bottomless. You really don't think that you're going to tell me what an orgasm is! You who've never undulated your vagina around a penis!"

"Hilda!"

"And a prude to boot! Get out of here, you little dunce! Go scrub the kitchen floor and don't show your face in here again. You hear? Don't show your face in here again. I want to be alone with Martinelli."

If it weren't for the way she hated me, I could have felt sorry for Audrey, so contorted was her face with suffering. Out of the corner of my eye I watched her leave, a small, old-fashioned silhouette followed by her long skirts that brushed against button boots from another century.

Her jet-black hair drawn over left cheek, Helsingforth, nude and sacerdotal, offered me her right profile. Her brows angry, she ate and drank with a look of not wanting me to talk to her.

I considered it as good as said. In silence, I sipped my tea and I ate my toast. I was astonished to have the presence of mind to savor the butter that Audrey had spread. At Blueville we never had anything but margarine.

"What are you thinking about, Doctor?" asked Helsingforth, throwing me an eagle's glance.

That did it! My turn had come. This Moloch constantly needed victims. I gathered my strength.

"About the butter on my bread."

"You don't see beyond the end of your nose."

"I'm lucky that way."

"Aren't you worried about the future?"

"No."

"Aren't you presumptuous?"

"I don't think so."

"You no doubt take yourself for my favorite."

"No."

"How long do you think this fickleness is going to last?"

"I don't know."

"And do you know what's going to happen afterward?"

"I haven't any idea."

"Would you like to know?"

"Only if you want to tell me."

"Well, I'm letting Audrey accuse you of rape. I'll corroborate her story and you'll be sentenced to prison and castration."

I limited my reply to a legal objection.

"It's California where they sentence people to castration for sexual offenses."

"Your information isn't up to date, Doctor. Under the Bedford regime, all the states, Vermont included, have come into line with California."

I remembered poor Mr. B. and I kept quiet.

"Well," she asked with a snicker, "what do you think about it?"

"Nothing."

"Do you think you'd like being a *castrato*?"

I decided to brighten up the conversation.

"Who knows? Maybe I'd also have a fine career in the Administration."

Helsingforth reacted in a way that I'd begun to know quite well: She laughed. But as soon as she'd laughed, she was angry with me for making her laugh. Her look hardened and she said in a cold voice, loaded with subtle animosity, "I can tell you with certainty, Doctor, as the situation has become quite clear. Your vaccine won't be produced either here or outside of the U.S. Surveillance will be increased while waiting for you to develop the vaccine. As of now, you are to consider yourself a prisoner."

Although these words taught me nothing that I hadn't already known in a haphazard way, they froze my blood. If the fiction about my freedom no longer seemed necessary to Helsingforth, it meant that the denouement was drawing near.

I said, dry-mouthed, "If you don't plan to use the vaccine, why are you letting me develop it?"

A curt laugh. "Come now, because it's security. And you may rest assured of one thing: As soon as it's ready, I'll put it someplace safe—and not necessarily here."

If I understood correctly, Bedford and Helsingforth didn't quite trust each other. Since I had nothing to lose, I decided to counterattack.

"How can you make yourself an accomplice to Bedford's genocide—you, most of all, who continues to have men on the sly?"

She laughed derisively. "That's not a good question. Men— I'll always find them. And 'love' isn't the right word, either."

"What's the right question?"

"This one: Why have I agreed to lose the huge sums that your vaccine could have brought me? Well, I'll tell you, Martinelli, I've reached a little compensation. That was the aim of my Washington trip and I achieved it."

I kept quiet. I'd learned to be afraid of cynics. I even prefer fanatics of Ruth Jettison's type. I feel nothing but contempt for a woman capable of auctioning off a vaccine that took such effort but mostly of trading millions of human lives for a sum of money.

"You're looking at me quite sternly," Helsingforth said with a wry smile. "You look like a judge. But I'm the judge! And the secular arm, too! You've been handed over to me, bound hand and foot, Martinelli, and believe me, I'm not giving anything away!"

She began laughing and showed her strong teeth.

"Come closer, Martinelli. The moment has come for me to eat you up."

She laughed again. I feigned thinking that she'd told me to bring my stool closer. I stood up, lifted it by one of its three legs—it was very heavy—and for an instant, a split second, I had an urge to swing it with all my might at her head.

I didn't do it. At that second I realized that it was almost impossible to improvise the role of a killer. I set down the stool, but I didn't get the time to sit on it. The glass door of the living room, at the other end of the pool, opened with a bang, and Audrey appeared, dressed in an old pair of black jeans and a sweater. She was very pale, almost cadaverous, her face taut, the neck muscles standing out, and she was heading toward us in a strange way, both hands behind her back as if they'd been tied prior to her execution.

That's just about what it was. I could tell just by seeing the look that Helsingforth, turning away from me, riveted on her. Poor Audrey couldn't have come at a worse moment.

She had about a dozen yards to cover to reach us—the length of the pool—and under Helsingforth's gaze—which I could no longer see because she turned her back on me but the expression of which I guessed—Audrey walked, straight and stiff, her hands behind her back. Her miotic eyes fixed on us unblinkingly gleamed with a fanatic flame. She was wan and she advanced, her chin thrust forward like a prow.

"Well, what are you coming in here for, Audrey?" Helsingforth asked with false sweetness. "I told you to scrub the kitchen floor. Have you done that?"

Audrey came to a halt two yards from her and said, without any humility, in a tone of voice that was passionately defiant, "No. I've been busy."

"Doing what?"

"Making a decision."

"Oh, that's fine!" exclaimed Helsingforth. "And have you made this decision?"

"Yes."

I came abreast of Helsingforth, though keeping myself out of her reach. I wanted to see her face. In two or three seconds the confrontation had attained an enormous degree of tension.

"Well, I hope you'll let me in on it tonight," Helsingforth said with the same ferocious irony. "I've noticed that your decisions are always original, no matter what stupidity you decide on. For instance, you break off with your fiancé"—Audrey winced—"or you have sex with Ruth Jettison. Or better still, you commit suicide."

"I'm going to tell you what I've decided," Audrey replied tonelessly but without her resolute look vacillating.

"Later! Later!" Helsingforth shouted with a little gesture of her hand as though brushing off a fly. "This isn't the right time. I'm getting ready to make love with Martinelli."

"It's about Martinelli."

"I can't believe it. You don't think much of the doctor. You're wrong. God knows," she went on with a little sneer, "I admire your intelligence, Audrey, but physically you're insipidity personified. And from that point of view, Martinelli has it all over a partner of your type. He's got everything you don't have. I'm not talking about his specific attributes. Martinelli has a good many other assets: He's got muscles, firm lips and a heavy growth of hair."

If Helsingforth's constantly false and exaggerated tone of voice hadn't nettled me, I might have admired her inventiveness in the domain of mental torture: the "firm lips," for instance. I saw Audrey's grow taut. With each new, treacherous blow, I saw Audrey blink and her white face quiver. She was erect, motionless, her hands behind her back. Tying her to the stake and bringing the torch near was all that she needed.

Although she was ferociously resolute (or perhaps precisely because of that) the words didn't come easily from her throat. Her lips were stuck one against the other and when she finally did open her mouth no sound was produced.

"Come now, Audrey, speak, speak," Helsingforth said. "You look like a fish out of water. This suspense is unbearable. Please speak. I can't understand what I can't hear."

"Hilda!" Audrey said in a low, toneless voice that was scarcely intelligible.

"Finally!" Helsingforth exclaimed.

"Hilda, please put a stop to your intrigue with Martinelli."

Helsingforth laughed. "An *intrigue!* Did I hear right? What a vocabulary! You're a century behind the times, Audrey! This is no intrigue but a simple variation in the techniques of orgasm. Must I repeat that the orgasm is qualitatively different—."

"Hilda!"

"Hilda, what?"

"Hilda, I'm asking you for the last time—send Martinelli away."

"For the last time?" Helsingforth said. "Tell me right away what's going to happen if I don't obey."

A silence, then Audrey replied in a toneless voice, "I'll kill myself."

"Oh, that's just great!" Helsingforth exclaimed. "So that's what you've come to! You give me an order and if I don't obey, you kill yourself. What childish blackmail. Didn't it ever occur to you that you haven't got a chance in a million of intimidating me?"

"It isn't blackmail," Audrey replied in a low voice. "It's just that I don't want to go through any more of what I've been through."

In saying this, pain had distorted her face and there could be no mistaking her voice.

"Do you mean, Audrey, that you suffer at the thought of Martinelli making love with me?" Helsingforth asked with feigned astonishment.

"You know quite well."

"Well, that's your business. It's none of mine. Straighten yourself out with your emotions."

A silence.

"Hilda," Audrey said in a low, restrained voice, "I'm going to kill myself."

Helsingforth shrugged her powerful shoulders.

"One more suicide with barbiturates. Two weeks in a hospital. And big expenses for me."

"I'll kill myself with this," Audrey said.

Both arms came out from behind her back and, in her left hand a small revolver appeared.

"Little vermin," Helsingforth said coldly, "you've gone through my purse again. After I forbid you to."

"I want an answer, Hilda," Audrey said, pressing muzzle of the revolver against her own chest.

Her voice trembled but not her hand. The appearance of the revolver had changed everything. Sweat ran down my back and my heart accelerated. At that instant I was certain Audrey would shoot. So was Helsingforth, I think, because she remained silent for a moment.

But when she spoke again it was to resume in a contemptuous, bantering tone of voice: "Audrey, you're useless. When someone wants to commit suicide, they shove the barrel of the revolver into their mouth or, if need be, they put it to their temple. But you, you'd rather drill a little hole any old place in your chest so that you won't be disfigured. And what's more, you make sure to kill yourself in the presence of a doctor. You think of everything."

I decided to do something right away and I did it vehemently: "I can't let you say something like that, Helsingforth! If Audrey puts a bullet in her chest, I can't do anything for her. And neither can Dr. Rilke at Blueville. She'd have to be taken to Montpelier. That is, assuming the bullet goes through a lung. If it goes through her heart, it's all over in a few seconds."

"Keep still, Martinelli," Helsingforth said, glancing at me with hatred. "Audrey doesn't even know where her heart is. Look at the barrel of the gun. It's much too far to the left."

I shouted, "It's horrible, it's diabolic, telling her that!"

Helsingforth turned a furious face to me. "For the last

time—keep still! Let me play this my way! You'll ruin every-thing with your stupid bumbling!"

When I looked at Audrey again, she had moved the barrel of her gun and had brought it more to the center of her chest in an infinitely more dangerous position. Sweat ran down my cheeks. I kept quiet. I sensed the uselessness of any action. And, strangely enough, Helsingforth also kept quiet.

"Well, are you satisfied?" asked Audrey. (Helsingforth's silence had given her the advantage and she sensed it.) "Is the barrel in the right place?"

Helsingforth remained silent. At that instant I was sure that the fear of a fatal outcome had taken hold of her because her contemptuous verve, which, a moment before, had seemed inexhaustible, ran dry all of a sudden. A second elapsed. Helsingforth seemed to grow smaller, her back bent. She turned to me and said wearily, "Go away."

I was amazed. She was capitulating.

Then it all happened in less than two seconds. With the muzzle of the pistol still pointed at her heart, Audrey's face grew relaxed and regained its color, and, throwing her head back, she alternately looked at us in triumph. This look, on her part, was an enormous error, I realized at once.

Helsingforth, drawing herself up to her full height, bellowed, "Doctor, you stay here!"

And taking a stride toward Audrey, bending forward, crim-son, the veins in her temples swollen, she cried—no, screamed—in a voice vibrant with hatred, "Audrey, I don't want blackmail! I won't let you tell me what to do! I've made a decision of my own. The doctor will come back as often as I like! He'll come back tomorrow and tomorrow and tomorrow!"

I don't know if Helsingforth meant to parody the lines from *Macbeth*, but on the last "tomorrow" a shot rang out and Audrey fell. In contrast with the suddenness of the shot—sharp but not loud—what amazed me about that fall was its slowness. At first I hadn't immediately understood that Audrey had fired. What I'd seen was the wavering of her body, the head thrown back, the neck that swelled and the lips that frantically drank in the air with a horrid sucking noise. Then her eyes glazed, the color left her face, her knees buckled. And, from there on, the fall. As in slow motion. Her legs gave way by degrees, her body folding up with a slight rotary movement and collapsing head first, not brutally but with a kind of grace. And as lightly as a scarf slipping off the back of a chair and dropping onto the floor.

Helsingforth let out a piercing screech, flung herself down on her knees beside the body and turned it over.

"Doctor!" she cried, her face desperate. "Do something, quickly!"

But there was nothing to do. She should have known! For the sake of form, I knelt on the other side of Audrey, raised her sweater and found the place where the bullet had entered. I didn't even need to bring my ear close; but I did anyway, because it was expected of me. I got to my feet. I looked at Helsingforth and shook my head.

She didn't say a word. She enveloped the frail body in her powerful arms and, effortlessly, she lifted it, carried it to the wicker chaise lounge and laid it down there. Then she collapsed at the foot of the bed and put her head beside Audrey's—which, in contrast, seemed as small as a child's—and began to moan.

It was a sinister moaning, at times exceeding the intensity that the ear can accept. It sounded like a pack of wild dogs baying together at the moon. At other moments her moans, sharp and hoarse all at once, gave way to more articulate lamentations where there were more or less recognizable words, fragments of sentences, tender names. Then the sounds were again lost in an animal scream that expressed such hopeless despair that it made my blood run cold. Helsingforth's face was sunken, hollowed, convulsed. Tears ran from her half-closed eyes. Most of all, I noticed her lips, hardened in the square grimace of the masks from Greek tragedy.

This mask gave forth without stop the same interminable psalmody, echoing lugubriously in the glassed-in room. I didn't capitalize on that instant of her trance to dress and slip away because I was afraid of attracting her attention and having her come rushing at me while both my hands were occupied. After the gun shot I'd hoped to see Jackie come running in. No, she couldn't have heard it. The picture windows of the pool must have been doubled or tripled for insulation, and the report of a low-caliber pistol hadn't managed to get through them. I must admit that I was both fascinated by the demented nature of Helsingforth's grief and, at the same time, struck by stupid astonishment. Dazed, I sat down on the stool. I couldn't get rid of the idea that it should be possible to go backward in time to undo the event.

Because, after all, it was absurd. It had all started as a game—scarcely more cruel than their usual games—and it had ended with a heart that emptied its blood on a marble floor.

Silence fell over us. Helsingforth was standing next to the chaise lounge where Audrey lay. She was as motionless as a statue, her face like stone, and her right eye was staring at me.

"It's your fault," she hissed.

"Oh, of course," I replied, getting to my feet and looking at her with a mixture of fury and fear. "I came here of my own free will! And it was also of my own free will that you got me mixed up in your private life!"

"You're not going to squirm out of it like that!" she said in a low and hissing voice. "The truth is that you played a devilish game. I was convincing Audrey of the foolishness of her plan and then you had to butt in. Not once but twice! Each time you made reality out of something that was only play-acting for her! She killed herself because you let yourself believe that she was going to!"

I was so indignant that I threw all caution to the wind.

"That's too easy!" I replied vehemently. "You're throwing your guilt on my shoulders! You provoked Audrey! You defied her, humiliated her, pushed her to the breaking point! What's more, you even corrected the position of the gun against her chest!"

"Keep quiet!" she screamed, wild-eyed, and, turning her back to me, she rushed to the place where a pool of blood was spreading.

I don't understand why she bent down.

Then it all happened very fast. I seized the stool on which I'd been sitting an instant before, swung it with both hands over my head and hurled it with all my might at her head—just as she was straightening up, revolver in hand. I didn't hit the target; she'd blocked the stool with her right arm, which fell back, broken and inert. Naked as I was, I went racing along the side of the pool, headed for the entrance. A shot rang out. I was outside. I ran as hard as I could and went down the trail that led to the stalls. Another shot rang out, then another. Behind me I heard someone running with heavy footfalls, and ahead of me, about thirty yards away, Jackie emerged, the carbine in her hands. She shouted: "Get down, Doctor! Get down!" I left the trail, dove into the tall grass and flattened myself on the ground. Two louder reports, then the dull thud of someone falling. It was over. My heart pounded against the tall grass. I pressed myself against it. I began to believe that I was alive.

15

"Are you all right?"

I rolled over on my back; Jackie's blond and suntanned face bent over me. Buttoned up tight in her reassuring uniform, she was looking at me anxiously with her gray eyes, the carbine under her arm.

"Are you all right, Ralph?"

I got up, tottering a little.

"Yes. I can't get over it. I can't understand how Helsingforth could have missed me. A woman like that must know how to shoot."

"She was shooting left-handed and on the run. Even so, I was frightened. You were in my line of fire and I couldn't get a clear shot at her. What about Audrey?" she continued, her watchful gray eyes fixed on the house.

"She killed herself."

Jackie lifted her brows.

"Out of jealousy. And very much encouraged by Helsingforth. In the name of brinkmanship, if you see what I mean."

"You can tell me about all that afterward, Doctor," Jackie broke in with an air of authority, glancing at her watch. "We've got a lot to do."

And, at once, she took the situation in hand, coolly, competently, with a force that I admired. I'd rather not dwell on the abominable task. Carrying—and, with regard to Helsingforth, dragging—the two bodies to the funeral pyre, piling them up and setting fire to the whole thing. I still have the splutter of frying in my ears and, in my nostrils, the odious smell of burning flesh from the holocaust. I can still see Jackie, searching among the hot fireplace's ashes with a shovel and putting aside the bones and the fragments of bones that had withstood the flames—actually, a very small heap when you think of the enormous power that Helsingforth wielded in her lifetime. Afterward, Jackie threw gasoline on these relics and burned them until completely consumed.

We still had to track down the empty shells—the ones from the revolver and those from the carbine—and wash away the puddle of blood at the side of the pool.

"I'll take care of that," Jackie said. "Meanwhile, you take a shower, get dressed and make us a cup of coffee. I'm going to need one."

I had carried out my domestic task when Jackie came back into the kitchen. There had been a hose, fortunately, and a drain not too far away. Just then the phone rang. There was a moment of stupor, then Jackie straightened up and said curtly, "I'll answer it."

I followed her into the living room and, as soon as she picked up the receiver, grabbed the earphone.

"Lieutenant Davidson speaking," Jackie answered in a clipped, military tone of voice.

"This is Mr. Barrow."

"Mr. Barrow, must I call Helsingforth?" Jackie asked tersely, decisively and almost threateningly.

I marveled at her aplomb.

"No, no," Barrow replied with a quaver in his suave voice. "You know she has forbidden us to call her. If I've taken the liberty of violating orders, it's because the helicopter patrolling the border has just radioed that they've spotted a fire close to her cabin. I was worried."

"The woodpile caught fire," Jackie answered. "Helsingforth, Audrey and Martinelli are there. It's practically out. No danger."

"That's good, that's good, that's good," Barrow said—and I don't know why that cascade of three "that's good"s reminded me of his three superimposed chins. "Lieutenant Davidson," he added and his voice was so suave, so light and so cautious that it seemed to be walking on egg shells, "do you know how long Helsingforth intends to stay with us?"

That "with us" was a masterpiece of courtesan affection.

"She's going away again with Audrey," Jackie replied in the same fast, businesslike way. "I'm supposed to pick them up in the car after supper and take them to the train. Do you have an urgent message to be transmitted to Helsingforth, Mr. Barrow?"

"No, no," answered Barrow, as frightened as if an egg shell had cracked under his feet, "and you don't even have to tell her that I called."

"Okay, Mr. Barrow," Jackie replied and she hung up.

"Ralph, we mustn't go back too soon, either," she resumed at once. "So we have time. Tell me everything that happened."

She listened to my detailed report, and when I'd finished she said seriously, "We knew that Helsingforth had 'sold' your vaccine to the Bedford Administration on her trip to Washington and that she'd received, in exchange, enormous financial compensation and tax privileges. We've got proof of this shameful transaction and we'll publish it at the right time. We've also found out that Helsingforth received practically carte blanche for eliminating you."

"Is that why you were so worried when you brought me here?"

"Yes, Ralph. And I also had a carte blanche for protecting you. It wasn't easy. I'd have willingly liquidated Helsingforth as soon as we got here. But Audrey was here. The entire time you were in the pool, I followed your movements with field glasses. Then the picture windows fogged up and I could hardly see anything when Audrey reappeared.

"And you didn't hear the shot?"

"No." She got to her feet. "One last look around the place before leaving, Ralph."

She went through all the rooms, her gray eyes alighting on everything. I was there but much more absently. When we were back in the foyer she grabbed her carbine and, with a quick movement of her hand, her head and her shoulder, slung it across her back.

"Jackie, just one thing," I said. "When do I leave Blueville? Do you know?"

She looked at me and inexplicably her eyes began to sparkle. "Tonight."

"I'm leaving tonight?"

She nodded. I looked at her incredulously.

"The twenty-eighth."

"Why?" she asked with a smile. "Doesn't the twenty-eight suit you?"

"The twenty-eighth suits me fine."

"I thought you were superstitious. At any rate, don't worry. It can't miss. I'm the one who set up the whole plan."

"I'm leaving with Dave, of course?"

Laughter. "You're leaving with Dave, but you're not leaving just with him."

"How's that? We won't be alone?"

"Don't look so worried, Ralph. 'We' has thought this out very carefully. You're going with Dave, with Burage . . ."

I exclaimed, "With Burage!"

"Hold on," Jackie said with a laugh, triumphant this time. "I haven't finished. You're going with Dave, with Burage and . . . with me."

I was dumfounded. "With you?"

"It's got to be that way," Jackie said, looking me in the eyes. She added, "It wouldn't be wise for me to stay in Blueville. I'm pregnant."

"Are you sure?" I asked with a gulp.

"Two weeks overdue on my period and the test was positive."

She unlocked the outside door and faced me again. Her eyes sparkled. "Come now, Ralph, don't give me that look. It's my concern, not yours."

She pursed her lips and puffed up her cheeks with a playful look.

"If it's a boy—and I hope it is—I'll call him Michael Bedford Davidson."

She emphasized the middle name, burst out laughing at her joke and gave me a very soldierly slap on the back. Then, with a quick movement of her shoulders, she pulled the carbine tighter against her back and walked briskly out into the sunlight, leaving me behind to lock the door. When I turned around, I saw her moving away in the direction of the stalls, her head high and her shoulders square.

When your escape has been planned by the leader of the militiawomen assigned to guard you, "it can't miss," as Jackie said. Nor was the escape terribly heroic, although, afterward, the Canadian press, then the European press, made a big fuss over it—a fuss cooked up in certain cases by the newsmen themselves. And one where the truth was stretched considerably. All the interviewers who—in Europe especially—raked me over the coals invariably praised me for the "find" that made my escape possible. Invariably, I answered that this trick hadn't come from me but from Burage. And invariably they continued to credit me for it in their articles. For the sake of simplicity, I suppose. Being the best known of the escapees, all the glory for the escape had to go to me, like a general who receives the glory for a battle that his subordinates have won.

Stripped of all the embellishments added subsequently, here's the truth: My role in this affair was limited to precisely what the others ordered me to do. And, actually, all the credit should go to the women: to Burage, who thought up the trick in question, and to Jackie, who, on the basis of that trick, worked out the details and set up the schedule.

Of course, the plan had been authorized by the general staff of "we," somewhere in the United States, as soon as they learned the vaccine was soon to be developed. But considerable initiative was left to the local level, and the means and date were decided at Blueville in several closed sessions, none of which exceeded half an hour.

When, later on, I asked Burage where "we" had found a place in Blueville safe enough to hold its meetings, she answered: in the wading pool when all the children were swimming. They made such a racket that any bugging became impossible. With that she looked at me with smiling eyes. I suppose you must have thought that we were gossiping. Yes, I said, with retrospective sheepishness. She laughed: cluck, cluck, cluck!

"Yes, that's it all right."

Burage laughed again.

"That's the impression we wanted to give. We knew that we could always count on old sexist reactions. In fact, our gossiping gave Mr. Barrow a handy pretext for teasing his wife."

"What? Mrs. Barrow was in on your closed sessions?"

Burage looked at me, a gleam dancing in her eyes. "Mrs. Barrow was the head of 'we' in Blueville."

She gave herself a little pause to enjoy my astonishment.

"It was Mrs. Barrow who recruited Rita. She had been caught in the act of going through her husband's wastepaper basket. And you know how Rita recruited Jackie." A little laugh. "And after Jackie, a good many others. Rita had a genius for this kind of work. Do you remember that Rita used to make dolls? Well, she had an almost infallible nose for detecting those single women whose maternal instinct had withstood Bedfordian propaganda. She would offer them one of her dolls and, if the reaction was right, the verbal approach began."

Mentally, I went over my self-criticism. I'd known that there had been a "doll episode" among the single women at the camp and that Mr. Barrow had finally outlawed—and I quote—this "ridiculous pastime." But for me (just as for him) it had seemed a trifling matter. I hadn't attached any importance to it. Only now did I realize its political implications. I looked at Burage with respect.

"And what happened after Mr. Barrow outlawed them?"

"Oh, it was wonderful!" Burage exclaimed, her eyes shining. "What a service the old *castrato* rendered our cause without knowing it! After he banned dolls they turned into clandestine objects, almost symbols of resistance. They became—in every sense of the word—the forbidden fruit. There were searches and in the course of these searches—we were forewarned by Mrs. Barrow—they invariably found dolls. But where? In the rooms of stool pigeons and Bedfordists, who were thereby eliminated at the same time. As for the dolls, it became sheer madness. Everyone started making dolls in secret, as well as sewing clothes and underwear for them. The single women got into the habit of meeting on the sly to trade and compare their 'babies.' Even the militiawomen began doing it! Jackie closed her eyes to it—or, rather, she closed only one—spotting 'good mothers' in the militia, pointing them out to Rita and then Rita would go right into action."

When I asked Burage how she'd thought of the trick for the escape, she replied, "Out of jealousy. I was horribly jealous, Ralph, jealous of all the women who came near you: Anita, Crawford, Helsingforth, Jackie, Pussy and, in particular, Bess. Yes, Bess! I know it's crazy. I don't know why. I had a fixation about Bess. I hated her without ever having laid eyes on the woman. It seemed very unfair that what was forbidden to an honest female lab technician was allowed for a whore. I knew from your description—you described her very well—that Bess was about my size and weight, that you might make fun of me, but one night, in my room, I disguised myself as Bess—false eyelashes, tons of eye shadow, lots of lipstick. Just then Jackie happened to come in. She burst out laughing and went to look for a blond wig she'd confiscated from a militiawoman. I put it on, and Jackie—who knew Bess from the checkpoint—swore that the resemblance was striking. She suggested that, in this getup, I should go to your quarters at nine o'clock and take 'a little sample' from you. Thinking about the idea from all its angles, we laughed like a couple of lunatics for an hour. It was just an outlet, I suppose, for the sexual frustration we were experiencing with more and more anxiety. Well, that night and the following nights, I fantasized that I'd eliminated Bess, that I was taking her place, that I came to your door. And so that's it, Ralph. There's nothing mysterious about it. The trick grew out of that daydream."

Now for the hour-by-hour scenario of the escape.

At 8:00 P.M., after supper, I told Dave to go straight to our quarters, and I went to the lab, where Burage, pale and tense, handed me the drugged whisky. I wasn't supposed to take along the vaccines. It had been agreed that she would take charge of them.

At 8:15 I was at home or, more precisely, in Dave's room.

And there, as Jackie had asked me to do, I sat down without speaking a word, took a sheet of paper and wrote with a felt pen what was going to happen and what, for his part, Dave had to do. I then handed him the sheet and watched him as he read it. He straightened up, blushed, puffed out his chest. His eyes began to shine. I saw a very happy boy before me. *Huckleberry Finn* was continuing, with his father and himself as heroes and, this time, not on a raft but nice and dry in a Ford pick-up truck. I leaned over his shoulder and underscored with my finger the "we" instructions that concerned him. His face glowing and enthusiastic, Dave read them over and over, and I noticed from the movement of his lips that he was learning them by heart. I was tempted to take him in my arms and kiss him, but I realized just in time that behavior so little in keeping with the stereotypes of adventure could only shock him. I went to the kitchen for matches and handed them to him. His face solemn and almost religious, Dave burned the sheet of paper. I didn't want to spoil beautiful moments by prolonging them. I left him. But, in leaving, I gave him a pat on the back and a wink, which I imagined was in the best movie tradition of austere friendship between men.

I went back into my room. I wasn't supposed to carry anything except my notes in a briefcase, so I had nothing to do until nine o'clock.

Those three quarters of an hour of idle waiting were the hardest moments of my escape. If I'd been a smoker, at least I could have availed myself of a favorite poison. But if that had been the case I probably wouldn't even have noticed I was smoking. I took the least harmful course: Instead of pacing up and down, I stretched out on the bed. And there, after a few minutes, I felt something that, to this day, still amazes me. I ran my eyes around the room and, all of a sudden, felt very keen, almost poignant regret at leaving it.

Yet there was nothing attractive about it. Cold in winter, hot in summer, simple furniture, little comfort, wan light through a single window. A forlorn view of barbed wire and the militia-women's barracks. And what memories were attached to that room! A bed where I'd had more insomnia and nightmares than restful sleep. A little table made of fake mahogany where

I'd often sat, without reading, without writing, mulling over my humiliations, eating my heart out waiting for Anita or anxiously anticipating the future. But, even so, it had been *my* place! The lair to which I had retreated to lick my wounds. And leaving it, I left a bit of my fur, my smell, my heat and a few months of my life.

When, at nine o'clock, Bess and Ricardo knocked at my door, I was feverish and happy enough to go back to the routine. In the kitchenette, I poured Ricardo the last glass of my unadulterated whisky. And I went to join Bess in my room, paying little attention to her professional zeal, even when she complained about the sluggishness of my reactions, claiming that there had been "competition." When we finally rejoined Ricardo in the kitchenette, it was with a trembling hand that I went to the lone cupboard in which the bottle of whisky given to me by Burage was locked. Although I had been assured there was nothing harmful in it, I felt like a Borgia when I poured them a full glass of the drugged whisky. And I wasted quite some time, once they had fallen asleep, their arms folded on the table, listening to their hearts and taking their pulse.

"Well, what are you waiting for?" asked Burage, coming into the kitchenette, bewigged and made up beyond recognition. Take off Ricardo's jacket and put it on."

The only suspenseful moment of the escape was at half past nine. Everything was ready: Burage behind the wheel of the Ford Transit panel truck; me next to her, a white medical cap down over my eyes and feigning intoxication; Dave in the back of the truck, wrapped head to toe in blankets; on his right, the freezer in which the vaccines had been placed next to Bess's test tubes—the former, I hoped, someday making the latter unnecessary.

The white panel truck stopped at the foot of the lookout tower. Daylight was fading and the lights of the camp were not yet turned on. Burage handed our two badges to the girl sentinel who inspected them at length before returning, almost grudgingly, our identity cards. Sprawling in my seat, I looked with only one eye at the militiawoman. It was enough, however, to tell that this big dried-up gawk with a pimply face was a troublemaker. She glanced suspiciously through the window.

"Why isn't the driver at the wheel?"

"Because he's drunk," Burage replied in a drawling, raucous voice.

"Why?"

"I can't stop the customers from giving him a drink," Burage said in a tone of voice that was incredibly accurate.

"Who gave him a drink?" the militiawoman asked accusingly.

"Dr. Martinelli."

"I'm going to report him for that," the militiawoman replied peevishly (she mustn't have liked me, God knows why).

"Sister, if I stopped the customers from drinking or from giving Ricardo drinks, I'd go out of business," Burage said.

The militiawoman blushed. I could see that this conversation with a woman of ill repute was an effort for her and that she wanted to call the meeting to an end. But she didn't. The more I looked at her, the less I liked that lantern jaw and those thin lips. She never gave up.

"I'm going to report the driver too."

"That's okay," Burage replied.

Here Burage made a mistake, the first since the start of the conversation. She shifted gears and revved up the motor. The militiawoman snapped, "Turn off that motor, get out and open the side door."

I forced myself to remain motionless, but my whole body grew tense and my heart pounded against my ribs. Silence. Burage switched off the motor and said in a drawling, sardonic voice, "Sister, there ain't nothing inside but sperm in a refrigerator."

The militiawoman winced as if she'd been insulted. But she didn't give any ground. Far from it.

"You heard me," she said.

"I'm sorry," Burage said raising her voice. "You ain't got no right messing around with my sperm in my refrigerator!"

"Do what I tell you," the militiawoman said.

"Well, if you insist, call the lieutenant," Burage replied with admirable sangfroid. "I'll only open it in front of her."

I was beside myself with apprehension and rage—especially against Jackie. She'd promised to be there when we went through the checkpoint. Because of her everything might be lost. What was she doing?

"Get out of there," ordered the militiawoman.

Burage obeyed, but she understood the stratagem. As she got out, she turned, leaned over, snatched the keys from the ignition and stuffed them in her pocket.

"Give me those keys," the militiawoman said furiously.

"Sister, this sperm is federal property," Burage answered. "Ain't nobody got the right to touch it—except me."

The militiawoman made an unexpected move. She grabbed her carbine and aimed the barrel at Burage's chest. I noticed that her hands were shaking.

"Give me those keys," she said white with anger.

I decided to do something. I slid over to Burage's seat behind the wheel, put a rather inebriated face to the window and said with a very inaccurate Spanish accent, "Señora soldada, you can't shoot Señora Bess. She's a federal employee."

"Don't call me 'señora,'" the militiawoman screamed.

A bigot on top of everything.

"Yes, señora," I replied with a stupid look.

Just then my elbow against the wheel triggered a brief honk. It was accidental, but I would exploit that chance: Overcome with weakness, I let my drunkard's head and both arms fall on the wheel. The Ford's horn sounded continuously, and its strident, monotone note drowned out the voice of the militia-woman, who, I suppose, was screaming orders and threats at me. Out of the corner of my eye I saw militiawomen come pouring out of their barracks. There were five or six of them, guns in their hands, very excited. A great commotion. Confusion. Shouts half covered by the horn. Various curses came my way. Several hands (and not the most gentle) shook me to make me let go of the wheel, but, despite the blows, I hung on until I finally saw Jackie. She came running from the camp at top speed, red-faced, her eyes blazing. Orders rang out. The guards, sheepish-looking, returned to their barracks. The mili-tiawoman stood frozen at attention. She was visibly shaken. So was Burage. Me too. Jackie had her hand over the car keys. She sent the militiawoman on duty to turn on the camp's lights, opened and closed the side door of the panel truck with a great slam, returned the keys to Burage and, bending down, said to me in a low, furious voice, "You didn't stick to my schedule. You were at the checkpoint five minutes too soon."

I glanced at my watch. She was right. It was Burage's fault, she'd rushed me when I listened to the hearts of the sleeping Bess and Ricardo. I straightened my white medical cap and got back on my seat. As I did so I realized I was bleeding from the mouth and my gums hurt. Those nice girls had punched me black and blue.

We drove. Blueville and its lookout tower receded behind us. I sponged my wound with my handkerchief. At the time I felt most humiliated—about the way I'd been treated, about my disguise, about my mustache, about the green rosette that burned my chest. If I hadn't been afraid of violating orders again, I would have thrown it out the window. Coming out of Blueville had cost me every scrap of pride.

The panel truck drove slowly over a dirt road—a few jolts. Burage ripped off her veil and her wig, shook out her dark auburn hair, turned to me and said suddenly in a furious voice, "I see that you're capable of using some initiative when it's a matter of going to your son's rescue!"

I jumped. That was the last straw! That was the height of injustice! As if I hadn't gone to her rescue, too! And as if "we," since the whole operation began, had given me the slightest say in the matter. I've caught you in the act, Burage, of reacting like a sexist! Like the women of the past, I was treated like a minor. I wasn't consulted, I was forbidden to undertake any action, and when I did nothing I was criticized for it. The handkerchief pressed to my lip, without a word, I ensconced myself in my corner and, turning my eyes as far as possible from the driver, looked at the night.

The prospects were dismal: Dave and the worry that I had about him. A jealous woman whose jealousy extended to Dave. Another woman, pregnant by me, who was escaping with us. Both of them claimed rights to me, since they were "protecting" me. Oh, I'd forgotten my sweet legitimate spouse, Anita, from whom, as far as I knew, I wasn't divorced. I had the feeling that I'd broken out of one jail only to land in another.

I looked at the night. My gums were bleeding. From time to

time I spat up a little blood into my handkerchief. As I think back, how bitter my first minutes of freedom seemed.

About a mile from Blueville, Burage brought the Ford truck to a halt, all lights out, on the right-hand shoulder of the road. We waited without speaking. A jeep appeared, and a face appeared at the window. It was Jackie. She passed us going very slow and waved for us to follow.

Three or four miles farther on the jeep left the highway and took a dirt road that snaked its way among the fir trees. Twilight, barely enough to drive without lights, brightened up all at once when we came out into a clearing. Jackie leaped from the jeep and came over to tell us curtly, "Don't get out of the Ford, don't talk and don't get excited if you hear gunfire."

With that, she went back to the jeep, stripped off her uniform, pulled on a pair of greenish Levi's that were baggy at the knees, a brown turtleneck sweater that had a russet armband on the left sleeve. Next she strapped on a revolver and gun belt, slung the carbine over her shoulder, rolled up her uniform, threw it into the back of the jeep and moved away, a walkie-talkie in her hand. I soon lost sight of her among the pines.

Another long wait. A violent firefight broke out. I reached for the handle of the door and Burage asked, "Where are you going?"

"To stay with Dave."

"Stay where you are. Didn't you hear the orders?"

I shrugged, got out of the Ford, opened the side door of the truck and, in a low voice, said a few words to Dave. I felt his face: He was perspiring under the blankets. I freed him and cocked my ear. The crash of gunfire went on. I went back to sit beside Burage, who said haughtily, "Great! Make yourself right at home. Slam the door!"

But what could the little noise that I'd made mean in the midst of that deafening firefight? It was so absurd that I didn't bother to reply. But I felt like gnashing my teeth. There was very little love, just then, between Burage and me.

The gunfire grew weaker, spaced itself out into three or four sporadic shots and stopped. I appreciated the value of the silence that followed, although I knew this consolation wouldn't last longer than the time it took me to become accustomed to it. Again, a long wait, then in the night, where some shreds of daylight remained, Jackie, decidedly darker, appeared, quick among the pines, without walkie-talkie, without weapons but with a dazzling smile, clearly visible when she came up to us.

"It's in the bag!" she said elatedly.

She started up the jeep, turned sharply and went back onto the highway, all lights blazing. We followed her.

A mile and a half farther on, an armed group stopped us or, rather, stopped Jackie. The headlights of the Ford illuminated the commando unit: girls and boys of twenty, dressed like Jackie was now, greenish jeans, brown sweater and russet armband. A girl broke away from the group and came up to the truck.

"You the doc with the vaccine?" she asked merrily.

"That's me."

"Stick your face up to the window so I can see you."

I obeyed.

"Well, Pop," she said, climbing onto the running board, "you sure look good." And she kissed me on the mouth.

I didn't know if I should be sad about the name or be delighted about the kiss. I asked, rather at random, "How are things in the guerrillas?"

She laughed. "It's a great life. We screw and we fight."

With that she laughed again and strode off, with a rolling gait, her torso at ease on her hips. She wasn't very clean, I guess. But her lips were fresh and her kiss tasted of grass. We drove slowly. The armed group waved their weapons when we went past them. For the first time I felt the breath of freedom. I threw a conciliatory glance at Burage. She was pale and tense behind the wheel.

The customs booth on the U.S. side was occupied by another armed group, more numerous than the first and much less exuberant. Among them I saw a few old-timers. And blackened, tired faces. Perhaps they had suffered casualties during the attack.

A very short stop at Canadian customs. Obviously they'd been waiting for us. A flashlight beam on my face and on Burage's, a wave, and we went through without showing any papers at all. Burage heaved a sigh and stopped the panel truck a few yards farther on.

"Ralph, would you take the wheel?"

We switched places, and I took the time to tell Dave that he could get rid of the blanket and make himself comfortable. When I started up, with Jackie's jeep ahead of me, we were preceded, accompanied and followed by a swarm of female motorcyclists. The protection was being continued, this time Canadian.

Sustained gunfire, but rather far away, broke out behind us.

"A counterattack?" I asked.

Burage looked at her watch and shook her head.

"No. A third commando unit is taking Blueville."

I lifted my brows. "What's the aim of that mission?"

"Three aims," replied Burage, pale and huddled up in her seat. I noticed that she spoke with extreme fatigue but that she hadn't lost any of her usual methodical self.

"First, to destroy the radio transmitter at Blueville. Second, to bring out the persons most endangered—Mrs. Barrow, Rita, Grabel, Pierce, Smith and the Stiens. Third, to get hold of the logbook for the Jespersen project. It goes without saying that Jespersen, himself, will be brought out, not at all in the same spirit as the others, and that we expect a statement and self-criticism from him."

I kept quiet. I marveled. "We" had overlooked nothing. With the denunciation of the Jespersen project, the war machine against Bedford had been reinforced with a mighty weapon.

That's what I was thinking about when Burage, her hands over her face, bent over and burst into sobs. For a moment I was speechless. Then I said gently, "Burage . . ."

"Leave me alone!" she answered through her hands.

Not an especially encouraging reaction. After a moment I advanced my right hand and touched her shoulder. My hand was thrust aside at once.

"Don't touch me, you damned sexist!" she said through her tears.

"What, again? What have I said . . ."

"You didn't say it—you were thinking it."

"Because now you can read my mind!"

"Spare me your heavy-handed humor."

Naturally, my humor could only be heavy-handed.

"And just what was it that I was thinking?"

"When I showed up at the checkpoint five minutes too early, you saw that as proof of female flightiness."

"Not at all. I was to blame as well."

She had full steam up.

"In the clearing you accused me of insensitivity when I wouldn't allow you to get out of the truck to cheer Dave up."

"No. You were just following orders. But I wasn't."

"And just now, when I started crying . . ."

"You're wrong. I was thinking that the culture in which we swim has allowed you to cry and not me!"

Saying that, I handed her my handkerchief, as white as Noah's dove. Her sobs grew sporadic. Her hands came down, her face appeared. After a few little rear-guard spasms, we were heading toward the calm. I myself had a lump in my throat— after all, in Homer, the heroes cry.

"Oh, Ralph," Burage said, "I was so frightened, so very frightened, when that big bitch ordered me to open the side door of the Ford!"

"You handled it very well."

"No, no, it was you, Ralph, who saved the day. You were magnificent! And it was so unexpected! Up to now, because you've been sensitive, I thought you were a bit of a coward."

"Thanks."

She hadn't heard. In her head, on her lips, my attributes were expanding visibly.

"Poor Ralph! How I suffered for you! And there you were, stoic under their blows! Hanging on to your steering wheel like a little bulldog."

"'Little' wasn't absolutely necessary."

She laughed, moved closer to me on the front seat and threw me a line. I caught it with my right hand. There we were, in port. Calm waters. Gentle breezes. We were moored side by side. I noticed that nothing further had been said about "being able of taking the initiative only to go to my son's rescue." Silence. Our two masts rocked side by side.

Furthermore, it wasn't long before I cast off my fingers. I

needed both hands to drive. But I felt relieved. With my eyes glued on the rear lights of the jeep and my ears full of the roaring of the motorcycles, I was having trouble keeping up a conversation.

After a three-hour drive, the jeep crossed an airfield—military, I believe—and led us straight into the maw of a transportplane that swallowed the truck. I supposed they needed it as "evidence." I pulled Dave out. He'd been fast asleep.

In the plane, however, he was wide awake. In his triangular face, his big eyes studded with black lashes were lively, inquisitive—and dropping with sleep as I was—I was infinitely grateful to Jackie for taking charge of him and giving him an epic account of what had happened. I collapsed into a seat, buckled my seat belt and closed my eyes.

"Ralph, this isn't the time to sleep," Burage said, sitting down beside me. "I've got work for you."

I raised my eyelids. This was a new-model Burage: her hair combed, her face smooth, her movements prompt, her speech clipped. She was so fresh-looking that she seemed to have emerged from a long sleep and a bath.

"Ralph, here's the text of your message for Canadian TV. Naturally, you mustn't read it. You have to look as if you're extemporizing. The flight is going to last half an hour. You'll be interviewed on landing. So you have half an hour to learn this text."

"You think of everything!" I said in a bad temper. "Are you the one who wrote this paper?"

"Oh, no! It was worked out at a much higher level. Don't think for a minute they're going to let you say just any old thing."

"I'm not an idiot!"

"Come now, dear little Ralph, you mustn't get angry."

She gently stressed "little," and leaning over, she swept my face with her magnificent auburn hair. I breathed in the smell of her hair and realized for the first time that it had been washed and scented. Thank God, femininity wasn't dead. What man would have thought of washing his hair before escaping? I looked at Burage. I cherished more than ever that indomitable sex.

In the vulgar version of the facts of life, they say that the man penetrates the woman. But couldn't it also be said that the woman "surrounds" the man? And that was precisely what Burage was doing—at that stage, psychologically. She enveloped me—a very pleasant sensation—with her hair, her eyes, her smile, her fingers. And let's not forget her voice, either.

She resumed. "You're not an idiot, but you're naïve politically. Ralph, with your acting ability, you're going to deliver this text to perfection. You've got to. Everything has been thought out very carefully. Every word counts."

16

Every word counted, all right. A week after my revelations, a revitalized Congress impeached President Bedford.

I don't deserve all the credit for it. My contribution was modest. I headed a team that developed the Encephalitis 16 vaccine. For the test, I was a tool in the hands of "we." To quote Burage, I was a tool equipped with a limited amount of know-how and capable of a certain margin of initiative while operating.

Furthermore, I was only the linchpin in the revelations that brought Bedford's downfall. I testified that Bedford, while trying to look as though she was subsidizing my research, had arranged with Helsingforth to keep the vaccine from being used.

Nevertheless, my testimony wouldn't have had such far-reaching effects if it hadn't been corroborated on Canadian TV by Mrs. Barrow. She reported conversations between Helsingforth and her husband that not only confirmed the plot against my vaccine but also against me personally.

With that, Jespersen—who, from the moment he fell into the hands of "we" and safe and sound in Canada, repudiated Bedfordism—willingly made public the aims of the project he'd headed: to make *Caladium seguinum* tasteless, colorless and odorless.

His self-criticism took the form of a press conference over Canadian TV. Jespersen was rudely shaken by the pack of reporters present there. He defended himself feebly, but this feebleness even lent some credibility to his defense: He hadn't had a clear picture, he said, of the use that the Bedford Administration could make of his discoveries. He gave the impression of being a good chemist who didn't want to see beyond his chemistry and who, out of personal convenience or sluggishness of mind, had erected an airtight partition between science and his conscience.

"We" finally produced its surprise witness on Canadian TV.: Alina Murdock, adviser to the President at the White House, twenty-eight years of age, single. She revealed in all its details, backed up by photocopies and tape recordings, the financial transaction under the terms of which Helsingforth promised the President not to start manufacturing the Encephalitis 16 vaccine.

This testimony made quite an impression on world public opinion; it put together all the pieces of a puzzle that, once reconstructed, gave a startling clear picture—the Bedford Administration, in the name of a depraved philosophy, had taken a series of measures that all tended to the extinction or, what amounted to the same, to the non-protection of the male population of the United States.

I expected that Jackie would also be called to testify, if only about Helsingforth's attempt to murder me. But this was not the case, and Burage explained to me that "we" had decided to remain silent, both about my personal relations with Helsingforth and about what had become of her and Audrey. The implicit thesis of "we" was, I believe, that Caesar's wife (in this case, me) must be above suspicion and that my image would have suffered too much from the violence and eroticism of this episode.[1]

Finally, it should be emphasized that the anti-Bedford operation wouldn't have been possible without efficient backing from the authorities in Ottawa.

---

[1]"We" also rejected the idea of using Stien's testimony on clones. They felt that it was inadvisable to discredit research that was dangerous only in the Bedfordian context.

In fact, "we" had long maintained close relations with President Colette Lagrafeuille, whose surprising epistolary idyll with the French President had been described to me by Anita, and who was, like her correspondent, quite an uncommon character. First of all, there was her size. Never had the word "little" been more aptly employed to designate a human being. The French-Canadians, who were grateful to the lady President for bearing a name that was indeed "one of theirs," affectionately dubbed her "that little bit of a woman." Without heels—and hers were certaintly high—she couldn't have stood more than four feet eleven. But she was so well built and her proportions so perfect that she gave the impression of being better "finished" than the invariably taller persons around her. When I was introduced to her—and I saw her several times, as she wanted to see me about a minor neurological condition—I was very much struck by the fine texture of her skin and the beauty of her complexion, mat and highly colored at the same time. She had a nose that could scarcely be called classical, broad at the base, turned up at the tip and, without marring her face, giving it a mischievous look. And finally—I kept the best for a tidbit—extremely attractive dark eyes, the myopia of which—she almost never wore glasses—was an added attraction.

Lagrafeuille was a member of Women's Lib, radically foreign to Bedford's fanaticism. And the analysis that she made of the relations between the two sexes proved quite different from Deborah Grimm's. Lagrafeuille said that men's misogyny was a prejudice, universal and superficial at the same time, yet hard to root out, especially where it was a fact of culture and not a reasoned position. It therefore made little sense to be angry with men about their sexism. It had been inculcated in them by a certain type of civilization and, while it governed their actions, it usually did so without their knowledge. Thus, it was sheer madness to reply to their misogyny with a misandry of the Bedfordian type. It wasn't a question of hating men but of reeducating them. Mend, not end, said Lagrafeuille, who, as far as she was concerned, had a great deal of friendship and respect for the human animal, men included, and was horrified at the idea of the "unisex parthenogenetic state" that Bedford was calling for.

This "little bit of a woman" had great courage. When the "Martinelli Scandal" broke, she reacted quite firmly to the pressures and threats from her powerful neighbor. After my first interview on Canadian television, Bedford made the most of her opportunities. The mass media, under her heel, immediately portrayed me as an unscrupulous individual who, not content with having stolen a vaccine belonging to the Helsingforth Company, was spreading the vilest calumnies about the White House, besmirching the good name of the employer that he'd swindled and was probably mixed up in her disappearance. At the same time, Bedford demanded my extradition, Mrs. Barrow's, Jespersen's and Alina Murdock's. Not obtaining satisfaction, she recalled her ambassador, threatened Lagrafeuille with an economic blockade and armed reprisals.

Actually, it wouldn't have been easy for her to mount a classical type of military operation against Canada just then. As soon as my revelations came out, they were picked up by the clandestine radio stations that "we" had set up in United States territory and were disseminated by millions of leaflets and pamphlets. At the same time, the anti-Bedfordian guerrillas took the initiative everywhere, reducing the government's female militia—in which desertions became wholesale—to defensive action.

Nevertheless, in view of the increasingly bellicose and hysterical statements that Bedford issued in the week preceding her impeachment, apocalyptic reprisals were to be feared when President Defromont gave a Paris press conference at which, reporting the serious dangers that menaced Canada, he announced that French atomic submarines were cruising off the Canadian coast and that France—as he put it—"would not stand by with her arms folded" if her ally were attacked.

Obviously, the pro-Bedfordian press had a field day denouncing one more time the braggadocio, megalomania and pro-Canadian chauvinism of France, as well as her perpetual meddling, on behalf of world conscience, in the business of others. But the rest of the world felt a certain relief. In England, whose foreign policy had nevertheless been so closely subjected to that of the United States, a *Times* editorial summed up the general feeling by saying that, while the French President's arrogance was insufferable at times—"That King of France who took himself for God Almighty"—one had to be grateful to him in this instance for having *mis le pied dans le plat* (put his foot in it). What lay concealed behind this convenient expression was the British Prime Minister's urgent warning to Bedford—not quite *dans le plat* but, at least, on its rim—not to initiate any military action against a Commonwealth nation.

Fortunately, Bedford's impeachment before the Senate of the United States, meeting as a high court and presided over by the Chief Justice of the Supreme Court, was able to dispel these fears. For, although Bedford continued to enjoy all the prerogatives of the Executive, it was clear that her authority had been too badly shaken and her political power too paralyzed for her to be able to take any serious foreign-policy action against her neighbor to the north.

In all likelihood the trial was going to drag on for some time, so I prepared myself for a long stay in Ottawa. Actually, nothing of the kind happened, but I nevertheless had the pleasure of seeing our vaccine go into production and the first vaccinations begin. Generally speaking, an epidemic can be considered as having been stemmed in a country when 30 percent of the people are vaccinated. This modest percentage had always surprised me and yet, in the case in point, it proved accurate once more. In Canada, the figures for deaths due to Encephalitis 16 kept on rising until we had reached the prophetic 30 percent. And once past this threshold, the number of cases daily became insignificant.

This news was broadcast by the clandestine radio stations of "we" in the United States and touched off a violent storm against Bedford. In normal times the ire of public opinion would doubtless have been expressed through the press to a large extent, but the latter was still muzzled by the special laws issued against it by Bedford and showed a timidity that was hardly in keeping with its traditions. Consequently, violence became the only means of expression for the huge crowds which, in most American cities, went into the streets and into public places to demand the importation of Canadian vaccine—and Bedford's resignation.

The rule proved true once more: To produce casualties at a

demonstration, just put armed police in front of it. If, in most of the big American cities, the disturbances ended with property damage but no bloodshed, it was because the female militia was too busy fighting guerrillas in the countryside to be able to intervene in the urban centers. On the other hand, in Washington, where Bedford had concentrated troops to protect herself, the demonstration degenerated into a riot and the riot into a pitched battle. A civil-war situation arose at the local level with the acts of cruelty on both sides that this type of situation produces.

Inert the first few days, Washington's black majority revolted abruptly on the fifth day and swarmed through the city. According to rumors going around among the blacks, Bedford, capitulating before the Senate's opposition, would soon be importing the Martinelli vaccine, but this importation was to be kept secret and the vaccine distributed only to whites. Bedford had given orders for employers to give black workers *Caladium seguinum* without their knowledge, in the colorless, odorless form that a scientist had just discovered.

This "news," I later learned, had no basis in fact, and "we" bore no responsibility for its diffusion. The rumors had appeared spontaneously among the blacks due to the overheating caused by the tense period and the blacks' age-old feeling of insecurity. Very symptomatic of the situation was the fact that, as long as the epidemic raged, there had been a kind of truce between blacks and whites in most states. But this truce ended as soon as it became a question of preventing the disease. Even before the vaccine appeared in the United States, black American men believed that it would not be made available to them.

By a reaction that can only be termed racist, the head of the female militia in Washington, Evelyn B. Cropper, committed an enormous error. She concentrated the bulk of her troops to meet the advancing blacks, in great numbers but unarmed, and to do this she borrowed soldiers from the front that she held against the white guerrillas, who were well supplied with submachine guns, grenades and bazookas. Naturally, the whites attacked in force everywhere, breaking through the depleted lines that had been left before them and, after a few hours of violent combat, managed to seize the White House grounds.

The excitement of these white guerrillas disappeared as soon as they were in control of the grounds. They didn't dare to enter the mansion to which they attached so many illustrious memories and they stared at it in silence, with obvious embarrassment and almost religious respect. Finally, not knowing what to make of their victory and not having the slightest intention of overthrowing the United States government or, still less, of molesting the lady President, they asked to be received in a delegation.

Bedford remained seated, impassive, in the Oval Office, the doors and windows closed. She asked to be given, beforehand, a list of the delegates. Surprisingly respectful of form, the rebels complied. When the list was given to Bedford after making the rounds of a number of hands, she read it attentively. There were five names. The first four were female. The fifth was a man's. Bedford asked if he was an A and, on receiving a negative reply, she turned livid with rage and curtly refused to receive the delegation.

What happened next was only to be expected. The White House was invaded, the few militiawomen defending it opened fire and were killed, the doors battered down and Bedford chased from room to room. In the confusion that ensued, without anyone knowing exactly if it were murder, suicide or accident, the President fell from an upstairs window.

Bedford, elected Vice President a year earlier on the Sherman ticket, had become President at his death. Bedford having died, her successor was to be the Speaker of the House, in accordance with the provisions of the Constitution.

The woman who, after Bedford, became the leader of the most powerful nation in the world was almost unknown by the general public. Her name was Elizabeth Hope. Divorced, remarried, then widowed in the first month of the epidemic, she was forty-eight years of age, had raised four children born of her two marriages and, before becoming a Senator, had skillfully managed a ready-to-wear business.

On the day that the new President of the United States was

sworn in, the little group of exiles from Ottawa boarded a plane for Washington. Burage, Barrow and Jackie were deliriously happy. Their courageous struggle had ended in victory. A new life was beginning for them and for the United States. Elizabeth Hope, the openly acknowledged but apparently cautious leader of the Senate's anti-Bedfordian opposition, had secretly been one of the national leaders of "we."

In comparison with these great events, my private life may seem relatively unimportant, but I should like to say a little about this, because what happened to me happened to the millions of men who had survived in the United States. The takeover by "we" changed my everyday existence completely, although in an entirely different way than Bedford had.

I had a foretaste of what lay in store for me from the first night that I spent in Ottawa after my escape. At 2:00 A.M., two double rooms separated by a bathroom were placed at our disposal in a suburban hotel, the grounds of which were crawling with guards. Like a modest American, I proposed sharing one of the rooms with Dave and leaving the other to Jackie and Burage. The two women smiled, looked at each other with an air that was both knowing and superior—as if they wouldn't even stoop, out of tactfulness, to challenge the hypocrisy of my proposal. And with that, Jackie said decisively, "Not at all. I haven't finished telling Dave the whole story. I'll share this room with him. And you'll take the other with Burage."

Which we did. God knows, I'd waited long enough for that moment. And now that it had come, I felt too exhausted to savor its joy. As soon as we were alone, Burage threw me a glance, just one, and, with an admirable sangfroid, made a realistic decision: She picked up the telephone and asked the desk to wake us at six in the morning.

"I'm going to let you get your beauty sleep until then," she said, hanging up and looking at me tenderly.

A week went by. A week during which the days seemed long and the nights short. I smile today as I recall the frame of mind that had been mine at the time. I'd had my share of failure and grief, and now I'd found Burage, she was everything good that a man could have wanted—"in every respect." What's more, Dave liked her; she'd hit it off with him. She was maternal and clever. In short, Burage, Dave and I, all in the same boat, were going to scud along with the wind behind us, toward the horizons of heaven. Happiness for three, a nuclear family, a little island of calm in the chaos of the world.

The third night, with Burage's head, *post amorem,* resting on my shoulder, I said, "I suppose Anita won't create any problems about giving me a divorce."

"Why—do you mean to ask for one?"

"As soon as possible. Does that surprise you?"

"It doesn't surprise me."

A silence, then she resumed. "But I don't see the point of it."

I moved away, raised myself on my elbow, looked at Burage and asked tonelessly, "Don't you love me enough to marry me?"

"I love you. Period."

"But not enough to marry me."

"That's got nothing to do with it."

A silence. I resumed, "It seems to me that when you love someone you want to live with him."

"But I'm planning to do that," Burage replied, considering me mischievously.

"But without marrying me?"

"No."

"Why?"

"Come now, Ralph, the traditional monogamous marriage is a completely outmoded structure."

Whether that was true or false, I didn't know. But I didn't like that kind of argument. No solid ground. Quicksand. Quagmire. Enough to keep you bogged down for hours. I got out of that dialectic swamp as quickly as possible and regained solid footing.

"What happens if we have a baby?"

"What's going to happen to Jackie's baby?"

I looked at her, bewildered. Why hadn't I remembered that? They told each other everything! I was the only one they hid things from! Like a baby . . . Like the baby I'd given Jackie or, rather, that she'd had me give her. Because, let's not exaggerate my initiative on that stormy night.

"I don't know," I answered, embarrassed. "I haven't asked her."

"What I would do myself," Burage said. "I'd give the baby my name and I'd raise it."

"Without my assistance?"

"With your kind assistance, if you wish, and for as long as we live together."

"And what if you leave me?"

An unexpected reaction: Burage covered my neck with fond little kisses.

"Oh, how sweet you are, Ralph! You can't even imagine that you're the one who might leave me!"

I hugged her. I cried over that, then over myself. Finally, I didn't know which of us I was crying over. Okay. Let's not rack our brains over it. We'll let that angel go by. Let's hope we'll see his sky-blue wings between her and me again. I looked at Burage gratefully. At least, there was someone who appreciated my good qualities. Not like Anita. With Anita, you scratched her charm a little and saw the hardness right away. A question of noses. Anita's, thin, slightly hooked, a bit pointy and, as I said, "delicately chiseled," had always seemed connected to a certain lack of feeling. How much more reassuring Burage's round nose or Colette Lagrafeuille's nose, turned up at the end.

"Well, if we split up," Burage resumed, "one thing is certain. I'll raise the child alone and without assistance."

"No alimony?"

"Absolutely not. A woman lowers herself by agreeing to be financially dependent on a man. She should make do with her own work."

"What about the right of visitation?"

"It isn't a right," she replied sharply, "and it isn't connected to the payment of alimony. It's an arrangement between us."

A silence. I said, "Still, it seems to me that I'm the one who becomes the minor and irresponsible member of the couple. I'd have a baby with you and I'd have no duty toward him."

"And no rights, either."

"In other words, I'd be a stranger to him."

"Not at all. You can take care of him as much as you like. What you lose is a double guardianship—over 'your' wife and 'your' child."

"You mean that all the power goes into the mother's hands, don't you?" I asked harshly.

"Yes."

Not a curt "yes" but a firm one.

"Then it's a matriarchy, isn't it?"

"Yes."

A pause to digest these two "yesses" and I continued: "But won't that set up a certain inequality between men and women right away, just the opposite of what's been going on up to now?"

"Yes," Burage replied honestly, "that's true. There is some injustice to it. And we've often argued over this among ourselves. But what can we do? All of us believe that this is the price of women's liberation."

"How convenient," I said, "and how easy, to resign yourself to an injustice when you benefit from it."

Burage didn't reply. I couldn't say if she'd decided to let me have the "last word" or if she preferred turning a deaf ear to my answer. If it were unwillingness, I must admit that it was an altogether male tactic: polite dismissal of the issue or what's worse, men's amused indulgence toward the age-old grievances of the second sex.

I wasn't out of the woods yet. In Ottawa, with Bedford still not impeached and "we" not yet in power in the United States, I went from one surprise to another in my private life.

On the eighth day, I was busy until quite late. I phoned the hotel to have the trio eat supper without me, and when I finally got back to my room I found the light out and the door unlocked. I wasn't going to wake Burage. I didn't switch on any lights, and I went into the bathroom to undress and shower. Having done this, I came back to the bed, still in the dark, and looked for my pajamas. No luck. The chambermaids in that hotel showed remarkable ingenuity for hiding things of this type.

I pressed the button on my little night-table lamp, and what I saw then made me forget about pajamas. In the bed next to mine, emerging from the sheets—blond hair. I recognized that color and hair style at once.

"Jackie!" I said.

Her head emerged, her eyes accommodated, and her first reflex—I'd have bet on it—was to laugh. She was a good-natured girl.

"Jackie! What are you doing here?"

She laughed again. "Oh, Ralph!" she said. "What a face you're making! How funny you look! To top it off, a naked man should never look surprised. The mixture is irresistible!"

"Jackie, where's Burage?"

"In the room next door, of course. Where do you expect her to be?"

"With Dave?"

"No. Dave now has a room of his own. He was very angry about sharing his quarters with a woman."

I was relieved. I might be old-fashioned, but I wouldn't have liked Dave to do too much wondering.

"But that doesn't tell me why you're here," I said.

She laughed louder. "What a question, Doctor! You're going to have to resume your studies! After all, this won't be the first night that we've spent together."

"What about Burage?" I asked. "Has she consented . . .?"

She exclaimed, "Why, of course! Ralph! What century do you think you're living in? I'll wager you see the situation in terms of adultery! Why not 'sinning' while you're at it? Ralph, you should be ashamed! You've got your head stuffed with old monogamous fripperies." With that, mystified, mocked, taken to task and, why not admit it, disappointed, I gave up my pajamas—what good would they have been?—and stuffed myself into my bed, where I was soon joined at a bound by Jackie. Yes, disappointed. Oh, I knew the charms of variety, having daydreamed about them often enough. But why did it have to be just then? When I was intoxicated with the discovery of Burage. Certainly, Jackie was a beautiful, wholesome girl, but she was completely without mystery. She marched toward pleasure like a good soldier marches toward cannon. And what's more, she was breaking up my honeymoon with Burage and all the delicious, delicate pleasure that I'd been anticipating.

The following day, early in the morning, Jackie, fresh and invigorated, was kind enough to take Dave on a walk around the city, and while I was shaving in our common bathroom, Burage made her appearance, wearing a black-and-gold bathrobe against which her dark auburn hair made a splendid effect. Do these pretty things come from Ottawa? What elegance for a Women's Lib militant! But, after all, why not? I looked fondly at Burage. She took a stand next to me and, her milky arms coming out of her wide sleeves, combed her sumptuous mane—energetically, methodically, diligently. I looked at her in the mirror that covered the wall in front of the double sink. A pretty picture that I'd have termed archaic, if I hadn't feared being accused of sexist nostalgia. How different was the process of Jackie, who, while whistling, gave her short hair a quick combing.

"Good morning, Ralph," Burage said serenely. "Sleep well?"

The tone of her voice was matter-of-fact, without the least impudence.

"I would have slept better if my roommate hadn't been switched. Of course, without telling me."

A little smile, but without losing her serenity.

"I'm sorry, Ralph. I meant to let you in on our decision myself. But you came in so late and I was dead-tired. I'd taken a tranquilizer."

"Of course," I said bitterly. "You let me in on decisions. You don't make them with me."

What could she do but—still smiling—take the offensive?

"Ralph, you wouldn't be a little hypocritical by any chance, would you? After all, you find Jackie pleasing. You've already had sex with her. Before me. In that famous little hut."

"It was Jackie who made the advances."

"Ralph, that's childish! It doesn't matter who did what to whom! The results are what count."

A silence.

"But, Burage—Jackie! With your consent! I thought you were jealous."

"Jealous—*me*?" Burage replied.

But her eyes were laughing as she said that. Clearly, these two women were making fun of me. Next to them, I felt like somebody who was indescribably funny, childish, backward, old-fashioned. In short, disdain tempered by affection. Because they loved me, too. Oh, yes! That dear little Ralph, so naïve, so sentimental. And always ready to do honor to his Latin virility. For it is Latin, of course. Southern Europe has its good sides.

I was going to try being serene, too.

"If my memory serves me, you were very jealous in Blueville. You created one scene after another."

"Oh, Blueville!" Burage replied.

She set down her hair brush on the sink. Her face changed. Her voice, too.

"In Blueville, Ralph, the situation was different. In Blueville, everybody got a piece of the 'poor beast,' except me. Bess! Jackie! Oh, I won't be forgetting Blueville! I suffered unimaginable sexual frustration. Every night I lay writhing on my bed for hours, calling you in the dark. Oh, Ralph, I remember that I would clutch the sheets with both hands and I'd repeat without stop in a low voice, because of the bugging, 'Give me a baby, Ralph, give me a baby!'"

I was touched by that speech. I unplugged my electric razor and, in my distraction put the razor into its case without cleaning it. I looked at Burage. Magnificent hair, blue eyes, milky complexion (and let's not forget that reassuringly round nose), all that against a charming decor of black-and-gold bathrobe. I felt a great surge within me. But just as the idea of taking her in my arms dawned on me, my excitement ebbed away. I thought to myself, Do I have the right to kiss her this morning? How have these two women shared me? A week apiece? And during the week that I devote to one, do I have the right to caress the other?

I controlled my irritation. I took up my electric razor again, opened it and cleaned it.

"Burage, you can't convince me. I'll never believe that you've given me away to Jackie of your own free will. I also notice that you took tranquilizers last night—you, who've been against them."

She had picked up her brush again, and although I'm a man, I'm not a fool. I knew that the brushing was over.

"Do you think you're making things any easier by that kind

of remark?" she finally asked in a slightly husky voice and avoiding my eyes in the mirror.

A little silence that made its weight felt. I wouldn't have wanted to exploit my advantage, but . . . I resumed in a neutral voice, "If you don't like it, why do you do it?"

Her lips grew taut, her blue eyes turned bluer, her hair became wild, a Gorgon or Maenad, depending on her mood. A storm was about to burst on me. I could feel it.

"Ralph, you're scatterbrained! Irresponsible! And politically illiterate! You have absolutely no idea of the situation. The United States has lost an enormous percentage of its male population. A percentage still not known with any degree of accuracy, since all of the Bedford Administration's statistics were falsified, you know this for a fact. I'm not even counting all those swarms of A's. In short, the task ahead of us is immense, Ralph, and under these conditions, what woman can claim to reserve a man all for herself?"

"What about artificial insemination?"

She shook her dark auburn hair violently.

"It's failed to a large extent. They found out under Bedford. The number of women who have had recourse to it is very small. The fact is that women are revolted at the idea of having a child by a man that they haven't known personally."

The "personally" was well put. And as hypocrisy, it was as good as mine. But that didn't matter. It was all clear now.

"And that's why 'traditional monogamous marriage is an outmoded structure,' I quoted not without irony. "Burage, who's saying that? 'We'?"

"Yes, 'we', but I agree with it," Burage said firmly.

With mingled feelings, I looked at that militant who was immolating her impassioned jealousy on the altar of the general interest.

"But in that case, it would seem that I'm very underworked for the moment," I said sarcastically. "Apparently two pregnant women aren't enough. Just as Leah and Rachel, in their contest of fertility, weren't enough to provide Jacob with an adequate family. They had to have helpers."

"We'll get them," Burage replied, compressing her lips.

I didn't say anything. I didn't smile. I revealed no feeling; I was neutral from head to foot. But just then something in me betrayed itself outwardly by a sign that was infinitesimal but enough to cause a spark.

The lightning struck.

"You needn't look so happy," Burage said, her hoarse voice bearing heaps of clouds and storms, "nor go to so much trouble to conceal the fact you're so happy. You aren't fooling anyone, I know you. You have neither morality nor shame. You're a gorilla, that's all. No, no, not a gorilla—that's too big. A chimpanzee! Just as furry, too. You're an animal, that's what! An animal whose lewdness has no limits. A worthy mate for Bess! A Ricardo before ablation! Your dream: that all the women in the world might have only one c--- so that you could screw them all in one fell swoop!"

This picture was too much for me. I left the room, I slammed the door. What Burage said was neither true nor false. It was beside the point. Like any human being—male or female—I could have many partners. But in the case in point, the night before, I hadn't wanted to see Burage replaced by any other woman. And, what's more, she knew it. But the division made and the sacrifice consented to, who could she blame but me?

As I expected after what Burage had told me in Blueville about "we" strategy, President Hope appointed a Cabinet in which all the members were women. She nevertheless made sure to put a few men into posts that were relatively minor but where, on the other hand, they were plainly visible. For example, she sent a man to represent the U.S. at the UN, dispatched a male ambassador to Paris in replacement of Anita and chose as White House press secretary a charming young man who had been an actor, learned by heart the text that had been written for him beforehand and invariably replied "no comment" to all questions that were put to him.

In losing her post in Paris, my wife (since, legally, she still was) hadn't fallen into disgrace. As a matter of fact, I would have been surprised if she had. Anita was one of these deep-sea fish that are good at swimming with the current and, when the tide runs out, refuse to allow themselves to be left stranded. In the last months of the Bedford Administration she had established profitable clandestine relations with "we," and when President Hope called her back from Paris, it wasn't a demotion. Anita was appointed White House adviser for foreign affairs. Perhaps the only such case in the annals of U.S. history, she served three successive Presidents in this capacity.

So I saw Anita again in Washington fairly often, since I'd gone back to my Wesley Heights home. I must admit—but I'll take this up a little later—that Anita managed to set up relations between us that astonished me.

Anita was one of the four—or, rather, one of the three— women advisers at the White House, the fourth being a man. Basically, he played the role that a high-ranking black officer plays in the U.S. Army—he was a token. He was there to show that the U.S. Army isn't racist and that even a black can become a general. Anita, who, in the beginning, hadn't had much respect for the fourth adviser—but she came around when his role began increasing—dubbed him uncharitably "the duty male," which wasn't kind either to Archibold C. Montague or to his sex.

At first, Anita said, nobody knew exactly what role Archie played among the female advisers. To be sure, he was always there, but he never opened his mouth and seemed to listen with equal deference to the often contradictory remarks that the female advisers and the President exchanged in his presence.

Nevertheless, he did not leave Elizabeth Hope's side and formed an amusing contrast with her. For Archie was sparkling and athletic at thirty-five, while Elizabeth Hope was heavy and wrinkled at fifty-five. He was as tall and slim as she was short and dumpy. And while the dresses that she hung over her back and her little belly seemed to have been sewn in haste and pulled on any old way, Archie was dressed from head to foot in the most exquisite fashion.

In three months Anita and the other female advisers had never seen Archie do anything but sit gracefully beside Elizabeth Hope, keep quiet with consummate dignity while the women talked and leap from his armchair, lighter in his hand, as soon as a cigarette appeared between the presidential lips. During all this time they had never heard him utter more than one sentence and then in a low voice as if *a parte*: "You're smoking too much, President." It should be noted that the "Mr.," which had formerly preceded "President," had been dropped as improper and the "Mrs." as sexist.

Elizabeth Hope had such a pragmatic turn of mind that everyone at the White House wondered why she tolerated an adviser at her side whose functions were mainly aesthetic. The mystery was solved when the new *Code of the Woman* took effect and President Hope took Archie as her companion. Proof that her penetrating eye had discerned the adviser's true merits.

Furthermore, some of these merits became evident quite quickly. Archie had an innate sense of priorities—always so important in Washington. With a little study he pierced and mastered all the enigmas of etiquette, and his natural tact did the rest. He always remembered the names of people, he knew how to listen, and he had a knack for saying things gracefully that committed no one. So he became a trump card for Elizabeth Hope when she resumed the White House receptions.

It should be said that, under Bedford, the receptions had fallen into a sorry state. As men were banned from them, the single women who met there made up for the absence of hated males by affecting hypervirility, which ruined their manners. They got into the habit, at the White House luncheons, of drinking to excess, sprawling out in their chairs and making scatological remarks. According to eyewitnesses, one of whom was an A that had been hired as headwaiter because he'd been a waiter at Maxim's, some of the women, as a sort of protest against masculine hypocrisy, "belched and farted at the table."

It goes without saying that nobody would have been allowed such excesses in front of President Hope's husband. Archie never stepped out of his domain, but in his domain he showed firmness.

To a Secretary of State who took the liberty of appearing at the White House in blue jeans and a turtleneck sweater—glorious souvenirs of her clandestine life—he did not hesitate to remark curtly yet courteously that this attire was no longer in fashion, peace having returned. A month later, as the social secretary of the President had used a vulgar word in his presence, he had the President fire her at once and, to the general satisfaction, took over the discharged woman's duties, performing them with an incomparable efficiency. Such a sense of decorum, together with so much beauty and an elegance that led people to call him "the world's best-dressed man," had done a great deal for his popularity. His photograph was seen more and more often in the magazines, followed by amiable comments, and six months after his marriage he was already being called the "First Gentleman."

At the beginning I suspected some derision in this title, the reference to ex-First Ladies being obvious, but Anita assured me that the women reporters who used the title had a sincere admiration for Archie.

Finally, we were all very happy that President Hope could fall back on the consolation of family affection, for she had to confront an extremely serious situation. In every country and more so in the United States, Encephalitis 16 had wreaked havoc among the male population. In the United States they didn't speak of the birth-rate problem, as they did in Europe. Using an expression full of resonances from history, the President had said that an absolute priority must be given to the "demographic reconstruction" of the United States.

The word was specifically American and the measures taken or, more precisely, the liberal philosophy from which they originated were in remarkable contrast with the solutions adopted elsewhere. In Europe, where the conservatism of mores was backed up by a long tradition, they thought that repopulation could be prompted by repressing abortion and homosexuality. President Hope took a harsh attitude to this repressive policy, which, to her, seemed to jeopardize every individual's inalienable right to his own body and to confiscate the reproductive organs of citizens for service to the state. Furthermore, the President felt that the incidence of contraception and abortion on demographic reconstruction was insignificant and that of homosexuality completely nonexistent. According to Hope, the vast majority of women in a country wanted children, and jailing the small minority who didn't want children wasn't going to make the others have more. What was needed was to give that minority advantages and benefits such that a large family need no longer be seen by the women as an overwhelming burden or lifetime slavery.

This was one of the goals that the new *Code of the Woman* set for itself. Promulgated during the first year of the Hope Administration, it reflected a historical event: At the end of the epidemic there had been no more American women in the home. The reign of the housewife was over; all women, except those in retirement, were working.

From this state of affairs, the *Code of the Woman* drew the conclusions that were imperative. Henceforth, women would declare their incomes separately, pay their taxes and give their names to their children, acting as sole legal guardian until the children reached the age of majority. The *Code of the Woman* recognized only one parent: the mother. And she alone benefited from the family allowances, social services and substantial tax reductions granted by the Hope Administration.

The father's role was defined only by preterition. Although the new Administration had abolished the laws against polygamy as unnecessarily repressive, nowhere was it indicated that the structure of marriage in the United States was slated for change. On the contrary, complete freedom was left to the couple—whether Catholic, Protestant or Jewish—to marry in the church of their choice. But the concept of "husband" and of "father" was implicitly abolished by virtue of the fact that the duties and rights attached to this double capacity were gone. The code did use the term "procreator," but the procreator didn't give his name to the woman that he had fertilized, nor to the children born of these relations. In addition, he couldn't declare those children on his income-tax statement and was neither obliged to provide for them nor to cohabit with their mother.

The only link that a man could establish with his offspring consisted of giving them his name as a middle name preceding the mother's. In this case, he was obliged to make out his will in their favor. Nevertheless, this demi-adoption involved no right for the adopting party. Furthermore, such arrangements could be made only at the written request of the mother, a request to which the procreator was in no way obliged to consent.

Obviously, this code marked the beginning of a sexual revolution without precedent in world history. But it was a revolution that did not reveal its name. The clever and completely unprovocative way in which the *Code of the Woman* was worded attested to what the old-fashioned sexist psychologists would have called the President's "feminine wile." At no time did the new legislation seem to touch the principle of monogamous marriage, but, on closer examination, it was nothing but an empty shell. Men, reduced to their biological role as reproducers, had ceased to exist as father. Their social power had been liquidated discreetly. Ousted from his managerial role, having ceased to be the nucleus of the family cell, he became a marginal element in society.

As Burage had warned, the idea of legal ownership, implicit in the "rights" of the father, died out along with those "rights." Only mothers had a definite social existence. They could live alone or with a man; it didn't matter. They still remained single women, since the guardianship and economic dependence on a man had ended.

These women were helped, of course, but by the community. The generous assistance, constant and many-sided, granted to mothers and single mothers (family allowances, premiums, tax reductions, neighborhood or town day-care centers operating around the clock) put "fathers" out of the picture and eventually led to the discreet nationalization of education.

These reforms might not have succeeded if, in financial terms, men still hadn't held the nation's main resources. It goes without saying that sooner or later money would have won back the positions that the laws had cost the ex-first sex. But this hypothesis seemed to have been ruled out forever. During the epidemic, women had inherited more than three quarters of the tools of production in the United States and had shown themselves to be capable of operating them. President Hope's new tax program would assure the continuation of this process. Tax reductions were granted to female owners of businesses and corporations where women held the majority of the shares and of the managerial positions. As taxes had become very high to offset the nation's new burdens, this measure led either to the closing of male businesses or to their transfer to women. Concurrently, inheritance taxes were considerably lightened when the property of mothers was left to female heirs. Certainly, a mother could still make her will in favor of her son, but this equity was a mere sham. The inheritance taxes paid by a male heir cost him more than half of the value of the estate, whereas the taxes that female heirs had to pay did not exceed 10 percent.

Thus, the *Code of the Woman* sets up, by simple tax legislation and without any statement of principle, a disguised birthright in favor of daughters. If the code is not revoked in the near future, these provisions will result in American women gaining a total stranglehold over the U.S. economy within two or three generations. Along with this, the code will assure the perpetuity of women's political power.

This process is not yet finished. At the present time it is still going on. But it is already clear that President Hope, by her powers of persuasion, her respect for the freedom of speech and her good relations with Congress, is succeeding where the previous Administration failed so miserably. Bedford's bigotry, the criminal misandry of her clique, the dream of Grimm and Jettison to establish—and I quote their idiotic pleonasm—a "unisex parthenogenic state" resulted in the United States being plunged into civil war. President Hope, on the other hand, understands that, as wronged as women have been over the centuries, no lasting social edifice could be built on hatred of men.

The *Code of the Woman* could doubtless be accused of creating a new imbalance by promoting the omnipotence of the ex-second sex. Only the future can tell if this imbalance contains the seeds of discord. But at least I can attest to the fact that this society is infinitely more pleasant to live in than the one in Blueville. Under President Hope, a man no longer feels hated, scorned, nor is his manhood and life constantly threatened. In the behavior of females with regard to men, I should almost say that, at present, there is an excess of love—a reaction, no doubt, with respect to Bedford's taboos against nature, along with the blossoming of an instinct that, in women, is no longer stifled by the traumatizing sense of her social inferiority.

As soon as I got back to Washington the whirlwind that we'd been through in Ottawa started in again: radio, television, press conferences, with one difference, however. In Ottawa I'd been the great man. In Washington it was Burage.

Furthermore, she shared that fame with Jackie, coming out of the shadows where she'd been in Ottawa, and with Mrs. Barrow. All three explained in great detail—for the added glory of "we"—how they had effectively protected me against the Bedfordists in Blueville before bringing off my escape.

I took part in these interviews, but, as they hardly ever asked me questions, I kept quiet. I noted that I was presented to the public as an object of pity rather than the hero of the story. On television the camera certainly was lavish with flattering close-ups of me—and while the lady interviewer didn't often let me speak, she made up for it with adulatory comments on my person. "We have Dr. Martinelli here and, as you can see, he's a very charming man." This was said in passing, placing her hand on my thigh and with a knowing wink that called the female viewers to witness my charms.

Furthermore, before the interview, Burage and Jackie had coached me. If I were asked any questions (and they'll have to say something about the famous vaccine!) try not to be too sexist-looking, whatever you do. What do you mean by that now? Come on, you know perfectly well, Ralph—arrogant, sure of yourself. Oh, I understand. I'm supposed to be the modest ingenue from Oscar Wilde's plays! The girl who always answers "Yes, Mama" to her mother!

Yet my mates had given me good advice. When I tried sexist arrogance six months later it didn't work. At my umpteenth televised interview—which was pre-recorded, if my memory serves me—the lady commentator introduced me once again as a "very charming man." A bit wounded, I broke in to say sharply, "And, I hope, a good scientist as well." The commentator looked at me, as though stunned by my aggressiveness. Next she smiled indulgently and said with an amused look, "Why, of course, Dr. Martinelli. Nobody here doubts your ability." With that, close-ups of the bellies of Jackie and Burage, both of whom were obviously pregnant at the time. I suppose that the M.C. and the camerawomen must have had a good laugh when they edited this little film afterward.

"You see?" Burage said furiously. "That's what you get when you let yourself go!"

Dave was delighted to be back in Washington in our Wesley Heights home, the big garden, the pool, his room—where a big black desk took up one whole wall—and, most of all, the TV, which he'd missed so badly in Blueville. In the beginning I wondered how he was going to take my cohabitation with two spouses. But when I cautiously sounded him out on this subject, I realized that my uneasiness was unfounded. Thanks to TV, thanks to school, Dave soon soaked up the main ideas about the Reconstruction. True, they didn't have to overcome, in him, an ingrained monogamous tradition as they did in me. I realized that I had set up a false problem, as I'd often done with him when, one day, returning from school, he announced triumphantly that three girls in his class had reserved him as procreator when he was "old enough."

Furthermore, he followed the pregnancies of my mates with the keenest interest, and to satisfy his insatiable curiosity about this, I decided to give him a little course in embryology on the blackboard in his room. I learned afterward that he'd repeated my course at school with a competence that won him the congratulations of his teacher. "All the same," Dave said, giving me an account of her praise, "it makes me sore when I think I'll never have a baby." And he concluded with melancholy: "It's pretty lousy to be a boy."

That's a remark he wouldn't have made a year before, or even in Blueville. The least that can be said is that the instruction the coeducational school dispenses nowadays doesn't encourage phallocracy among the boys.

As to his personal relations with Burage and Jackie, they have been so good that I'm almost jealous. From the way he buried himself in the down and warmth of their affection, I realized how badly, after his mother's death, he'd missed a female presence. With regard to Jackie and Burage, he is always very demanding, very greedy for contact, and, to get his way, I've noticed that he turns his bare-faced charm on them. What's more, it works quite well. And he monopolizes their time and attention, with a secret preference (which I've spotted) for

Burage. Yet, of the two—even for him—Jackie is the easiest to get along with: always happy, even-tempered, free of complexes, absolutely imperturbable, never quarrels, whereas Burage can be very touchy at times and shows fight. But Burage has a trait that Dave appreciates. In her moments of tenderness, she is more tender and she "envelopes" him more. He must feel that this makes up for the few slaps he receives.

I've noticed with a great deal of pleasure that his present happiness hasn't made him forget Mutsch, who gave him such good lessons in Blueville. He writes to her often and to Harvard, where Stien has resumed his teaching. Mutsch answers him with lengthy letters that are methodical and almost familial. Dave also writes to Joan Smith. I was imprudent enough to tell him that if I were actually put in charge of a research center in Washington, I would try to put together my old team from Blueville, with Smith, Pierce and Grabel. Since that day, almost every week, he's been asking me for news about that plan and if we're going to be seeing the Smiths again soon. I must admit that Jackie is scarcely less impatient. She'd be thrilled to meet "Rita" again. Me, too. Burage, on the other hand, isn't saying anything, and I know why. She holds Rita's inquisitive nature against her.

Someone, on the other hand, who overjoyed us when she swooped down on us unexpectedly was Dorothy Barrow. I put her up at Wesley Heights, and I regretted that she couldn't stay in Washington for more than two weeks. But the governor of the state of Ohio had just died and she wanted to run for the office. Dorothy Barrow, with whom I'd traded smiles at Blueville without ever speaking to her, surprised me, when I got to know her better, by her boundless energy. During the short time she stayed in Washington she divorced Mr. Barrow—the *Code of the Woman* making it easier for the wives of A's to separate from their infertile husbands—plowed through an enormous amount of political work with President Hope and got herself with child by me.

She also asked me, on the forms, to give my name as middle name to the future child.

Jackie and Burage had made the same request, and I'd

agreed, not without repugnance, because it meant dividing Dave's inheritance by three. I had to agree to divide it by four. After all, Mrs. Barrow had been the head of "we" and I knew well enough (and they'd told me enough!) how "we" had protected me in Blueville.

What surprised me was that Mrs. Barrow, even before the birth of the child, coupled my name to hers as a middle name and began calling herself, throughout her long election campaign, Dorothy Martinelli Mortimer, the latter being her maiden name.

There was nothing legal about that procedure. It was nevertheless a practice that showed a tendency to spread. The administrative forms required of women no longer asked if they were married or single (reputedly sexist distinctions) but, rather, if they were mothers. And the status of mother gave so many advantages and conferred so much social prestige that women who still weren't mothers but were mothers-to-be pointed out the fact by giving themselves as middle name the last name of the adopted procreator of their future child.

Obviously, in the case of Dorothy Martinelli Mortimer, there was a political afterthought in the adoption of my name as middle name. At the time I was as famous in the United States as a hit singer, and Dorothy added a romantic luster to her brand image by portraying herself to the electorate as pregnant by the man she'd protected in Blueville.

After her election Dorothy came back to Washington often enough, always in a hurry and busy and always between planes, but, as short as her stopovers were, she found the means, if I may put it this way, to avail herself of her rights to my bed. Actually, it wasn't a chore. I wouldn't have wanted to cohabit with Dorothy—her energy would have worn me out—but I always came back to her with friendship, with pleasure. And—why not admit it?—Dorothy had a physiological peculiarity that I found very much to my liking. She was one of those women about whom a great writer said very neatly: "Their orgasms have the straightforwardness of a good handshake."

In the early days of our move to Washington, Anita, back from Paris and named presidential adviser, phoned me. I gave her a rather chilly reception, accused her vehemently of deserting me, and without listening to her explanations, hung up. Burage, who was standing there and who'd picked up the earphone, grew indignant over my behavior, so little in keeping, she emphasized, with the modesty of my sex. Anita was a damned opportunist, certainly, but no one could deny that she'd done her best to protect me in Blueville.

I roared, "That's just it! I'm fed up with being protected!"

Burage shrugged. "Keep quiet, Ralph," she said with a superior air. "You talk nonsense." With that, Jackie appeared in the room, her pregnancy beginning to show under her captain's uniform (she'd been promoted), but the perpetual nausea she felt in no way altered her good humor. Burage told her about my glorious deed, and Jackie burst out laughing. "Come now, Ralph," she said, "how infantile can you get! You mustn't let your sensitivity get the best of you! You just can't start fighting with a presidential adviser. Besides, we won't let you do it."

Two days later, Anita, evangelic, phoned me back. And, well reprimanded between times, I apologized. "No, Ralph, your reaction was quite understandable. Would you like to have lunch at the Chinese restaurant tomorrow? I'm buying. The epidemic killed off old Mr. Twang, so he couldn't have been all that old." Laugh. "But Mrs. Twang is still there with that fascinating little slit in the hem of her dress." Laugh. "And then, of course, I'll be there too."

I got there late. Anita was seated at an upstairs table, thumbing through a magazine. Unchanged. Dark auburn hair, green eyes and that nose so well chiseled that I liked less since I'd gotten to know Burage's. Also unchanged was her attire: black sheath dress and little white collar, almost in uniform. A terribly competent look. And her eyes that went through me, quick as a sword, and sized me up as I moved toward her. She got up with eagerness, it seemed—perhaps a carefully planned eagerness—and kissed me on the mouth. A shock. Even so, as I recall, before the kiss, there'd been the look. She sat back down, seized my right hand, turned to me.

"Why, you're splendid, Ralph! Your eyes bright, your coat glossy! Anyone can see at a glance that you're kept very well by your women"—laugh—"pampered, brushed, fed. And what elegance! I'm so glad that these short jackets close-fitting at the waist have replaced the old suit coats. The new style is more flattering to lean and muscular men of your type. Especially when it's worn with skin-tight trousers like yours. Ralph, you've got the buttocks of a toreador! Not to mention your other assets." Laugh. "Frankly, when I saw you coming in, my mouth watered. My only regret: that you still aren't wearing the German-style codpiece. They're starting to be the rage in New York, and personally I think they're awfully seductive."

Mrs. Twang had come to take our order. It was still the same archaic smile that she folded and unfolded at will but not at all the same impassiveness. As my gaze automatically roved down to the little slit in the hem of her dress, she gave me such an aggressive, seductive look that I was flabbergasted. As soon as she left the room, Anita (I thought I was hearing Burage!) cautioned me to be more reserved and prudent.

"You'll get yourself kidnapped, Ralph. There's a lot of that going on right now. Gangs of three or four women. Oh, it's nothing like the case of that Mr. B., you remember? They don't use brutality or torture. The procreator is released with every consideration once he's performed his function. There's just no way of stopping these women. We're going through such a maternity craze that it's just impossible! There isn't a judge anywhere, right now, who'd dare convict pregnant women for kidnapping, since they claim that they've done it out of patriotic duty 'in the spirit of the Reconstruction.' Seriously, Ralph, you should put those bedroom eyes of yours in your pocket when there's a woman around or, at any rate, keep looking at the ground. I advise you not to come back to eat alone at Mrs. Twang's. As a general rule, I'd say it's inadvisable for you to go out alone. You should ask Captain Davidson to give you an escort. That would be safer."

"You know Jackie?"

"Of course. Burage, too. What a charming woman. And what a tribute to me, dear Ralph, your choosing a woman who resembles me." Laugh. "We have the same hair."

"She doesn't resemble you—her eyes, her nose . . ."

Anita's fingertip ran over her finely drawn nostril.

"Well, maybe her nose," she said with a vain little movement that was astonishing from a politician.

With that, she took from her purse a tiny box that she gave me as a "mini-gift." I had an urge to refuse, but I didn't dare, she seemed so anxious for me to accept. And when I'd opened the package, naturally, it was too late. It wasn't a "mini-gift" but a gold signet ring with my initials engraved on it. They're coming back into fashion, Anita assured me, slipping it onto my little finger and kissing me once more.

Having banded me like some fowl and having recovered her equanimity after that kiss of peace, she began downing a great quantity of eggrolls (my own share would also meet the same fate) while confiding to me the great plans that she'd dreamt up for me.

At the White House, she'd made the acquaintance of a recent oil millionairess, a widow of course. This "oilionairess," who wasn't young any more, had a yen to leave her name to posterity in the form of a scientific foundation. I suggested to her—what could be more fitting?—an institute for research into diseases of the encephalon. Right here in Washington. With you to head it. It's going to work, I think.

I listened and made little grateful murmurs. I could do no more. Like all great men, Anita had gotten into the habit of the monologue. What's more, she congratulated me on my silence: "You listen so well, Ralph, and you've got such beautiful eyes when you listen to me."

From the Institute—not yet off the ground but which she was already describing to me as finished—Anita moved to a more immediate project, on which she had her heart set just as much and which also supposed my cooperation: She wanted to have a child by me.

I was thunderstruck. "*You!* A child?"

"Why? Don't you think I can have one?"

"Oh, of course. But it's so opposed to your philosophy of life."

"My philosophy has changed," Anita replied solemnly. "And so have the times. And along with them, the set-up of society. Babies are no longer incompatible with a political career. On the contrary."

In passing I savored that "on the contrary," as was only fitting.

"You mustn't forget," Anita said in the style of Elizabeth Hope's last speech (but, after all, she might have been the one who'd written it), "that demographic reconstruction has absolute priority in our time. No American woman, however highly placed she may be, will be able to walk with her head high unless she's a mother. The President, unfortunately—" she lowered her voice—"in view of her age . . . But we who are her advisers, we must set the example. Look, Ralph, you're going to see something that won't be official for another week." Without removing the object from her purse, she showed it to me in the palm of her hand. It was a crimson badge on which the gold letters "MAR" stood out.

"What does MAR mean?"

"Mothers of the American Reconstruction. The only ones entitled to wear the badge," she told me with an envious expression in her green eyes and wistfully putting it back into her purse, "are the American women who become pregnant during the first year of the Reconstruction."

I promised myself to tell Burage and Jackie about that. They were going to be delighted—especially Jackie, who, as a soldier, had to have a weakness for insignia.

"But why me?" I asked. "After all, there are still some men left."

She laughed. "Because we're married, Ralph! Legally! And, as far as I know, you don't intend to get a divorce." (How did she know?)

She laughed again. "Please, don't make that face! I have no intention of disturbing the arrangement of your life. You cohabit with two charming women. That's very fine the way it is. I've always lived alone, as you know. Ralph, I ask nothing more of you than your friendship and a child. I already have your name."

A gentle reminder and how enlightening. But of course! Patriotic duty! Elizabeth Hope, we are yours! The pioneers of the fertility rush! The very first mothers of the Reconstruction! But let's not forget to bear a child that bears my name. To be linked in this way—with Jackie, with Burage, with Barrow—to a historic episode of the anti-Bedfordian resistance, the very woman who, in the beginning, resisted so little . . . I looked with admiration (and a little horror) at the crafty politician who hid behind those beautiful green eyes and that pretty nose.

Anita took my hand and squeezed it forcefully in hers. "You'll say yes, won't you, Ralph?"

Caressed, banded, even "institutified" in advance, how could I say no? But even so I felt, well rooted within me, even if it was rather bicephalic, solid conjugal loyalism.

"As far as I'm concerned, yes, Anita, gladly." That took a bit of an effort to say. "But I must consult my mates."

She laughed. "You needn't bother, Ralph. It's already been done."

"What's that—already been done?"

"I had tea with them yesterday."

And they hadn't told me anything about it! I could have roared! And I would have roared, I think, if Mrs. Twang hadn't come into the room just then bringing the check. I lowered my eyes at once and kept them lowered until Anita had paid and the little ogress in the slitted dress had left the room. I noticed that Anita had unashamedly gone over the check before paying it. She might be the President's adviser, but she could still protect her interests.

"Well, then, it's all set," Anita said cheerfully. "I'll give you a lift!"

"Where to?"

"My place."

"What?" I asked. "Right now?"

"Why not now? This comes just at the right time. I'm in a fertile period. Ralph, I'm kidnapping you! Just let me make a few phone calls, and we're on our way."

Without waiting for my answer, she got to her feet and went to the other end of the room to pick up the receiver. I wasn't at all convinced that this came "just at the right time" but, quite to the contrary, that the date for our encounter had been calculated *ad hoc.*

Her voice clear, her speech distinct, her tone decisive, Anita spoke into the phone. A woman of action and one who, with me, had quickly dispatched her business. Just long enough to down a few shrimp eggrolls, and there I was, in her purse along with the MAR badge.

She made not one but several calls. So as not to seem to be listening, I flipped through the pages of advertising in the magazine that Anita had left on the seat.

A sign of the new times, nothing but men—handsome, muscular, hairy. An ad for a deluxe bathroom (with gilded pipes and fittings), a well-endowed fellow with dark hair seated on the rim of a blue bathtub, naked or almost, a narrow towel flung over his pudenda but in a way that the shape and size of them could be guessed. His confident pose and his friendly eyes gave you the impression that, in buying the bathtub, this vigorous procreator could be given to you as a bonus. Further on, a blond man, also nude, but decently, turned your way a muscular buttock and a hairy armpit in order to assure you that the deodorant he was using made it possible to perspire without offending anyone. And there it was, in a full-page ad, an impressive assortment of German-style codpieces, photographed close up with their contents. By way of reference, in the center, the German-style codpiece such as it can be seen in sixteenth-century paintings—in Germany, of course, the caption assures us, but also in Flanders and in France under Charles IX—these erudite explanations lending dignity to the return of this "charming mode" (*sic*) so well-suited to our time. Thus, no more laces that were so hard to untie but a zipper concealed under a becoming embroidery. Two schools: the codpiece in the same material and color as the skintight pants. Or the codpiece in contrasting material "which emphasizes the bulge" (*sic*). Sophisticates may prefer the "bon ton" (*sic*) of different material but in a color matching the pants. Nothing had been overlooked, not even the falsie codpiece, a discreet cross-section diagram of which was shown, with an "extra-large bulge" that would give timid men new confidence. Yes, just looking at those ads dispelled any illusions I might have: The opposite sex was the dominant one.

Anita finished her phoning, and now I had a call to make to postpone an appointment. Less patient or in greater haste, Anita told me that she was going for the car and driver, parked a hundred yards down the block, and that I should meet her there as soon as I was done.

I should have waited for her in front of the restaurant.

Because I hadn't anticipated that, halfway to the car, I'd have to pass a good twenty women construction workers who were taking a break sitting on the curb. By the time I'd seen them it was too late. I had to keep going. Which I tried to do with my eyes lowered, feigning indifference. But I would never have dreamt what happened next. Up to then, on my strolls, it had never gone beyond a few grazing touches, heckling, whistles or even once or twice vulgar propositions. But this time it may have been the beautiful sunshine, the fact that they had nothing to do on their break or that there were few passers-by at that hour. As soon as they spotted me coming, the women workers stared at me and looked me up and down with eyes like saucers, and as soon as I came within earshot they heckled me. It was an incredible outburst. There was something contemptuous and sadistic in that exposure of their thoughts, a kind of verbal rape the violence of which frightened me. I turned a deaf ear to them and went on. I didn't dare quicken my pace. I wouldn't have wanted to provoke them by seeming to run away. Wasted effort. A tall girl loomed up ahead of me, her face covered with freckles. Her piercing blue eyes were coming out of their sockets. She was drenched with sweat, and, blocking my way, she shouted, amid laughter and encouragement, "Girls, I'm going to treat myself to this little sweetie!" She grabbed me by the arms, hugged me and kissed me on the mouth. Her lips were hot and she gave off a strong odor. I struggled. I cried out and broke away from her, but other hands seized me. Screaming, the girls rushed to the attack, clustering in bunches around me. "Hey, shortie!" the blond girl said amid the laughter, locking her left arm over my throat. "You got to help us do our patriotic duty!"

A black Plymouth made its tires screech against the curb as it jolted to a stop. A short, strident blast of the horn. A militia-woman leaped out. A fierce shout. I was freed.

I dove into the back seat under the last jeers, two or three of which were intended for Anita and tinged with social bitterness. The militiawoman started up while the furies hammered the fenders with both fists. I sprawled out in the back of the car, breathless, disheveled, my heart pounding. I was trembling with rage and, why not confess it, with fear as well. Oh, I could have put two or three of those girls out of action but, aside from the fact that I hate to strike women (an outmoded taboo, I suppose), they would have overwhelmed me.

"Come, now," Anita said, "get hold of yourself, Ralph. And do button your fly. They only wanted to fool around with you. We don't get the kidnappings from those kind of girls. They haven't got the means or the spare time—or the private houses to carry out a proper abduction. But that ought to teach you a lesson, Ralph. You simply must ask Jackie to provide you with a female escort—and do it today. You just can't continue going out alone on the streets of Washington, even by day."

The postponement of my appointment and my stop at Anita's—longer than usual—had knocked my schedule for a loop and, after a quick sandwich, I got home late. "I was beginning to worry," Burage said, opening the door for me. "Jackie has to work late and I've put Dave to bed. It wasn't easy. He wanted to wait up for you."

I stripped naked, showered and, in my pajamas, half a glass of whiskey in my hand, collapsed on the sofa and gave Burage the account that she was waiting for. I was so tired that I didn't even take her to task for having had tea with Anita without telling me.

A silence. She made no comments and I said after a moment, "I have the feeling that I've sold myself for an Institute."

Burage shrugged irritably. "That's ridiculous. You're dramatizing. After all, Anita is legally your wife."

"I have only one wife and you know who she is."

"I said legally."

"Who was it that advised me against a divorce?"

"Come on, Ralph, let's not go into that again. The divorce was impossible, whether you wanted it or not. There would have been political overtones. You would have looked as though you were throwing Anita back into the darkness of Bedfordism, after the President had decided to salvage her. And then, frankly, what do you have against Anita? Even from Paris, she never stopped urging Bedford to have them leave you alone."

I jumped up. "But that changes everything! I didn't know about that! Who did you hear this from?"

"From Dorothy."

"And you didn't say a word about it to me!"

"Maybe it's asking too much of me to keep on singing Anita's praises," Burage replied, tossing her hair.

I kept quiet. I looked at her. My great Burage, who'd just been appointed to an important position at the top of HEW— gradually, by means of sweetness, obstinacy, gentle reproach and all the feminine arts of persuasion, I'll have to get you first, not to hide things from me; second, not to make decisions concerning me behind my back. We'll discuss that cup of tea with Anita. Not tonight. Tonight, because you've just said something true—the truth of the woman piercing the shell of the militant. I feel myself melting.

"Burage," I said half in earnest, half in jest, "what if we gave all this up? What if we went away?"

"Who's 'us'?"

"You, Dave and me."

"The nuclear family," Burage replied but without the virulent sarcasm that was to be feared.

"Why not?"

"Yes," she said with a softened irony, "why not? Only where?"

"Wherever you want—Europe."

"Oh, Europe!" Burage replied. "With the repressive laws they've just enacted?"

"Africa?"

"To wind up in a culture that has contempt for women?"

At that point I stopped the game. But it was a game in which I'd sensed her profound complicity.

"Why only the three of us?" she resumed, returning the service obligingly. "Why not Jackie too? Poor Jackie."

I silently appreciated that pity. But as Burage was looking at me, awaiting an answer, I said, "I like Jackie a lot. But, as they say, three's a crowd. It seems to me that she's here to give our life the appearance of respectability."

Burage burst out laughing. "Oh, you are funny, Ralph! 'The appearance of respectability!' And actually it's all so true!"

She stopped, just in time. She wouldn't go any further. Even alone with me, even rid of bugging, she wasn't going to criticize the philosophy of "we," the *Code of the Woman* and the mystique of the Reconstruction. Hail, President Hope, we who are about to rebuild the nation salute you!

She took my hand and heaved a gentle sigh.

"Ralph, you can't keep on going out alone. You've got to make up your mind to ask Jackie for that escort."

A squeeze of her hand, to which I responded. Another sigh. No more dream of escape for the escapees from Blueville. It's the sad truth: Wherever you go, the barbed wire follows you. Burage would continue to work for HEW and to militate. And I, the ex-profiteer of a misogynic culture, would continue the apprenticeship, which had been so well started in Blueville, of a subtly lower position. And what's more, I would go on bearing, as best I could, my new status as sex object. Without overdeveloping my narcissistic instincts, I hope. And to the extent that it was possible, without developing a paranoiac persecution complex.

If I were a Christian, I'd say that I was expiating. And frankly, I've become increasingly aware of it with each passing day, now that the roles have changed. There is plenty to atone for.

I looked at Burage and squeezed her fingers once more. No, I certainly won't be going away. I've lost a lot. But there's still one thing I've got that can't be taken away from me. You, Burage.

You . . . and the secret couple we form, in the midst of official collectivization.